Sisters

Kathleen Norris

Sisters

Contact:
BibliotechPress@gmail.com

ISBN: 978-1-61895-018-5

TO
FRANCES ROSE BENET

Dear mother of my mother's child, to you
The tribute brings not praise from me alone,
Still clings some grace of hers to what I do,
And the gift comes in her name, as my own.

CHAPTER I

Cherry Strickland came in the door of the Strickland house, and shut it behind her, and stood so, with her hands behind her on the knob, and her slender body leaning forward, and her breath rising and falling on deep, ecstatic breaths. It was May in California, she was just eighteen, and for twenty-one minutes she had been engaged to be married.

She hardly knew why, after that last farewell to Martin, she had run so swiftly up the path, and why she had flashed into the house, and closed the door with such noiseless haste. There was nothing to run for! But it was as if she feared that the joy within her might escape into the moonlight night that was so perfumed with lilacs and the scent of wet woods. In this new happiness of hers a fear was already mingled, a sweet fear, truly, and a delicious fear, but she had never feared anything before in her life. She was afraid now that it was all too wonderful to be true, that she would awaken in the morning to find it only a dream, that she would somehow fall short of Martin's ideal— somehow fail him—somehow turn all this magic of moonshine and kisses into ashes and heartbreak.

She was a miser with her treasure, already; she wanted to fly with it, and to hide it away, and to test its reality in secret, alone. She had come running in from the wonderland down by the gate, just for this, just to prove to herself that it would not vanish in the commonplaceness of the shabby hall, would not disappear before the everyday contact of everyday things.

There was moonlight here, too, falling in clear squares on the stairway landing, white and mysterious and bewitching, but on the other side of the hall was wholesome, cheerful lamplight creeping in a warm streak under the sitting-room door.

Dad was in the sitting room, with the girls. The doctor's house was full of girls. Anne, his niece, was twenty-four; Alix, Cherry's sister, three years younger—how staid and unmarried and undesired they seemed to-night to panting and glowing and glorified eighteen! Anne, with Alix's erratic help, kept house for her uncle, and was supposed to keep a sharp eye on Cherry, too. But she hadn't been sharp enough to keep Martin Lloyd from asking her to marry him, exulted Cherry, as she stood breathless and laughing in the dark hallway.

Cherry had never had any other home than this shabby brown bungalow, and she knew every inch of the hall, even without light to see it. She knew the faded rugs, and the study door that swallowed up her father every day, and the table where Alix had put a great bowl of buttercups, and the glass-paned door at the back through which the doctor's girls had looked out at many a frosty morning, and red sunset, and sun-steeped summer afternoon. But even the old hall had seemed transformed to-night, lighted with a beauty quite new, scented with an immortal sweetness.

Hong came out of the dining room; the varnished buttercups twinkled in a sudden flood of light. He had come to put a folded tablecloth into the old wardrobe that did for a sideboard, under the stairs. Cherry, descending to earth, smiled at him, and crossed the hall to the sitting-room door.

An older woman might have gone upstairs, to dream alone of her new joy, but Cherry thought that it would be "fun" to join the family, and "act as if nothing had happened!" She was only a child, after all.

Consciously or unconsciously, they had all tried to keep her a child, these three who looked up to smile at her as she came in. One of them, rosy, gray-headed, magnificent at sixty, was her father, whose favourite she knew she was. He held out his hand to her without closing the book that was in the other hand, and drew her to the wide arm of his chair, where she settled herself with her soft young body resting against him, her slim ankles crossed, and her cheek dropped against his thick silver hair.

Alix was reading, and dreamily scratching her ankle as she read; she was a tall, awkward girl, younger far at twenty-one than Cherry was at eighteen, pretty in a gipsyish way, untidy as to hair, with round black eyes, high, thin cheek-bones marked with scarlet, and a wide, humorous mouth that was somehow droll in its expression even when she was angry or serious. She was rarely angry; she was unexacting, good-humoured, preferring animals to people, and unconventional in speech and manner. Her father and Anne sometimes discussed her anxiously; they confessed that they were rather fearful for Alix. For Cherry, neither one had ever had a disquieting thought.

Anne, smiling demurely over her white sewing, was a small, prettily-made little woman, with silky hair trimly braided, and a rather pale, small face with charming and regular features. She was not considered exactly pretty; perhaps the contrast with Cherry's unusual beauty was rather hard on both the older girls; but she was so perfectly capable in her little groove, so busy, contented, and necessary in the doctor's household, that it was rather a habit with all their friends to praise Anne. Anne had "admirers," too, Cherry reflected, looking at her to-night, but neither she nor Alix had ever been engaged—engaged—engaged!

"Aren't you home early?" said Doctor Strickland, rubbing his cheek against his youngest daughter's cheek in sleepy content. He was never quite happy unless all three girls were in his sight, but for this girl he had always felt an especial protecting fondness. It seemed only yesterday that Cherry, a rosy-cheeked sturdy little girl in a checked gingham apron, had been trotting off to school; to him it was yesterday that she had been a squarely-built baby, digging in the garden paths, and sniffing at the border pinks. He had followed her exquisite childhood with more than a father's usual devotion, perhaps because she really had been an exceptionally endearing child, perhaps because she had been given him, a tiny crying thing in a blanket, to fill the great gap her mother's going had left in his heart. He had sympathized with her microscopic cut fingers, he had smiled into her glowing, damp little face when she stuttered to him long tales of bad doggies and big 'ticks; he had brought her "jacks" and paper-dolls and hair ribbons; he loved the diminutive femininity of the creature; she was all a woman, even at three. Alix he proudly called his "boy"; Alix used hair ribbons to tie up her dogs, and demanded hip boots and an air rifle and got them, too, and used them, but when he took Alix in his arms she was apt to bump his nose violently with her hard young head, to break his glasses, or at best to wriggle herself free. Little Cherry, however, was 'fraid of dogs, she told her father, and of guns, and she would curl up in his arms for happy half-hours, with her gold curls sprayed against his shoulder, and her soft little hand tucked into his own.

"Mr. Lloyd had to take the nine o'clock train," Cherry answered her father dreamily, "and he and Peter walked home with me!" She did not add that Peter had left them at his own turning, a quarter of a mile away.

"I thought he wasn't going to be at Mrs. North's for dinner," Anne observed quietly, in the silence. She had been informally asked to the Norths' for dinner that evening herself, and had declined for no other reason than that attractive Martin Lloyd was presumably not to be there.

"He wasn't," Cherry said. "He thought he had to go to town at six. I just stopped in to give them Dad's message, and they teased me to stay. You knew where I was, didn't you—Dad?" she murmured.

"Mrs. North telephoned about six, and said you were there, but she didn't say that Mr. Lloyd was," Anne said, with a faint hint of discontent in her tone.

Alix fixed her bright, mischievous eyes upon the two, and suspended her reading for a moment. Alix's attitude toward the opposite sex was one of calm contempt, outwardly. But she had made rather an exception of Martin Lloyd, and had recently had a conversation with him on the subject of sensible, platonic friendships between men and women. At the mention of his name she looked up, remembering this talk with a little thrill.

His name had thrilled Anne, too, although she betrayed no sign of it as she sat quietly matching silks. In fact, all three of the girls were quite ready to fall in love with young Lloyd, if two of them had not actually done so.

He was a newcomer in the little town, a tall, presentable fellow, ready with laughter, ready with words, and always more than ready for flirtation. He admitted that he liked to flirt; his gay daring had quite carried Anne's citadel, and had even gained Alix's grudging response. Cherry had not been at home when Martin first appeared in Mill Valley, and the older girls had written her, visiting friends in Napa, that she must come and meet the new man.

Martin was a mining engineer: he had been employed in a Nevada mine, but was visiting his cousin in the valley now before going to a new position in June. In its informal fashion, Mill Valley had entertained him; he had tramped to the big forest five miles away with the Stricklands, and there had been a picnic to the mountain-top, everybody making the hard climb except Peter Joyce, who was a trifle lame, and perhaps a little lazy as well, and who usually rode an old horse, with the lunch in saddle-bags at each side. Alix formulated her theories of platonic friendships on these walks; Anne dreamed a foolish, happy dream. Girls did marry, men did take wives to themselves, dreamed Anne; it would be unspeakably sweet, but it would be no miracle!

And Anne, always busy and happy and helpful, was more so than ever, unpacking the delicious lunch, capably arranging for everybody's comfort and pleasure, looking up with innocent surprise when Martin bent over her as she fussed and rearranged baskets.

"I thought YOU were gathering wood!"

"Did you, indeed? Let the other fellows do that. I shan't be here forever, and I'm privileged."

"Would you like me to give you something else to do?"

"No, ma'am, I'm quite happy, thank you!"

Not much in the words to remember, truly, but the tone and the look went straight to Anne's close-guarded heart. Every time she looked up at the mountain, rearing its dark crest above the little valley, they had come back to her.

That was all several weeks ago, now. It was just after that mountain picnic that Cherry had come home; on a Sunday, as it chanced, that was her eighteenth birthday, and on which Martin and his aunt were coming to dinner. Alix had marked the occasion by wearing a loose velvet gown in which she fancied herself; Anne had conscientiously decorated the table, had seen to it that there was ice-cream, and chicken, and all the accessories that make a Sunday dinner in the country a national institution. Cherry had done nothing helpful.

On the contrary, she had disgraced herself and infuriated Hong by deciding to make fudge the last minute. Hong had finally relegated her to the laundry, and it was from this limbo that Martin, laughing joyously, extricated her, when, sticky and repentant, she had called for help. It was Martin who untied the checked brown apron, disentangling from the strings the silky gold tendrils that were blowing over Cherry's white neck, and Martin who opened the door for her sugary fingers, and Martin who watched the flying little figure out of sight with a prolonged "Whew-w-w!" of utter astonishment. The child was a beauty.

But if she was beautiful when flushed and cross and sticky, there was no word for her when she presently came demurely downstairs, her exquisite little red mouth still pouting, her bright head still drooping sulkily, but her wonderful eyes glinting mischief, and the dark, tumbled apron replaced by thin white ruffles that began at Cherry's shoulders and ended above her ankles. Soft, firm round chin, straight little nose, blue eyes ringed with babyish shadows; Martin found them all adorable, as was every inch of the slender, beautifully made little body, the brown warm hand, the clear, childish forehead, the square little foot in a shining slipper.

Her eighteenth birthday! He learned that she had just put up her hair, indeed, after dinner, her father made her tumble it down in a golden mop again. "Can't lose my last girl, you know," he said to Mrs. North, Martin's aunt, seriously. Martin had been shown her birthday gifts: books and a silver belt buckle and a gold pen and stationery and handkerchiefs. A day or two later she had had another gift; had opened the tiny Shreve box with a sudden hammering at her heart, with a presage of delight. She had found a silver-topped candy jar, and the card of Mr. John Martin Lloyd, and under the name, in tiny letters, the words "O fudge!" The girls laughed over this nonsense appreciatively, but there was more than laughter in Cherry's heart.

From that moment the world was changed. Her father, her sister, her cousin had second place, now. Cherry had put out her innocent little hand, and had opened the gate, and had passed through it into the world. That hour was the beginning, and it had led her surely, steadily, to the other hour to-night when she had been kissed, and had kissed in return.

Nobody dreamed it, she told herself with innocent exultation, looking at Alix, sunk into her chair ungracefully, and at Anne, peacefully sewing. They thought of her as a child—she, who was engaged to be married!

"So—we walk home with young men?" mused the doctor, smiling. "Look here, girls, this little Miss Muffet will be cutting you both out with that young man, if you're not careful!"

Alix, deep in her story, did not hear him, but Anne smiled faintly, and faintly frowned as she shook her head. She considered Cherry sufficiently precocious without Uncle Lee's ill-considered tolerance. Anne had often told him that Cherry was the "pink-and-white type" that would attract "boys" soon enough without any encouragement from him. But he persisted in regarding her as nothing more than a captivating baby!

He would have had them always children, this tender, simple, innocent Doctor Strickland. He was in many ways a child himself. He had never made money in his profession; he and his wife and the two tiny girls had had a hard enough struggle sometimes. Anne and her own father had joined the family eight years ago, in the same year that the Strickland Patent Fire Extinguisher, over which the doctor had been puttering for years, had been sold. It did not sell, as his neighbours believed, for a million dollars, but for perhaps one tenth of that sum. It was enough, and more than enough, whatever it was. After Anne's father died it meant that the doctor could live on in the brown house under the redwoods, with his girls, reading, fussing with a new invention, walking, consulting with Anne, laughing at Alix, and spoiling his youngest- born.

The house was shingled, low, framed in wide porches, smelling within and without of the sweet woods about it. Here the Stricklands weathered the cold, damp winters, when the trees dripped and the creeks swelled, and here they watched the first emerald of spring breaking through the loam of a thousand autumns; here they hunted for iris and wild lilac in April, and hung Japanese lanterns through the long, warm summers. It was a perfect life for the old man; it was only lately that he begun uneasily to suspect that they would some day want something more, that they would some day tire of empty forest and blowing mountain ridge, and go away from the shadow of Mt. Tamalpais, and into the world.

Anne, now—was she beginning to fancy this young Lloyd? Doctor Strickland was surprised with the fervour with which he repudiated the thought. Anne had been admired, she must go to her own home some day. But her uncle hoped that it would be a neighbouring home; this young engineer, who had drifted already into a dozen different and distant places, was not the man for staid little Anne. He was twenty-eight years old, but it was not the discrepancy in years that mattered. The doctor had himself been twelve years older than his wife. No, it was something less tangible—

"What did you want to see Mr. Lloyd about to-morrow, Dad?" Cherry interrupted his thoughts to ask.

"The rose vine!" her father reminded her.

"You'll never get that back on the roof!" Alix looked up to assure him discouragingly. "I told you, when you were pruning it," she added vivaciously, "that you were cutting too deep. No—you knew it all! Now the first wind brings it down all over the place, and you get exactly what you deserve!"

Her tone was less harsh than her words; indeed, it was the tone he loved from her, that of a devoted but long-suffering mother. She came to Cherry's hassock, and dropped on it, and rested her untidy head against his knee.

"Anne aided and abetted me!" said the doctor meekly.

"To the extent of handing you your shears!" Anne said promptly.

"No, but really you know, Dad, you were a pig-headed little creature to do that!" Alix said musically. "You might just as well cut it down at the roots and plant another double banksia."

"I rather thought that Lloyd might have some idea of a tackle—or a derrick or something—" submitted her father vaguely.

"Well, if anybody can—" Anne conceded, laughing. "What did he say about coming over, Cherry?"

But Cherry had not been listening, and the conversation was reviewed for her benefit. She remarked, between two rending yawns, that Mr. Lloyd was coming over to-morrow at ten o'clock, and Peter, too—

"Peter won't be much good!" Alix commented. Cherry looked at her reproachfully.

"You're awfully mean to Peter, lately!" she protested. Her father gave her a shrewd look, with his good-night kiss, and immediately afterward both the younger girls dragged their way up to bed.

Alix and Cherry shared a bare, woody-smelling room tucked away under brown eaves. The walls were of raw pine, the latticed windows, in bungalow fashion, opened into the fragrant darkness of the night. The beds were really bunks, and above her bunk each girl had an extra berth, for occasional guests. There was scant prettiness in the room, and yet it was full of purity and charm. The girls sat upon their beds while they were undressing, and plunged upon their knees on the bare pine floor and rested their elbows upon the faded patchwork quilts while they said their prayers. Mill Valley was so healthful a little mountain village that among her two thousand residents there was only one doctor, the old man who sat by the fire downstairs, and he had formally retired from general practice. The girls, like all their neighbours, were hardy, bred to cold baths, long walks, simple hours, and simple food. In the soft Western climate they left their bedroom windows open the year round; they liked to wake to winter damp and fog, and go downstairs with blue finger-tips and chattering teeth, to warm themselves with breakfast and the fire.

So Alix said nothing when Cherry went to the window to-night, and knelt at it, looking out into the redwoods, and breathing the piney air. In the silence of the little room the girls could hear a swollen creek rushing; rich, loamy odours drifted in from the forest that had been soaked with long April rains. Cherry saw a streak of light under the door of Hong's cabin, a hundred yards away; there was no moon, it was blackness unbroken under the trees. The season was late, but the girls felt with a rush of delight that summer was with them at last; the air was soft and warm, and there was a general sense of being freed from the winter's wetness and heaviness.

Alix rolled herself in a gray army blanket, and was asleep in some sixty seconds. But Cherry felt that she was floating in seas of new joy and utter delight, and that she would never be sleepy again.

Downstairs Anne and the doctor sat staidly on, the man dreaming with a knotted forehead, the girl sewing. Presently she ran a needle through her fine white work with seven tiny stitches, folded it, and put her thimble into a case that hung from her orderly workbag with a long ribbon.

"Wait a minute, Anne," said the doctor, as she straightened herself to rise. "This young Lloyd, now—what do YOU think of him?"

She widened demure blue eyes.

"Should you be sorry if I—liked him, Uncle Lee?" she smiled.

The old man rumpled his silver hair restlessly.

"No-o," he said, a little ruefully. "I suppose it'll be some man some day, my dear. I've been thinking—even little Cherry seems to be growing up!"

Anne, who modelled her deportment somewhat upon the conduct of Esther in "Bleak House," came to the hassock at his knee, and sat there, looking up at him with bright affection and respect.

"Cherry's only a child," she assured him, "and Alix will not be ready to give her heart to any man for years to come! But I'm twenty-four, Uncle. And sometimes I feel ready to—to try my own wings!"

He smiled at her absently; he was thinking of her mother, an articulate, academic, resolute woman, of whom he had never been fond.

"That's the way the wind blows, eh?" he asked kindly.

Anne widened her pretty eyes.

"Well—you see how much he's here! You see the flowers and books and notes. I'm not the sort of girl to wear my heart on my sleeve," Anne, who was fond of small conservational tags, assured him merrily. "But there must be some fire where there's so much smoke!" she ended.

"You're not sure, my dear?" he asked, after some thought.

"Oh, no!" she answered. "It's just a fancy that persists in coming and going. You know, Uncle Lee," Anne pursued, confidentially, "I've always had rather a high ideal of marriage. I've always said that the man I would marry must be a big man—oh, I don't mean only physically! I mean morally, mentally—a man among men!"

"And you think young Lloyd—answers that description, eh?"

"I think he does, Uncle Lee," she answered seriously. And immediately afterward she got to her feet, saying brightly, "Well! we mustn't take this too gravely—yet. It was only that I wanted to be open and above-board with you, Uncle, from the beginning. That's the only honest way."

"That's wise and right!" her uncle answered, in the kindly, absent tone he had used to them as children, a tone he was apt to use to Anne when she was in her highest mood, and one she rather resented.

"Cherry, now—" he asked, detaining her for a moment. "She—you don't think that perhaps Peter admires her?"

"PETER!" Anne echoed amazedly, and stood thinking.

Peter was more than thirty years old, thin, scholarly, something of a solitary, the sweet, dreamy, affectionate neighbour who had shared the girls' lives for the past ten years. Cherry had bullied Peter since her babyhood, ruined his piano with sticky fingers, trampled his rose-beds, coaxed him into asking her father to let her sit up for dinner. For some reason she could not, or would not, define, Anne liked the idea of Cherry and Peter falling in love—

"Somehow one doesn't think of Peter as marrying any one—" she said slowly, still trying to grasp the thought. "He's so—self- sufficient," she added, shaking her head. "You—you WOULDN'T like that, Uncle?"

"Peter is a dear fellow," the doctor mused. "But Cherry—why, she's barely eighteen! He—" The old man hesitated, began again: "I suppose there's no reason why Peter shouldn't kiss her, in a— brotherly sort of way?" he submitted doubtfully.

"Did he kiss her?" Anne exclaimed.

"I don't know that he did," Cherry's father said hastily.

"But what made you think he did?" the girl persisted.

"Just a fancy," he assured her. "Just an old father's fear that she is growing up too fast!"

"Because we all, and you especially, spoil her," Anne reminded him, smiling. "Peter," she added thoughtfully, "has kissed us all, now and then!" She stooped for a dutiful good-night kiss, and was gone. And as she went, lightly and swiftly across the hall, up the stairway with her shoulders erect, and methodically and prettily moved about her brushing and folding and disrobing, she saw herself engaged to be married, saw herself veiled and mystical in white, on her Uncle's arm, heard the old neighbours and friends saying that little Anne Strickland had gone to her own home, and had won the love of a fine man.

Downstairs, the doctor sat on, thinking, and his face was grave. He was thinking of little Cherry's goodnight kiss, half an hour ago. She had rested against his arm, and he had held her there, but what had been the thoughts behind the blue eyes so near his own? Perhaps Anne was right—perhaps Anne was right. But he realized with a great rush of fear that some man had kissed Cherry to-night, had held her against a tobacco-scented coat, and that the girl was a woman, and an awakened woman at that. Cherry— kissed a man! Her father's heart winced away from the thought.

Young Lloyd and Peter had walked home with her. But if Anne was right in her maidenly suspicions of Lloyd's intentions, then it must have been Peter who surprised little Cherry with a sudden embrace. Lloyd had been hurrying for a train, too; the case looked clear for Peter.

And as he came to his conclusions, a certain relief crept into the old man's heart. Peter was an odd fellow; he was ten years too old for the child. But Peter was a lover of books and gardens and woods and music, after all, and Peter's father and this old man musing by the fire had been "Lee" and "Paul" to each other since boyhood. Peter might give Cherry a kiss as innocently as a brother; in any case, Peter would wait for her, would be all consideration and tenderness when he did win her.

"But I think perhaps she might go down to the San Jose school for half a term," her father reflected. "Six months there did wonders for Alix. No use precipitating things—the next few years are pretty important for all the girls. We mustn't let her fancy that the first man who turns her head with compliments is the right partner for life! Alix, now—somehow she wasn't like Cherry, at eighteen."

He smiled at a sudden memory of Alix, who was chicken-farming at that age, and generally unpleasantly redolent of incubators, chopped feed, and mire. He seemed to remember Alix shouting that if Peter Joyce was going to LIVE in their house, she would move somewhere else! Cherry was different.

Cherry, he reflected fearfully, was as pretty as her mother had been at eighteen, with the same rounded chin and apricot cheeks, and the same shadowed innocent blue eyes with a film of corn- coloured hair blown across them. She had the strange, the indefinable quality that without words, almost without glances, draws youth toward youth, draws admiration and passion, draws life and all its pain. Her father for the first time to-night formulated in his heart the thought that she might be happily married—

Married—nonsense! Why, what did she know of life, of submission and courage and sacrifice? At the first strain, at the first real test, she would want to run home to her Daddy again, to "stop playing"—! It would be years, many years, before the snowy frills, and the pale gold head, and the firm, brown little hand would be ready for that!

Not many hours after he went slowly up to bed morning began to creep into the little valley. The redwoods turned gray, and then dark green, the fog stirred, and a first shaft of bright sunlight struck across a shoulder of the hills, and pierced the shadows about the brown bungalow. Alix, at her early bath, heard quail calling, and looked out to see the last of the fog vanishing at eight o'clock, and to get a wet rush of fragrance from the Persian lilac, blooming this year for the first time. At half-past eight she came out into the garden, to find her father somewhat ruefully studying the tumbled ruins of the yellow banksia rose. The garden was still wet, but warming fast; she picked a plume of dark and perfumed heliotrope, and began to fasten it in his coat lapel while she kissed him.

"We'll never get that back on the roof, my dear boy," Alix said maternally.

Her father pursed his lips, shook his head doubtfully. The rose, a short, week ago, had been spreading fan-like branches well toward the ridge-pole, a story and a half above their heads. But the great wind of yestereve that had ended the spring and brought in the summer had dragged it from its place and flung it, a jumble of emerald leaves and sweet clusters of creamy blossoms, across the path and the steps of the porch. Alix looked up at the outward curve of the reversed branches, bent almost to the splitting point in the unfamiliar direction, and whistled. She tentatively tugged at a loose spray, and stood biting her thumb.

"Why it should have kept its place for fifteen years and then suddenly flopped, is a mystery to me!" she observed resentfully.

"Well, the truth is," her father confessed, "you were quite right last night. When I pruned it, a week ago, I may have undermined it."

"You never will listen to reason!" his daughter remarked absently, her attention distracted by the setter puppy who came clumsily gambolling toward her. "Hello, old Bumpydoodles!" she added, with rich affection, kissing the dog's silky head, and burying both hands in his feathered collar. "Hello, old Buck!"

"Alexandra, for heaven's sake stop handling that brute!" said Peter Joyce disgustedly, coming up the path. "I dare say you've not had your breakfast, either. Go wash your hands! 'Morning, Doctor!"

Father and daughter turned to smile upon him, a tall, lean man, with a young face and a finely groomed head, and with touches of premature silver at his temples. He was very much at home here, had been their closest friend for many years.

He was a bachelor, just entering his thirties, a fastidious, critical, exacting man by reputation, but showing his best side to the Stricklands. They had a vague idea that he was rich, according to their modest standard, but he apparently had no extravagant tastes, and lived as quietly, or more quietly, than they did. He had a brown cabin, up on the mountain, where two or three Portuguese boys and an old, fat Chinese cook managed his affairs, and he sometimes spoke of friends at the club, or brought two or three men home with him for a visit. But for the most part he liked solitude, books, music, dogs, and his fireside. The old doctor's one social enjoyment was in visiting Peter, and the younger man went to no other place so steadily as he came to the old house under the redwoods.

The girls accepted him unquestioningly, sometimes resenting his frank criticism, sometimes grateful for the entertaining he delighted to do for them, but most often ignoring him, as if he had been an uncle whose place and standing in the domestic circle was unquestioned, but who did not really enter into their young plans and lives. He was whimsically, good-naturedly disapproving of Alexandra, and he frankly did not like Anne, but he had always been especially indulgent to Cherry, and had taken the subject of Cherry's schooling and development very seriously. And Cherry treated him, in return, as if she had been his demure and mischievous and affectionate daughter.

"'Morning, Peter!" said Doctor Strickland now, smiling at him. "Have you had yours?"

"My house," said Mr. Joyce fastidiously, "is a well-managed place."

"Of course," Alix said, panting from her welcome to the dog, and laughing at the newcomer without resentment, "of course it is, for the President Emeritus of the Maiden Ladies' Guild is running it!"

"Don't be insulting," Peter answered, in the same mood. "Say," he added, pursing his lips to whistle, as he looked at the rose tree, "did Tuesday's wind do that?"

"Tuesday's wind and Dad," Alix answered. "Will it go back, Peter?"

"I—I don't know!" he mused, walking slowly about the wreck. "If we had a lever down here, and some fellow on the roof with a rope, maybe."

"Mr. Lloyd is coming over!" Alix announced. Peter nodded absently, but the mention of Martin Lloyd reminded him that they had all dined at his house on the very evening when the mysterious gale had commenced, and with interest he asked:

"Cherry catch cold coming home Tuesday night?"

"No; she squeezed in between Dad and me, and was as warm as toast!" Alix answered casually. "How'd you like Mr. Lloyd?" she added.

"Nice fellow!" Peter answered. Alix grinned. She had before this accused Peter of violent partisanship with his own sex. He criticized women severely; the Strickland girls had often been angry and resentful at his comments upon the insincerity, extravagance, and ignorance of their own sex, but with Peter, all men were worthy of respect, until otherwise proved.

"He's awfully nice," Alix agreed.

"Who is he?" Peter asked curiously. "Where are his people and all that?"

"His people live in Portland," the girl answered. "He's a mining engineer, and he's waiting now to be called to El Nido; he's to be at a mine there. He's lots of fun—when you know him, really!"

"Talking of the new Prince Charming, of course," Anne said, joining them, and linking an arm in her Uncle's and in Alix's arm. "Don't bring that puppy in, Alix, please! Breakfast, Uncle Lee. Come and have another cup of coffee, Peter!"

"Prince Charming, eh?" Peter echoed thoughtfully, as they all turned toward a delicious drift of the odour of bacon and coffee, and crossed the porch to the dining room. "I was going down for the mail, but now I'll have to stay and see this rose matter through! Thanks, Anne, but I'll watch you."

"Afraid of getting fatter?" Alix speculated, shaking out her napkin. "You ARE fatter," she added, with a calm conviction.

"Do you always say the thing that will give the most offence?" Peter asked, annoyed. "Where's Cherry?" he added, glancing about.

Cherry answered the question herself by trailing in in a Japanese wrapper, and beginning to drink her coffee with bare, slender arms resting on the table. Nobody protested, the adored youngest was usually given her way. Alix's indifference to the niceties of her toilet had been seriously combated, years ago, but Cherry was so young, and so pretty in any dress or undress, that it was impossible to regard her little lapses with any gravity. Moreover, the family realized perfectly that Alix would have clipped her thick hair, and taken to bloomers or knickerbockers outright, at the slightest encouragement, and would gladly have breakfasted in a wrapper, or in her petticoats, or while about the woods with her dogs, whereas nobody could know Cherry and not know that every weakness of which the feminine heart is capable, for frills and toilet waters, creams and laces, was dormant under the childish negligence.

"I heard you all laughing, under the window and it—woke—me—up!" Cherry said dreamily.

"It seems to me," Anne, who had been eying her uneasily, said lightly, "that someone I know is getting pretty old to come downstairs in that rig when strangers are here!"

"It seems to me this is just as decent as lots of things—bathing suits, for instance!" Cherry returned instantly, gathering the robe about her, and giving Anne a resentful glance over her blue cup.

"Peter, are you a stranger?" Alix said. "If Peter's a stranger," she added animatedly, "what is an intimate friend? Peter walks through this house at all hours; you can't wash your hair or do a little ironing without having Peter under your feet; he borrows money from me; he bullies Hong about wasting butter—"

"Also you borrow money from me, my child, don't forget that," Peter interrupted serenely, peeling an apple. "I don't come to see YOU, Alix."

"I have a rope somewhere—" the doctor ruminated. "Where did I put that long rope—what did I have it for, in the first place—"

"You had it to guy the apple tree," Alix reminded him. "Don't you remember you got a regular ship's cable to tie that tree, and it never worked? The tree that died after all—"

"Ah, yes!" said her father, his attentive face brightening. "Ah, yes! Now WHERE is that rope?" But even as Alix observed that she had seen it somewhere, and advanced a tentative guess as to the cellar, his eyes fell upon Cherry, and went from Cherry's absorbed face—for she was dreaming over her breakfast—to Peter, and he wondered if Peter HAD kissed her.

"Come on, let's get at it!" Alix exclaimed with relish. She loved a struggle of any description, had prepared for this one with sleeves rolled to the elbows, and had put on heavy shoes and her briefest skirt. "Come on, Sweetums," she added, to the dog, who had somehow wormed his way into the dining room, and was beating the floor with an obsequious tail. She caught his forepaws, and he whipped his beautiful tail between his legs, and looked about with agonized eyes while she dragged him through a clumsy dance. "He's the darlingest pup we ever had!" Alix stated to Cherry, who was departing for the upper regions and a complete costume.

"He needs a bath," Anne observed coldly, and Peter's abrupt shout of laughter made Alix flush angrily.

"Bring your cigarette out here, Peter," the old doctor said, crossing the garden to look in the abandoned greenhouse for his rope. "We're in no hurry," he said. "We may as well wait until Lloyd comes along; the fellow's arms are like flails. You—-" the old man opened a reluctant door, peered into a glassed space filled with muddy shelves and empty flower-pots and spiderwebs. "It's not here," he stated. Then he began again, "You brought Cherry home last night?" he asked.

"As a matter of fact, I didn't," Peter answered, in his quick, precise tones. "I came with Lloyd and Cherry as far as the bridge, then I cut up the hill. Why?" he added sharply. "What's up?"

"Nothing's up," Doctor Strickland said slowly. "But I think that Lloyd admires—or is beginning to admire—her," he said.

"Who—Cherry!" Peter exclaimed, with distaste and incredulity in his tone.

"You don't think so?" the doctor, looking at him wistfully, asked eagerly.

"Why, certainly not!" Peter said quickly. "Certainly not," he added, frowning, with his eyes narrowed, and his look fixed upon the vista of woodland.

"I had a fancy that he might have been putting notions into her head," her father said, anxious to be reassured.

"But—great Scott!" Peter said, his face very red, "she's much younger than Anne and Alix—"

"It doesn't always go by that," the doctor suggested.

"No, I know it doesn't," Peter answered in his quick, annoyed fashion.

"I should be sorry," Cherry's father admitted.

"Sorry!" Peter echoed impatiently. "But it's quite out of the question, of course! It's quite out of the question. You mustn't— we mustn't—let ourselves get scared about the first man that looks at her. She—she wouldn't consider him for an instant," he suddenly decided in great satisfaction. "You mustn't forget that she has something to do with it! Very fastidious, Cherry. She's not like other girls!"

"That's true—that's true!" Doctor Strickland agreed, in great relief. They turned back toward the garden, in time to meet Alix and several dogs streaming across the clearing. Over the girl's shoulder was coiled the great rope; she leaped various logs and small bushes as she came, and the dogs barked madly and leaped with her. Breathless, she stumbled and fell into her father's arms, and both men had the same thought, one that made them smile upon her tomboyishness indulgently: "If this is twenty-one— eighteen is three long years younger and less responsible!"

CHAPTER II

Immediately they gathered by the fallen rose vine, all talking and disputing at once. Alix and the dogs added only noise to the confusion; the men debated, measured, and doubted; Anne, busy with household duties, came and went smilingly. About them stretched the forest, wrapped in the summer morning stillness that is really compounded of a thousand happy sounds. There was no fog now; warm spokes of sunshine fell brightly into the dim, glowing heart of the woods; bees and birds murmured on short journeys; aromatic sweetness drifted on the air.

They had known a thousand such mornings, the doctor and his girls, still, exquisite, happy, dedicated to some absurd undertaking. They had built chicken pens, they had dammed or cleared the creek, they had felled bay-trees, and lopped the lower branches of the redwoods, they had built roaring bonfires, or painted the porch floor, and many times they had roasted chops or potatoes at the brick oven, and feasted royally in the open forest.

A light rope was tied; an experimental tug broke it like a string, tumbling Alix violently in a sitting position, and precipitating her father into a loamy bed. Anne, who was bargaining with a Chinese fruit vendor frankly interested in their undertaking, had called that she would help them in a second, when behind Alix, who was still sitting on the ground, another voice offered help.

A young man had come into the doctor's garden; work was stopped for a few minutes while they welcomed Martin Lloyd.

He was tall and fair, broad, but with not an ounce of extra weight, with brown eyes always laughing, and a ready friendliness always in evidence. He was dressed becomingly to-day, in a brown army shirt open at the throat, and shabby golf trousers that met his thick woollen stockings at the knee. Anne's heart gave a throb of approval as she studied him; Alix flushed furiously, scowled a certain boyish approval; Cherry had not come down.

"Can you help us?" The doctor echoed his question doubtfully. "I don't know that it can be done!" he admitted.

"This shameless old man has just confessed that he gouged the heart out of the poor tree a week ago," Alix said, getting to her feet. "That's the first use he put his birthday knife to! And Anne stood here and abetted him, as far as I can find out!"

"How you garble things, Alix!" Anne said, giving her hand to Martin. "I came out here to find my uncle busily pruning and chopping the dead underwood away, but I had no more to do with it than you had!"

"What's that you're eating—an apricot?" Martin said to Anne, in his laughing way. "I was going to say that if it was a peach, you are a cannibal!"

"Oh, help!" Alix ejaculated, with a look of elaborate scorn.

"No, but where were you last night?" Martin added in a lower tone when he and Anne could speak unnoticed. The happy colour flooded her face.

"I have to take care of my family SOMETIMES!" she reminded him demurely. "Wasn't Cherry a good substitute?"

"Cherry's adorable!" he agreed heartily.

"Isn't she sweet?" Anne asked enthusiastically. "She's only a little girl, really, but she's a little girl who is going to have a lot of attention some day!" she added, in her most matronly manner.

Martin did not answer, but turning briskly toward the doctor, he devoted himself to the business in hand. Peter had climbed on an inverted barrel, to inspect and advise. Alix dashed upstairs for nails and hammer; the doctor whittled pegs; Martin measured the comparative strength of ropes and branches with a judicial eye and hand. Anne flitted about, suggesting, commenting, her pretty little head tipped to one side.

They were all deep in the first united tug, each person placed carefully by the doctor, and guys for the rope driven at intervals decided by Martin, when there was an interruption for Cherry's arrival on the scene. With characteristic coquetry she did not approach, as the others had, by means of the front porch and the garden path, but crept from the study window into a veritable tunnel of green bloom, and came crawling down it, as sweet and fragrant, as lovely and as fresh, as the roses themselves. She wore a scant pink gingham that had been a dozen times to the tub, and was faded and small; it might have been a regal mantle and diadem without any further enhancing her extraordinary beauty. Her bright head was hidden by a blue sunbonnet, assumed, she explained later, because the thorns tangled her hair; but as, laughing and smothered with roses, she crept into view, the sunbonnet slipped back, and the lovely, flushed little face, with tendrils of gold straying across the white forehead, and mischief gleaming in the blue, blue eyes was framed only in loosened pale gold hair.

Years afterward Alix remembered her so, as Martin Lloyd helped her to spring free of the branches, and she stood laughing at their surprise and still clinging to his hand. "The day we raised the rose tree" had a place of its own in Alix's memory, as a time of carefree fun and content, a time of perfume and sunshine—perhaps the last time of its kind that any one of them was to know.

Cherry looked at Martin daringly as she joined the labourers; her whole being was thrilling to the excitement of his glance; she was hardly conscious of what she was doing or saying. Under her father's direction she tied ropes, presently was placed with her arms clasped tightly about a great sheaf of vines, ready for the united tug. Martin came close to her, in the general confusion.

"How's my little sweetheart this morning?"

Cherry looked up, her throat contracted, she looked down again, unable to speak. She had been waiting for his first word; now that it had come it seemed so far richer and sweeter than her wildest dream.

"How can I see you a minute?" Martin murmured, snapping his big knife shut.

"I have to walk down for the mail—" stammered Cherry, conscious only of Martin and herself.

Both Peter and her father were watching her with an uneasiness and suspicion that had sprung into being full-blown. Both men were asking themselves what they knew of this strange young man who was suddenly a part of their intimate little world.

He was simply a man; not unusual in any apparent way. He was ready with his words, fairly good-looking, clean and muscular, his evident lack of polish in languages and letters atoned for by his quick wit, and by a certain boyish artlessness and ingenuousness. He represented himself as about to receive an excellent salary at the mine at El Nido, two thousand a year, but also admitted cheerfully that he was always "broke." He had distinguished himself at college, but had left it after only two years, upon being offered a promising position. There was nothing especially to admire in him, nothing especially to blame; under other circumstances Peter and the doctor might have pronounced him as one of the least interesting of human specimens. The beauty of childhood and adolescence were gone, the ripeness given by years and suffering was wanting; Martin Lloyd was just, as he himself laughingly remarked, "one of the fellers."

Peter had secretly criticized him because he used the words "'phone" and "photo" and "'Frisco," but in justice he had to admit to himself that there was no particular significance to the criticism. He also, in his secret heart, had a vague, dissatisfied feeling that Lloyd was a man who held women, as a class, rather in disrespect, and had probably had his experiences with them, but there was no way of expressing, much less governing, his conduct toward Martin by so purely speculative a prejudice. The young man had dined at his house a few nights ago, had shown an admiration, if not an appreciation, for music, had talked with sufficient intelligence about political matters, mining, and—what else? photography, and pullman cars, and the latest wreck off Bolinas— just the random conversation that was apt to trail through a country dinner. He had told a Chinese joke well, and essayed an Irish joke not so successfully. Peter, somewhat appalled, in the sunny garden, struggling with the banksia, decided that this was not much to know of a person who might have the audacity to fall in love with an exquisite and innocent Cherry. After all, she would not be a little girl forever, some man would want to take that little corn-coloured head and that delicious little pink-clad person away with him some day, to be his wife—

And suddenly Peter was torn by a stab of pure pain, and he stood puzzled and sick, in the garden bed, wondering what was happening to him.

"Listen—want a drink?" Alix asked, coming out with a tin dipper that spilled a glittering sheet of water down on the thirsty nasturtiums. "Rest a few minutes, Peter. Dad wanted a pole, and Mr. Lloyd has gone up into the woods to cut one."

"And where's Cherry?" Peter asked, drinking deep.

"She went along—just up in the woods here!" Alix answered. "Dad had to answer the telephone, but they're going to yell if they need help! WELL!" and Alix, panting, sat down on a log, "are we going to do it?"

"We ought to go up and help Lloyd," Peter decreed. "Which way did he go?"

"I don't know, darling!" Alix answered, leaning back, crossing her ankles, and yawning. "But they'll be back before you could get there. They've been gone five minutes!"

Only five minutes, but they were enough to take Cherry and her lover out of sight of the house, enough to have him put his arm about her, and to have her raise her lips confidently, and yet shyly, again to his. They kissed each other deeply, again and again. The girl was a little confused and even a little uneasy as he continued the tight grip on his arm about her, and her upward look found his eyes close to her own.

Their talk was incoherent. Cherry was still playing, coquetting and smiling, her words few, and Martin, having her so near, could only repeat the endearing phrases that attempted to express to her his love and fervour.

"You darling! Do you know how I love you? You darling—you little exquisite beauty! Do you love me—do you love me?" Martin murmured, and Cherry answered breathlessly:

"You know I do—but you know I do!"

Presently he selected the sapling redwood, and brought it down with two blows of his axe. The girl seated herself beside him, helped him strip the trunk, their hands constantly touching, the man once or twice delaying her for one more snatched and laughing kiss.

"But, Martin, you've been engaged before?" Cherry asked.

"Never—on my honour! But yes, I was once, too, years ago. I want to tell you about that—"

He told her, her grave face bent over the redwood boughs she was tearing. She nodded, flushed, paled. He had met this girl at his mother's, do you see? And she was a cute little thing, don't you know? Her name was Dorothy King, and when he went back to college she had promised to write, do you see? But she hadn't written for weeks, and then she had written to say that she was engaged to another man, a man named— named—he had forgotten the name. But she had married him all right—-

And Cherry looked up, laughing almost reproachfully. How could he ever forget her married name! Cherry said that she suspected that Martin hadn't really cared, and he said no, but he had wanted to tell her about it all the same, because knowing her had made him want really to be honest—and to be good—

Tears stood in his eyes, and she forgave him his admiration for Dorothy King, and said that she knew he was good. And Martin said that he was going to make her the happiest wife a man ever had.

Dragging the stripped tree, they ran down the sharp hill to the house just as Anne came out to announce luncheon. Peter was wandering off in the woods nearby, but came at Alix's shrill yell of summons, and looked relieved when he saw Cherry and Martin not even talking to each other. They had been gone only ten minutes.

Anne, who did not like Peter, had decided not to ask him to stay, but Peter had calmly taken his usual place, and had annoyed Anne with his familiar questioning of Hong as to the amount of butter needed in batter bread. It was a happy meal for everyone, and after it they had attacked the rose bush again, with aching muscles now, and in the first real summer heat. It was three o'clock before, with a great crackling, and the scream of a twisted branch, and a general panting and heaving on the part of the workers, at last the feathery mass had risen a foot—two feet- -into the air, had stood tottering like a wall of bloom, and finally, with a downward rush, had settled to its old place on the roof. Hong was pressed into service now, and with Martin, was on the roof, grappling with a rope, shouting directions. A shower of tiny blossoms and torn leaves covered the steps of the office- porch, the garden beds were trampled deep, the seven labourers breathless and exhausted. But the rose vine was in place! Alix shouted congratulations to Martin as he busily roped and tied the recaptured masses in their old position. Anne had vanished for sandwiches; Peter was being scientifically bandaged by the doctor. Cherry stood looking up at the roof; she did little talking; she watched Martin during every second he spent there.

Her small heart was bursting with excitement. He had found easy opportunities to talk to her a dozen times under cover of the general noise. He had said wonderful and thrilling things.

"How is my own girl? Sweetheart, you're the sweetest rose of them all! Cherry, do you suppose they can see from our faces how happy we are?" Little sentences that meant nothing when other lips spoke them, but that his voice made immortal.

Looking up at him, she thought of the glorious days ahead. How they would all wonder and exclaim; yes, and how the girls would envy her! Little Cherry, just eighteen, going to be married, and married to a man that Alix or Anne would have been only too glad to win! A real man, from the outside world, a man of twenty-eight, ten years older than she was. And how the letters and presents and gowns and plans would begin to flutter through the bungalow—she would be married in cafe-au-lait rajah cloth, as Miss Pinckney in San Francisco was; she would be Mrs. Lloyd! She could chaperone Alix and Anne—

There was a rending, slipping noise on the roof, a scream from Martin, and shouts from the doctor and Peter. With a great sliding and rushing of the refractory sprays, and with a horrifying stumbling and falling, down came Martin, caught in a great rope of the creeper, almost at her feet.

A time of great running and calling ensued. Cherry dropped on her knees beside him, and had his head on her arm for a moment; then her father took her place, and Alix, with an astonished look at the younger girl's wet eyes, drew her sister away. Immediately afterward Martin sat up, looked bewilderedly about from one face to another, looked at his scratched wrist and said "Gee!" in a thoughtful tone. Anne, coming out with sandwiches, joined in the general laugh.

"You scared Cherry out of ten years' growth!" Alix reproached Martin.

"I—I thought he might have hurt himself!" Cherry said, in the softest of little-girl voices, and with her shy little head hanging. Anne decided that it was becoming her clear duty to talk to Cherry.

"My dear," she said, later that same afternoon, when by chance she was alone with her little cousin, "don't you think perhaps it would be a little more dignified to treat Mr. Lloyd with more formality? He likes you, dear, of course. But a man wants to respect as well as like a pretty girl, and I am afraid—Uncle has noticed it!" she interrupted herself quickly, as Cherry tossed her head scornfully. "He spoke of it last night, and Alix tells me that you are calling Mr. Lloyd 'Martin!' Now, dearie, Martin Lloyd is fully ten years—-"

"Then Alix is a tattle-tale!" Cherry said childishly.

"I don't know about that," Anne said gently, although perhaps it would have been more generous in her to add that Alix had made the comment gleefully, and almost admiringly. "But that isn't important. The point is that you are only a young girl—"

"I wish you would all mind your own royal business for about five seconds!" Cherry said, rudely and impatiently. She was in her own room, rummaging on the upper shelf of the closet for a certain hat. She secured the hat now, and ran unceremoniously away from her admonitor, to join Alix, Peter, and Martin for the daily ceremony of walking into the village for the mail.

Anne followed her downstairs sedately, perhaps a little dashed presently to discover that this dignified proceeding had lost her the walk. They were all gone. The house was very still, early summer sweetness was drifting through wide-opened windows and doors; the long day was slowly declining. In the woods close to the door a really summery hum of insect life was stirring. Hong, in dull minor gutturals, jabbered somewhere in the far distance to a friend. Anne peeped into the deserted living room, softened through all its pleasant shabbiness into real beauty by the shafts of sunset red that came in through the casement windows; and was deliberating between various becoming occupations—for Martin might walk back with the girls—when her uncle called her.

He was sitting in the little room that was still called his office, but that was really his study now, and the late afternoon light, through the replaced rose vine, streamed in on the shabby books and the green lampshade and the cluttered desk.

"Anne—you weren't there when that young chap tumbled. But I've been worrying about it a little. There's no question—there's no question that she—that Cherry—called him by his name. 'Martin,' she called him."

Anne had crossed to the shadowy doorway; she stood still.

"It can't be!" protested the doctor, uneasily. "Did Alix say anything to you about it?"

"She said that," Anne admitted, drily.

"You've not noticed anything between him and Cherry?" pursued the doctor. "A girl might call a man by his name, I suppose—"

"I don't think there has been anything to notice," Anne stated, in a level tone.

"You don't?" the doctor echoed, in relief, peering at her. She could meet his look with a smile, but in her heart were the same thoughts that Cherry had been innocently indulging, under the rose vine an hour ago, and the dream that had been Heaven to Cherry was Purgatory to Anne. Cherry married, Cherry receiving cups and presents and gowns, Cherry, Mrs. Lloyd, with a plain gold ring on her young, childish hand, Cherry able to patronize and chaperone Alix and Anne—! "I half fancied that it might be you, Anne," her uncle added, "although I know what a sensible little head you have!" "I'm afraid I'm a trifle exacting where men are concerned!" Anne said, understanding perfectly that her pride was being shielded, but hurt to the heart, nevertheless.

"Well, it must be stopped, if it has begun," decided her uncle. "I can't permit it—I'd forgotten how the little witch grows!"

"He isn't as eligible for Cherry as for me, then?" Anne asked lightly. But her smile disarmed the unsuspicious old man, and he answered honestly:

"You're quite different, Anne. You were older at eighteen than she'll be at twenty-four; you could hold your own—you could, in a way, make your own life! She—why, she's only an innocent little girl; she's got dolls in the attic; we were teasing her about turning up her hair last week!"

Again Anne was silent. It occurred to her to laugh at the absurdity of these quick suspicions, but they had already seized upon her with the curious tenacity of truth; already she had accepted the fact that what yesterday would have been the unbelievable maximum of humiliation and hurt was true to-day, and less than the whole bitter truth!

She was not in love with Martin Lloyd; she was not as susceptible as the much younger Cherry, and she had not had his urging to help her to a quick surrender. But for the first time in her life she had seen an absolutely suitable man, a man whose work, position, looks, name, and character fitted her rather exacting standard, and for the first time she had let herself think confidently of being wooed and won. It was all so right, so dignified, so fitting. She had been the light of her uncle's eyes, and the little capable keeper of his house for years; she had been reminding her own friends of this frequently during the past year or two; now she was ready to step into a nest of her own.

Standing there in the doorway, she tasted the last bitter dregs of the dream. It was all over. Anne was at the age that sets twenty-five years as the definite boundary of spinsterhood. She would be twenty-five in August.

Alix came in from her walk glowing, and full of a great discovery.

"Dad," she said eagerly, taking her place at the supper table, "what do you think! I'll bet you a dollar that man is falling in love with our Cherry!"

Anne, at the head of the table, looked pained, but there was genuine apprehension in the doctor's face.

"Where is your sister?" he asked.

"Down there by the gate," Alix answered. "They're gazing soulfully into each other's eyes, and all that! Peter went home. But CHERRY- -with a beau! Isn't that the ultimate extension of the limit! I'm crazy about it—I think it's great. An engineer, Dad, and Mrs. North's nephew, and he has a fine job in a mine somewhere," she summarized enthusiastically, "you couldn't ask anything better than that, could you? Could you, Dad? I love weddings! This'll be the third I've been to!"

"All this seems to have come up very suddenly," the doctor said, dazedly, rumpling his gray hair with a fine old hand. "I don't imagine your sister is taking it as seriously as you and Anne seem inclined to—-"

"Oh, does Anne think so!" Alix exclaimed.

"I think Cherry is one of the fortunate girls destined to drift along the surface of life," Anne said, "and to accept wifehood quite simply. I only wish I were that type—"

"Oh, Nancy, what rot you talk every time you remember you had a year at college!" Alix said, lightly. "Can't you let the poor kid fall in love without yapping about types and biology and the cosmic urge—-"

"Really, Alix, you use extraordinary language!" Anne remonstrated, glancing at her uncle with outraged dignity. "And I am not aware that I spoke of biology or the cosmic urge!" But her tone was not as impersonal as her words, and she was flushed and even agitated. "Shan't we begin, Uncle Lee?" she asked, patiently. "If Cherry is just down at the gate there, she'll only be another minute—"

She was interrupted by Cherry herself. The girl came to the porch door, and as she hesitated there a minute, with her smiling eyes seeking her father's face, they saw that by one firm, small hand she drew her lover beside her. Martin Lloyd's smiling face showed above hers in the lamplight.

"Dad!" said Cherry, with a childish breath. "Dad! I've brought Martin to supper!"

CHAPTER III

The three at the table did not move for perhaps twenty slow seconds. Doctor Strickland, who had pushed back his chair, and whose hands were resting on the table before him, stared at them steadily. Anne, with a quick little hiss of surprise, smiled faintly. Alix, the unstilted, widened her eyes, and opened her mouth in unaffected astonishment. For there was no mistaking Cherry's tone.

"Doctor," said Martin, coming in, "this little girl of yours and I have something to tell you!" The old man looked at him sharply, almost sternly, looked about at the girls' faces, and was silent. But he tightened his arm about Cherry, who had fluttered to the arm of his chair.

"Are you surprised, Daddy?" Cherry laughed, with all a child's innocent exultation. The next instant Anne and Martin were shaking hands, and Alix had enveloped Cherry in an enthusiastic embrace.

"Surprised!" exclaimed Alix. "Why, aren't you surprised yourself!"

Her sister flushed exquisitely, and Martin laughed.

"We're just about knocked silly!" he confessed, and all the girls laughed joyously.

There followed a delighted confusion of talk, when each in turn remembered what she had noticed, what she had suspected, and what her first emotion had been at this moment or that. Meanwhile a place was made for Martin, and biscuits and omelette and honey and tea were put into brisk circulation. Cherry left her place beside her father, with a final kiss, and took her own chair, all dimples, flushes, smiles, and shy confidence.

"And what are your plans?" Anne asked maternally, as she poured tea.

Her uncle, who had been silent during the excitement, mildly interposed:

"I think we needn't go too fast, young people! You've only known each other a few weeks, after all; you must be pretty sure of yourselves before taking anything like a decisive step. Plenty of time—plenty of time. Mr. Lloyd can go back to his mine, and Cherry will wait for him—"

Cherry's wild-rose face coloured, and her whole body drooped.

"But I can be getting ready, and I can tell people, Dad?" she pleaded.

"We'll see," her father promised her, soothingly. He had promised her thus vaguely when, as an imperative baby years ago, she had wanted the impossible. But she was not a baby now.

"Ah, now—that won't do!" she pouted.

"You must give me a little time to get used to the idea of losing my baby, pretty," her father said. "I confess that this thing seems to have come upon me rather unexpectedly. Mr. Lloyd here and I must have some talks about his plans—"

"I know exactly how you feel, Doctor," Martin said, sensibly and sympathetically. "I realize that I should have come to you first, and asked to pay my respects to your daughter—laugh, why don't you?" he added to Alix, from whom an abrupt and startling laugh had indeed escaped in good-natured scorn.

"Nobody does that any more!" the girl said, in self-defence. "It sounded so old-fashioned!"

"Perhaps nobody does it any more, but I should have done it," Martin said briskly and seriously. "Except that it all came over me with such a rush. A week ago Cherry was only a most attractive child, to me. I'd spoken to my aunt about her and had said that I envied the man that was some day to win her, and that was all! Then the time came for me to get back to work—and I found I couldn't go! I couldn't leave her. However, I expect to be back here some time in the fall, and I thought to myself that I'd see her then, and perhaps, THEN—And then came last night, when I began to say good-byes, and—it happened! I know that you all hardly know me, and I know that Cherry is pretty young to settle down, but I think I can satisfy you, Doctor, that you give her into safe hands, and I believe she'll never regret trusting me!"

He had gotten to his feet as he spoke, and was holding the back of his chair, looking anxiously and eagerly into the old man's eyes. His tone, in spite of his effort to keep it light, had taken on a depth and gravity quite new to his hearers, and as Cherry, sitting next him, and fired through all her girlish being by his eloquence, turned to lay a small, warm hand on his own, the tears came to his eyes.

"Well—" said the doctor, touched himself, and in his gentlest tone, "well! It had to come, perhaps, I can't promise her to you very soon, Mr. Lloyd. But if you both are willing to wait, and if time proves this to be the real feeling, I don't believe you'll find me hard on you!"

"That's all I ask, sir!" Martin said, resuming his seat and his dinner. And for the rest of the meal harmony and gaiety reigned.

Alix shot an occasional glance at Anne, who was flushed, but as usual busy and charming over the tea cups. Alix knew that Anne was inwardly writhing; indeed she felt a sort of emotional shock herself. Yesterday the mere talk of a lover for any one of them was delightfully thrilling and vague—to-night Cherry was actually engaged! The older girls' romantic speculations were flat enough now; Cherry had the actual thing.

There was no jealousy in Alix's heart, as there definitely was in Anne's, of the man. But Alix felt envious of the superior experience—why, he would kiss Cherry! No man had ever kissed Alix. Cherry would be the admired and envied girl among all the girls; married at eighteen, it was so beautifully flattering and satisfying to be married young!

She looked at her father's face, a troubled face to-night. He was watching the lovers regretfully; he did not disguise it. Their quick plans, the readiness with which they solved the tremendous problems to come, the light-heartedness with which they were hurrying toward the future— had he and the older Charity been like that, twenty-five years ago, when they had had supper at her mother's house, and told the great news? He remembered himself, an eager, enthusiastic lover—had he really given better promise then than this handsome young fellow was giving to-night? He tried to remember the older Charity's mother; what she had said, what expression her face had worn, and it seemed to him that he could dimly recall reluctance and pain and gravity in that long-ago look.

After dinner Cherry and Martin, in all the ecstatic first delight of recognized love, went out to the wide front porch, where there were wicker chairs, under the rose vines. Alix alone laughed at them as they went. Anne, with a storm in her heart, played noisily on the piano, and the doctor, after giving the doorway where Cherry had disappeared a wistful look, restlessly took to his armchair and his book, in such desolation of spirit as he had not known since the dark day of her mother's death.

The next day Alix and the engaged pair walked up to invite Peter to a tennis foursome on the old Blithedale court. It was a Saturday, and as he usually dined with them, or asked them to dine with him on Saturday, they were not surprised to find him busy with a charcoal burner, under the trees, compounding a marvellous dish of chicken, tomatoes, cream, and mushrooms, or to have his first words a caution not to tip things over if they wanted any dinner. His Chinese cook was hovering about, but Peter himself was chef.

"Stop your messing one second!" Alix said, catching him by the arm. And as he straightened up she added, with a little awkward laugh, "Congratulate these creatures—they—they're going to be married! Why don't you congratulate them!"

Peter gave one long look at Martin and Cherry, who stood laughing, but a little confused and self-conscious, too, in the grassy path. With a shock like death in his heart, he realized that it was all over. Their protection of her, their suspicions, had come too late. Blind child that she was, she was committed to this fascinating and mysterious adventure.

His face grew dark with a sudden rush of blood. "Peter hates to have any one else know a thing before he does!" Alix explained this later. But he went to them quickly, and shook hands with Martin, and was presently reproaching Cherry for her secretiveness in his old, or almost his old, way.

"Of course nobody's to know—Dad insisted on that!" said Cherry's soft, proud little voice.

"Did you suspect yesterday, Peter?" Alix asked, tasting the sauce, and bunching her fingers immediately afterward to send a rapturous kiss into the air as an indication of its deliciousness. "Yesterday when they went off after the tree, I mean?"

"I had my own suspicions!" he returned, and Cherry—his little, gay, lovely Cherry!—laughed happily. He arranged that they were to play the tennis here on his own courts, and later dine with him, but under his hospitality and under the golden beauty of the day it was all pain—pain—pain. It was agony to see her with him, beginning to taste the rapture of love given and returned; it was agony to have the conversation return always to Martin and Cherry, to the first love affair. When they wandered away to the brook, and stood talking, the girl's head dropped, her cheek flushed, but her face raised quickly now and then for a flashing look, Peter felt that he could have killed this newcomer, this thief, this usurper of the place that he himself might have filled.

"Dad's always said he disapproved of long engagements," Alix commented, amusedly, "but you ought to hear him now! This thing— he won't even call it an engagement—it's an understanding, or a preference— is to be a profound secret, and Cherry's to be twenty- one before any one else but ourselves knows—"

"Your father is quite right!" Peter said sharply, in his most elderly manner. They were resting after the first set, and Cherry and Martin, in the opposite court, were out of hearing.

"When your hair gets tossed back that way," Alix observed innocently, "lots more gray shows! I think you're turning gray pretty young, Peter, aren't you? Are you forty yet? You're not forty, are you?"

"I'm thirty-six," Peter answered briefly. "My father was gray at twenty-seven!" he added, after a pause.

"I have a gray hair," Alix started. "People talk about the first gray hair—"

Peter did not hear her. There was beginning of a little hope in his heart. Girls did not always fulfill their first engagements, did not often do so, in fact. The thing was a secret; it might well come to nothing, after all.

That was the beginning, and after it, although it was arranged between them all that nothing should be changed, and that nobody but themselves should share the secret, somehow life seemed different. Two or three days after the momentous day of the raising of the rose tree, Martin Lloyd went to his mine at El Nido, and the interrupted current of life in the brown bungalow supposedly found its old groove.

But nothing was the same. The doctor, in the first place, was more silent and thoughtful than the girls had ever seen him before. Anne and Alix knew that he was not happy about Cherry's plans, if the younger girl did not. He sighed, sat silently looking off from his book in the summer evenings, fell into deep musing even at his meals. With Alix only he talked of the engagement, and she knew from his comments, his doubtful manner, that he felt it to be a mistake. The ten years' difference between Cherry and Martin distressed him; he spoke of it again and again. In June he sent Cherry to a long-planned house-party at Menlo Park, but the girl came back after the third day. "I didn't have any fun," she confessed, "I had to tell Olive, about me and Martin, I mean. The boys there were all KIDS!"

Cherry was changed, too, and not only in the expected and natural ways, Alix thought. She had always had a generous share of the family devotion, but she entirely eclipsed the others now. Her daily letter from Martin, her new prospects, not only increased her importance in the other girls' eyes, but innocently inflated her own self-confidence. She received a diamond ring, and although at her father's request she did not show it for a few weeks, eventually it slipped mysteriously from the little chamois bag on her neck, and duly appeared on her left hand. She had promised to keep the engagement "or understanding, or preference," a profound secret, but this was impossible. First one intimate friend and then another was allowed to gasp and exclaim over the news. The time came when Anne decided that it was not "decent" not to let Martin's aunt know of it, when all these other people knew. Finally came a dinner to the Norths', when Cherry's health was drunk, and then the engagement presents began to come in.

"But it's July now," Cherry said, innocently, "and I think we were pretty smart to keep it a secret so long! Don't you, Dad? And we've been engaged three months, now, so that it looks as if waiting wasn't going to change our minds, doesn't it?"

He could not chill her gay confidence; he had always spoiled her. Her father only looked tenderly into the blue eyes, and tightened his big arm protectingly about the slender young shoulders. But he was deeply depressed. There seemed nothing to say. Cherry was of age; she was sure of herself. She was truly in love with this presentable young man. Doctor Strickland felt that he did not know Martin—the man to whom he gave his lovely daughter he would have hoped to know intimately for years. There was nothing to be said against young Lloyd. It was only—mused the doctor, aghast—only what was being done in the world every day. But he was staggered by the bright readiness with which all of them—Cherry, Martin, the other girls—accepted the stupendous fact that Cherry was to be married.

She was quite frankly and delightedly discussing trousseau now, too entirely absorbed in her own happiness to see that the other girls had lives to live as well as she. Did Anne mind if she divided her share of the silver from theirs; did Alix think she would ever want any of Mother's lace?

"I got my cards yesterday," she said one day, "I was passing the shop, and I thought I might as well! The woman looked at me so queerly; she said: 'Mrs. John Martin Lloyd. Are these for your mother?' 'No,' I said, 'they're for me!' I wish you could have seen her look. Martin says in to-day's letter that he thinks people will say I'm his daughter, and Alix—he says that you are to come up to visit us, and we're going to find you a fine husband! Won't it be funny to think of your visiting ME! Oh, and Anne—did you see what Mrs. Fairfax sent me? A great big glorious fur coat! She said I would need it up there, and I guess I will! It's not new, you know, she says it isn't the real present, but it can be cut down and it will look like new."

And so on and on. The other girls listened, sympathized, and rejoiced, but it was not always easy. They could not get Cherry to be interested in any of their plans for week-end house-parties, climbs, or picnics; indeed, even to themselves their own lives seemed a trifle dull by contrast.

Anne, as usual, took her part in the summer activities of the village; she and Alix put on their white gowns and wide hats, and duly descended to strawberry fetes and church fairs and concerts, and duly laughed disarmingly when old friends expressed their pleasant suspicions of Cherry.

But Alix voiced their feelings one summer afternoon when she was sauntering into the village at her cousin's side, and began for the first time a faint criticism of Martin.

"What makes Dad mad," Alix opined, "is that Martin had it all arranged before he asked him! Took advantage of Dad, in a way. I don't think he would have felt so if they both were kids, but after all, Martin's twenty-eight—" Her voice fell. "Anne," she began, hesitatingly, "sometimes when Mrs. North says so gaily that Martin was a TERROR in college, and kept his whole family worrying, I feel sort of sorry for Cherry! She doesn't know as much of life as we do," twenty-one-year-old Alix finished soberly.

"I know!" Anne said quickly, perhaps a little glad to find a point where Cherry needed sympathy.

"I have a feeling that Dad thinks," Alix pursued, "that it was just because it was Cherry's first beau-I mean that Cherry waked up suddenly, don't you know? It was as if she said to herself, 'Why, I'm a woman! I can get kissed and get married and all the rest of it!'—I'm expressing this beautifully," stumbled Mix.

"I often wonder Uncle Lee doesn't forbid it!" Anne said. She had never had even a flitting thought of such a thing before, but she spoke now as if the engagement had had her heartiest disapproval from the first.

"Oh, no—why should he!" Alix remonstrated. "Martin may be the best man in the world for her. I confess," the girl added frankly, "I can't stand his aunt. I always used to like Mrs. North, too. But lately, when she's begun to tell Cherry that he is extravagant, and she must save his money for him, and that he's often been in love before, but this time she's sure it is the real thing, and that Martin has his father's delicate stomach—-"

Anne laughed out, in a merry fashion not usual with her of late.

"Oh, Alix, she DIDN'T!"

"Oh, yes, she did! And it makes me sort of sick. What does Cherry care about anybody's delicate stomach!" Alix fell silent, broke out again abruptly: "Anne—do you suppose she'll have a baby?"

Anne flushed. She considered this remark rather indelicate, and yet she liked Alix's recognition of her superior knowledge of the subject.

"I think it very likely!" she answered calmly, after a moment's hesitation. Her first impulse had been to answer, "I think it very unlikely!"

"She doesn't know anything about babies!" Alix said, somewhat worried.

"I don't, either!" Anne confessed with honesty, her brow troubled. "I've read things, here and there. I know SOMETHING, of course. But I don't know much!"

"We've all read Dickens—and the Classic Myths, and things," Alix submitted. "And of course she went with us the day Dad took us to Faust! Is that about all there is to it, Nance?"

"Just—about, I guess!" Anne answered briefly. Both girls' faces were red. They had rarely touched upon these and kindred subjects in their talks with each other; they had never discussed them with any one else. Anne liked to fancy herself rather worldly wise; Alix had an independent brain and tongue. But in their household there was no older woman to illumine their confused guessing with an occasional word now and then, even if an unusually wholesome out-of-door life had not distracted their attention from the problems raised in books, and their isolation had not protected them from the careless talk of other girls of their ages.

August brought Martin, and more changes. He was delighted with his work in the El Nido mine, the "Emmy Younger," and everything he had to say about it was amusing and interesting. It was still in a rather chaotic condition, he reported, but the "stuff" was there, and he anticipated a busy winter. He was to have a cottage, a pretty crude affair, in a few weeks, right at the mine.

"How does that listen to you?" he asked Cherry. Cherry was sitting beside him, at the dinner table, on the first night of his arrival. She was thrilling still to the memory of his greeting kiss, its fresh odour of shaving soap and witch hazel, and the clean touch of his smooth-shaven cheek. She gave her father a demure and interrogative glance. Martin, following it, immediately sobered.

"Just what is your position there?" the doctor asked, pleasantly.

"A little bit of everything now," Martin answered, readily and respectfully. "Later, of course, I shall have my own special work. At present I'm doing some of the assaying, and have charge of the sluice-gang. They want me to make myself generally useful, make suggestions, take hold in every way!"

"That's the way to get on," the older man said, approvingly. Cherry looked admiringly, with all her heart in her eyes, at her husband-to-be; the other girls were impressed, too. Martin brought a new element, something masculine and modern, to their quiet dinner table. Dad and Peter were men, to be sure, but they were different. They were only a little more dear and amusing and real than the men in Dickens' novels, long familiar and beloved in the household. But Martin made the girls feel suddenly in touch with real life.

He had kissed Alix and Anne, upon arriving, and they liked it. Both the older girls, in fact, were so impressed with the brilliancy of Cherry's prospects, with the extraordinary distinction she possessed in having a promised husband, with whom to walk about the woods and to talk of the future, that they could forgive Cherry for being wrapped in a sort of dream. Her new name, her new state, her new clothes, and home and position filled her thoughts, and theirs. Martin had not been with them more than a few hours before the engagement was openly discussed, and there were constant references to Cherry's marriage.

It was a cool evening, and after dinner they all gathered about the fire; Martin and Cherry murmuring together in the ingle seat, and the others only occasionally drawing them into the general conversation. Peter and the Norths had come in for coffee, Mrs. North giving Cherry a maternal kiss as she greeted her. Alix thought that she had never seen her sister look so pretty; Cherry was wearing a new dress, of golden-brown corduroy velvet, with a deep collar and cuffs of old embroidery that had belonged to her mother. Her silk stockings were brown, and her russet slippers finished with square silver buckles. But it was at the lovely face that Alix looked, the earnest, honest blue eyes, the peach-bloom of the young cheeks, and the drooping crown of shining hair.

Somehow, a few days later, wedding plans were in the air, and they were all taking it for granted that Cherry and Martin were to be married almost immediately; in October, in fact. The doctor at first persisted that the event must wait until April, but Martin's reasonable impatience, and Cherry's plaintive "But why, Daddy?" were too much for him. Why, indeed? Cherry's mother had been married at eighteen, when that mother's husband was more than ten years older than Martin Lloyd was now.

"Would ye let it go on, Peter, eh?" the doctor asked, somewhat embarrassed, one evening when he and Peter were walking from the train in the late September twilight.

"Lord, don't ask me!" Peter said, gruffly. "I think she's too young to marry any one—but the mischief's done now! You can't lock a girl in her room, and she's the sort of girl that wouldn't be convinced by that sort of argument if you did!"

"I think I'll talk to her," her father decided. "Anything is better than having her make a mistake. I think she'll listen to me!" And a day or two later he called her into the study. It was a quiet autumn morning, foggy yet warm, with a dewy, woody sweetness in the air.

"Before we decide this thing finally," the doctor said, smiling into her bright face, "before Martin writes his people that it's settled, I want to ask you to do something. It's something you won't like to do, my little girl. I want ye to wait a while—wait a year!"

It was said. He watched the brightness fade from her glowing face, she lowered her eyes, the line of her mouth grew firm.

"Wait until you're twenty, dear. That's young enough. I've been planning a full winter for you girls; I wanted to take a house in town, entertain a little, look up a few friends! You trust me, Cherry. I only ask you to take a little time—to be sure, dear!"

Silence. She shrugged faintly, blinked the downcast eyes as if tears stung them.

"I know you don't like Martin, Dad!" she said, tremulously.

"No, no, my darling—you mustn't say that!" he said, in distress. "I like him very much—I think he's a thoroughly fine fellow! I could wish—just with an old father's selfishness—that he was a neighbour, that he didn't plan to take you away entirely. That's natural, before I give him the thing I hold most precious in the world. And that's just it, Cherry. Wait a year or two, and perhaps it will be possible to establish him here near us. You'll have a little money, dear, and Martin says himself that he would much prefer office work to this constant changing. Marriage is a great change, anyway. Everything is different; your point of view, your very personality changes with it. You'll be lonely, my dear. You'll miss your sister and Anne, and all the old friends. There are cases where it must be so, of course. But in your case—"

He stopped, discouraged. She was sitting opposite him at the shabby writing table, her elbows resting upon it, her full lips pouting with disappointment. Perhaps the one phrase of her new plans that pleased Cherry most was that she was to be carried entirely away from the familiar atmosphere in which she would always be "little Cherry," and subject to suggestions and criticisms. Now she began slowly to shake her head.

"Can't take your old father's word for it?" Doctor Strickland asked.

"It isn't that, Dad!" she protested eagerly and affectionately. "I'll wait—I have waited! I'll wait until Christmas, or April, if you say so! But it won't make any difference, nothing will. I love him and he loves me, and we always will.

"You don't know," Cherry went on, with suddenly watering eyes, "you don't KNOW what this summer of separation has meant to us both! If we must wait longer, why, we will of course, but it will mean that I'll never have a happy instant! It will mean that I am just living along somehow— oh, I won't cry!" she interrupted, smiling with wet lashes, "I'll try to bear it decently! But sometimes I feel as if I COULDN'T bear it—"

A rush of tears choked her. She groped for a handkerchief, and felt, as she had felt so many times, her father's handkerchief pressed into her hand. The doctor sighed. There was nothing more to be said.

So he gave Cherry a wedding check that made her dance with joy, and there was no more seriousness. There were gowns, dinners, theatre-parties, and presents; every day brought its new surprise and new delight to Cherry. She had her cream-coloured rajah silk, but her sister and cousin persuaded her to be married in white, and it was their hands that dressed the first bride when the great day came, and fastened over her corn-coloured hair her mother's lace veil.

It was a day of soft sweetness, not too brightly summery, but warm and still under the trees. Until ten o'clock the mountain and the tops of the redwoods were tangled in scarfs of white fog, then the mellow sunlight pierced it with sudden spectacular brightening and lifting.

The little brown house was full of flowers and laughter and coming and going. Anne and Alix, flushed and excited in their bridesmaids' gowns, were nervous and tired. They had made lists and addressed envelopes, had decorated the house, had talked to milliners and florists and caterers and dressmakers, had packed and repacked Cherry's trunk and boxes. Cherry was tired and excited, too, but had no realization of it; she was carried along upon a roseate cloud of happiness and excitement.

Martin's mother and stepfather had come down from Portland, and were friendly, and pleased with everything.

"His mother," Alix told Peter, "is the sort of handsome person who keeps a boarding-house and marries a rich, adoring old Klondike man."

"Is that what she did?" Peter whispered, amused.

"She's only sixteen years older than Martin is!" Alix confided further. "She kissed Cherry and said, 'You're just a baby doll, that's what you are!' And he calls me 'Ma'am,' and Cherry 'Sister!' They've got two little children, a boy and a girl. Dad likes them both."

"Well, that's good!" Peter approved. "Does Cherry?"

"Oh, anything that belongs to Martin is perfect!" Alix answered, in indulgent scorn, as she abruptly departed to see to some detail concerning the carriages, the music, or the breakfast. She and Anne were in a constant state of worry during the morning; their plans for seating two score of persons were changed twenty times; they conspired in agitated whispers behind doors and in the pantry.

But the first wedding went well. At twelve o'clock Charity Strickland became Charity Lloyd, and was kissed and toasted and congratulated until her lovely little face was burning with colour, and her blue eyes were bewildered with fatigue. She stood in the drawing-room doorway, her bouquet with its trailing ribbons in her gloved hands, and as each one of all the old friends and neighbours made some little pre-arranged speech of an amusing or emotional nature, she met it with a receptive word or smile, hardly conscious of what she did or said. Sometimes she freed her feet from the folds of her lacy train, and sometimes gave Martin a glance backward and upward over her shoulder, once asking him to hold her flowers with a smile that several guests afterward remarked showed that those two couldn't see anything in the world but each other.

At two o'clock there were good-byes. Cherry had changed the wedding satin for the cream-coloured rajah silk then, and wore the extravagant hat. It would be many years before she would spend twenty-five dollars for a hat again, and never again would she see bronzed cocks feathers against bronzed straw without remembering the clean little wood-smelling bedroom and the hour in which she had pinned her wedding hat over her fair hair, and had gone, demure and radiant and confident, to meet her husband in the old hallway.

She was confusedly kissed, passed from hand to hand, was conscious with a sort of strange aching at her heart that she was not only far from saying the usual heart-broken things in farewell, but was actually far from feeling them. She laughed at Alix's last nonsense, promised to write—wouldn't say good-bye—would see them all soon—was coming, Martin—and so a last kiss for darling Dad, and good-bye and so many thanks and thanks to them all!

She was gone. With her the uncertain autumn sunshine vanished, and a shadow fell on the forest. The mountain, above the valley, was blotted out with fog. The brown house seemed dark and empty when the last guests had loitered away, and the last caterer had gathered up his possessions and had gone. Hong was prosaically making mutton broth for dinner; pyramids of sandwiches and little cakes stood on the sideboard.

Up in Cherry's room there was a litter of tissue papers, and pins and powder were strewn on the bureau. The bed was mashed and disordered by the weight of guests' hats and wraps that had lain there. A heap of cards, still attached to ribbons and wires, were gathered on the book-shelf, to be sent after Cherry and remind her of the donours of gifts and flowers.

Across the lower bed that had been Cherry's a pale blue Japanese wrapper had been flung. The girls had seen her wear it a hundred times; she had slipped into it to change her gown a few hours ago. Anne, excited and tired, picked it up, stared vaguely at it for a few minutes, and then knelt down beside the bed, and began to cry. Alix, the muscles about her mouth twitching, stood watching her.

"Funerals are gay compared to the way a wedding feels!" Alix said finally. "I've eaten so much candy and wedding-cake and olives and marrons, and whipped cream and crab salad that my skin feels like the barrel of a musical box! I'm going to take a walk! Come on, Nancy."

"No, I don't want to!" Anne said, wiping her eyes, and sitting back on her heels, with a long sigh and sniff. "I've got too much to do!"

Alix descended to find her father and Peter discussing fly- fishing, on the porch steps. The doctor had changed his unwonted wedding finery for his shabby old smoking jacket, but Peter still looked unnaturally well dressed. Alix stepped down to sit between them, and her father's arm went about her. She snuggled against him in an unusual mood of tenderness and quiet.

"Be nice to me!" she said, whimsically. "I'm lonely!"

"H'm!" her father said, significantly, tightening his arm. Peter moved up on the other side and locked his own arm in her free one. And so they sat, silent, depressed, their shoulders touching, their sombre eyes fixed upon the shadowy depths of the forest into which an October fog was softly and noiselessly creeping.

CHAPTER IV

Meanwhile, the hot train sped on, and the drab autumn country flew by the windows, and still the bride sat wrapped in her dream, smiling, musing, rousing herself to notice the scenery. The lap of the cream-coloured gown held magazines and a box of candy, and in the rack above her head were the new camera and the new umbrella and the new suitcase.

When Martin asked her if she liked to be a married woman, travelling with her husband, she smiled and said that it seemed "funny." For the most part she was silent, pleased and interested, but not quite her usual unconcerned self. She and Alix, taking this trip, would have been chattering like magpies. She and Martin had their dinner in the train, and then she did brighten, trying to pierce with her eyes the darkness outside, and getting only a lovely reflected face under bronzed cocks feathers, instead. After dinner they had a long, murmured talk; she began to droop sleepily now, although even this long day had not paled her cheeks or visibly tired her.

At ten they stumbled out, cramped and over-heated, and smitten on tired foreheads with a rush of icy mountain air.

"Is this the pl-l-ace?" yawned Cherry, clinging to his arm.

"This is the place, Baby Girl, El Nido, and not much of a place!" her husband told her. "That's the Hotel McKinley, over there where the lights are! We stay there to-night, and drive out to the mine to-morrow. I'll manage the bags, but don't you stumble!"

She was wide-awake now, looking alertly about her at the dark streets of the little town. Mud squelched beneath their feet, planks tilted. Beside Martin Cherry entered the bright, cheerful lobby of a cheap hotel where men were smoking and spitting. She was beside him at the desk, and saw him write on the register, "J. M. Lloyd and wife." The clerk pushed a key across the counter; Martin guided her to a rattling elevator.

She had a fleeting thought of home; of Dad reading before the fire, of the little brown room upstairs, with Alix, slender in her thin nightgown, yawning over her prayers. A rush of reluctance—of strangeness—of something like terror smote her. She fought the homesickness down resolutely; everything would seem brighter to- morrow, when the morning and the sunshine came again.

There was a brown and red carpet in the oblong of the room, and a brown bureau, and a wide iron bed with a limp spread, and a peeling brown washstand with a pitcher and basin. The boy lighted a flare of electric lights which made the chocolate and gold wallpaper look like one pattern in the light and another in the shadow. A man laughed in the adjoining room; the voice seemed very near.

Cherry had never been in a hotel of this sort before; she learned later that El Nido was extremely proud of it, with its rattling elevator and its dining room on the "American Plan." It seemed to her cheap and horrible; she did not want to stay in this room, and Martin, tipping the boy and asking for ice-water, seemed somehow a part of this new strangeness and crudeness. She began to be afraid that he would think she was silly, presently, if she said her prayers as usual.

In the morning Martin hired a phaeton, and they drove out to the mine. It had rained in the night, and there were pools of water on the soft dirt road, but the sky was high and blue, and the air tingled with sweetness and freshness after the shower. Cherry had had a good breakfast, and was wearing a new gown; they stopped another phaeton on the long, pleasant drive and Martin said to the fat man in it:

"Mr. Bates, I want to make you acquainted with my wife!"

"Pleased to meet you, Mrs. Lloyd!" said the fat man, pleasantly. Martin told Cherry, when they passed him, that that was the superintendent of the mine, and seemed pleased at the encounter. And Cherry smiled up at the blue sky, and felt the warmth and silence of the day saturate her whole being. Presently Martin put his arm about her, and the bay horse dawdled along at his own sweet will, while Martin's deep voice told his wife over and over again how adorable and beautiful she was, and how he loved her.

Cherry listened happily, and for a little while the old sense of pride and achievement came back—she was married, she was wearing a plain gold ring! But after a few days that feeling vanished forever, and instead it began to seem strange to her that she had ever been anything else than Martin's wife. The other women at the mine were married; she was married; and nobody seemed to think the thing remarkable in them, or in her. She was, to be sure, younger and prettier than any of the others, but the men she met here were not the sort whose admiration would have satisfied her innocent ambition to have Martin's friends flock about her adoringly, and more than that, they knew her to be newly married, and left the young Lloyds to their presumably desired isolation. And very soon Cherry found herself a little housewife among other housewives, much more praised if she made a good shortcake than because the tilt of her new hat was becoming.

For several days she and Martin laughed incessantly, and praised each other incessantly, while they experimented with cooking, and ate delicious gipsy meals. In these days Martin was always late at the mine, and every evening he came home to find that ducks, or a jar of honey, or a loaf of cake, had been contributed to Cherry's dinner by the interested women in the near-by cottages. In all, there were not a dozen families at the "Emmy Younger," and Cherry was watched with interest and sympathy during her first efforts at housekeeping.

By midwinter she had settled down to the business of life, buying bacon and lard and sugar and matches at the store of the mine, cooking and cleaning, sweeping and making beds. She still kissed Martin good-bye every morning, and met him with an affectionate rush at the door when he came home, and they played Five Hundred evening after evening after dinner, quarrelling for points, and laughing at each other, while rain sluiced down on the "Emmy Younger," and dripped on the porch. But sometimes she wondered how it had all come about, wondered what had become of the violent emotions that had picked her out of the valley home, and established her here, in this strange place, with this man she had never seen a year ago.

Of these emotions little was left. She still liked Martin, she told herself, and she still told him that she loved him. But she knew she did not love him, and in such an association as theirs there can be no liking. Her thoughts rarely rested on him; she was either thinking of the prunes that were soaking, the firewood that was running low, the towels that a wet breeze was blowing on the line; or she was far away, drifting in vague realms where feelings entirely strange to this bare little mining camp, and this hungry, busy, commonplace man, held sway. Cherry was in the position of a leading lady mysteriously forced into a minor role; she had never known what she wanted in life, and was learning now in a hard school.

The first time that she quarrelled with Martin, she cried for an entire day, with the old childish feeling that somehow her crying mattered, somehow her abandonment to grief would help to straighten affairs. The cause of the quarrel was a trifle; her father had sent her a Christmas check, and she immediately sent to a San Francisco shop for a clock that had taken her fancy months before.

Martin, who chanced to be pressed for money, although she did not know it, was thunderstruck upon discovering that she had actually disposed of fifty dollars so lightly. For several days a shadow hung over their intercourse, and when the clock came, as large as a banjo, gilded and quaint, he broke her heart afresh by pretending not to admire it.

But on Christmas Eve he was delayed at the mine, and Cherry, smitten suddenly with the bitterness of having their first Christmas spoiled in this way, sat up for him, huddled in her silk wrapper by the air-tight stove. She was awakened by feeling herself lowered tenderly into bed, and raised warm arms to clasp his neck, and they kissed each other. The little house was warm and comfortable, they had a turkey to roast on the morrow, and ranged on the table were the home boxes, and a stack of unopened envelopes waiting for Christmas morning.

The next day they laughed at the clock together, and after that peace reigned for several weeks. But it was inevitable that another quarrel should come and then another; Cherry was young and undisciplined, perhaps not more selfish than other girls of her age, but self-centred and unreasonable. She had to learn self- control, and she hated to control herself. She had to economize when poverty possessed neither picturesqueness nor interest. They were always several weeks late in the payment of domestic bills, and these recurring reminders of money stringency maddened Cherry. Sometimes she summed it up, with angry tears, reminding him that she was still wearing her trousseau dresses, and had no maid, and never went anywhere—!

But she developed steadily. As she grew skilful in managing her little house, she also grew in the art of managing her husband and herself. She became clever at avoiding causes of disagreement; she listened, nodded, agreed, with a boiling heart, and had the satisfaction of having Martin's viewpoint veer the next day, or the next hour, to meet her own secret conviction. Martin's opinion, she told herself wearily, as she swept and cooked and marketed busily, didn't matter anyhow. He would rage and storm at his superiors, he would threaten and brood, and then it would all be forgotten, time after time after time. Silent, absent-minded, looking closely at a burn upon her smooth arm or pleating her checked apron, Cherry would sit opposite him at his late lunch.

"I suppose you don't agree with me?" he would interrupt himself to ask scowlingly.

"Mart—" The innocent blue eyes would be raised vaguely. "I don't know anything about it, dear. If Mr. Taylor—"

"Well, you know what I tell you, don't you?"

"Yes, dear. But—"

"For God's sake don't call me DEAR when you—"

"Mart!" Her dignity always rose in arms. "Please don't get excited."

"Well!" His tone would be modified, as the appetizing little meal was dispatched. "But Lord, you do make me so mad, sitting there criticizing me—I can always tell when you're in sympathy with me- -my Lord, I wish you had to go up against these fellows sometimes- -" The grumbling voice would go on and on; Cherry would pause at the door, carrying out plates, to have him finish a phrase; would nod sympathizingly as she set his dessert before him. But her soul was like some living thing spun into a cocoon, hearing the sounds of life only vaguely, interested in them not at all.

Martin seemed satisfied, and all their little world accepted her as a matter of course. Pretty little Mrs. Lloyd went every morning into the Company Store as the only store at the mine was called, and smiled over her shopping; she stopped perhaps at the office to speak to her husband; she met some other woman wheeling a baby up to the cottages, and they gossiped together. She and her husband dined and played cards now and then with a neighbour and his wife, and they gave dinners in return, when the men praised every dish extravagantly, and the woman laughed at their greedy enthusiasms. Like the other women, she had her small domestic ambitions; Mrs. Brown wanted a meat-chopper; Mrs. White's one desire was to have a curly maple bedroom set; Mrs. Lloyd wanted a standing mahogany lamp for the sitting room.

But under it all Cherry knew that something young and irresponsible and confident in her had been killed. She never liked to think of the valley, of the fogs and the spokes of sunlight under the redwood aisles, of Alix and the dogs and the dreamy evenings by the fire. And especially she did not like to think of that eighteenth birthday, and herself thrilling and ecstatic because the strange young man from Mrs. North's had stared at her, in her sticky apron, with so new and disturbing a smile in his eyes.

CHAPTER V

So winter passed at the mine, and at the brown house under the shoulder of Tamalpais. Alix still kept her bedroom windows open, but the rain tore in, and Anne protested at the ensuing stains on the pantry ceiling. Creeks rushed swollen and yellow; fog smothered the mountain peak; the forest floor oozed moisture. Spring came reluctantly; muddy boots cluttered the doctor's hearth, for he and Alix and Peter tramped for miles through the woods and over the hills, bringing home trillium and pungent wild currant blossoms, and filling the house with blooms.

Cherry's wedding, once satisfactorily over, was a cause of great satisfaction to her sister and cousin. They had stepped back duly, to give her the centre of the stage; they had admired and congratulated, had helped her in all hearty generosity. They had listened to her praises of Martin and his of her, and had given her more than her share of the household treasures of silver spoons and yellowed old lace.

And now that she was gone they enjoyed their own lives again, and cast over hers the glamour that novelty and distance never fail to give. Cherry, married and keeping house and managing affairs, was an object of romantic interest. The girls surmised that Cherry must be making friends; that everyone must admire her; that Martin would be rich some day, without doubt. When her letters came, there was always animated chatter about the fire.

Cherry wrote regularly, now and then assuring them that she was the same old Cherry. She described her tiny house right at the mine, looking down at the rough scaffoldings that covered the mouth of the tunnels, and the long sheds of the plant, and the bare big building that was the men's boarding-house. Martin's associates brought her trout and ducks, she wrote; she and Martin had driven three hundred miles in the superintendent's car; she was preparing for a card party.

"Think of little old Cherry going off on week-end trips with three men!" Alix would say proudly. "Think of Cherry giving a card party!" Anne perhaps would make no comment, but she often felt a pang of envy. Cherry seemed to have everything.

Alix was working hard with her music this winter, aided and abetted by Peter, who was tireless in bringing her songs and taking her to concerts. Suddenly, without warning, there was a newcomer in the circle, a sleek-headed brown-haired little man known as Justin Little.

He had been introduced at some party to Anne and Alix; he called; he was presently taking Anne to a lecture. Anne now began to laugh at him and say that he was "too ridiculous," but she did not allow any one else to say so. On the contrary, she told Alix at various times that his mother had been one of the old Maryland Percies, and his great-grandfather was mentioned in a book by Sir Walter Scott, and that one had to respect the man, even if one didn't choose to marry him.

"Marry him!" Alix had echoed in simple amazement. Marry him—what was all this sudden change in the household when a man could no sooner appear than some girl began to talk of marriage? Alix had always rather fancied the idea that all girls had an opportunity of capriciously choosing from a dozen eligible swains, but Cherry had quickly anchored herself to the first strange man that appeared, and here was Anne dimpling and looking demure over a small, neat youth just out of law school. Certainly the little person of Justin Little was a strange harbour for all Anne's vague dreams of a conquering hero. Stupefied, Alix watched the affair progress.

"I don't imagine it's serious!" her father said on an April walk. Peter, tramping beside them, was interested but silent.

"My dear father," the girl protested, "have you listened to them? They've been contending for weeks that they were just remarkably good friends—that's why she calls him Frenny!"

"Ah—I see!" the doctor said mildly, as Peter's wild laugh burst forth.

"But now," Alix pursued, "she's told him that as she cannot be what he wishes, they had better not meet!"

"Poor Anne!" the old doctor commented.

"Poor nothing! She's having the time of her life," her cousin said unfeelingly. "She told me to-day that she was afraid that she had checked one of the most brilliant careers at the bar."

"I had no idea of all this!" the doctor confessed, amazed. "I've seen the young man—noticed him about. Well—well—well! Anne, too."

"You and me next, little sweetums," suggested Peter, dropping down beside the doctor, who had seated himself, panting, upon a log.

Alix, the dog's silky head under her hand, was resting against the prop formed by a great tree trunk behind her shoulders, and looking down at the two men. She grinned.

"Nothingstirring, Puddeny-woodeny!" she answered, blandly.

The old man looked from Peter's smiling, indifferent face to his daughter's unembarrassed smile; shook his head in puzzled fashion, and returned to his pocket the big handkerchief with which he had been wiping his forehead.

"There ye are!" he said, shrugging. "Cherry goes gaily off with a man she's only known for a few weeks; Anne dresses up this new fellow with goodness knows what qualities; and you and Alix here, neighbours all your lives, laugh as if marriage was all a joke!"

"Our marriage would be, darling," Alix assured him. "But, Dad, if you would like me to marry Peter, by George, I will!" she added, dutifully. "Peter, consider yourself betrothed! Bucky," she said to the dog, "dat's oo new Daddy!"

Neither man paid her the slightest attention. Peter scraped a lump of dried mud from the calf of his high boots, and the doctor musingly looked back along the rough trail they had climbed.

"I'd have felt safer—I'd feel very safe to have one of my girls in your care, Peter," the older man said at last, thoughtfully. "I hate to see them scatter. Well!"

He sighed, smiled, and got to his feet. "That's not in our hands," he said, cheerfully.

Alix, without moving, sent her glance from his face to Peter's, and their eyes met. Only a few words, spoken half in earnest, on a spring morning tramp, and yet they had their place, in her memory and Peter's, and were to return to them after a time, and influence them more seriously than either the man, or the grinning girl, or the old man himself ever dreamed.

The glance lasted only a second, then Alix, who had been carefully removing burrs from the soft tangle of the dog's tasselled ears, took the trail again with great, boyish springs of her bloomered legs.

"Father," said she, "am I to understand that you disapprove of my choice?"

"I hope," her father answered, seriously, "that when you do marry you will get a man half as good as Peter!"

"Thank you!" Peter said, gravely, more as a rebuke to the incorrigible Alix than because he was giving the conversation much attention.

Alix had time for no comment, for at this moment she placed her foot upon an unsubstantial root and slid down upon the two men with such an unpremeditated rush of heavy boots, wet loam, loosened rocks, and cascading earth, that the footing of them all was threatened, and it was only after much shouting, staggering, balancing, and clutching that they resumed their climb. Peter was then nursing a wrist that had been wrenched in the confusion, looking away from it only to give the loudly singing Alix an occasional resentful glance.

"You could omit some of those cries!" he presently observed.

"I thought you liked 'The Lotos Flower'?" Alix called back.

"I just proved that I do," Peter said neatly, and the doctor, and Alix herself, laughed joyously.

In June came the blissful hour in which Anne, all blushes and smiles, could come to her uncle with a dutiful message from the respectfully adoring Justin. Their friendship, said Anne, had ripened into something deeper.

"Justin wants to have a frank talk with you, Uncle," Anne said, "and of course I'm not to go until you are sure you can spare me, and unless you feel that you can trust him utterly!"

"And remember that you aren't losing a daughter, but gaining a son—Oh, help!" Alix added. Anne gave her a reproachful glance, but found it impossible to be angry with her. She was too genuinely delighted with her cousin's happiness and too helpful with all the new plans. Anne's engagement cups were ranged on the table where Cherry's had stood, and where Cherry had talked of a coffee-coloured rajah silk Anne discussed the merits of a "smart but handsome blue tailormade."

The wedding was to be in September, not quite a year after Cherry's wedding. Alix wrote her sister pages about it, always ending with the emphatic declaration that Cherry must come down for the wedding.

Cherry read of it with a strange pang. Somehow it robbed her own marriage of flavour and charm to have Anne so quickly following in her footsteps. She was homesick. She dreamed continually of the cool, high valley, the scented aisles of the deep forest, the mountain rearing its rough summit to the pale blue of summer skies.

June passed; July passed; it was hot at the "Emmy Younger." August came in on a furnace breath; Cherry felt headachy, languid, and half sick all the time. She hated housekeeping in this weather; hated the smells of dry tin sink and wooden floor, of milk bottles and lard tins. Martin had said that he could not possibly get away, even for the week of Anne's wedding, but Cherry began to wonder if he would let her go alone.

"If he doesn't, I shall be sick!" she fretted to herself, in a certain burning noontime, toward the middle of August. Blazing heat had been pouring over the mine since six o'clock; there seemed to have been no night. Martin, who had been playing poker the night before, was sleeping late this morning. He was proud of the little wife who so generously spared him for an occasional game, and always allowed him to sleep far into the following morning. Other wives at the mine were not so amiable where poker was concerned. But Martin, coming home at three o'clock, dazed with close air and cigar smoke, had awakened his wife to tell her that he would be "dead" in the morning, and Cherry had accordingly crept about her own dressing noiselessly, had darkened the bedroom, and eaten her own breakfast without the clatter of a dish, putting the coffee aside to be reheated for him when he awakened. Now she was sitting by the window, panting in the noon heat, and looking down upon a dazzle of dust and ugliness and smothering hotness. She was thinking, as it chanced, of the big forest at home, and of a certain day—just one of their happy days!— only a year ago, when she had lain for a dreamy hour on the soft forest floor, staring up idly through the laced fanlike branches, and she thought of her father, with his mild voice and ready smile; and some emotion, almost like fear, came over her. For the first time she asked herself, in honest bewilderment, why she had married.

The heat deepened and strengthened and increased as the burning day wore on. Martin waked up, hot and headachy, and having further distressed himself with strong coffee and eggs, departed into the dusty, motionless furnace of out-of-doors. The far brown hills shimmered and swam, the "Emmy Younger" looked its barest, its ugliest, its least attractive self. Cherry moved slowly about the kitchen; her head ached; it was a day of sickening odours. The ice man had failed them again, the soup had soured, and after she had thrown it away Cherry felt as if the grease and the smell of it still clung to her fingers.

There was a shadow in the doorway; she looked up surprised. For a minute the tall figure in striped linen and the smiling face under the flowery hat seemed those of a stranger. Then Cherry cried out, and laughed, and in another instant was crying in Alix's arms.

Alix cried, too, but it was with a great rush of pity and tenderness for Cherry. Alix had not young love and novelty to soften the outlines of the "Emmy Younger," and she felt, as she frankly wrote later, to her father, "at last convinced that there is a hell!" The heat and bareness and ugliness of the mine might have been overlooked, but this poor little house of Cherry's, this wood stove draining white ashes, this tin sink with its pump, and the bathroom with neither faucets nor drain, almost bewildered Alix with their discomfort.

Even more bewildering was the change in Cherry. There was a certain hardening that impressed Alix at once. There was a weary sort of patience, a disillusioned concession to the drabness of married life. Alix, after meeting some of the other wives at the mine—there were but five or six—saw that Cherry had been affected by them. There was general sighing over the housework, a mild conviction that men were all selfish and unreasonable. "And I must say," Alix's first letter to her father admitted, "that the men here are all dogs, except the ones that are under dogs!"

But she allowed the younger sister to see nothing of this. Indeed, Cherry so brightened under the stimulus of Alix's companionship that Martin told her that she was more like her old self than she had been for months. Joyously she divided her responsibilities with Alix, explaining the difficulties of marketing and housekeeping, and joyously Alix assumed them. Her vitality infected the whole household, and, indeed, the mine as well. She flirted, cooked, entertained, talked incessantly; she bullied Martin and laughed at him, and it did him good.

Perhaps, thought Alix, rather appalled at Cherry's attitude, Cherry had been too young for wifehood. Sometimes she spoiled and humoured Martin, and sometimes quarrelled with him childishly, scolding and fretting for her own way, and angry with conditions over which neither he nor she had any control. Alix was surprised to see the old pout, and hear the old phrase of Cherry's indulged girlhood: "I don't think this is any FUN!"

"Anne isn't one half as clever or as pretty as Cherry, but she'll make a better wife!" was Alix's conclusion. She gave them spirited accounts of Anne's affair. "He's a nice little academic fellow," she said of Justin Little. "If he had a flatiron in each hand he'd probably weigh close to a hundred pounds! He's a—well, a sort of DAMP-LOOKING youth, if you know what I mean! I always want to take a crash towel and dry him off!"

"Fancy Anne with a shrimp like that!" Cherry said, with a proud look at her own man's fine height.

"Anne was delicious!" Alix further revealed. "They used to take dignified walks on Sundays. I used to tease her, and she'd get so mad she'd ask Dad to ask me to be more refined. She said that Mr. Little was a most unusual man, and it was belittling to his dignity to have me suppose that a man and a woman couldn't have an intellectual friendship. This in May, my dear, and after the thing was settled and Anne had cried, and written notes, and Justin had gone to Dad and asked where he could buy a second-hand revolver—"

"Oh, Alexandra Strickland, you're making up!" Cherry went back naturally to the old nursery phrase.

"Honestly—cross my heart!" Alix assured her. "That's the way they managed it; they solemnly discussed it and worked it out on paper, and Justin's mother called on Anne—she's an awful old girl, too, she looks like a totem pole—and Anne called on his aunts, and then he asked Dad, 'as Anne's male relative,' he said, and it was all settled. And THEN—THEN Anne became the mushiest thing I ever saw! And not only mushy, Cherry, but proudly and openly mushy. She'd catch Justin's hand up, at the table, and say 'Frenny—'"

"'Frenny?'" echoed Cherry, who had laughed until actual tears stood in her eyes.

"That's short for 'friend,' do you see? Because of this platonic intellectual friendship that started everything, you know. She'd catch up his hand and say, 'Frenny, show Uncle what an aristocratic hand you've got.' My dear, she'll keep me awake nights repeating things he's said to her: 'He's so wonderful, Alix. He's the simplest and at the same time the cleverest man I ever knew.'"

"He sounds awful to me," Cherry said.

"He's not, really. Only it seems that he belongs to the oldest family in America, or something, and is the only descendent—"

"Money?" Cherry asked, interestedly.

"No, I don't think money, exactly. At least I know he is getting a hundred a month in his uncle's law office, and Dad thinks they ought to wait until they have a little more. She'll have something, you know," Alix added, after a moment's thought.

"Your cousin?" Martin asked, taking his pipe out of his mouth.

"Well, her father went into the fire-extinguisher thing with Dad," Alix elucidated, "and evidently she and Justin have had deep, soulful thoughts about it. Anyway, the other day she said—you know her way, Cherry—'Tell me, Uncle, frankly and honestly, may Justin and I draw out my share for that little home that is going to mean so much to us—'"

"I can hear her!" giggled Cherry.

"Dad immediately said that she COULD, of course," Alix went on. "He's going to look the whole thing up. He was adorable about it. He said, 'It will do more than build you a little home, my dear!'"

"We'll get a slice of that some time," Cherry said, thoughtfully, glancing at her husband. "I don't mean when Dad dies either," she added, in quick affection. "I mean that he might build us a little home some day in Mill Valley."

"Gee, how he'd love it!" Alix said, enthusiastically.

"I married Cherry for her money," Martin confessed.

"As a matter of fact," Cherry contradicted him, vivaciously, animated even by the thought of a change and a home, "we have never even spoken of it before, have we, Mart?"

"I never heard of it before," he admitted, smiling, as he knocked the ashes from his pipe. "If I leave the 'Emmy Younger' in October, and go into the Red Creek proposition, I shall be making a good deal myself. But it's pleasant to know that Cherry will come in for a nest-egg some day!"

"Mart doesn't care a scrap for money!" Cherry said to her sister, in the old loyal way. Since Alix's arrival she had somehow liked Martin better. Perhaps Alix brought to her sister with a whiff of the old atmosphere, the old content, the old pride, and the old point-of-view. Presently the visitor boldly suggested that they should both go home together for the wedding, and Martin, to Cherry's amazement, agreed good-naturedly.

"But, Mart, how'll you get along?" his wife asked, anxiously. She had fumed and fussed and puttered and toiled over the care of these four rooms for so long that it seemed unbelievable that her place might be vacated even for a day.

"Oh, I'll get along fine!" he answered, indifferently. Cherry, with a great sigh of relief and delight, abandoned the whole problem; milk bottles, fire wood, groceries, dust, and laundry slipped from her mind as if they had never been. On the last day of August, in the cream-coloured silk and the expensive hat again, yet looking, Alix thought, strangely unlike the bride that had been Cherry, she and her sister happily departed for cooler regions. Martin took them to the train, kissed his sister-in-law gaily, and then his wife affectionately,

"Be a good little girl, Babe," he said, "and write me!"

"Oh, I will—I will!" Cherry looked after him smilingly from the car window. "He really is an old dear!" she told Alix.

CHAPTER VI

But when at the end of the long day they reached the valley, and when her father came innocently into the garden and stood staring vaguely at her for a moment—for her visit, and the day of Alix's return had been kept a secret—her first act was to burst into tears. She clung to the fatherly shoulder as if she were a storm- beaten bird safely home again, and although she immediately laughed at herself, and told the sympathetically watching Peter and Alix that she didn't know what was the matter with her, it was only to interrupt the words with fresh tears.

Tears of joy, she told them, laughing at the moisture in her father's eyes. Hanging on his arm, she went back into the old sitting room again, under the banksia rose; went up the brown stairway to the old, clean, woody-smelling bedroom. Her hat and wraps went into the closet; she danced and exclaimed and exulted over every familiar detail.

She and Alix ran downstairs before supper, and into the garden, and Cherry drew deep, refreshing breaths of the cool air and laughed over every bush and flower. Peter came out to join them, her father came down, and she kissed him again; she could not be close enough to him. She had a special joyous word for Hong; she laughed and teased and questioned Anne, when Anne and Justin came back from an afternoon concert in the city, with an interest and enthusiasm most gratifying to both.

After dinner she had her old place on the arm of her father's porch chair; Alix, with Buck's smooth head in her lap, sat on the porch step beside Peter, and the lovers murmured from the darkness of the hammock under the shadow of the rose vine. It was happy talk in the sweet evening coolness; everybody seemed harmonious and in sympathy to-night. Alix asked Peter's advice regarding her White Minorcas and respectfully promised to act upon it, and Cherry showed him a new side, an affectionate, little sisterly deference and confidence quite different from her old childish sulkiness and pretty caprice.

"Bedtime!" said her father presently, and she laughed in sheer pleasure.

"Daddy—that sounds so nice again!"

"But you do look fagged and pale, little girl," he told her. "You're to stay in bed in the morning."

"Oh, I'll be down!" she assured him. But she did not come down in the morning, none the less. She was tired in soul and body, and glad to let them spoil her again, glad to rest and sleep in the heavenly peace and quiet of the old home.

Midsummer heat was upon the little valley, but here under the redwoods there was always coolness; delicious odours of warm sap and loamy sweetness drifted into Cherry's darkened room; the morning was fresh and foggy, and the night before she had smiled drowsily to stir from first sleep and find her father bending over her, drawing up an extra blanket in the old way. All night long she slept deeply and sweetly, as she had slept through all the nights of childhood; it was ten o'clock when Alix came smiling in with a breakfast tray. Presently she carried it away, and Cherry, with a deep sigh from the fullness of her content, turned on her side and drowsed again.

Waking, after a while, she locked her hands under her head, and lay listening happily to the old and familiar sounds of home. She heard Hong bargaining in his own minor chatter with a fruit vendor, and Alix and her father chuckling over some small confidence in the porch. She heard the subdued clink of dishes, the squawk of a surprised chicken, and the girls' murmuring voices.

It was Saturday, Cherry remembered, when Peter's voice suddenly sounded above the others and was hastily hushed for her sake; Peter was always there at three o'clock on Saturdays. There was another voice, too, pleasant and crisp and even a trifle fastidious; that must be Justin.

Late in the afternoon, rested, fresh, and her old sweet self in the white ruffles, she came down to join them. They had settled themselves under the redwoods, Anne and Justin, Peter and Alix and Buck, the dog, all jumped up to greet her. Cherry very quietly subsided into a wicker chair, listened rather than talked, moved her lovely eyes affectionately from one to another.

Peter hardly moved his eyes from her, although he did not often address her directly; Justin was quite obviously overcome by the unexpected beauty of Anne's cousin; Anne herself, with an undefined pang, admitted in her soul that Cherry was prettier than ever; and even Alix was affected. With the lovely background of the forest, the shade of her thin wide hat lightly shadowing her face, with the dew of her long sleep and recent bath enhancing the childish purity of her skin, and with her blue eyes full of content, Cherry was a picture of exquisite youth and grace and charm. It was not the less winning because she seemed genuinely unconscious of it to-day; perhaps before the girls and Anne's precise little fledgling lawyer no self-conscious thought of conquest had entered her head.

The dog had gone to her knee and laid his bronze mane against the white ruffles, and while she listened and smiled, she idly fondled and petted him with her childish, ringed hand.

"And the next experience is to be at Red Creek?" Justin asked, delighted with this addition to the family circle and beaming about upon everyone.

"Mr. Lloyd is there now," Cherry smiled. "Do you know Red Creek?— I'll have to call you Justin, since you're going to be my cousin so soon," she interrupted herself to say shyly.

"No—I—er—I—er—don't!" Justin stammered.

Anne said vivaciously:

"Of course you're to call him Justin! And he's to call you Cherry, too—those are my orders, Frenny, and don't you dare disobey!"

"But did you get onto the artful and engaging smile Justin gave Cherry?" Alix giggled later to Peter. She and Peter were in the pantry, deep in the manufacture of a certain sort of canape. "Why, he was all in a heap over her!" continued Alix elegantly, as she sampled a small piece of smeared toast with a severe and wrinkled brow. "Try a little mustard in it," she suggested, adding confidentially, "You know Cherry is really too pretty for any use! The rest of us can diet for complexion or diet for figures, and this hat will be becoming or that dress will always look well—but Cherry, why, she just knocks us all galley-west! What's the use of struggling and brushing your hair and worrying about your clothes, when a girl like Cherry will come along and sit down and have everybody staring!"

"She is, of course, quite extraordinary!" Peter conceded as he punched two small holes in the top of a tin of olive oil. The oil welled up through the holes and he wiped his fingers on a corner of Alix's apron.

"It's just the difference," Alix said, "between being nice looking, which half the women in the word are, and being a beauty. I remember that when Cherry was only about ten I used to look at her and think that there was something rather—well, rather arresting about her face. It was such an aristocratic little face. I remember her in those old bluejacket blouses—"

"Yes, I do, too!" Peter said quickly, straightening up from restoring the vinegar demijohn to an obscure position in a lower cupboard. "Well— These have to go in the oven now; I'll take them out. Aren't you going to change for dinner? It's after six now!"

"Since you ask me, I'll see what frock Deshabille has laid out!" Alix yawned, disappearing in the direction of the sitting room, where he found her a few minutes later absorbed in a book.

The evening was cooler, with sudden wind and a promise of storm. They grouped themselves about a fire in the old way; Anne and Justin sitting close together on the settle, as Martin and Cherry had done a year ago. Cherry sat next her father with her hand linked in his; neither hand moved for a long, long time. Alix, sitting on the floor, with her lean cheeks painted by the fire, played with the dog and rallied Peter about some love affair, the details of which made him laugh vexedly in spite of himself. Cherry watched them, a little puzzled at the familiarity of Peter beside this fire; had he been so entirely one of the family a year ago? She could almost envy him, feeling herself removed by so long and strange a twelvemonth.

"Be that as it may, my dear," said Alix, "the fact remains that you taught this Fenton woman to drive your car, didn't you? And you told her that she was the best woman driver you ever knew, a better driver even than Miss Strickland; didn't you?"

"I did not," Peter said, unmovedly smoking and watching the fire.

"Why, Peter, you did! She said you did!"

"Well, then, she said what is not true!"

"She distinctly told me," Alix remarked, "that dear Mr. Joyce had said that she was the best woman driver he ever saw."

"Well, I may have said something like that," Peter growled, flushing. Alix laughed exultingly. "I tell you I loathe her!" he added.

"Daddy, we have a lovely home!" Cherry said softly, her eyes moving from the shabby books and the shabby rugs to Alix's piano shining in the gloom of the far corner. It was all homelike and pleasant, and somehow the atmosphere was newly inspiring to her; she had felt that the talk at dinner, the old eager controversy about books and singers and politics and science, was—well, not brilliant, perhaps, but worth while. She was beginning to think Peter extremely clever and only Alix's quick tongue a match for him, and to feel that her father knew every book and had seen every worthwhile play in the world.

Martin, whose deep dissatisfaction with conditions at the "Emmy Younger Mine" Cherry well knew, had entered into a correspondence some months before relative to a position at another mine that seemed better to him, and instead of coming down for a day or two at the time of Anne's wedding, as Cherry had hoped he might, wrote her that the authorities at the Red Creek plant had "jumped at him," and that he was closing up all his affairs at the "Emmy Younger" and had arranged to ship all their household effects direct to the new home. He knew nothing of Red Creek, except that it was a small inland town in the San Joachim region, but Cherry's delight at the thought of any alternative for the "Emmy Younger" was a revelation to Alix. Martin told his wife generously that he hoped she would stay with her father until the move was accomplished, and Cherry, with a clear conscience, established herself in her old room. She wrote constantly to her husband and often spoke appreciatively of Mart's kindness.

Anne's marriage took place in mid-September. It was a much more formal and elaborate affair than Cherry's had been, because, as Anne explained, "Frenny's people have been so generous about giving him up, you know. After all, he's the last of the Littles; all the others are Folsoms and Randalls. And I want them to realize that he is marrying a gentlewoman!"

The older Littles and all the Folsoms and Randalls came to the wedding, self-respecting, thrifty people who were, for the most part, as Alix summarized it, "buying little homes on the installment plan in desirable residential districts of Oakland and Berkeley." There were bright-faced school teachers, in dark plaid silk waists, and young matrons in carefully planned colour schemes of brown and gray; and they all told Alix and Cherry about the family, the members who were daughters of the Revolution, and the members who belonged to the Society of the Daughters of Officers of the Civil War.

Cherry and Alix went upstairs after the ceremony as Alix and Anne had done a year ago, but there was deep relief and amusement in their mood to-day, and it was with real pleasure in the closer intimacy that the little group gathered about the fire that night.

After that life went on serenely, and it was only occasionally that the girls were reminded that Cherry was a married woman with a husband expecting her shortly to return to him. When she and Alix took part in the village fairs and bazaars, Alix was still a little thrilled to see their names in print, "Miss Strickland and her sister Mrs. Lloyd, who is visiting her," but to Cherry all the romance seemed to have vanished from her new estate. November passed, and Christmas came, and there was some talk of Martin's joining them for Christmas. But he did not come; he was extremely busy at the new mine and comfortable in a village boarding-house.

It was in early March that Alix spoke to her father about it; spoke in her casual and vague fashion, but gave him food for serious thought, nevertheless.

"Dad," said Alix suddenly at the lunch table one day when Cherry happened to be shopping in the city, "were you and Mother ever separated when you were married?"

"No—" the doctor, remembering, shook his head. "Your mother never was happy away from her home!"

"Not even to visit her own family?" persisted Alix.

"Not ever," he answered. "We always planned a long visit in the East—but she never would go without me. She went to your Uncle Vincent's house in Palo Alto once, but she came home the next day--didn't feel comfortable away from home!"

"How long do you suppose Martin will let us have Cherry?" Alix asked.

Her father looked quickly at her and a troubled expression crossed his face.

"The circumstances seem to make it wise to keep her here until he is sure that this new position is the right one!" he said.

"If I know anything about Martin," Alix said, "no position is ever going to be the right one for him. I mean," she added as her father gave her an alarmed look, "I simply mean that he is that sort of man. And it seems to me—odd, the way he and Cherry take their marriage! Now when she got here, five months—six months ago," Alix went on as her father watched her in close and distressed attention, "Cherry was always talking about going back to Mart—every time he sent her money she would say that she ought to keep it for a sudden summons. But she doesn't do that now. You've been giving her her own allowance right along, and she has settled down just as she was. A day or two ago Martin sent her twenty dollars and she has gone into town to spend it to-day—"

She hesitated, shrugged her shoulders.

"You think she ought to go back?" her father asked.

"No, I don't think so!" Alix answered, eagerly. "I don't think anything about it. But—but IS that marriage? Is that really for better or for worse? I mean," she interrupted herself hastily, "as time goes on it will get harder and harder for her; there will seem to be less and less reason for going! Mrs. Brown was talking to me about it yesterday, and she asked in that catty, smiling way she has—"

"Trust the women to gossip!" the doctor said, impatiently.

"Well, nobody minds their gossip!" his daughter assured him. "And for my part I think it's a shame that a girl can't come back home as simply as that, if she wants to!" she added, boldly.

"Don't talk nonsense!" her father said, mildly. "You think," he added, reluctantly, "that it wasn't a good thing for her, eh?"

"Well—" Alix began. "She doesn't seem like other married women," she said, doubtfully. "And the only thing is, will she ever want to go back, if she isn't rather—rather coerced. Martin is odd, you know; he has a kind of stolid, stupid pride. He wrote her weeks ago and asked her to come, and she wrote back that if he would find her a cottage, she would; she couldn't go to his boarding-house, she hated boarding! Martin answered that he would, some day, and she said to me, 'Oh, now he's cross!' Now, mind you," Alix broke off vehemently, "I'd change the entire institution of marriage, if it was me! I'd end all this—"

"Well, we won't go into that!" her father interrupted her, hastily, for Alix had aired these views before and he was not in sympathy with them. "And I guess you're right: the child is a woman now, with a woman's responsibilities," he added. "And her place is with her husband. They'll have to solve life together, to learn together. I'll speak to Cherry!"

Alix, watching him walk away, thought that she had never seen Dad look old before. She saw the shadow on his kind face all the rest of that day.

It was only the next morning when he opened the question with Cherry.

It was a brilliant morning, with spring already in the air. Cherry, on the porch steps, was reading a letter from Martin. Her father sat down beside her. She had on one of her old gowns, and bathed in soft sunlight, looked eighteen again. Emerald grass was already filming the ground about the house; from under the deep rich brown of the forest flooring spring had thrust a million tiny spears of green. The redwoods wore plushy plumes of blue new foliage, and a wild lilac at the edge of the clearing drifted like pale smoke against the dark woods. Everywhere life was soaking and bursting after heavy rains; the very posts of the garden fence were sprouting little feathery tips. The air was sweet and pungent and damp and fresh, the sky high and blue, and across the granite face of Tamalpais a last scarf of mist was floating.

"Well, what has Martin to say?" asked the doctor.

"Oh, he doesn't like it much!" Cherry said, making a little face. "He describes the village as perfectly hopeless. He's moved into the little house in E Street, and gotten two stoves up."

"And when does he want his girl?" her father pursued.

"He doesn't say," Cherry answered, innocently. "I think he is really happier to have me here, where he knows I am well off!" she said. "I know I am," she ended after a moment's thought.

Her father was conscious of a pang; he had not even formed the thought in his own mind that Cherry was unhappy. He was as trusting and as innocent as his daughters in many ways; he shrank from the unwelcome facts of life. His own childhood had been hard and disciplinary, and at Cherry's age he had been concerned only with realities, with the need of food and clothes and shelter. That a life could be spoiled simply by contact with an unsympathetic personality was incomprehensible to him. The child, he told himself, had a good husband, a home and health, and undeveloped resources within herself. It was puzzling and painful to him to realize that there was needed something more—and that that something was lacking. He felt a sudden anger at Martin; why wasn't Martin managing this affair!

"Mart doesn't mention any time!" he mused.

"Thanks to you!" Cherry said, dimpling mischievously. "He wrote quite firmly, just before Christmas," she added, "but I told him that Dad had been such an angel and liked so much to have me here- -" And Cherry's smile was full of childish triumph.

"My dear," her father said, spurred to sudden courage by a realization that the matter might easily become serious, "you mustn't abuse his generosity. Suppose you write that you'll join him—this is March—suppose you say the first of April?"

Cherry flushed and looked down. Her lips trembled. There was a moment of unhappy silence.

"Very well, Dad," she said in a low voice. A second later she had jumped to her feet and vanished in the house. Her father roamed the woods in wretched misgivings, coming in at lunch time to find her in her place, smiling, but traces of tears about her lovely eyes.

Nothing more was said for a day or two, and then Cherry read aloud to the family an affectionate letter in which Martin said that everything would be ready for her whenever she came now.

CHAPTER VII

The last day of March and of Cherry's visit broke clear and blue, and with it spring seemed to have come on a rush of perfume and green beauty. Days had been soft and warm before; this day was hot, and flushed with colour and splendour. There were iris in the dewy grass under the oaks, but in the sunshine every trace of winter's damp had disappeared. Larks whirled up from the fields, and the bridal-wreath and syringa bushes were mounds of creamy bloom.

Alix and Cherry washed each other's hair in the old fashion, and came trailing down with towels and combs to the garden. The doctor joined them in the midst of their tossing and spreading, and sat smoking peacefully on the porch steps.

"Oh, heavens, how I love this sort of weather!" Alix exclaimed, flinging her brown mane backward, her tall figure slender in a faded kimono. She sat down crosswise on her chair, locked her arms about its back, dropped her face on them, and yawned luxuriously. "Dad and Peter," she went on, suddenly sitting erect, "will get all this nice clean hair full of cigar smoke to-night, so what's the use, anyway?"

"To-night's the night we go to Peter?" Cherry stated rather than asked. "Do you remember," she glanced at her father, who was reading his paper, "do you remember when Dad always used to scold us for being rude to Peter?"

"Well, I'd rather go to Peter's for dinner than anywhere else I ever go!" Alix remarked, dreamily. "Seriously, I mean it!" she repeated as Cherry looked at her in amused surprise. "In the first place, I love his bungalow—tiny as it is, it has the whole of a little canyon to itself, and the prettiest view in the valley, I think. And then I love the messy sitting room, with all the books and music, and I love the way Peter entertains. I wish," she added, simply, "that I liked Peter half as well as I do his house!"

"Peter's a dear!" Cherry contended.

"Oh, I know he is!" Alix said, quickly. "Peter's always been a dear, of course. But I mean in a special sense—" finished Alix with an entirely unembarrassed grin.

Cherry, through a glittering cloud of hair, looked at her steadily. Suddenly she gave an odd laugh.

"Do you know I never thought of Peter like that?" she said.

Alix nodded with a cautious look at her father who was out of hearing.

"No, nor I! We've always taken him rather for granted," she admitted. "Only I've been rather wishing, lately, that Peter wasn't such an unflattering, big-brotherish, every-day-neighbour sort of person."

Still Cherry regarded her steadily with an awakening look in her eyes.

"Why lately?" she asked.

"Because," said Alix, briskly and unromantically, "I think Peter would like me to—well, to stop taking him for granted!"

"But Peter's lame—" Cherry submitted, doubtfully.

"You can't call a shortness left from a broken leg LAME!" Alix protested. "Peter isn't brawny, but he's never been ill. And he's not a child. He's thirty-seven. And I imagine he's awfully lonely. And then I imagine it would please Dad—" "Dad has always been ridiculously fond of him," Cherry said, thoughtfully. Peter— possibly in love with Alix! She had never even suspected it. Peter's attitude toward them all had been more paternal than anything else. Cherry and her sister could not remember life without Peter, but he had always been Dad's friend, rather than theirs. He had rebuked them; he had patiently asked them not to chatter so; he had criticized their grammar and their clothes and their friends.

Peter and Alix. Well, there was something rather pleasant in the thought after all, if Alix didn't mind his ugliness and thinness. Cherry thought about it all day. She had had no thought of money a year or two ago; but she was more experienced now. And Peter was rich.

Ordinarily she would have said that she was not going to change for Peter's dinner; but this afternoon, without mentioning the fact, she quietly got into one of her prettiest dresses; a dress that had been made in the long-ago excitement of trousseau days. Peter as a rather autocratic and critical neighbour was one thing; as a possible brother-in-law he was another.

She came downstairs to find her father waiting, and they walked away through the woods together. Alix had already gone up to Peter's house to play tennis. They walked slowly through the lovely aisles of the trees, crossing a road or two, climbing steadily upward under great redwoods. The forest was thinning with oaks and madrone trees, and they found the sunlight again high on the crest of the ridge before a turn of the trail brought them in view of Peter's bungalow. It was a shabby little place, all porch and slope of rough brown roof, set in a wilderness of wild flowers and overlooking long descending slopes of hillside that stretched far away to the very bay and marshes at the ocean mouth.

To-night the spring sunshine streamed across it with broad shadows, the mountains' rough crest stood against a wide expanse of sunset sky. Cherry's skirt brushed the gold dust from masses and masses of buttercups. The tennis was over, but just over; Peter and Alix were sitting, still panting, on the rail of the wide, open porch, and shouted as the others came up.

"You missed doubles!" called Alix. "The grandest we ever did! Doubles with the Thompsons and three sets straight to us—six-two, six-two, and six-two again! They've gone. Oh, heavens, I never had such tennis. Oh, Peter, when you stood there at the net and just curved your hand like a cup"—Alix gave an enthusiastic imitation- -"and over she went, and game and set!"

Cherry, sinking white and frilly into a chair, smiled indulgently. The walk had given her a wild-rose colour, and even Alix was struck with her extraordinary beauty. Alix had wheeled about on the rail to face the porch, and Peter had gotten to his feet and was hospitably pushing basket chairs about. Now he gave Alix a critical look.

"You're disgracefully dirty!" he said, fraternally.

"I know it," she answered, calmly. "Have I time to tub?"

"All the time in the world!" he answered.

"Are any clothes of mine here?" further demanded Alix, rising lazily.

"Yes, there's a blouse. It's in the linen closet; ask Kow for it or get it yourself when you get your towels. You left it the day you changed here after we all climbed the mountain. I hope you people are going to get enough to eat," Peter added, flinging himself into a chair beside Cherry.

"He's been cooking it since breakfast!" Alix remarked, departing. Peter laughed guiltily, and Cherry, too. It was only an exaggeration of the simple truth. He loved to cook, and his meals were famous.

"It's very pleasant to me to have Alix so much at home here," Cherry said, when Alix was gone, and the doctor wandering happily about the garden. "I don't know what we'd do if any one ever usurped our places here!"

She had said it deliberately; the fascination of her recent discovery was too strong to resist. The man flushed suddenly. For a full minute he did not speak, and Cherry was surprised to find herself a little thrilled and even frightened by his silence.

"What put that into your head?" he asked, presently, smoking with his eyes fixed upon the valley far below.

"Just—being here," she answered. And as he glanced over his shoulder he met her smile.

"You've been here a thousand times without ever paying me a compliment!" he reminded her.

Cherry considered this, her brows drawn a trifle together.

"Perhaps," she offered, presently, "it's because there are so many changes, Peter; my marriage, Anne's—everything different! It just came to me that it is nice to have this always the same."

"Perhaps Alix will come up here and help keep it so some day," the man said, deliberately. Cherry's look of elaborate surprise and pleasure died before his serious glance. She was silent for a moment.

"Why don't you ask her?" she said in a low, thoughtful tone, trembling, eager to preserve his mood without a false note.

"I have," he answered simply. Cherry's heart jumped with a sudden unexpected emotion. What was it? Not pleasure, not all surprise— surely there could be no jealousy mixed with her feeling for Peter's plans? But she was dazed with the rush of feeling; hurt in some fashion she could not stop to dissect now. Only this morning she had felt that Peter was not good enough for Alix; now, suddenly, he began to seem admirable and dear and unlike everybody else—

"And she said no?" she stammered in confusion.

"She said no. Or, at least, I intimated that I was a lonely old affectionate man with this and that to offer, and she intimated that that wasn't enough. It was all—" he laughed—"It was all extremely sketchy!"

"Peter, but what does she want?" There was actual sisterly indignation in Cherry's tone.

"Oh, Alix is quite right!" he answered, lightly. "I ought to have said— I ought to explain—that I had told her, only a few days previously, that I had always loved somebody else!"

"Oh-h-h!" Cherry was enlightened. She visualized an affair in the last years of the old century for Peter.

"Oh, and—and she didn't love you?" Cherry asked.

"The lady? She was unfortunately married before I had a chance to ask her," said Peter.

"Oh-h-h!" Cherry said again, impressed, "and you'll never get over it?" she asked, timidly. "Peter, I never knew that!" she added as he was silent. "Does—does Dad know?"

"Nobody knows but Alix, and she only knows the bare facts," he assured her.

"Oh!" Cherry could think of nothing to add to the sympathetic little monosyllable. Twilight was reaching even the hilltop, the canyons were rilling with violet shadows; the sweet, pungent odour of the first dew, falling on warm dust, crept across the garden.

"Finished with the shower!" shrieked Alix from the warm darkness inside the doorway. "Hurry up, Peter, something smells utterly grand!"

"That's the chicken thing!" Peter shouted back, springing up to disappear in the direction of the bathroom. Cherry sat on, silent, wrapped still in the new spell of the pleasant voice, the strangely appealing and yet masterful personality.

The dinner straggled as all Peter's dinners did; Alix mixed a salad-dressing; Peter himself flashed in and out of the tiny, hot kitchen a hundred times. Kow, in immaculate linen, came back and forth in leisurely table-setting. Suddenly everything was ready; the crisp, smoking-hot French loaf, the big, brown jar of bubbling and odorous chicken, the lettuce curled in its bowl, the long- necked bottles in their straw cases, and cheeses and crackers and olives and figs and tiny fish in oil and marrons in fluted paper that were a part of all Peter's dinners.

After dinner they watched the moon rise, until Alix drifted in to the piano and Peter followed her, and the others came in, too, to sit beside the fire. As usual it was midnight before any one thought of ending one of Peter's evenings.

And all through the pleasant, quiet hours, and when he bundled them up in his own big loose coats to drive them home, Cherry was thinking of him in this new light; Peter loving a woman, and denied. The knowledge seemed to fling a strange glamour about him; she saw new charm in him, or perhaps, as she told herself, she saw for the first time how charming he really was. His speech seemed actually the pleasanter for the stammer at which they had all laughed years ago; the slight limp lent its own touch of individuality, and the man's blunt criticisms of books and music, politics and people, were softened by his humour, his genuine humility, and his eager hospitality.

Next day she took occasion to mention Peter and his affairs to Alix. Alix turned fiery red, but laughed hardily.

"If he considers that an offer, he can consider it a refusal, I guess," she said, boyishly embarrassed. "I like him—I'm crazy about him. But I don't want any party in ringlets and crinolines to come floating from the dead past over my child's innocent cradle—"

"Alix, you're awful!" Cherry laughed. "You couldn't talk that way if you loved him!"

"What way?" Alix demanded.

"Oh, about his—well, his children!"

"I should think that would be just the proof that I do love him," Alix persisted idly in her musical, mischievous voice. "I certainly wouldn't want to talk of the children of a man I DIDN'T- -"

"Oh, Alix, don't!" Cherry protested. "Anyway, you know better."

Alix laughed.

"I suppose I do. I suppose I ought to be a mass of blushes. The truth is, I like kids, and I don't like husbands—" Alix confessed, with engaging candour.

"You don't know anything about husbands!" Cherry laughed.

"I know lots of men I'd like to go off with for a few months," Alix pursued. "But then I'd like to come home again! I don't see why that isn't perfectly reasonable—"

"Well, it's not!" Cherry declared almost crossly. "That isn't marriage. You belong where your husband is, and you—you are always glad to be with him—"

"But suppose you get tired of him, like a job or a boarding-house, or any of your other friends?" Alix persisted idly.

"Well, you aren't supposed to!" Cherry said, feebly. Alix let her have the last word; it was only due to her superior experience, she thought crossly. But half an hour later, lying wakeful, and thinking that she would miss dear old Cherry to-morrow, she fancied she heard something like a sob from Cherry's bed, and her whole heart softened with sympathy for her sister.

They came downstairs together the next day in mid-afternoon, both hatted and wrapped for the trip, for Peter was to take Cherry as far as Sausalito in the car, and Martin by a fortunate chance was to meet them there at the ferryboat for San Francisco. Mill Valley was not more than an hour's ride from the ferry. Alix was to drive down and return with Peter. Cherry said good-bye to her father in the porch; she seemed more of a puzzled child than ever.

"I've had a wonderful visit, Dad—" she began bravely. Suddenly the tears came. She buried her face against her father's shabby old office coat and his arms went about her. Alix laughed awkwardly, and Peter shut his teeth. Anne, who had very properly come over to say good-bye to her cousin, got in the back seat of the car and Alix took the seat beside her.

"Take a picture of Peter and me with the suitcases!" she said. "We must look so domestic!"

"Get in here, Cherry," Peter said, opening the door of the seat beside his own. "Doctor, we'll be back in about an hour—"

"Without Cherry!" her father said with a rueful smile.

"Without Cherry!" Peter echoed, looking at her gravely.

It was then that Cherry saw in Peter's expression something that she did not forget for many, many months—never quite forgot. He wore a rough tramping costume to-day, a Sunday, and he was halfway up the porch steps, ready to carry bags to the waiting motor car. His eyes were fixed upon her with something so yearning, so loving, so troubled in their gaze that a thrill went through Cherry from head to foot. He instantly averted his look, turned to the car, fumbled with the gears; they were off. He was to drive them all the way to Sausalito; Alix commented joyously upon the beauty of the day.

Cherry, tied trimly into a hat that was all big daisies, was silent for a while. But when Alix and Anne commenced an interested conversation in the back seat, she suddenly said regretfully:

"Oh, I hate to go away this time! I mind it more even than the first time!"

Peter, edging smoothly about a wide blue puddle, nodded sympathetically, but did not answer.

"I envy Alix—" Cherry said in idle mischief. She knew that the subject was not a safe one, but was irresistibly impelled to pursue it.

"Alix?" said Peter, after a silence long enough to make her feel ashamed of herself.

"Yes. Her young man lives in Mill Valley, right near home!" elucidated Cherry.

"Am I Alix's young man?" he asked, amused.

"Well, aren't you?"

"I don't know. I've never been any one's young man," said Peter.

"Whoever the woman who treated you meanly is—I hate her!" Cherry began again. "Unless," she added, "unless she was very young, and you never told her!"

This time he did not answer at all, and they spun along in utter silence. But when they were nearing Sausalito, Cherry said almost timidly:

"I think perhaps it would make her happy—and proud, to know that you admired her, Peter. I don't know who she is, of course, but almost any woman would feel that. This visit, somehow, has made me feel as if you and I had really begun a new friendship on our own account, not just the old friendship. And I shall often think of that talk we had a week ago, and—think of you, too. N-n-next time you fall in love I hope you will be luckier!"

Silence. But he gave her his quick, friendly smile. Cherry dared not speak again.

"Last stop—all out!" Alix exclaimed. "You get tickets, Peter. Hurray, there's Martin!"

Unexpectedly Martin's big figure came toward them from the ferry gate. Some ore from the mine had to be assayed in San Francisco, and he had volunteered to make the trip so that he might meet his wife and bring her back with him to Red Creek. Time hanging on his hands in the city, he had crossed the bay for the pleasure of the return trip with Cherry. He met them beamingly. There was a little confusion of greeting and good-byes. Alix and Peter watched the others at the railing until the ferryboat turned. Martin smiled over Anne's head; Cherry, both little white-gloved hands on the rail, blue eyes and a glint of bright hair showing under the daisies on her hat, her small figure enveloped in a big loose coat, looked as if she would like to cry again.

"It must be fun to be married, and go off to strange places with your beau!" Alix decided. "I'm hungry, Peter; let's go over there and treat ourselves to fried oysters!"

"Let's go home," he said, unsympathetically. "I'm not hungry."

"Oh, VERY well!" Alix agreed, airily, jumping into the seat beside him. "Though what has given you a grouch I really am at a loss to imagine!" she added under her breath.

"I don't hear you!" shouted Peter, who was suddenly rushing the engine.

"You weren't intended to!" she shouted back. And until they were halfway home, and Alix laughed out in sudden shame and good-nature not another word was spoken. The bright weather had changed suddenly, and a wet spring cloud was spreading over the sky.

"Love me, Peter?" Alix asked, suddenly.

"Not always!" he answered, briefly and sincerely. Fog was creeping over the marshes, the air was full of damp chill. A memory of the coat-enveloped figure and the blue eyes that smiled wistfully under a daisied hat was wringing his heart.

"Listen," began Alix again. "Let's stop for Dad, it's going to pour. And let's go up to your house to eat?"

Silence.

"We can play duets all evening!" Alix added, temptingly.

"Little and Anne coming back?" Peter asked, unwillingly.

"No; they're dining with the Quelquechoses—those bright-faced, freckled cousins of his," Alix answered.

"I don't know that I've got anything up there to eat!" Peter said, gloomily.

"Ooo—say!" Alix said, brightening suddenly with her incorrigible childishness of expression. "Kow's got eggs and cream, hasn't he? I'll make that new thing I was telling you about—it's delicious. Oh, and an onion—" she broke off in concern.

"He has an onion," Peter admitted. "What dish?" he asked, interested in spite of himself, as Alix fell into a rapturous reverie.

"Well, you fry a chopped onion," Alix began, "and then you have a lot of hard-boiled eggs—" In another moment they were deep in culinary details.

CHAPTER VIII

Martin's work was in the Contra Costa Valley, and he and Cherry had a small house in Red Creek, the only town of any size near the mine. Red Creek was in a fruit-farming and dairy region and looked its prettiest on the spring evening when Cherry saw it first. The locusts were in leaf and ready to bloom, and the first fruit blossoms were scattered in snowy whiteness up and down the valley.

Her little house was a cottage with a porch running across the front where windows looked out from the sitting room and the front bedroom. Back of these rooms were a dark little bathroom that connected the front bedroom with another smaller bedroom, a little dining room and a kitchen. Almost all the houses in Red Creek were duplicates, except in minor particulars, of this house, but this particular specimen was older than some of the others and showed signs of hard usage. The kitchen floor was chipped and stained, and the bathroom basin was plugged with putty; there were odd bottles partly full of shoe polish and ink and vinegar, here and there; and on the shelves of the triangular closet in the dining room were cut and folded pieces of spotted white paper.

Martin, man-fashion, had merely camped in kitchen and bedroom while awaiting his wife; but Cherry buttoned on her crisp little apron on the first morning after her arrival, and attacked the accumulated dishes in the sink, and the scattered shirts and collars bravely. It was a cold, raw morning, and she went to and fro briskly, burning rubbish in the airtight stove in the sitting room, and keeping a good wood fire going in the kitchen, and feeling housewifely and efficient as she did so.

After a lunch for which she was praised and applauded in something of the old honeymoon way, she walked to market, passing blocks of other little houses like her own, with bare dooryards where nipped chrysanthemums dangled on poles, and where play wagons, puddles of water, and picking chickens alternated regularly. Other marketing women looked at Cherry with the quickly averted look that is only given to beauty; but the men in the shops wrote down the new name and address with especial zeal and amiability. She remembered the old necessities, bacon and lard and sugar and matches; she recovered the kitchen clock from its wrapping of newspaper, and wound it, and set it on the sink shelf; she was busy with a hundred improvements and cares, and was almost too tired, when Martin came home to dinner, to sit up and share it with him.

It was warm in the dining room and Cherry yawned over her dessert, and rose stiff and aching to return to the kitchen with plates and silver, glasses and food, to shake the tablecloth, to pile and wash and wipe and put away the china, to brush the floor and the stove, and do the last wiping and wringing, and to turn out the gas, and go in to her chair beside the airtight stove.

Martin handed her half his paper and Cherry took it, realizing with cheerful indifference that there was a streak of soot on one cuff, and that her hands were affected by grease and hot water. She read jokes and recipes and answers to correspondents, and small editorial fillers as to the number of nutmegs consumed in China yearly, and the name and circumstances of the oldest living man in England. A new novel was in her bedroom, but she was too comfortable and too tired to go get it, and at ten she rose yawning and stumbling, and went to bed. Breakfast must be on the table at half-past seven, for Martin left for the mine at eight, and she had had a hard day.

For a few weeks the novelty lasted and Cherry was enthusiastic about everything. She looked out across her dishpan at green fields and the beginning of the farms; she saw the lilacs burst into fragrant plumes on the bare branches of her dooryard trees; spring flushed the whole world with loveliness, and she was young, and healthy, and too busy to be homesick.

Martin left the house at eight and was usually at home at five. He would sometimes come into her kitchen while she finished dinner, and tell her about the day, and then suggested that they go to the "pictures" at night. But although Cherry and Alix often had coaxed their father into this dissipation in Mill Valley, it was different there, she found. That was a small colony of city people, the theatre was small, and the films carefully selected. One sat with one's neighbours and friends. But here in Red Creek the theatre was a draughty barn, and the farm workers, big men odorous of warm, acid perspiration, pushed in laughing and noisy; the films were of a different character, too, and advertised by frightful coloured posters at the doors. Martin himself did not like them; indeed, he and Cherry found little to like in either the people or the town.

It was a typical railroad town of California. It was flat, dusty, all its buildings of wood. There were some two thousand souls in Red Creek; two or three stores, a bakery from which the crude odour of baking bread burst every night; saloons, warehouses, a smithy, a butcher shop open only two days a week, a Chinese laundry from which opium-tainted steam issued all day and all night; cattle sheds, pepper trees, wheat barns, and a hotel of raw pine, with a narrow bedroom represented by every one of the forty narrow windows in its upper stories, and a lower floor decorated with spittoons. Back of the crowded main street was another street, beside which Main Street's muddy ugliness was beautiful. Here was another saloon, and rooms above it, and several disreputable cottages about which Cherry sometimes saw odd-looking women.

Not everyone in Red Creek was poor, by any means. It was a district bursting with prosperity; all summer long wheat and fruit and butter and beef poured through it out into the world. Down the road a mile or two, and back toward the far hills, were comfortable ranches where trees planted fifty years before had grown to mammoth proportions, and where the women of the family cultivated gardens. Every family had pigs and cattle and fine horses, and mud-spattered motor cars were familiar sights in Red Creek's streets.

Cherry used to wonder why anybody who could live elsewhere lived here. When some of the ranch girls told her that they always did their shopping in San Francisco, she marvelled that they could reconcile themselves to come home.

The days went on and on, each bringing its round of dishes, beds, sweeping, marketing, folding and unfolding tablecloths, going back and forth between kitchen and dining room. Martin's breakfast was either promptly served and well cooked, in which case Martin was silently satisfied, or it was late and a failure, when he was very articulately disgusted; in either case Cherry was left to clear and wash and plan for another meal in four hours more. She soaked fruit, beat up cake, chopped boxes into kindlings, heated a kettle of water and another kettle of water, dragged sheets from the bed only to replace them, filled dishes with food only to find them empty and ready to wash again.

"I get sick of it!" she told Martin.

"Well, Lord!" he exclaimed. "Don't you think everybody does? Don't I get sick of my work? You ought to have the responsibility of it all for a while!"

His tone was humorously reproving rather than unkind. But such a speech would fill Cherry's eyes with tears, and cause her to go about the house all morning with a heavy heart.

She would find herself looking thoughtfully at Martin in these days, studying him as if he were an utter stranger. It bewildered her to feel that he actually was no more than that, after two years of marriage. She not only did not know him, but she had a baffled sense that the very nearness of their union prevented her from seeing him fairly. She knew that she did him injustice in her thoughts.

It MUST be injustice, decided Cherry. For Martin seemed to her less clever, less just, less intelligent, and less generous than the average man of her acquaintance. And yet he did not seem to impress other people in the way he impressed her.

He was extraordinarily healthy, and had small sympathy for illness, weakness, for the unfortunate, and the complaining. He was scrupulously clean, and Cherry added that to his credit, although the necessity of seeing that Martin's bath, Martin's shaving water, and Martin's clean linen were ready complicated her duties somewhat. He was not interested in the affairs of the day; politics, reforms, world movements generally found him indifferent, but he would occasionally favour his wife with a sudden opinion as to China or intensive farming or Lloyd's shipping. She knew when he did this that he was quoting. He whistled over his dressing, read the paper at breakfast, and was gone. At noon he rushed in, always late, devoured his lunch appreciatively, and was gone again. At night he was usually tired, inclined to quarrel about small matters, inclined to disapprove of the new positions of the bedroom furniture, or the way Cherry's hair was dressed.

He loved to play poker and was hospitable to a certain extent. He would whistle and joke over the preparations for a rarebit after a game, and would willingly walk five blocks for beer if Cherry had forgotten to get it. On Sunday he liked to see her prettily gowned; now and then they motored with his friends from the mine; more often walked, ate a hearty chicken dinner, and went to a cold supper in the neighbourhood, with "Five Hundred" to follow. At ten their hostess would flutter into her kitchen; there would be lemonade and beer and rich layer cake. Then the men would begin to match poker hands, and the women to discuss babies in low tones.

Cherry never saw her husband so animated or so interested as when men he had known before chanced to drift into town, mining men from Nevada or from El Nido, or men he had known in college. They would discuss personalities, would shout over recollected good times, would slap each other on the back and laugh tirelessly.

She thought him an extremely difficult man to live with, and was angered when her hints to this effect led him to remark that she was the "limit." They had a serious quarrel one day, when he told her that she was the most selfish and spoiled woman he had ever known. He called her attention to the other women of the town, busy, contented women, sending children off to school, settling babies down for naps in sunny dooryards, cooking and laughing and hurrying to and fro.

"Yes, and look at them!" Cherry said with ready tears. "Shabby, thin, tired all the time!"

"The trouble with you is," Martin said, departing, "you've been told that you're pretty and sweet all your life—and you're SPOILED! You are pretty, yes—" he added, more mildly. "But, by George, you sulk so much, and you crab so much, that I'm darned if I see it any more! All I see is trouble!"

With this he left her. Left her to a burst of angry tears, at first, when she dropped her lovely little head on the blue gingham of her apron sleeve and cried bitterly.

The kettle began to sing on the stove, a bee came in and wandered about the hot kitchen; the grocer knocked, and Cherry let the big lout of a boy stare at her red eyes uncaring.

Then she went swiftly into the bedroom and began to pack and change. She'd SHOW Martin Lloyd—she'd SHOW Martin Lloyd! She was going straight to Dad—she'd take the—take the—

She frowned. She had missed the nine o'clock train; she must wait for the train at half-past two. Wait where? Well, she could only wait here. Very well, she would wait here. She would not get Martin any lunch, and when he raged she would explain.

She finished her packing and put the house in order. Then, in unaccustomed mid-morning leisure, she sank into a deep rocker, and began to read. Quiet and shade and order reigned in the little house. Outside in the shaded street the children went shouting home again; a fishman's horn sounded.

Steps came bounding up to Cherry's door; her heart began to beat; a knock sounded. She got to her feet, puzzled; Martin did not knock.

It was Joe Robinson, his closest friend at the mine. His handsome, big-featured face was full of concern.

"Say, listen, Mrs. Lloyd; Mart can't get home to dinner," said Joe. "He don't feel extra well—he was in the engine room and he kinder—he kinder—"

"Fainted?" Cherry asked, sharply, turning a little pale.

"Well, kinder. Lawson made him lay down," Joe said. "And he's coming home when the wagon comes down, at three o'clock. He says to tell you he's fine!"

"Oh, thank you, Joe!" Cherry said. She shut the door, feeling weak and frightened. She flew to unpack her bag, hung up her hat and coat, darkened the bedroom and turned down the bed; waited anxiously for Mart's return. Mrs. Turner came in with the baby, a gentle, tired woman, with a face always radiant with joy. Mrs. Turner had seven children, and had once told Cherry that she had never slept a night through since the first year of her marriage. She never changed a baby's gown or rolled a batch of cookies without a deep and genuine love for the task; she could not unbutton the twisted collar from a son's small neck without drawing his freckled cheek to her hungry lips for a kiss, or ask one of her black-headed, bright-eyed daughters to hang up a dish towel without adding: "You're a darling help to your mother!"

The Turners lived next door to the Lloyds, in a shabby two-story house, and though Cherry and her neighbour spoke a different language, they had grown fond of each other. Cherry had sometimes timidly touched upon the matter that was always troubling her, with the older woman. But Mrs. Turner had little to say regarding her feeling for the lean, silent, somewhat unsuccessful man who was the head of her crowded household. She seemed to take it for granted that he would sometimes be unreasonable.

"Papa gets so mad if anything gets burned!" she would say, with her gentle laugh. And once she added the information that her husband's mother had been a wonderful manager. "Men are that way!" was her comment upon the difficulties of other wives. But once, when there was a wedding near by, Cherry, with others in the church, saw the tears in Mrs. Turner's eyes as she watched the bride. "Poor little innocent thing!" she had whispered with a tremulous smile.

She was deeply concerned over the news from Martin, and when Cherry had met his limp form at the front door, and had whisked him into a cool bed, and put chopped ice on the aching forehead, and gotten him, grateful and penitent, off to sleep, her neighbour came over again to whisper in the kitchen.

"He's all right," Cherry smiled. "He was so glad to get to bed, and so appreciative!" she added in a motherly tone.

"You look as if you hadn't a thing in the world to do!" the older housekeeper commented, glancing about the neat, quiet kitchen.

"I believe I like sick nursing!" Cherry smiled back.

For a day or two Martin stayed in bed and Cherry spoiled and petted him, and was praised and thanked for every step she took. After that they took a little trip into the mountains near by, and Cherry sent Alix postcards that made her sister feel almost a pang of envy.

But then the routine began again, and the fearful heat of midsummer came, too. Red Creek baked in a smother of dusty heat, the trees in the dry orchards, beside the dry roads, dropped circles of hot shadow on the clodded, rough earth. Farms dozed under shimmering lines of dazzling air, and in the village, from ten o'clock until the afternoon began to wane, there was no stir. Flies buzzed and settled on screen doors, the creek shrunk away between crumbling rocky banks, the butcher closed his shop, and milk soured in the bottles.

The Turners, and some other families, always camped together in the mountains during this season, and they were off when school closed, in an enviable state of ecstasy and anticipation. Cherry had planned to join them, but an experimental week-end was enough. The camp was in the cool woods, truly, but it was disorderly, swarming with children, the tents were small and hot, the whole settlement laughed and rioted and surged to and fro in a manner utterly foreign to her. She returned, to tell Martin that it was "horribly common," and weather the rest of the summer in Red Creek.

"Mrs. Turner is the only woman that I can stand," said Cherry, "and she was always cooking, in an awful cooking shed, masses and masses of macaroni and stewed plums and biscuits—and all of them laughing and saying, 'Girlie, I guess you've got a hollow leg!' Dearie, I couldn't eat any more without busting!' And sitting round that plank table—"

Martin shouted with laughter at her, but he sympathized. He had never cared particularly for the Turners; was perfectly willing to keep the friendship within bounds.

He sympathized as little with another friendship she made, some months later, with the wife of a young engineer who had recently come to the mine. Pauline Runyon was a few years older than her husband, a handsome, thin, intense woman, who did everything in an entirely individual way. She took one of the new little bungalows that were being erected in Red Creek "Park," and furnished it richly and inappropriately, and established a tea table and a samovar beside the open fireplace. Cherry began to like better than anything else in the world the hours she spent with Pauline. She would have liked to go every day, and every day argued and debated the propriety of doing so, in her heart.

Not since the days of her engagement to Martin, and then only on a few occasions, had she felt the thrill that she experienced now, when Pauline, with her dark eyes and her frilly parasol, wandered in the kitchen door, to sit laughing and talking for a few minutes, or when she herself dressed and crossed the village, and went up past the packing plant and the storage barns to the two small cement gate posts and the length of rusty chain that marked the entrance to Red Creek "Park." Then there would be tea, poetry, talk, and the flattery that Pauline quite deliberately applied to Cherry, and the flattery that Cherry all unconsciously lavished on her friend in return.

Pauline read Browning, Francis Thompson, and Pater, and introduced Cherry to new worlds of thought. She talked to Cherry of New York, which she loved, and of the men and women she had met there. She sometimes sighed and pushed the bright hair back from Cherry's young and innocent and discontented little face, and said, tenderly, "On the stage, my dear—anywhere, everywhere, you would be a furore!"

And thinking, in the quiet evenings—for Martin's work kept him later and later at the mine—Cherry came to see that her marriage had been a great mistake. She had not been ready for marriage. She would sit on the back steps, as the evenings grew cooler, and watch the exquisite twilight fade, and the sorrow and beauty of life would wring her heart.

Darkness came, the Turner children shrieked, laughed, clattered dishes, and were silent. Cherry would sit on, her arms wrapped in her apron, her eyes staring into the young night. In the darkness she could only see the great shadows that were the Adams' windmill, and the old Brown barn, and the Cutters' house down the back road. The dry earth seemed awake at night, stretching itself, under brown sods, for a great breath of relief in the merciful coolness. Cherry could smell grapes, and smell the pleasant wetness of the dust where the late watering cart had passed by, after sunset. The roads were too hot for watering all day long, and this sweet, wet odour only came with the night.

A dream of ease and adoration and beauty came to her. She did not visualize any special place, any special gown or hour or person. But she saw her beauty fittingly environed; she saw cool rooms, darkened against this blazing midsummer glare; heard ice clinking against glass; the footsteps of attentive maids; the sound of cultivated voices, of music and laughter. She had had these dreams before, but they were becoming habitual now. She was so tired—so sick—so bored with her real life; it was becoming increasingly harder and harder for her to live with Martin; to endure and to struggle against the pricks. She was always in a suppressed state of wanting to break out, to shout at him brazenly, "I don't care if your coffee is weak! I like it weak! I don't care if you don't like my hat—I do! Stop talking about yourself!"

Various little mannerisms of his began seriously to annoy her; a rather grave symptom, had Cherry but known it. He danced his big fingers on the handle of the sugar spoon at breakfast, sifting the sugar over his cereal; she had to turn her eyes resolutely away from the sight. He blew his nose, folded his handkerchief, and then brushed his nose with it firmly left and right; she hated the little performance that was never altered. He had a certain mental slowness, would blink at her politely and patiently when she flashed plans or hopes at him: "I don't follow you, my dear!" This made her frantic.

She was twenty, undisciplined and exacting. She had no reserves within herself to which she could turn. Bad things were hopelessly bad with Cherry, her despairs were the dark and tearful despairs of girlhood, prematurely transferred to graver matters.

Martin was quite right in some of his contentions; girl-like, she was spasmodic and unsystematic in her housekeeping; she had times of being discontented and selfish. She hated economy and the need for careful managing.

In October Alix chanced to write her a long and unusually gossipy letter. Alix had a new gown of black grenadine, and she had sung at an afternoon tea, and had evidently succeeded in her first venture. Also they had had a mountain climb and enclosed were snapshots Peter had taken on the trip.

Cherry picked up the little kodak prints; there were four or five of them. She studied them with a pang at her heart. Alix in a loose rough coat, with her hair blowing in the wind, and the peaked crest of Tamalpais behind her—Alix busy with lunch boxes— Alix standing on the old bridge down by the mill, A wave of homesickness swept over the younger sister; life tasted bitter. She hated Alix, hated Peter, above all she hated herself. She wanted to be there, in Mill Valley, free to play and to dream again—

A day or two later she told Martin kindly and steadily that she thought it had all "been a mistake." She told him that she thought the only dignified thing to do was to part. She liked him, she would always wish him well, but since the love had gone out of their relationship, surely it was only honest to end it.

"What's the matter?" Martin demanded.

"Nothing special," Cherry assured him, her eyes suddenly watering. "Only I'm tired of it all. I'm tired of PRETENDING. I can't argue about it. But I know it's the wise thing to do."

"You acted this same way before," Martin suggested, after looking back at his paper for a few seconds.

"I did not!" Cherry said, indignantly. "That is not true."

"You'd go back to your father, I suppose?" Martin said, yawning.

"Until I could get into something," Cherry replied with dignity. A vague thought of the stage flitted through her mind.

"Oh!" Martin said, politely. "And I suppose you think your father would agree to this delightful arrangement?" he asked.

"I know he would!" Cherry answered, eagerly.

"All right—you write and ask him!" Martin agreed, good-naturedly. Cherry was surprised at his attitude, but grateful more than surprised.

"Not cross, Mart?" she asked.

"Not the least in the world!" he answered, lightly.

"Because I truly believe that we'd both be happier—" the woman said, hesitatingly. Martin did not answer.

The next day she sat down to write her father. The house was still. Red Creek was awakening in the heavenly October coolness, children chattered on the way to school, the morning and evening were crisp and sharp.

Cherry stared out at a field of stubble bathed in soft sunshine. The hills to-day were only a shade deeper than the pale sky. Along the road back of the house a lumber wagon rattled, the thin bay horses galloping joyously in harness. Pink and white cosmos, pallid on clouds of frail, bushy green, were banked in the shade of the woodshed.

She meditated, with a troubled brow. Her letter was unexpectedly hard to compose. She could not take a bright and simple tone, asking her father to rejoice in her home-coming. Somehow the matter persisted in growing heavy, and the words twisted themselves about into ugly and selfish sounds. Cherry was young, but even to her youth the phrases, the "misunderstood" and the "uncongenial," the "friendly parting before any bitterness creeps in," and the "free to decide our lives in some happier and wiser way," rang false. Pauline had been divorced, a few years ago, and the only thing Cherry disliked in her friend was her cold and resentful references to her first husband.

No, she couldn't be a divorced woman. It was all spoiled, the innocent past and the future; there was no way out! She gave up the attempt at a letter, and began to annoy Martin with talk of a visit home again.

"You were there six months ago!" Martin reminded her.

"Eight months ago, Mart."

"What you want to go for?"

"Oh, just—just—" Cherry's irrepressible tears angered herself almost as much as they did Martin. "I think they'd like me to!" she faltered.

"Go if you want to!" he said, but she knew she could not go on that word.

"That's it," she said at last to herself, in one of her solitary hours. "I'm married, and this is marriage. For the rest of my life it'll be Mart and I—Mart and I—in everything! For richer for poorer, for better for worse—that's marriage. He doesn't beat me, and we have enough money, and perhaps there are a lot of other women worse off than I am. But it's—it's funny."

CHAPTER IX

In January, however, he came home one noon to find her hatted and wrapped to go.

"Oh, Mart—it's Daddy!" she said. "He's ill—I've got to see him! He's awfully ill."

"Telegram?" asked Martin, not particularly pleased, but not unsympathetic either.

For answer she gave him the yellow paper that was wet with her tears. "Dad ill," he read. "Don't worry. Come if you can. Alix."

"I'll bet it's a put-up job between you and Alix—" Martin said in indulgent suspicion.

Her indignant glance sobered him; he hastily arranged money matters, and that night she got off the train in the dark wetness of the valley, and was met by a rush of cool and fragrant air. It was too late to see the mountain, lights were twinkling everywhere in the dark trees. Cherry got a driver, rattled and jerked up to the house in a surrey, and jumped out, her heart almost suffocating her.

Alix came flying to the door, the old lamplight and the odour of wood smoke poured through. There was no need for words; they burst into tears and clung together.

An hour later Cherry, feeling as if she was not the same woman who waked in Red Creek this same morning, and got Martin's eggs and coffee ready, crept into her father's room. Alix had warned her to be quiet, but at the sight of the majestic old gray head, and the fine old hands clasped together on the sheet, her self-control forsook her entirely and she fell to her knees and began to cry again.

The nurse looked at her disapprovingly, but after all it made little difference. Doctor Strickland roused only once again, and that was many hours later. Cherry and Alix were still keeping their vigil; Cherry, worn out, had been dozing; the nurse was resting on a couch in the next room.

Suddenly both daughters were wide awake at the sound of the hoarse yet familiar voice. Alix fell on her knees and caught the cold and wandering hand.

"What is it, darling?" The old, half-joking maternal manner was all in earnest now.

"Peter?" he said, thickly.

"Peter's in China, dear. You remember that Peter was to go around the world? You remember that, Dad?"

"In the 'Travels with a Donkey,'" he said, rationally.

The girls looked at each other dubiously.

"We all read that together," Alix encouraged him.

"No—" he said, musingly. They thought he slept again, but he presently added, "Somewhere in Matthew—no, in Mark—Mark is the human one—Mark was as human as his Master—"

"Shall I read you from Mark?" Alix asked, as his voice sank again. A shabby old Bible always stood at her father's bedside; she reached for it, and making a desperate effort to steady her voice, began to read. The place was marked by an old letter, and opened at the chapter he seemed to desire, for as she read he seemed to be drinking in the words. Once they heard him whisper "Wonderful!" Cherry got up on the bed, and took the splendid dying head in her arms, the murky winter dawn crept in, and the lamp burned sickly in the daylight. Hong could be heard stirring. Alix closed the book and extinguished the lamp. Cherry did not move.

"Charity!" the old man said, presently, in a simple, childish tone. Later, with bursts of tears, in all the utter desolation of the days that followed, Cherry loved to remember that his last utterance was her name. But Alix knew, though she never said it, that it was to another Charity he spoke.

Subdued, looking younger and thinner in their new black, the sisters came downstairs, ten days later, for a business talk. Peter had been named as one executor, but Peter was far away, and it was a pleasant family friend, a kindly old surgeon of Doctor Strickland's own age, or near it, and the lawyer, George Sewall, the other executor, who told them about their affairs. Anne, as co-heiress, was present at this talk, with Justin sitting close beside her. Martin, too, who had come down for the funeral, was there.

Cherry was white, headachy, indifferent; she seemed stunned by her loss; but Alix's extraordinary vitality had already asserted itself, and she set herself earnestly to understand their somewhat complicated affairs.

The house went to the daughters; there were books and portraits for Anne, a box or two in storage for Anne, and Anne was mentioned in the only will as equally inheriting with Alexandra and Charity. For some legal reason that the lawyer and Doctor Younger made clear, Anne could not fully inherit, but her share would be only a trifle less than her cousins'.

Things had reached this point when Justin Little calmly and confidently claimed that Anne's share was to be based upon an old loan of Anne's father to his brother, a loan of three thousand dollars to float Lee Strickland's invention, with the understanding that Vincent Strickland be subsequently entitled to one third of the returns. As the patent had been sold for nearly one hundred and fifty thousand dollars, one third of it, with accumulative interest for ten years, of which no payment had ever been made Anne, was a large proportion of the entire estate, and the development of this claim, in Justin Little's assured, woodeny voice, caused everyone except the indifferent Cherry to look grave.

The estate was not worth one hundred and fifty thousand dollars now, by any means; it had been reduced to little more than two thirds of that sum, and Anne's bright concern that everyone should be SATISFIED with what was RIGHT, and her ingenuous pleasure in Justin's cleverness in thinking of this possibility, were met with noticeable coldness.

If Anne was wrong, and the paper she held in her hand worthless, each girl would inherit a comfortable little fortune, but if Anne was right, Cherry and Alix would have only a few thousand dollars apiece, and the old home.

The business talk was over before any of them realized the enormity of Anne's contention, and Anne and Justin had departed. But both the old doctor and the lawyer agreed with Martin that it looked as if Anne was right, and when the family was alone again, and had had the time to digest the matter, they felt as if a thunderbolt had fallen across their lives.

"That Anne could DO it!" Alix said, over and over. Cherry seemed dazed, spoke not at all, and Martin had said little.

"People will do anything for money!" he observed once drily. He had met Justin sternly. "I'm not thinking of my wife's share—I didn't marry her for her money; never knew she had any! But I'm thinking of Alix."

"Yes—we must think of darling Alix!" Anne had said, nervously eager that there should be no quarrel. "If Uncle Lee intended me to have all this money, then I suppose I must take it, but I shan't be happy unless things are arranged so that Alix shall be COMFORTABLE!"

"B-but the worst of it is, Alix!" Cherry stammered, suddenly, on the day before she and Martin were to return to Red Creek, "I—I counted on having enough—enough to live my own life! Alix, I can't—I can't go back!"

"Why, my darling—" Alix exclaimed, as Cherry began to cry in her arms. "My darling, is it as bad as all that!"

"Oh, Alix," whispered the little sister, trembling, "I CAN'T bear it. You don't know how I feel. You and Dad were always here; now that's all gone—you're going to rent the house and try to teach singing—and I've nothing to look forward to—I've nobody!"

"Listen, dear," Alix soothed her. "If they advise it, and especially if Peter advises it when he gets back, we'll fight Anne. And then if we win our fight, I'll always keep the valley house open. And if we don't, why I'm going to visit you and Martin every year, and perhaps I'll have a little apartment some day—I don't intend to board always—"

But she was crying, too. Everything seemed changed, cold and strange; she had suspected that Cherry's was not a successful marriage; she knew it now, and to resign the adored little sister to the unsympathetic atmosphere of Red Creek, and to miss all the old life and the old associations, made her heart ache.

"There's—there's nothing special, Cherry?" she asked after a while.

"With Martin? Oh, no," Cherry answered, her eyes dried, and her packing going on composedly, although her voice trembled now and then. "No, it's just that I get bad moods," she said, bravely. "I was pretty young to marry at all, I guess."

"Martin loves you," Alix suggested timidly.

"He takes me for granted," Cherry said, after a pause. "There doesn't seem to be anything ALIVE in the feeling between us," she added, slowly. "If he says something to me, I make an effort to get his point of view before I answer. If I tell him some plan of mine, I can see that he thinks it sounds crazy! I don't seem very domestic—that's all. I—I try. Really, I do! But—" and Cherry seemed to brace herself in soul and body—"but that's marriage. I'll try again!"

She gave Alix a long kiss in parting, the next day, and clung to her.

"You're the dearest sister a girl ever had, Alix. You're all I have, now!"

"I'll write you about the case, and wire you if you're needed, and see you soon!" Alix said, cheerfully. Then she turned and went back into the empty house, keeping back her tears until the sound of the surrey had quite died away.

CHAPTER X

Alexandra Strickland, coming down the stairway of the valley house on an April evening, glanced curiously at the door. Her eyes moved to the old clock, and a smile tugged involuntarily at the corners of her mouth. Only eight o'clock, but the day had been so long and so quiet that she had fancied that the hour was much later, and had wondered who knocked so late.

She crossed to the door and opened it to darkness and rain, and to a man in a raincoat, who whipped off a spattered cap and stood smiling in the light of the lamp she held. Instantly, with a sort of gasp of surprise and pleasure and some deeper emotion, she set down the lamp, and held out her hands gropingly and went into his arms. He laughed joyously as he kissed her, and for a minute they clung together.

"Peter!" she said. "You angel—when did you arrive and what are you doing, and tell me all about it!"

"But, Alix—you're thin!" Peter said, holding her at arm's length. "And—and—" He gently touched the black she wore, and fixed puzzled and troubled eyes upon her face. "Alix—" he asked, apprehensively.

For answer she tried to smile at him, but her lips trembled and her eyes brimmed. She had led the way into the old sitting room now, and Peter recognized, with a thrill of real feeling, the shabby rugs and books and pictures, and the square piano beside which he had watched Cherry's fat, childish hand on the scales so many times, and Alix scowling over her songs.

"You heard—about Dad?" Alix faltered now, turning to face him at the mantel.

"Your father!" Peter said, shocked.

"But hadn't you heard, Peter?"

"My dear—my dearest child, I'm just off the steamer. I got in at six o'clock. I'd been thinking of you all the time, and I suddenly decided to cross the bay and come straight on to the valley, before I even went to the club or got my mail! Tell me—your father—"

She had knelt before the cold hearth, and he knelt beside her, and they busied themselves with logs and kindling in the old way. A blaze crept up about the logs and Alix accepted Peter's handkerchief and wiped a streak of soot from her wrist, quite as if she was a child again, as she settled herself in her chair.

Peter took the doctor's chair, keeping his concerned and sympathetic eyes upon her.

"He was well one day," she said, simply, "and the next—the next, he didn't come downstairs, and Hong waited and waited—and about nine o'clock I went up—and he had fallen—he had fallen—"

She was in tears again and Peter put his hand out and covered hers and held it. Their chairs were touching, and as he leaned forward, their faces might almost have touched, too.

"He must have been going to call someone," said Alix, after a while, "they said he never suffered at all. This was January, the last day, and Cherry got here that same night. He knew us both toward morning. And that—that was all. Cherry was here for two weeks. Martin came and went—"

"Where is Cherry now?" Peter interrupted.

"Back at Red Creek." Alix wiped her eyes. "She hates it, but Martin had a good position there. Poor Cherry, it made her ill."

"Anne came?"

"Anne and Justin, of course." Peter could not understand Alix's expression. She fell silent, still holding his hand and looking at the fire.

He had not seen her for nearly six months; he had been all around the world; had found her gay, affectionate letters in London, in Athens, in Yokohama. But for three months now he had been away from the reach of mails, roughing it on a friend's hemp plantation in Borneo, and if she had written, the letter was as yet undelivered. He looked at her with a great rush of admiration and affection. She was not only a pretty and a clever woman; but, in her plain black, with this new aspect of gravity and dignity, and with new notes of pathos and appeal in her exquisite voice, he realized that she was an extremely charming woman.

More than that, she stood for home, for the dearly familiar and beloved things for which he had been so surprisingly homesick. His mountain cabin and the old house in San Francisco on Pacific Avenue; she belonged to his memories of them both; she was the only woman in the world that he knew well.

Before he said good-bye to her, he had asked her to marry him. He well remembered her look of bright and interested surprise.

"D'you mean to tell me you have forgotten your lady love of the hoop-skirts and ringlets?" she had demanded.

"She never wore ringlets and crinolines!" he had answered.

"Well, bustles and pleats, then?"

"No," Peter had told her, frankly. "I shall always love her, in a way. But she is married; she never thinks of me. And I like you so much, Alix; I like our music and cooking and tramps and reading— together. Isn't that a pretty good basis for marriage?"

"No!" Alix had answered, decidedly. "Perhaps if I were madly in love with you I should say yes, and trust to little fingers to lead you gently, and so on—"

He remembered ending the conversation in one of his quick moods of irritation against her. If she couldn't take anybody or anything seriously—he had said.

Poor Alix—she was taking life seriously enough to-night, Peter thought, as he watched her.

"Tell me about Cherry," he said.

"Cherry is well, but just a little thin, and heart-broken now, of course. Martin never seems to stay at any one place very long, so I keep hoping—"

"Doesn't make good!" Peter said, shaking his head.

"Doesn't seem to! It's partly Cherry, I think," Alix said honestly. "She was too young, really. She never quite settles down, or takes life in earnest. But he's got a contract now for three years, and so she seems to be resigning herself, and she has a maid, I believe."

"She must love him," Peter submitted. Alix looked surprised.

"Why not?" she smiled. "I suppose when you've had ups and downs with a man, and been rich and poor, and sick and well, and have lived in half-a-dozen different places, you rather take him for granted!" she added.

"Oh, you think it works that way?" Peter asked, with a keen look.

"Well, don't you think so? Aren't lots of marriages like that?"

"You false alarm. You quitter!" he answered.

Alix laughed, a trifle guiltily. Also she flushed, with a great wave of splendid young colour that made her face look seventeen again. "Your father left you—something, Alix?" Peter asked presently, with some hesitation.

"That," she answered frankly, "is where Anne comes in!"

"Anne?"

"Anne and Justin came straight over," Alix went on, "and they were really lovely. And they asked me to come to them for a visit—but I couldn't very well; they live with his mother, you know, Amanda Price Little, who writes the letters to the Chronicle about educating children and all that. Doctor Younger and George Sewall were here every day; you and George were named as executors. I was so mixed up in policies and deeds and overdue taxes and interest and bonds—"

"Poor old Alix, if I had only been here to help you!" the man said. And for a moment they looked a little consciously at each other.

"Well, anyway," the girl resumed hastily, "when it came to reading the will, Anne and Justin sprung a mine under us! It seems that ten years ago, when the Strickland Patent Fire Extinguisher was put upon the market, my adorable father didn't have much money—he never did have, somehow. So Anne's father, my Uncle Vincent, went into it with him to the extent of about three thousand dollars—"

"Three thousand!" Peter, who had been leaning forward, earnestly attentive, echoed in relief.

"That was all. Dad had about three hundred. They had to have a laboratory and some expensive retorts and things, it seems. Dad did all the work, and put in his three hundred, and Uncle Vincent put in three thousand—and the funny thing is," Alix broke off to say, musingly, "Uncle Vincent was perfectly splendid about it; I myself remember him saying, 'Don't worry, Lee. I'm speculating on my own responsibility, not yours.'"

"Well?" Peter prompted, as she hesitated.

"Well. They had a written agreement then, giving Uncle Vincent a third interest in the patent, should it be sold or put on the market—"

"Ha!" Peter ejaculated, struck.

"Which, of course, was only a little while before Uncle Vincent died," Alix went on, with a grave nod. "The agreement lay in Dad's desk all these years—fancy how easily he might have burned it many's the time! But he didn't. George Sewall says that Anne is right."

"But wasn't Anne third heiress anyway, under his will? I know I've heard—"

"Certainly she was. But a third interest now, in a diminished estate that began at something less than one hundred and fifty thousand dollars, is quite different from a third of it ten years ago, plus compound interest," Alix said, bringing her clear brows together with a quizzical smile. "They've broken the will."

Peter, in the silence, whistled expressively.

"Gee—rusalem!" he exclaimed. "What does it come to?"

At this Alix looked very sober, gazed down at the fire, and shook her head.

"All he had!" she answered, briefly.

Peter was silent, looking at her in stupefaction.

"Almost, that is," Alix amended more cheerfully. "As it was—we should have had more than thirty thousand apiece. As it is, Anne gets it all, or if not quite all, nearly all."

"Gets!" he echoed, hotly. "How do you mean?"

"It seems to be perfectly just," the girl answered, rather lifelessly. But immediately she laughed. "Don't look so awful, Peter. In the first place, Cherry and I still have the house. In the second place, I am singing at St. Raphael's for five hundred a year, and singing other places now and then."

"Alix, aren't you corking!" he said, with his pleasantest smile.

"Am I?" she asked, smiling. But immediately the smile melted, and her lips shook. "Anyway, I'm glad you're home again, Peter!" she added.

"Home again," he answered, half-angrily. "I should hope I am—and high time, too! Has this—this money been turned over to Anne?"

"Not yet. Nobody gets anything until the estate is cleared—a year or more from now."

"And do you tell me that she will have the effrontery to take it?"

"Rather! She said to me, 'Isn't it wonderful that Justin saw it at once, and I never would have seen it!' She was quite sweet and merry over it—"

"Great Lord! Does she know that it's practically all your father had?"

Alix hesitated.

"Well, you see there had been mismanagement, Peter. Dad speculated, and lost some. And we were a pretty heavy expense for a good many years. I hated to expose the whole thing, and George— he's been splendid—said that they probably had a perfectly valid claim, anyway. There are some things to be thankful for," Alix added, dashing the sudden tears from her eyes, "and one is that Dad never knew it!"

"I can't tell you how surprised I am at Anne," Peter said.

"Well, we all were!" Alix confessed. "But it's just Anne's odd little self-centred way," she added. "It was here, and she wanted it. She belongs heart and soul to the Little family now, and she is quite triumphant over being of so much help to Justin. They're to build a house in Berkeley. Anne has it all worked out!" Alix said, with amused distaste. "Well—I let Hong go, and as soon as I can rent this house, I'm going to New York."

"Why New York, my dear girl?"

"Because I believe I can make a living there, singing and teaching and generally struggling with life!" she answered, cheerfully. "Cherry gets most of the money—they are always somewhat in debt, and I imagine that the reason she is able to have a nice apartment and a maid now is because she knows it is coming—and I get the house, and enough money to keep me going—say, a year, in New York."

"Do you want to go, Alix?" he said, affectionately.

"Yes, I think I do," she answered. But her eyes watered. "I do—in a way," she added. "That is, I love my singing, and the thought of making a success is delightful to me. But of course it means that I give up everything else. I can't have home life, and—and the valley—for years, four or five anyway, I'll have to give all that up. And I'm twenty-seven, Peter. And I'd always rather hoped that my music was going to be a domestic variety—"She stopped, smiling, but he saw the pain in her eyes. "George Sewall most kindly asked me to mother his small son—" she resumed, casually. "But although he is the dearest—"

"Sewall did!" Peter exclaimed, rather struck. "Great Scott! his father is one of the richest men in San Francisco."

"I know it," Alix agreed. "And he is one of the nicest men," she added. "But of course he'll never really love any one but Ursula. And I felt— oh, I felt too tired and alone and depressed to enter upon congratulations and clothes and family dinners with the Sewalls," she ended, a little drearily. "I wanted—I wanted things in the old way—as they were—" she said, her voice thickening.

"I know—I know!" Peter said, sympathetically. And for a while there was silence in the little house, while the rain fell steadily upon the dark forest without, and soaked branches swished about eaves and windows. "Can you put me up to-night?" he asked, suddenly. He liked her frank pleasure.

"Rather! I think Cherry's room was made up fresh last Monday," she told him. "And to-morrow," she added, with a brightening face, "we'll walk up to your house, and see what six months of Kow's uninterrupted sway have done to it!"

"That's just what we'll do!" he agreed, enthusiastically. "And we'll have some music—"

She had risen, as if for good-nights, and was now beside the old square piano, where she had placed the lamp.

"I haven't touched it—since—" she said, sadly, sitting on the stool, and with her eyes still smiling on him, putting back the hinged cover. And a moment later her hands, with the assurance and ease of the adept, drifted into one of the songs of the old days.

"Do you remember the day we put the rose tree back, Peter?" she asked. "When Martin was almost a stranger? And do you remember the day Cherry and I fell into the Three Wells and you and Dad had to disappear while we dried our clothing on branches of trees? And do you remember the day we made biscuits, over by the ocean?"

"I remember all the days," he answered, deeply stirred.

"We didn't see all this, then," Alix mused, still playing softly. "Anne claiming everything for her husband, you and I here talking of Dad's death, and Cherry married—" She sighed.

"She's not happy?" he questioned quickly.

Alix shrugged, pursing her lips doubtfully.

"She's not unhappy," she told him, with a troubled smile. "It's just one of those marriages that don't ever get anywhere, and don't ever stop," she added. "Martin has faults, he's unreasonable, and he makes enemies. But those aren't the faults for which a woman can leave her husband. Oh, Peter," she added, laying a smooth warm hand on his, and looking straight into his eyes with her honest eyes, "don't go away again! Stay here in the valley for a week or two, and help me get everything worked out and thought out—I've been so much alone!"

"Dear old Alix!" he said, sitting down on the bench beside her and putting his arm about her. She dropped her head on his shoulder, and so they sat, very still, for a long minute. Alix's hand went to her own shoulder, and her fingers tightened on his, and she breathed deep, contented breaths, like a child.

"Somebody ought to wire Mrs. Grundy, collect," she said, after awhile.

"We will defy Mrs. Grundy, my dear," Peter said, kissing the top of a soft brown braid, "by trotting off hand in hand tomorrow and getting ourselves married. Why, Alix, he gave us his consent years ago—don't you remember?"

"He DID wish it!" she said, and burst into tears.

"I seem to be doing things in a slightly irregular manner," she said to him the next day, when they had gotten breakfast together, and were basking in the sunlight of the upper deck of the ferryboat, on their way to the city. "I spend the night BEFORE my marriage alone—alone in a small country house hidden in the woods—with my betrothed, and propose to buy my trousseau immediately after the ceremony!"

"I feel like saying to you what the dear old French archbishop said to the small child," Peter smiled, marvelling a little nonetheless at her untouched serenity. "He was speaking to all the children in some institution, and came to this little one: 'ET TU ETES NEGRE? AH, BIEN—BIEN, CONTINUEZ—CONTINUEZ!' It's what makes you yourself, Alix, doing everything just a little differently."

"Marrying you, far from seeming a radical or momentous thing to do," she assured him, "seems to me like getting back into key— getting out of this bad dream of loneliness and change—securing something that I thought was lost!"

Her voice fell to a dreamy note, and she watched the gulls, wheeling in the sunshine, with thoughtful, smiling eyes. The man glanced at her once or twice, in the silence that followed, with something like hesitation, or compunction, in his look.

"Look here, Alix—let's talk. I want to ask you something. Or, rather, I want to tell you something—or, rather—"

"CONTINUEZ—CONTINUEZ!" she said, laughing, as he hesitated.

"There's never been anything—anything to tell you—or your father, if he was here," Peter said, flushed and a trifle awkward, "I'm not that kind of a man. I was a crippled kid, as you know, all for books and music and walks and older people. But there HAS been that one thing—that one woman—"

Flushed, too, she was looking at him with bright, intelligent eyes.

"But I thought she never even knew—"

"No, she never did!"

Alix looked back at the gulls.

"Oh, well, then—" she said, indifferently.

"Alix, would you like to know about her?" Peter said bravely. "Her name—and everything?"

"Oh, no, please, I'd much rather not!" she intercepted him hastily, and after a pause she added, "Our marriage isn't the usual marriage, in that way. I mean I'm not jealous, and I'm not going to cry my eyes out because there was another woman—is another woman, who meant more to you, or might have! I'm going into it with my eyes wide open, Peter. I know you love me, and I love you, and we both like the same things, and that's enough."

Three weeks later he remembered the moment, and asked her again. They were in the valley house now, and a bitter storm was whirling over the mountain. Peter's little cabin rocked to the gale, but they were warm and comfortable beside the fire; the room was lamp- lighted, scented by Alix's sweet single violets, white and purple, spilling themselves from a glass bowl, and by Peter's pipe, and by the good scent of green bay burning. The Joyces had had a happy day, had climbed the hills under a lowering sky, had come home to dry clothes and to cooking, for Kow was away, and had finally shared an epicurean meal beside the fire.

Peter was wrapped in deep content; the companionship of this normal, pretty woman, her quick words and quick laugh, her music, her glancing, bright interest in anything and everything, was the richest experience of his life. She had said that she would change nothing in his home, but her clever white fingers had changed everything. There was order now, there was charming fussing and dusting, there were flowers in bowls, and books set straight, and there was just the different little angle to piano and desk and chairs and tables that made the cabin a home at last. She wanted bricks for a path; he had laughed at her fervent, "Do give me a whole carload of bricks for Christmas, Peter!" She wanted bulbs to pot. He had lazily suggested that they open the town house while carpenters and painters remade the cabin, but she had protested hotly, "Oh, do let's keep it just as it always was!"

Smiling, he gave her her way. She amused him day after day. He watched her, marvelling at the miracle that was woman. He heard her in the kitchen, interrogating the Chinese: "You show me picture your little boy!" He heard her inveigling Antone, the old Italian labourer, into confidences.

Tonight he watched her in great satisfaction; he liked to have her here in his home, one of the pretty Stricklands, Peter Joyce's wife. Nobody else was here, nobody else belonged here, they were masters of their own lives. She quite captivated him by her simplicity and frankness; she washed her masses of brown hair and shook it loose in the sunshine, and she came in wet more than once, and changed her shoes before the fire—just as she had years ago, when she was a madcap little girl running wild through the woods.

They had been talking of Cherry, as they often did. Alix's favourite topic was her little sister; she had almost a maternal pride and fondness where Cherry was concerned. Today she had been house-cleaning, and had brought some treasures downstairs. She had showed Peter Cherry's old exercise books: "Look, Peter, how she put faces in the naughts and turned the sevens into little sail- boats! And see the straggling letters—'Charity Strickland!' I've always hated to destroy them. She was such a lazy, cunning little scholar!"

Peter, smiling at the old books, had remembered her, a small, square Cherry, with a film of gold falling over a blazing cheek, and mutinous blue eyes. Ah—the wonderful eyes were wonderful even then—

The date gave him a moment's shock. Only eight—only seven years ago she had been a schoolgirl! Cherry was not yet twenty-three—

"I wish she had married a little differently," Alix said, thoughtfully. "Cherry isn't exacting. But she does like pretty gowns and pretty rooms, and to do things as other girls do!"

"You should have married the mining engineer," he told her. "Red Creek would have had no terrors for you!

"I should have loved it!" she agreed, carelessly.

A curious expression flashed into her face. She was smiling; but immediately the smile faded, and she looked back at the fire with puzzled eyes.

"If I loved a man, Peter, the place and the house and the money wouldn't matter much!" she answered after awhile, in a slightly strained voice.

"Perhaps," he suggested, still thinking of Cherry, "that's the trouble!"

She gave him a quick, almost frightened look.

"The—the trouble?" she stammered. And with a little ashamed laugh she added, "What trouble?"

For a long time he looked at her in silence, at first puzzled, gradually fitting meaning and interpretation to his words and her own. Presently their eyes met, and with her little gruff boyish laugh she came over to the low seat at his knee.

"You see that there is something just a little wrong, then?" she asked.

"Between you and me, Alix?" he questioned in return, his fine hand tight upon hers, and his affectionate, brotherly look searching her face.

"Well, don't you, Peter?" she countered.

"I hadn't noticed anything, my dear, except that you are making a lonely, solitary man a very happy one," he answered, with his grave smile.

"But that—" she contended, with scarlet cheeks, but bravely "— that isn't marriage!"

"What ought marriage be?" he smiled, half humouring her, half concerned.

For answer she looked keenly, almost wistfully, into his face. He had noticed this look more than once of late.

"I don't know," she said softly, after awhile, with a little discouraged shrug of her shoulders. "I always thought that when a man and a woman liked each other—oh, thoroughly—liked the same things, had everything in common, that that was enough. And—for the woman I was a month ago, it would have been enough, Peter!" she added in a puzzled tone.

"You've changed then, Mrs. Joyce?"

"That's it," she agreed. "I'm not the same woman. I couldn't, as a girl, estimate what life was going to be as a wife."

"Perhaps no girl can," he suggested, interested now.

"Well, that's just what I'm thinking, Peter!" she smiled, a little ruefully. And again she gave him the look that was new, that was not all timid nor wistful nor appealing, yet somehow partook of all three. "You see, you feel that nothing can change you," she elucidated further, "and you are perfectly sure of yourself, from your old standpoint. And then the— well, the mental and spiritual and physical miracle of marriage DOES change you, and it is as if you had entered into a contract for a totally strange woman!"

She was so intent, so bright and earnest, as she turned a fire- flushed face to his, that he felt an odd moisture pricking his eyes.

"Alix," he said, affectionately, "where do I fail you?"

For a moment she was silent, her bright eyes fixed on his. Gradually the serious look on her face lightened, and her customary smile twitched at the corners of her mouth.

"I married you under a misapprehension," she said. "I thought you had about three hundred dollars a year! It appears that you have more than that every month—every week, for all I know—"

"You knew my mother had that old Pacific Avenue place!" he answered with concern. "I never for one second deceived—"

"Oh, you idiot!" Alix laughed. "I don't mind being rich at all, I like it. I don't want to live in the city, or join women's clubs, and all that, but I like having my own check-book—truly, I do! As for all the silver and portraits and rugs and things, why, we may like them some day."

He was not listening to her; there was a sorry look in his eyes.

"You know, Alix," he said, suddenly, "you've made life a different thing to me. I never had any woman near me before, and to hear your voice about the house, and your piano, and your laugh—why, it's wonderful to me. I've been alone here so many years, not knowing really how much of life I missed, and you've brought it all to me. Why, even to have Mrs. Florence at the post office ask me for 'Mrs. Joyce,' gives me a warm, happy sort of feeling! I—" he stroked the smooth hand under his own; there was real emotion in his voice, "I'd do a good deal to show you how grateful I am, old girl," he finished. "I wish you could tell me where I fail, and I'd move heaven and earth to please you!"

"The point is," Alix said, with her mischievous smile, as she twisted the heavy ring he wore, "do I fail you? I know I don't flush with delight when you give me a smile, and tremble with fear at your frown! I know that the smell of my hair doesn't make you turn pale, and the touch of my hand make you dizzy! There's no fury, fire, and madness—"

She laughed, and he laughed, too, a little reproachfully.

"You never will be serious for more than two minutes, Alexandra, my child!" he said.

Alix did not answer. She sat staring at the fire for another minute or two, and her eyes brightened childishly, had he but seen them. But she did not give another look at him. With a great fling of her arms she rested her head between two elbows for a second, tousled her hair, and yawned.

"I'm going to bed!" she announced. "I'm so glad I married a man who is accustomed to banking the fire and opening windows and putting out lamps every night. You," she had reached the door of their room now, and already the silky braids were freed, and tumbled about her shoulders, "you spoil me, Pete!" she said, between them. "Our marriage may be different, but it has its good points!"

"Sure you're happy?" he smiled.

The familiar little answer came confidently. He heard her humming as she undressed in a shaft of moonlight; she was never serious long.

One May day they were picnicking in the big forest. It was a day of spongy dampness underfoot, sweet and wild with breezes, blue of sky, and still cold in the shade, if it was heavenly warm in the sun. Alix, who was hot and panting from the scrambling and slipping downhill, hung on a bank, with her arm crooked about a sapling oak, for support, her hat slipped back and hanging childishly about her neck, and her already brief tramping skirt displaying an even unusual amount of sensibly booted leg. Below her Peter on the bank of the stream was gathering firewood. Shafts of sunlight filtered through the arches of the redwoods high above the creek, and fell here and there upon the busy currents of the water. Presently sunshine turned the flames of the brush fire to pink, a dense column of white smoke rose fragrantly between the dark-brown, furry trunks.

They had been talking doubtfully of the recent developments of what Justin and Anne Little called with relish the Strickland Will Case. Peter, who had for several weeks been investigating the matter, with a deepening conviction that it was a deuced awkward affair, had smiled a most pleasant smile as Alix enlarged upon the delight of giving the whole fortune, should they get it, to Cherry.

"For Cherry," she said, still hanging on her bank, "isn't like most married women. She hates self-denial and economy—Dad always made life too easy for us, you know. It wasn't even as if she had had my mother's example before her; she really knew nothing of domestic responsibility!"

"But what about you," Peter asked, smiling, "you seem to take kindly enough to matrimony!"

"My case is different," Alix said, unembarrassed, getting down to come stand beside him at the fire. "I married an old man for his money!"

"Do you know," he said, putting his arm about her, "I like you! You'll no sooner get hold of your money, if you do—than you'll want to turn it all over to Cherry! You're a devoted sister, do you know it?"

"I'm a devoted wife!" she answered, with an upward glance. But a second later her mood changed; she was off to try the experiment of crossing the stream upon the treacherous surface of a fallen tree. He watched her; her cautiously advancing foot, her hand tightly grasping an upright branch, her eyes flitting from the water below to the rough bridge before her. She was completely absorbed.

"You can't do it!" Peter called, annoyed at the senseless risk she took when she placed her foot tentatively upon the curved side of a log. "There's no foothold there!"

"Come save me!" she shrieked in the old way, with the old laugh of terror and delight. He jumped to her rescue, clearing the creek in a shallow place with two splashing bounds, and catching her before her laughing cry had fully died away in the silent arches of the forest.

"You maniac!" he scolded, as warm, tumbled, and penitent she half slipped and half yielded herself to his hold. "Come over here now, and sit down, and unpack the eats! I can't have my wife drowned before my eyes—"

The title brought a sudden flood of colour to her face; she meekly seated herself beside him on a great log, and he locked his arm about her.

They sat so long in the wet, sweet, sun-warmed forest, hands clasped, that nesting birds flew boldly about them, unafraid, and two wildcats, trotting softly in single file, green eyes blinking, passed within a few inches of them unseeing.

"This," said Peter, after awhile, "is pleasant."

He thought she did not answer, except by a faint tightening of her fingers. But deep down in her heart she said:

"This—is marriage."

CHAPTER XI

Cherry had a flat now in Red Creek "Park." It differed from an apartment because it had no elevator, no janitor, no steam heat. These things were neither known nor needed in the crude mining town; the flat building itself was considered a rather questionable innovation. It was a wooden building, three stories high, with bay windows. There were empty lots each side of it, but the sidewalls were on property boundaries, and had windows only where the building jutted in, and there was a small gate, and a narrow cement walk pressing tightly on one side. Cherry had watched this building going up, and had thought it everything desirable. She liked the clean kitchen, all fresh white woodwork, tiles, and nickelplate, and she liked the big closets and the gas- log. She had worried herself almost sick with fear that she would not get this wonderful place, and finally paid twenty-five dollars for the first month's rent with a fast-beating heart. She had the centre floor.

From her windows she looked down at the "Park." All the other buildings were wooden bungalows, in many places the sidewalks were wooden, too, and the centre of the street was deep black dust in summer and churned black mud in the winter. The little houses gushed electric light, which was cheap; the street itself was unlighted.

But after the excitement of moving in died away, she hated the place. She had enough money to hire a maid now, and she had a succession of slatternly, independent young women in her kitchen, but she found her freedom strangely flat. She detested the women of Red Creek. Cherry went to market, to buy prunes and lard and apples and matches again, but this took little time, and otherwise she had nothing to do.

Now and then a play, straight from "a triumphant year on Broadway" came to town for one night; then Martin took his wife, and they bowed to half the men and women in the house, lamenting as they streamed out into the sharp night air that Red Creek did not see more such productions.

The effect of these plays was to make Cherry long vaguely for the stage; she really did not enjoy them for themselves. But they helped her to visualize Eastern cities, lighted streets, restaurants full of lights and music, beautiful women fitly gowned. After one of these performances she would not leave her flat for several days, but would sit dreaming over the thought of herself in the heroine's role.

One day she had a letter from Alix; it gave her a heartache, she hardly knew why. She began to dream of her own home, of the warm, sweet little valley whose breezes were like wine, of Tamalpais wreathed in fog, and of the ridges where buttercups and poppies powdered a child's shoes with gold and silver dust. Alix had been ill, and she and Peter had been away—a few brief weeks—to Honolulu and return. Cherry crushed the letter in her hand; she knew suddenly that she had always been jealous of Alix. Alix wrote gaily that she had asked Peter if he did not want to send Cherry a kiss, and he had said that his face was too dirty; he was moving geraniums. And for all that day, whenever Cherry thought of Peter, it was with his hands and even his face spattered with the dark earth of the mountain garden. The thought gave her a genuine thrill, and the next day she deliberately thought of him again, but the thrill was not so keen, and gradually she forgot him.

But the letter stayed in her thoughts, and she began to hunger for home. Nothing that Red Creek could offer shook her yearning for the remembered sweetness and beauty of the redwoods, and the great shade of the mountain. She wanted to spend a whole summer with Alix.

She was athirst for home, for old scenes and old friends and old emotions. She had only to hint to Alix to receive a love letter containing a fervent invitation. So it was settled. With a sort of feverish brevity Cherry completed her arrangements; Martin was to use his own judgment in the matter of boarding or keeping the flat. Some of their household goods were stored; Cherry told him that she would come down in September and manage all the details of settling afresh, but she knew that her secret hope was that she might never see Red Creek again. It was all quickly arranged; perhaps he was not sorry to have her go, although he kissed her good-bye affectionately, and wandered away from the station in a rather lonely frame of mind when she was gone.

A friend of his had asked him to dine that same evening, "with a couple of queens." Martin had realized long ago, as Cherry did, that their marriage was not an entirely successful one, but he still considered her the most beautiful woman he had ever known, and had never desired any other. But to-night he thought he would telephone King and perhaps dine with him—the girls might be amusing. Anyway, Cherry was happy and was having her own way, and he had three months in which to try having his own again.

Alix met her sister at the ferry in San Francisco on a soft May morning. She was an oddly developed Alix, trim and tall, prettily gowned and veiled, laughing and crying with joy at seeing Cherry again. Peter, she explained between kisses, had had to go to Los Angeles three days ago, had been expected home last night, and was not even aware yet that Cherry was definitely arriving.

"Of course he knew that you were coming, but not exactly when," Alix said, as she guided the newcomer along the familiar ferry place on to the big bay steamer for Mill Valley. Cherry drew back to exclaim, to marvel, to exult, at all the well-remembered sights and sounds and smells.

"Oh, Alix—Market Street!" she exclaimed. "And that smell of leather tanning, and that smell of bay water and of coffee! And look—that's a cable-car!"

"We'll come over to San Francisco soon, and you'll see the new hotels," Alix promised when they were seated on the upper deck, with the blue waters of the bay moving softly past them. Cherry's happy eyes followed a wheeling gull; she felt as if the world was suddenly sunshiny and simple and glorious again. "But now, I thought the best thing was to get you home," Alix went on, "and get you rested."

"Oh, Sis, that's what I want!" Cherry answered Her lip trembled, and tears came into her eyes. "You don't know how homesick I've been," she said, feeling it more and more every minute. "I feel as if I'd never really drawn a full breath since I went away!"

"I can't live in cities," Alix said, simply. "Peter has a house, you know, in the city," she added, nodding toward the hilly silhouette of San Francisco, as the boat ploughed steadily past it. "We were there one winter, and in a way it was pleasant. It was easier, too. But more than a year ago we came back to the valley, and I think it will be a long time before we want to leave it again!"

"I can't get used to the idea of you and Peter—married!" Cherry smiled.

"We're well used to it," Alix declared, smiling, too. But a little sigh stabbed through the smile a second later. Cherry's exquisite eyes grew sympathetic; she suspected from the letter Alix had written that there would be no nursery needed in the mountain cabin for awhile, and she knew that to baby-loving Alix this would be a bitter cross.

"Well, you see I've not seen you since the month Daddy died!" Cherry reminded her. They fell to talking of their father; drifted to Anne and Anne's limitations and complacencies. "And is it funny to you to be a rich man's wife?" Cherry pursued.

"Peter's not rich," Alix answered, laughing. "We have enough, and more than enough, and if I HAD ambitions about rugs and linen and furs, I could have them! But unfortunately neither one of us is interested in those things. I get a few new songs; Peter gets a few new books; we both get a catalogue and pick out plants, and that's about the extent of our dissipation! The things I want," Alix finished, "can't be bought for money!"

"I know!" Cherry said, a warm little hand quickly touching her sister's.

"But to have you here, Cherry dearest!" Alix said, joyfully, "and to think of what it means to us both! My dear, the walks and talks and fires and music and dinners—"

"And duets," Cherry said, with her old fresh laugh. "Don't forget 'tu canta rio sul tuo liuto!' and 'Oh, wert thou in the cauld, cauld blast!'"

"Oh, Cherry, how utterly delicious it is!" Alix said, gathering wraps and bags for the change from the boat to the train that would land them in twenty minutes at the little station in Mill Valley.

Sausalito, fragrant with acacia and rose blooms, rose steeply into the bright sunshine beyond the marshes skirting the bay glittering in light. Cherry's eager eyes missed nothing, and when they left the train at Mill Valley, and the mountain air enveloped them in a rush of its clear softness and purity, she was in ecstasies. She welcomed the waiting red setter as a beloved friend, and leaned from the shabby motor car, delighted at every landmark.

"Alix—the post office, and the blacksmith's, and how the hill has been built up, each side of the steps! And is that the Kelley's— and the O'Shaughnessys'—but look at the size of the trees!"

They came to the woods, by the skeleton of the old Spanish mill, and she fell silent, and the blue eyes that penetrated the layers upon layers of soft greenness over her head brimmed with happy tears. The sweet breath of the forest fell like a cool hand upon her tired forehead; her heart began to dance in the old, irresponsible way.

Presently, straight ahead, and rising sharply over them, was the sun-bathed mountain, clear to-day, even soft and kindly in the flood of early summer sunshine. It was cool in the woods, even though warm light was pushing its way through the redwoods here and there, but when they emerged from the trees, and took the winding dirt road that rose to the hilltop, suddenly the day seemed hot. Alix, driving, threw off her coat, and Cherry felt the moisture prick her forehead.

She gave an exclamation of delight when they reached the cabin. It was a picture of peaceful beauty in the summer noon. There were still buttercups and poppies in the fields, and in the garden thousands of roses were growing riotously, flinging their long arms up against the slope of the low brown roof, and hanging in festoons from the low branches of the oaks. Beyond the house the mountain rose; from the porch Cherry could look down upon the familiar valley, and the rivers winding like strips of blue ribbon through the marshes, and the far bay, and San Francisco beyond.

Inside were shady rooms, bowls of flowers, plain little white curtains stirring in the summer breeze, peace and simplicity everywhere. Cherry smiled at the immaculately clad Chinese stirring something in a yellow bowl in a spotless kitchen whose windows showed manzanita and wild lilac and madrone trees; smiled at the big, smoked fireplace where sunlight fell straight on piled logs down the chimney's great mouth; smiled as she went to and fro on journeys of investigation. But the smile quivered into tears when she came to her own room, just such a room as little Charity Strickland had had, only a few years ago, with white hangings and unpainted wood, fresh air streaming through it, and redwoods outside.

"Oh, Alix—I never missed Dad before! But to have him out there, fussing at something under the trees—to have him call us—'Where are the girls—I want a girl!'"

"I know—" Alix's own eyes filled. She sat on Cherry's bed while the younger woman changed her dusty travelling clothes for a worn but beautiful linen gown, and they said that they would go soon to the little Sausalito cemetery and see that Dad's favourite heliotrope was flourishing.

The exquisite day went its peaceful course. Cherry was too tired for walking, except on a laughing garden-round, when Alix showed her every separate bush and tree with pride. For the most part she lay in a deep porch chair, drinking in the beauty and serenity of the June afternoon, breathing, above the sweet garden odours of lilac and verbena and mignonette, the piney fragrance of the forest. Alix, coming and going, watched her affectionately. The little languid arm in its transparent sleeve, the drooping, beautiful head, the slender, crossed ankles were always a picture.

"You are like a boat just reaching harbour," Alix said, sympathetically. "Sails furled, anchor down, just resting."

"I feel like one," Cherry answered, lifting lazy blue eyes. "A month of this will make me over!"

"A month!" the older sister echoed, indignantly, disappearing kitchenward on some errand. Presently the supper table was laid at Cherry's side, bees shot like bullets through the garden, birds settled for the night. Supper was ready; still there was no haste, no stir, no apparent effort.

Alix came to her own porch chair for the long twilight. She brought Cherry a fluffy shawl; they were almost silent, and as the last light faded from the hills, and the valleys were flooded with violet shadow, the mountain chill came down, and the stars and the valley lights began to prick the dark.

The sisters came in blinking, in the old way, and in the old way were amazed to see that the clock's hands stood at ten.

"And I meant you to go early to bed!" Alix exclaimed, but Cherry with her good-night kiss answered gratefully:

"Ah, but I feel that I am going to sleep to-night! I've not been sleeping well—"

"Haven't?" Alix asked, in quick concern.

"Not lately!"

Cherry stumbled into the airy, dark, sweet little bedroom, and somehow undressed and crept between the cool sheets of the bed that stood near Alix's on the wide sleeping porch. Her last thought was for the heavenly redwoods so close to her; she slept, indeed, for almost twelve unbroken hours.

She came wandering out to the porch at eleven o'clock, the old, smiling, apologetic Cherry, with her skin dewy from a bath, and her corn-coloured hair freshly brushed, and her linen gown as pink as the Perkins rose that was blooming over her head.

"Oh, Sis, I do feel so deliciously lazy and happy and rested and— and everything!" said Cherry, as she settled herself at the porch table where service for one was spread. "Oh, Alix—apricots! You remember everything," she added, with a look all affectionate appreciation. Alix, panting from exertions in the garden, dropped, trowel in hand, upon the upper step, to watch her smilingly.

"Cherry, you're prettier than ever!" Alix said, eyeing the white hands so busy with blue china, and the bright head dappled with shade and sunshine coming through the green rose vine.

"Am I?" Cherry said, pleased. "I thought myself that I looked nice this morning," she added, innocently. "But it is really because the air of this place agrees with me, it makes my skin feel right and my eyes feel right; it makes me feel normal and smoothed out somehow!" And Cherry looked down at the green and glitter of the valley, looked up past solemn files of redwoods at the mountain, cameo-cut this morning against a cloudless sky, and sighed a great sigh of content that seemed to go from her heels to the crown of her head. "I have never been really well and really happy anywhere else!" she declared, out of deep peace and content.

"Oh, there's no place in the world like it!" Alix agreed, rubbing some dried mud from the back of her hand with the trowel. "Peter and I are always deciding to try New York, or to try San Francisco, or Southern California, but somehow we don't! If Martin continues to migrate every little while, I wish you could have a little house here. Then for part of the time at least we could be together."

"The old house," Cherry said, dreamily.

"Well, why not?" Alix echoed, eagerly. "It's in pretty bad shape, after being empty so long, but it would make darling home again! Would Martin object?"

The old spoiled Cherry, with the pretty petulant frown and shrug of years ago! "Martin knows what he could do," she drawled, naughtily.

"Martin would be here—some of the time?" Alix asked, a little anxiously.

Cherry filled her coffee cup a second time, gave Kow an appreciative smile as he put a hot French loaf before her, and said indifferently:

"Martin has a constitutional objection to whatever pleases me, and would find some objection to any plan that gave me pleasure!" Her tone was light, but there was a bitter twitch to her lips as she spoke.

"Oh, Cherry!" Alix said, distressed.

"However, I'm not going to talk about Martin!" the younger sister decreed, gaily. "I'm too utterly and absolutely happy!"

There was a worried little cloud on Alix's forehead, but it lightened steadily, as the happy morning wore on, and half an hour later, when she and Cherry were sailing a frog on a shingle, on the busy little stream that poured down the hill near the cabin, both were laughing like children again.

It was here that Peter found Cherry. Alix had met him at the house, given him a scrutinizing look with her quick kiss, questioned him about his trip, and reported all well with the house and garden.

"And now come down to the creek," she had said, mischievously. "The Bateses are here—"

"Not Alice Bates?" he had asked, quickly, and at her apologetic nod he added disgustedly: "Oh, thunder!"

"Oh, don't—she'll hear you!" said the beaming Alix, warningly. Peter's eyes, as he crossed the porch, were gloomy and he said "Thunder!" again under his breath.

They followed a rough little trail past stumps where nasturtiums and alyssum mingled with the underbrush, and were in the redwoods, and at the brookside. Peter saw a slender girl in pink pushing a plank about with a pole. She turned in surprise to face him.

"Cherry!" he said, and as Alix laughed delightedly, he gave his wife a glance, and said, "You liar!"

Cherry came up to him, and he took both her hands, and after a second of hesitation kissed her. She freed one hand to put it on his shoulder, and, standing so, she seriously returned his kiss. For a moment his arm encircled her waist; he had forgotten how blue her eyes were, with just a film of corn-coloured hair loosened above them, and what husky, exquisite, childish notes were in her voice.

"Cherry—this is the nicest thing that has happened for a long, long while!" he said.

"You and Alix are angels to let me come!" Cherry answered, as they turned, and with laughter and eager, interrupted talking went back to the house.

"And how do you think your big sister looks?"

"Oh, Alix is wonderful!" Cherry said. Indeed she had been looking at Alix with secret surprise and admiration since her arrival. Alix had always been different from Cherry, but in her own way she was amazing. Where Cherry had but one expensive waist, but one beautiful gown, but two or three elaborate sets of filmy lingerie, accumulated slowly and laundered by herself when she washed her silk stockings, Alix, like a child, changed her fresh, simple linen every day, jumped from one crisp tub suit to another, wore untrimmed straw hats that she bought in the village for fifty cents apiece. Alix apparently never considered the relation of her clothing to her own personality; she simply chose the simple colours and styles she liked, and aspired only to be always fresh and trim.

So with her house. She did not have one or two priceless tablecloths to be used on occasions with satin underlaid, and crystal and cut-glass; her china was all used every day, and her table linen cheap and plentiful and lavish. Meals were always simple and hearty and delicious; but Alix had not time for fancy touches; hated, as she frankly admitted, "all that stuffed celery and chopped nut and halved cherry business! If soup isn't good without whipped cream and sherry in it, it's pretty poor soup!"

Cherry had laughed at her, even years ago, for her point of view, but sometimes she had felt it to be almost an advantage. At all events, she had not been twenty-four hours in Alix's house without perceiving that her sister was singularly free and unruffled, unlike the women of her generation. Alix did not put all the time she saved to good use, although she puttered away in the garden, spent an hour or two each day at the piano, and was, as she confided to Cherry, writing a novel. But she was always gay and always fresh, and enjoyed every moment of the day.

Four years younger, yet Cherry felt older than she. Alix's nature was uncomplicated by any consciousness of self. Again like a child, she only wanted people to love each other and be happy, and that the sun should shine. She was equally content, whether she was helping Peter to pile wood, tramping in the deluging summer rains, or dreaming over a book through the long evenings, with her shabby slippers to the fire. An exquisite spring morning, with wet earth, rising mists, and shafts of pure, warm sunlight, made her sing like the forest birds all about her, but even on the coldest and blackest of winter nights, when the storm made the lamp-light fluctuate alarmingly, and trees creaked over the cabin, she would look up from the piano to say contentedly: "Well, I'd rather be here than anywhere else, anyway!"

Naturally, she was unsympathetic. If people were in pain, or cold, or hungry, Alix could sympathize. But for mental and spiritual troubles she had small sympathy.

"Almost everybody in the world could live as simply as we do!" she told Peter.

"It costs us about four thousand a year!" he said.

"Well, it NEEDN'T. We could buy fewer clothes, and keep only one cow, and let the cook go! We'd be just as happy."

"To some people," Peter had objected, doubtfully, more than once, "there are other things than clothes and food!"

"What things?"

"Well, various things."

"We have books, flowers, music, all out-of-doors," Alix protested, briskly.

"Sympathy, my dear—interpretation self-expression!"

"Tommyrot!" she had responded without animosity. He realized with surprise, not many months after their marriage, that she meant what she said. If she ate and slept and walked and read with her usual healthy relish, she needed nothing more. She was the least exacting of wives. If he was late for a meal, she smiled at him absently, or if, after they had entertained, he apologetically approached her with some reference to an unfortunate sentence or circumstances, she would meet him with a cheerful:

"Angel boy, I never heard you even, or if I did I don't remember it—even if I had heard it, it's true!"

She was one of the rare women who can take marriage calmly, as a matter of course; she had done so since the hour that made her his wife. At her illness she had rebelled; she hated nurses and their fuss, she said. She was perverse with doctors. In an unbelievably short time her magnificent constitution had responded; she was well again, at his side at the steamer rail, as eager for the sights and sounds and smells of Hawaii as if she had never heard of a sick room.

Her only sentiment was for the babies and small animals. She would cuddle rabbits or birds against her brown, lean cheek, and hug her setter enthusiastically. Peter suffered an agony of sympathy whenever she spoke of a child.

"I'd hate all the preliminary fussing, Pete—we both would! But oh, if the Lord would send me six or eight of them!"

Then and then only did the bright eyes and the confident voice soften, and then only was Alix no longer a flat, straight, splendid boy, but a woman indeed.

CHAPTER XII

Cherry, Peter saw at once, was different in every way. Cherry was full of softness, of ready response to any appeal, of sympathy and comprehension. She had been misunderstood, unhappy, neglected; she had developed through suffering a certain timidity that was almost a shrinking, a certain shy clinging to what was kind and good.

Her happiness here was an hourly delight to both Alix and himself. She seemed to flower softly; every day of the simple forest life brought her new interest, new energy, new bloom. She and Alix washed their hair again, dammed the creek again, tramped and sang duets again. Sometimes they cooked, often they went into the old senseless spasms of laughter at nothing, or almost nothing.

One evening, when in the sitting room there was no other light than that of the fire that a damp July evening made pleasant, about a week after her arrival, Cherry spoke for the first time of Martin. She had had a long letter from him that day, ten pages written in a flowing hand on ten pages of the lined paper of a cheap hotel, with a little cut of the building standing boldly against a mackerel sky at the top of each page. He was well, he had some of his dinners at the hotel, but lived at home; he had been playing a little poker and was luckier than ever. He was looking into a proposition in Durango, Mexico, and would let her know how it panned out. The letter ended with the phrases: "Have a good time, Babe, and write me. Send me a line when you can. I have been running some with Joe King, but I am not strong for that crowd." It was signed: "Aff'tly, Mart."

Peter had been playing the piano lazily when the letter was tossed to Cherry by Alix, who usually drove into the village every morning after breakfast for marketing and the mail. He had seen Cherry glance through it, seen the little distasteful movement of the muscles about her nose, and seen her put it carelessly under a candlestick on the mantel for later consideration. At luncheon she had referred to it, and now it evidently had caused her to be thoughtful and a little troubled. An open book was in her lap; she and Alix had gone through the farce of saying that they would read without speaking until Peter had finished some business telephoning; now he had joined them, but still she did not read and seemed disinclined for talk.

"Mart may go to Mexico!" she said, presently, with a sigh.

"To stay?" Peter asked, quickly.

Cherry shrugged.

"As much as he stays anywhere!" she answered, drily.

"H'm! Does that mean you?" Alix asked.

"I suppose that's the plan," Cherry said, lifelessly.

"It's a rotten country," Peter offered, thoughtfully. "At least I should think it would be," he added, more moderately, "to select for a permanent home."

"I always say that a place where the natives are black, or yellow, isn't fit for white people, or the natives would BE white!" Alix explained, brightly.

"All mining towns are horrible!" Cherry said with gloomy fervor. "They're raw, crude, coarse places, and the people in them are just as bad!"

Peter had a moment of pity for her, so young, so helpless, so tied.

"Perhaps he won't want you until he is sure of staying!" he offered.

"Oh, Mart always thinks the last thing is the permanent thing!" his wife answered, wearily. "He says he'll want me to join him about the middle of August."

"Oh, help!" Alix said, disgustedly.

Cherry was silent a few minutes, and Peter smoked with his eyes on the fire. Alix glanced from one to the other, sighed, and glanced down at her magazine.

"If——" Cherry said presently, "If I get my money I'll have enough to live on, won't I, Peter?"

"You'll have about forty thousand dollars—yes, at five per cent, you could live on that. Especially if you lived here in the valley," Peter answered, after some thought.

"Then I want you to know," Cherry went on quietly, with sudden scarlet in her cheeks, "that I'm going to tell Martin I think we have tried it long enough!" Peter looked gravely at her, soberly nodded, and resumed his study of the fire. But Alix spoke in brisk protest.

"TRIED it! You mean tried marriage! But one doesn't try marriage! It's a fact. It's like the colour of your eyes."

"As a matter of fact, it isn't anything of the kind," Cherry said, mildly.

"Lloyd has given you cause, eh?" Peter took his pipe out of his mouth long enough to ask, briefly.

"Not—not in the way you mean—" she answered, glad to be discussing the topic.

"H'm," Peter muttered. It was almost as if he were disappointed.

"But, Peter," Cherry went on hesitatingly, appealingly, "it is no more a marriage than if we both had—had done everything and anything! He doesn't—oh, love!" Cherry interrupted herself scornfully on the word. "Of COURSE he doesn't love me," she said. "But it isn't only that, it's that we differ in every way about everything! His friends, his ideas, his feelings about things—I can't tell you how we jar and jar on each other! No," said Cherry, beginning to cry a little, "he hasn't been unfaithful; I almost wish he had—"

"Cherry!" Alix protested, with affectionate reproach.

"Alix," the little sister pleaded, eagerly, "you don't know what it is—you don't know what it is! Always meeting people I don't like, always living in places I hate, always feeling that my own self is being smothered and lost and shrunk, always listening to Mart complaining and criticizing people—-"

"Don't appeal to Alix!" Peter said. "She doesn't care what she does or where she lives. She fraternized with every old maid school teacher on the steamer, and a booze-fiend, and a woman whose husband was a native of Borneo; and she would pick out the filthiest lairs in Honolulu and ask me if it wouldn't be fun to live there!"

They all laughed; then Peter added, seriously:

"I'll go this far, Cherry. Lloyd married you too young."

"Oh, far too young!" she agreed, quickly. "The thing I—I can't think of," she said, "is how young I was—only a little girl. I knew nothing; I wasn't ready to be anybody's wife!"

Something in the poignant sorrow of her tone went straight to their hearts, and for the first time Peter had an idea of the real suffering she had borne. Alix's mouth was rather firmly shut, her eyes a little narrowed, her face rather sad, as she looked into the fire.

"If I had a child, even, or if Martin needed me," Cherry said, "then it might be different! But I'm only a burden to him——"

"His letter doesn't sound as if he thought of you as a burden," Alix suggested, mildly.

"Ah, well, the minute I leave him he has a different tone," Cherry explained, and Peter said, with a glance almost of surprise at his wife:

"It's an awfully difficult position for a woman of any pride, dear!"

Alix, kneeling to adjust the fire, as she was constantly tempted to do, met his look, and laid a soot-streaked hand on his knee.

"Pete, dearest, of course it is! But—" and Alix looked doubtfully from one to the other—"but divorce is a hateful thing!" she added, shaking her head, "it—it never seems to me justifiable!"

"Divorce is an institution," Peter said. "You may not like it any more than you like prisons or mad-houses; it has its uses."

"People get divorces every day!" Cherry added. "Isn't divorce better than living along in marriage—without love?"

"Oh, love!" Alix said, scornfully. "Love is just another name for passion and selfishness and laziness, half the time!"

"You can say that, because yours is one of the happy marriages," Cherry said. "It might be very different—if Peter weren't Peter!"

As she said his name she sent him her trusting smile, her blue eyes shone with affection, and the exquisite curve of her mouth deepened. Peter smiled back, and looked away in a little confusion.

"I can't imagine the circumstances under which I shouldn't love you and Peter!" Alix summarized it, triumphantly.

"And Martin?" Peter asked.

"Ah, well, I didn't marry Martin!" his wife reminded him quickly. "I didn't promise to love and honour Martin in sickness and health, for richer for poorer, for better for worse—by George!" Alix interrupted herself, in her boyish way, "those are terrific words, you know. And a promise is a promise!"

"And even for infidelity, you don't believe people ought to separate?" Cherry asked.

"Nonsense!" Peter said.

"But you said—that Martin never—"

"No, I'm not speaking of Martin now!"

"Well, wouldn't that come under 'worser'?" Alix asked.

"But, my child," Peter expostulated kindly, "my dear benighted wife—there is such a thing as a soul—a mind—a personality! To be tied to a—well, to a coarsening influence day after day is living death! It is worse than any bodily discomfort—"

"I don't see it!" Alix persisted. "I think there's a lot of nonsense talked about the fammy oncompreezy—but it seems to me that if you have a home and meals and books and friends and the country to walk in, you—"

"Oh, Heavens, Alix, you don't know what you're talking about!" Cherry interrupted her, impatiently. "Let Peter here go off with some chorus girl, and see how long you—"

"It's all very well in books," Alix interrupted her sister in turn. "But in real life I don't believe a woman ever bothers to think whether her husband ever murmurs her name in dreams or not. I know I take Peter as much for granted as I do Tamalpais; if he ever leaped from the track, and stole or got drunk or wandered off after some petticoat, I'd FIX him! I'd be furious, but I don't see myself leaving him."

Peter's brief shout of laughter rang out.

"The awful thing about that female is that it is true," he told Cherry. "If I ever stray from the path of virtue, she'll scare me to death."

"Sometimes I think your marriage is as—as queer as my own," Cherry said, looking from one to the other.

Nothing more was said for several days upon the subject of a possible divorce. The weather continued perfect, and the little house-party on the mountaintop was complete in itself. Cherry often went into the village with Alix, to be sure; once they all went to a charity affair at Blithedale; sometimes a few women drove up the winding road in the afternoon, and there were ginger- ale and cookies on the porch; but most of the time the two sisters were alone, with Peter joining them in the afternoons.

One afternoon Peter crossed the porch, tired and hot, and found everything apparently deserted. He dropped into a chair, and was still breathless from the rapid climb up-hill, when stray notes from the piano reached his ears; a chord, a carefully played bit of bass; then a chord again. Then slowly, but with dainty accuracy and even feeling, Cherry began to play a strange little study of Schumann. Peter knew that it was Cherry, because Alix's touch was always firm and sure; more than that, he himself had played this same bit no longer ago than last night, and he remembered now that Cherry had asked him just what it was.

He experienced a sudden and pleasing emotion; he did not stop to analyze it. But he had been ruffled in spirit a moment before; Alix had known he was to come on this train, and had not met him with the car, and while he really did not mind the walk up, he disliked the feeling that they had entirely forgotten him.

The car was gone from its usual stand under a live oak, but everybody had not forgotten him nevertheless. Cherry was deliberately recalling the mood and moment that also recalled him. And as the notes came slowly, but precisely, from the cool, darkened living room, with its fragrant masses of sweet peas and fluted Martha Washington geraniums, Peter felt contented and serene. He looked up at the rise of Tamalpais, only half a tone darker than the pale blue sky to-day; he looked off at the range toward the ocean, where shimmers of heat were quivering upward; and then he settled himself back luxuriously in his great wicker chair and shut his eyes. Still the plaintive air came, as caressing as a touch.

Presently there was silence; then Cherry tried another little study, and finished it, and the hot summer stillness reigned again. The valley swam under a haze of pure heat; a buzzard hung motionless over the cabin, and the dry air was sweet with resinous scent of pines and manzanita and even of tarweed.

With a sense that he had been dozing, if only for a few minutes, Peter opened his eyes. Framed in the cabin doorway, poised like a butterfly against the dark background of the room, stood Cherry. He knew that she had been standing so for some time, for a full minute, perhaps more.

She was looking straight at him; one hand was hanging at her side, the other laid over her heart, as if she had involuntarily put it there when she saw him. Her corn-coloured hair was a little loosened; she was not smiling. She wore something limp and transparent, of white, he thought, or pale, pale blue, like the sky, with faint stripes making her figure look more slender even than it was.

They looked at each other in a silence that grew more and more awkward by great plunges. Peter had time to wish that he had kept his eyes shut, to wish that he had smiled when he first saw her— he could not have forced himself to smile now—to wonder how they were ever to speak— where they were rushing—rushing—rushing— before she turned noiselessly and vanished into the dim room.

Peter lay there, and his heart pounded. For a few minutes his senses whirled so madly that he felt suffocated. He dared not sit up, he dared not stir; from head to foot thrilling waves of surprise, and even a little of terror, went over him.

Never in his life had he experienced this sort of feeling before. He knew that he hated it, even while his whole spirit sang and soared in the new ecstasy. A moment ago he had been a tired man, fretted because his wife forgot to meet him; now there was something new in the world. And rapidly all the world became only a background, only a setting, for this extraordinary sensation. He sat up, after awhile, looked at the familiar porch, with the potted flowers, and Alix's boxes, where bachelor's-buttons, marguerites, and geraniums had been alternated to make a touch of patriotic colour on July Fourth. The hills beyond still swam in the hot sunlight, the mountain rose into the blue, but the light that changes all life lay over them for Peter.

He said to himself that it was awkward—he did not know how he could enter that door and talk to Cherry. And yet he knew that that meeting of Cherry, that the common exchange of words and glances, that the daily trifling encounters with Cherry were all poignantly significant now. Or if he did not fully sense all this yet he felt thrilled to the soul with the knowledge that she was there, back in the shadowy house somewhere, with the pale striped gown and the disordered corn-coloured hair, and that somehow they must meet, somehow they must talk together.

He felt no impulse toward hurry. He might sit on this porch another hour, might saunter off toward the creek. It mattered nothing; the hour was steadily approaching when she must reappear.

Alix drove in, full of animated apologies. She managed the car far better than he, and no thought of an accident had troubled him. But she explained that she had been to get eggs for a setting hen, and Antone had stopped her and told her that the new calf had been prematurely born, out on the hills, and had "been gone for die," and so she had driven over to Juanita, and gotten the calf.

And there the calf was, two days old, and as pretty as only a baby deer or a baby Jersey can be, roped by his woodeny little legs, and laid stiffly in the tonneau, with utter terror in his liquid dark eyes.

"Die, nothing!" Alix said, emphatically, as she tenderly lifted the calf out of the car. "I'm going to take him up to the barn; you run tell Kow that Missy wants warm milk. Then you come on, Pete—and tell me what you think!"

"Here—" Peter said, authoritatively, shouting the message, and taking the calf from her arms; they were laughing as they entered the dry, hot darkness of the stable. Alix's riding horse put a Roman nose reproachfully over the bitten barrier of his box-stall.

"We've got company for you, Creep-mouse!" Peter, panting from his heavy burden, announced. "Poor little feller!" he said to the calf.

"He's all right." Alix, rustling straw, said, confidently. "You know he must be a twin," she said to Peter, "for that brute of a mother of his was contentedly wandering up to the ridge, where the breeze is, and she certainly had another little calf cavorting about her—oh, thanks, Cherry! Here's the milk, Peter. See if the poor little beast will suck your fingers!"

Peter took the brimming blue bowl from Cherry's fingers. She had come like a shadow into the barn, her eyes were on the tipped surface of the milk. She lowered it carefully into his hold, and he felt the cool softness of her yielding fingers; he did not meet her eyes, partly because he gave her face only one glance. They all knelt about the calf, who after a few feeble struggles to escape altogether resigned himself, and lay looking at them with terrified eyes.

"He's too weak to stand on his legs, perhaps I should have had the mother brought in," Alix said, anxiously. "But he's a beautiful little thing, the prettiest she's ever had, except that he's so thin! Isn't he cute, Cherry?"

"He's—darling!" Cherry's voice, with its young cadences always ready to escape from the riper tones of womanhood, echoed oddly under the low, shingled roof of the barn. And again life seemed full of surprise and thrill to Peter. He wanted to say something to her; could think of nothing, and so was unusually silent throughout the ceremonies of getting the calf to suck Alix's fingers, getting him tied in a manner that should hold him without danger of strangulation, and bedding him comfortably on sacks and straw. Cherry was silent, too, but Alix talked briskly, and the necessity for constant effort and movement filled all possible gaps.

The evening was warm, one of the two or three warm evenings that marked the height of summer even in the high valley. While the three sat on the wide, unroofed porch, loitering over their coffee, a great, yellow-red moon rose slowly over the hill, and floated silently above them. Presently its light flooded the landscape, and strange and romantic vistas appeared between the redwoods aisles, and the tops of the forest trees far below them showed in a brilliant gray light, soft and furry. The whole world seemed to be lifted and swimming in vaporous brightness. There was not a breath of air in the garden; roses and wallflowers stood erect in a sort of luminous enchantment. Moonlight sank through the low twisted branches of the near-by oaks and fell tangled with black and lacy shade through the porch rose vine.

Alix sat on the porch rail, every line of crisp skirt and braided head revealed as if by daylight, but Cherry's pale striped gown was only a glimmer in the deepest shade of the vine. Peter, smoking, sat where he could not but see her; they had hardly looked at each other directly since the long, strange look of this afternoon; they had exchanged hardly a word.

A black cat crept across the grass, her body dragging stealthily on crouched legs, boldly silhouetted in the moonshine, invisible in the shade. Alix defeated her hunting plans by flinging a well- aimed pebble into the shrubbery ahead of her. The cat, dissembling, lay down in the dry grass, cleaned a paw, and coquetted with her tail.

"Town to-morrow, Pete?" Alix said, after a silence during which she had locked her arms behind her head, stared straight above her at the path the moon was making through faint stars, and yawned. "I've got to go in to a meeting of the hospital board."

"I didn't know you were on it," Cherry said.

"Peter's mother was, and hence I am," Alix said, virtuously. Cherry felt an old little prick of jealousy. Alix was strangely indifferent to the position she held.

"I go in to have luncheon with Mary" Cherry said. "I wish we could all lunch together!"

"I'll blow you girls to a meal at Frank's—" Peter began, and interrupted himself, "Oh, but you can't, Cherry!"

"And our meeting is at twelve; we'll have lunch at the hospital," Alix added. "Wouldn't you think we'd have enough of each other, we three?" she said, amusedly, beginning, in the reprehensible manner of girlhood, to roll the black scarf that had been knotted about her rolled bluejacket's collar, and to remove the pins from her hair. "But I hate to be in town and not see you both! Good-night, beloveds. I'm dead. Don't sit out here mooning with Pete all night, Cerise!"

Peter said to himself that now Cherry would go, too, but as the screen door banged lightly after Alix, and the dull glimmer of Cherry's striped gown did not move in the soft shadow, a sudden reluctance and distaste seized him. He had been subconsciously aware of her all afternoon; he had known a delicious warmth and stir at his heart that he had not analyzed, if indeed it could be analyzed. Now suddenly he did not want the beauty and bloom and charm of that feeling touched. His heart began to beat heavily again, and he knew that he must stop the unavailing game now.

But he had not reckoned on Cherry. She twisted in her chair, and he heard a child's long, happy sigh.

"Oh, so am I tired, too!" she breathed, reluctantly. "I hate to leave it—but I've been almost asleep for half an hour! You can have all the moonlight there is, Peter." Her white figure fluttered toward the door. "Good-night!" she said, drooping her little head to choke a yawn. A moment later he heard her laughing with Alix.

"You fool—you fool—you fool!" Peter said to himself, and he felt an emotion like shame, a little real compunction that he could so utterly misread her innocence. He felt it not only wrong in him, but somehow staining and hurtful to her.

CHAPTER XIII

Again Peter reckoned without Cherry. It was only the next day, when he was entering the Palace court for his lunch, that he experienced a sudden and violent emotion. His thoughts were, at the moment, far from Cherry, and he had fancied himself in a hurry. But every other feeling but excitement was obliterated at the sight of a slender, girlishly made woman, in a pongee gown, and a limp brown hat covered with poppies, waiting in the lounge.

Peter went toward her, and the colour rushed into Cherry's face. Half a dozen women had been furtively studying her, and one of them now said to a man, "Yes, she really is—extraordinarily pretty." But Cherry and Peter saw and heard them not. It was the first time they had accidentally encountered each other, and it had a special place of its own in the history of their lives.

The surprise of it kept them laughing, hands clasped, for a minute; then Cherry said:

"I was to lunch here with Mary Cameron. But she's full twenty minutes late!"

"Lunch with me," Peter substituted, promptly.

"She'll probably be along—" Cherry said, vaguely, looking at a clock. "You hate her, don't you?" she added, looking up from under the poppies at Peter.

"I don't like her," he admitted, with a boy's grimace.

"Then suppose we don't lunch here?" Cherry suggested, innocently. Peter laughed joyously, and tucking her little gloved hand under his arm, led her away. They went to Solari's, and had a window table, and nodded, as they discussed their lunch, at half a dozen friends who chanced to be lunching there, too. But it was a thrilling adventure, none the less, and after the other tables were empty, and when the long room was still, they talked on, trifling with cheese and crackers, Peter watching her as he smoked, Cherry's head bent over her plate.

She had said that she wanted to tell him "all about it," and Peter, with quick knowledge that she meant the unhappiness of her marriage, nodded a grave permission.

"I've made a failure of it!" Cherry said, sadly. "I know I ought to struggle on, but I can't. Just a few days of it, just a few weeks of it make me—make me a different woman! I get nervous, I get hysterical, I don't sleep! I have no individuality, Peter, I have no personality! As for my dignity—my privacy—"

Her face was scarlet, and for a moment she stopped speaking.

"Just tell me an alternative!" she said, after awhile. "It CAN'T be that there is no other life for me than going back. Peter, I'm only twenty-four!"

"I know you are," he said, with a brief nod.

"Why, everyone has some alternative," Cherry pleaded. "It can't be that marriage is the only—the only irrevocable thing! If you had a partner that you couldn't go on with, you could come to SOME agreement! You could make a sacrifice, but somehow you could end the association! Peter," she said, earnestly, "when I think of marketing again—six chops and soup-meat and butter and baking powder—I feel sick! When I think of unpacking the things I've washed and dusted for five years—the glass berry bowl that somebody gave us, and the eleven silver tea-spoons—I can't bear it!"

"You don't love him!" Peter said.

"I don't hate him," she answered quickly. "Indeed I don't. And it isn't just the place and the life, Peter! I could be happy in two rooms—somewhere—anywhere—But not—with HIM. Oh, Peter, if I hadn't done it—if I hadn't done it!" And Cherry knotted her fingers together, and her voice thickened and stopped.

Her beauty, as she pushed her plate aside and leaned toward him, was so startling that Peter, a lighted match half-raised to a fresh cigarette, put the match down aimlessly, and looked thoughtfully at the cigarette, and laid that down, too, without the faintest consciousness of what he was doing. The day was warm, and there was a little dampness on her white forehead, where the gold hair clung to the brim of the drooping hat. Her marvellous blue eyes were ringed with soft violet shadows, as if a sooty finger had set them under the dark brown arch of the brows. The soft curve of her chin, the babyish shortness of her upper lip, and the crimson sweetness of the little earnest mouth had never seemed more lovely than they were to-day. She was youth incarnate, palpitating, flushed, unspoiled.

For a moment she looked down at the table, and the colour flooded her face, then she looked him straight in the eyes and smiled. "Well! Perhaps it will all work out right, Peter," she said, with the childish, questioning look that so wrung his heart. She immediately gathered her possessions together to go, but when they stepped into sunshiny Geary Street it was three o'clock, and Peter suggested that they walk down to the boat.

To them both the hour was memorable, and the street and park and the tops of tall buildings, flooded with the sunlight of a summer afternoon, were Paradise. Cherry only knew that she felt strangely thrilled and yet at peace; Peter's heart was bursting with love of the world, love of this romantic city, with its flower market blazing in the sun, and with the ferry clock tower standing high above the vista of Market Street. He seemed floating rather than walking, and when, at crossings, he could help Cherry for a few steps, felicity swelled in his soul almost like pain.

They met Alix on the boat, but she did not ask any embarrassing questions; she sat between them on the upper deck, blinking contentedly at the blue satin bay, her eyes following the wheeling gulls or the passage of ships, her mind evidently concerned only with the idle pleasantness of the moment. And always, for Peter, there was the same joyous sense of something new—something significant—something ecstatic in life.

From that hour he was never quite at ease in Cherry's company, and avoided being alone with her even for an instant, although her presence always caused him the new and tingling delight. He read her honest blue eyes truly, and knew that although, like himself, she was conscious of the new sweetness and brightness of life, she had never entertained for an instant the flitting thought that it was Peter's feeling for her that made it so. She thought perhaps that it was the old childish happiness that she had known in the valley, the freedom and leisure and irresponsibility of the old days.

One day she made Alix and Peter laugh by reciting for them long passages from "Paolo and Francesca." They were walking, and had stopped to rest and get breath on a steep climb. Cherry's tender voice, half-amusedly and half-seriously repeating the passionate lines, lingered in Peter's mind like a sort of faint incense for hours.

"It's lovely," said Cherry in the garden that night, when he spoke to her about it, "but it's not Shakespere, of course," she surprised him by adding. Cherry had developed, he thought, she had cared nothing for Shakespere years ago. Immediately she began the immortal phrases:

> 'Tis but the name that is mine enemy,
> Thou art thyself, though, not a Montague ...
> ... And for that name which is no part of thee Take all myself!

Peter's heart began to thump again. They were alone in the garden; it was dark to-night, warm and starry.

"Now that you and I are brother and sister," Cherry said, after a silence, "tell me—it went across my mind once, and then I didn't think of it for years. But tell me, was it me with whom you were— you fancied you were in love, all those years ago?"

She looked innocently up at him in the gloom, and laughed. Peter did not speak for a few seconds.

"Yes, it was always you!" he said then, briefly.

Cherry laughed again, a little amused and exultant laugh. But immediately she stopped laughing, and said, vexedly:

"I was a fool to ask you that! I don't know why I did. Just sheer egotism—and I hate women who dwell on their own foolish old love affairs, too!"

Peter, as ashamed as she of the moment's weakness, laughed, too.

"You could hardly call it that!" he objected, mildly.

"You could hardly call it anything!" she agreed, in relief. "Does Alix know?" she asked, quickly.

"There wasn't much to tell," he reminded her, as they went back to the house through the ranks of wet wallflowers and roses.

"Nothing!" she said again, quickly.

And when they entered the house he was strangely disturbed to see a look of something like shame, something confused and embarrassed on her usually frank little face, and to realize that she was conscientiously avoiding his eyes. After she and Alix had gone to bed he got down the little red volume that was marked "Romeo and Juliet," and found the score of lines that she had quoted, and marvelled that the same words could seem on the printed page so bare, and sound so rich and full in Cherry's voice out under the stars.

The next day she talked in a troubled, uncertain way of going back to Red Creek and he knew why. But Alix was so aghast at the idea, and Peter, who was closing Doctor Strickland's estate, was so careful to depart early in the mornings, and return only late at night, that the little alarm, if it was that, died away. Martin's plans were uncertain, and Cherry might be needed as a witness in the Will Case, if Anne's claims were proved unjustified, so that neither Peter nor Cherry could find a logical argument with which to combat Alix's protests against any change.

The next time that Cherry went into town, Alix did not go, and Peter, sitting on the deck of the early boat with her, asked her again to have luncheon with him. Immediately a cloud fell on her face, and he saw her breast rise quickly.

"Peter," she asked him, childishly, looking straight into his eyes, "why didn't we tell Alix about that?"

Peter tried to laugh and felt himself begin to tremble again.

"About what?" he stammered.

"About our having been three hours at lunch last week?"

"Why—I don't know!" Peter said, smiling nervously.

She was silent, and they parted without any further reference to meeting for lunch. But every time he was summoned to the telephone Peter felt a thrill of expectation, and at noon his office swam suddenly before his eyes when the lovely voice was really addressing him. She was at the ferry, Cherry said; she had finished shopping, and was going home.

"That's fine!" Peter said, quite as he would have said it a month ago. But he was shaking as he went back to his work.

That night, when Alix had gone to bed, he entered the sitting room suddenly to find Cherry hunting for a book. She had dropped on one knee, the better to reach a low shelf, and was wholly absorbed in the volume she had chanced to open.

When she heard the door open she turned, and immediately became very pale. She did not speak as Peter came to stand beside her.

"Cherry—" he said in a whisper, his face close to hers. Neither spoke again for awhile. Cherry was breathing hard, Peter was conscious only of a wild whirling of brain and senses.

They remained so, their eyes fixed, their breath coming as if they had been running, for endless seconds.

"You remember the question you asked me this morning?" Peter said.

"Do you remember? Do you remember?"

Cherry, her cold fingers still holding the place in the book she had been reading, went blindly to the fireplace.

"What?" she said, in the merest breath. "What?"

"Because," Peter said, following her, a sort of heady madness making him only conscious of that need to hear from her own lips that she knew, "because I didn't answer that question honestly!"

It mattered not what he said, or what he was trying to express; both were enveloped in the flame of their new relationship; surprise and terror were eclipsing even the strange joy of their discovery.

"I must go home—I must go back to Mart to-morrow!" Cherry said, in a whispered undertone, as if half to herself. "I must go home to Mart to-morrow! I—let's not—let's not talk!" she broke off in quick interruption, as he would have spoken. "Let's—I'd rather not! I—where IS my book? What was I doing? Peter—Peter—"

"Just a minute!" Peter protested, thickly. "Cherry—I want to speak to you—will you wait a minute?"

She was halfway to the door; now she paused, and looked back at him with frightened eyes. Peter did not speak at once; there was a moment of absolute silence.

CHAPTER XIV

And in that moment Alix came in. She had said good-night half an hour before; she was in her wrapper, and her hair fell over one shoulder in a rumpled braid. Cherry, sick with fright, faced her in a sort of horror, unable to realize, at the moment, that there was nothing betraying in her attitude or Peter's, and nothing in her sister's unsuspicious soul to give significance to what she saw in any case. Peter, more quickly recovering self-control, went toward his wife.

Alix saw neither clearly, her eyes were full of tears, and she had a paper in her hand.

"Pete!" she said. "Cherry! Look at this! Look at this!"

She held the paper out to them, but it was rather at her that they looked, as all three gathered near the hearth again.

"I happened to finish my novel," Alix said, "and I reached for Dad's old Bible—it's been there on the shelf near my bed ever since I was married, and I've even read it, too! But look what was in it—there all this time!"

"What is it?" Cherry asked, as Peter, in a sudden and violent revulsion of feeling, took the paper and bent toward the lamp to read it.

"By George!" he said, suddenly, his eyes still running over the half-sheet. "By George, this is wonderful!"

"It's Uncle Vincent's receipt to Dad for that three thousand that is making all the trouble!" Alix exulted to the still bewildered Cherry. "It's been there all this time—and Cherry," she added, in a voice rich with love and memory, "THAT'S what he meant by saying it was in Matthew, don't you remember? Doesn't it mean that, Pete? Isn't it perfectly clear?"

"It means only about fifty thousand for you and Cherry," Peter answered. "Yes sir, by George—it's perfectly clear! He paid it back—every cent of it, and got his receipt! H'm—this puts rather a crimp in Little's plans—I'll see him to-morrow. This calls off his suit—"

"REALLY, Pete!" Alix asked, with dancing eyes. "And it means that you can keep the old house, Cerise," she exclaimed, triumphantly, "and we can be together part of the year anyway! Oh, come on, everybody, and sit down, and let's talk and talk about it! Let me see it again—'in recognition of all claims against the patent extinguisher aforementioned'—sit down, Pete, it's only ten o'clock! Let's talk. Aren't you simply WILD with joy, Cherry?"

But she told Peter later that she had been surprised at Cherry's quietness; Cherry had looked pale and abstracted, and had not seemed half enthusiastic enough.

"Though very probably," mused Alix, "it brought back Dad's death, and saddened her in that way, and more than that, I know she is worried all the time about feeling as she does toward Martin, and perhaps he'll feel that she ought to put this into some horrible mining scheme! Cherry is not mercenary, I'll say that for her."

"What will you do with all yours?" Peter asked.

"I wish we three could go about the world together," Alix answered. "I'd love to see Japan and India—I'd like to see burning-ghats on the sacred Gunga!" she added, cheerfully. "But I don't know—money doesn't buy you much!" she yawned. "Perhaps I'll go to some Old Ladies' Home, and give each of the old girls one hundred dollars a quarter—wouldn't they have fun, buying scarfs and wool and caps?"

"Their families would immediately remove them, for the revenue," Peter suggested. He was grinning at her; he felt suddenly the wholesomeness and safety of her absurdity and originality. He liked the characteristic earnestness with which, in the very act of snapping off her bedroom light, before going out to the sleeping-porch, she widened her eyes at him, and frowned in concentrated thought.

"Then I'll give them fifty dollars a quarter!" she decided. "Just enough to buy them some little things, you know, brass tea- kettles, flannel underwear, whatever they wanted! Presents—they must always want to be making Christmas presents." And she yawned again. "Shut your door, Pete, if you read," she said. "The light shines against the trees, and it's right in my eyes!" But ten minutes later he heard her call through the door, "Or I could give it on condition that they stayed in the home and didn't let their families get it!" and grinned again over his book.

After that there was silence, and gradually the little sounds of the summer night made themselves heard again. Alix's light was out. Cherry came, trailing her thin wrapper, to the porch bed opposite her sister's bed and slipped into it with only a brief good-night. But Peter read on deep into the first hours of the morning.

Kow Yu, flinging the striped blue tablecloth over the porch table the next day at the noon hour, and clinking knives and forks, was questioned by his master.

"You go catchem 'nother plate, Kow!" Peter said.

"Missy no come!" Kow answered, unruffled. "Him say no can come!"

"Cherry!" Peter shouted. "Did Alix say she wasn't coming to lunch?"

"N-n-not to me!" Cherry answered from the garden. She came up to the porch, with her hands full of short-stemmed roses.

"Him go flend house," Kow elucidated. "Fiend heap sick!"

"Mrs. Garvin?" Cherry questioned. "Did she stay at Mrs. Garvin's for lunch? Perhaps it's the Garvin baby," she added to Peter. "She said she was going to stop in!"

"I'll find out!" Peter was conscious that everything was beginning to tremble and thrill again, as he went to the telephone. "Why, yes," he said, coming back to the porch, "the baby arrived just before she got there, and they were all upset. She's in her glory, of course. Says that she'll be home to supper, even if she goes back!"

"Oh!" Cherry said, in a small voice. She sat down at the table, and shook out her napkin. Peter sat down, too, and, as usual, served. Kow came and went, and a silence deepened and spread and grew more and more terrible every instant.

It was a Sunday, foggy and overcast, but not cold. The vines about the porch were covered with tiny beads of moisture; among the bushes in the garden little scarfs and veils of fog were caught, and from far across the ridge the droning warning of the fog horn penetrated, at regular, brief intervals.

"Cherry," Peter said, suddenly, when the silent meal was almost over, "will you talk about it?"

"Talk—?" she faltered. Her voice thickened and stopped. "Oh, I would rather not!" she whispered, with a frightened glance about.

"Listen, Cherry!" he said, following her to the wide porch rail, and standing behind her as she sat down upon it. "I'm sorry! I'm just as sorry as I can be. But I can't help it, Cherry. And I would like—I do think it would be wiser, just to—to look the matter squarely in the face, and—and perhaps discuss it for a few minutes, and then END it."

She gave him a fleeting glance over her shoulder, but she did not go away. Peter sat down behind her on the rail, and she turned to face him, although her troubled eyes were still averted.

"Cherry," he said then, "I'm as surprised as you are—I can't tell you when it—it all happened! But it—" Peter folded his arms across his chest, and with a grimly squared jaw looked off into the misty distance—"it is there," he finished.

"Oh, I'm so sorry!" Cherry whispered, on a breath of utter distress. "I'm so sorry! Oh, Peter, we never should have let it happen—our caring for each other!—we never should have allowed ourselves to think—to dream— of such a thing! Oh, Peter, I'm so sick about it," Cherry added, incoherently, with filling eyes. "I'm just sick about it! I know—I know that Alix would never have permitted herself to—I know she wouldn't!"

He was close to her, and now he laid his hand over hers.

"I care—" he said, quite involuntarily, "I have always cared for you! I know it's madness—I know it's too late—but I love every hair of your beautiful head! Cherry—Cherry—!"

They had both gotten to their feet, and now she essayed to pass him, her face white, her cheeks blazing. He stopped her, and held her close in his arms, and after a few seconds he felt her resisting muscles relax, and they kissed each other.

For a full dizzy minute they clung together, arms locked, hearts beating madly and close, and lips meeting again and again. Breathless, Cherry wrenched herself free, and turned to drop into a chair, and breathless, Peter stood looking down upon her. About them was the silence of the dripping garden; all the sounds of the world came muffled and dull through the thick mist.

Then Peter knelt down beside her chair, and gathered her hands together in his own, and she rested her forehead on his, and spent and silent, leaned against his shoulder. And so they remained, not speaking, for a long while. Kow clinked dishes somewhere in a faraway kitchen, and the fog-horn boomed and was still-boomed and was still. But here on the porch there was no sound.

"Cherry, tell me that you care for me a little?" Peter said after awhile, and he felt as if he met a new Cherry, among all the strange new Cherries that the past bewildering week had shown him, when she answered passionately:

"Oh, Peter—Peter—if I did not!"

He tightened his fingers about her own, but did not answer, and it was presently Cherry who broke the brooding, misty silence again.

"What shall we do?" she asked, in a small, tired voice.

Peter abruptly got to his feet, took a chair three feet away, and with a quick gesture of his hand and toss of his head, flung back his hair.

"There is only one thing to do, of course!" he said, decidedly, in a voice almost unrecognizably grim. "We mustn't see each other—we mustn't see each other! Now—now I must think how best to manage that!"

Her eyes, heavy with pain, were raised to meet his, and she saw his mouth weaken with a sudden misgiving, and she saw him try to steady it, and look down.

"I can—I shall tell Alix that this new business needs me in town for two or three nights," he said, forcing himself to quiet speech, but with one fine hand propping his forehead as if it ached. "I'll stay at the club."

"And as soon as I can go," Cherry added, feverishly, "I shall join Martin. I suppose Alix would think it was perfectly idiotic for me to go now, just when the whole thing can be closed up so quickly, and Martin, too—" her voice trailed away vaguely. She fell silent, her eyes absent and full of pain. Suddenly they widened, as if some pang had suddenly shaken her into consciousness again. "Well, I'll go back," she began again, bravely, "I'll leave you power—what do they call it?—power to act for me. I can do that, can't I? I'll wire Martin to-morrow—this is Sunday, and I'll go on Wednesday!" And as she looked off across the green spaces of fog-wreathed hills and valleys, they seemed to turn suddenly glaring and ugly to her, and she felt a great weariness and heartsickness with life.

Peter sprang over the porch rail, and vanished, walking with swift energy up the trail that led toward the mountain. Cherry knew that he would walk himself tired; she longed to walk, too, to plunge on and on through the foggy depths of the hills, striding, stumbling, getting breathless and weary in body, while somehow—somehow!— this confusion and exhaustion cleared away from mind and soul. And yet beyond the horror and shame and regret she felt something was thrilling, exulting, and singing for joy.

For the rest of that day she lived in a sort of daze of emotion, sometimes she seemed to be living two lives, side by side. In the one was her old happy relationship with Alix, and even with Peter, the old joking and talking, and gathering for meals, the old hours in the garden or beside the fire, and in the other was the confused and troubled and ecstatic consciousness of the new relationship between Peter and herself, the knowledge that he did not merely admire her, did not merely feel for her an unusual affection, but that he was consumed by a burning adoration of her slightest motion, the turn of her wrist, the smile she gave Kow at breakfast time, the motion she made when she stooped to tie her shoe, or raised her arm to break an apple from the low, dusty branches. The glory of being so loved enveloped her like a great shining garment, and her cheeks glowed softly rosy, and there was a new and liquid softness, a sort of shining glitter, in her blue eyes.

Peter was quiet that evening, and was gone the next morning when the sisters came out to breakfast. His absence was a real relief to Cherry, who felt curiously tired and spent after a wakeful night, and looked pale. Alix, busy with a new venture in duck raising, noticed nothing, and Cherry could lie idly in the hammock all morning, sometimes frowning, and shutting her eyes at some sudden thought, otherwise smiling and dreaming vaguely, and always hearing Peter's voice, in words so charged with new magic that the mere recollection of them almost suffocated her with emotion.

He had left a message to the effect that he would not be at home that night, and at four o'clock telephoned confirming the message. Alix chanced to answer the telephone, and Cherry, who was in her room, heard Peter's name, and stood still, listening with a shock of disappointment. She did not want him to come home, she was hardly conscious of any desire or dread; her only thought was that he was there—now—at the telephone, and in a moment Alix would have hung up the receiver, and she, Cherry, would not have spoken to him, would not have heard his voice!

But at eight o'clock that evening, when she and Alix were sitting on the porch, when the last ebbing pink of the sunset had faded, and great spiders had ventured forth into the dusk and the dews, there was a sudden hail at the gate, and Cherry knew that it was he! A flood of utter, irrational happiness rose in her heart; she had been racked with hunger for the sound of that voice; she had been restless and unsatisfied, almost feverish with longing and doubt; now peace came again, and content.

He came up to them, his glance resolutely averted from Cherry, explaining that he was lonesome, assuring them that everything went well, and making them laugh with an account of Justin Little's reception of the new turn of affairs. Alix asked a hundred questions; laughed and rejoiced.

"To-morrow let's go down and see the old house," suggested Alix, "I guess it's in pretty bad shape, for we couldn't rent it. At least Pete and I didn't think it was worth while to do all the plastering and painting they wanted! But we'll do it now, Cherry; we'll fix it all up, and then every summer, and perhaps some winters—at least if Mart isn't too far away—you can live there. Did you see Anne, Peter?" she asked, suddenly.

"No, just Justin. He seemed absolutely dumbfounded," Peter said. "He looked at the paper, read it, laughed, and said—in that little nervous, smiling way of his—that he felt it to be by no means conclusive—"

"I can hear him!" giggled Alix.

"And I guess both you girls will have to come in in a day or two," Peter continued.

"Cherry's going in to the dentist to-morrow," said Alix.

"Oh, so I am!" Cherry said, in a rather strained voice.

She did not look at Peter, nor did he at her, but they felt each other's thoughts like a spoken word.

"Had you forgotten?" Alix asked. "I may go with you," she added, carelessly.

"Oh, do come!" Cherry said, eagerly. "I—I hate so going alone!"

"I've not a thing in the world to do in town, but I'll browse along those old book stores in Third Street," Alix mused.

But in the morning she had changed her mind. She was a trifle late to breakfast, and Cherry and Peter had a chance minute or two alone.

"Cherry," he said then, "I'm going to lunch at the St. Francis. Will you meet me there?"

"No, I can't!" Cherry whispered, unhappily.

"Well, I'll be there," Peter said, in a dull, steady voice. They did not look at each other as Cherry began, with trembling white ringers, to strip the black fine skin from a fig.

A moment later Alix joined them. She had come in from her ducks, and ate but a hasty and indifferent breakfast so that she might the sooner begin to prepare their meal. The ducks had been regaled of late on the minced remains of all the family meals, Alix spending an additional half-hour at the table while she cut fruit- rinds, cold biscuits, and vegetables into small pieces, for her gluttonous pensioners.

"Wait for the ten o'clock train, Pete, and go in with Cherry!" said Alix, holding a small piece of omelet close to the nose of the importunate Buck. "Go on, be a sport!—DON'T YOU DARE," she added, to the dog, who rolled restless and entreating eyes, banged his tail on the floor, and allowed a faint, disconsolate whimper to escape him. "I don't think I'll go in," she explained, "for I have about a week's work here to do. Those Italian boys are coming up to thin the lettuce, and Kow is going to put up the peaches, and if you both are gone I can have a regular orgy of housekeeping—really, I'd rather. Here, take it—the dear old Buckboy—well, did he get so mad he couldn't see out of his eyes!" she added, affectionately, to Buck, as the omelet disappeared with one snap of his jaws. She folded his two fringed ears into his eyes, and laid her face against his shining head. "Well, this isn't feeding the ducks!" she finished, jumping up. "Come see them, Pietro, they're too darling!"

"They're extremely dirty and messy," Peter complained, following with Cherry nevertheless, to see her scatter her chopped food carelessly on the surface of the little pond, the struggling bodies of the ducklings, and the bobbing downy heads alike. With quacking and wriggling and dabbling, the meal was eaten, and Alix, scraping the bowls for last fragments, and blinking in a flood of sunlight, laughed exultantly at the exhibition.

Peter left them there, without one word or look for Cherry, who went back to the house with her sister in a most agitated and wretched state of mind. She had the telephone in her hand, to cancel the engagement with her dentist, when Alix suddenly consented to accompany her into town; "and at lunch-time we'll take a chance on the St. Francis, Sis," Alix said, innocently, "for Peter almost always lunches there!"

Feeling that the question was settled, yet restless and unsatisfied still, Cherry dressed for town; they climbed into the car; Alix's firm hands, in yellow chamois gloves, sparched at the wheel; the die was cast.

Yet at the station another change of plan occurred, for as Alix brought the car to the platform Anne came toward them from the arriving train, a gloved and demure and smiling Anne, anxious, she explained, to talk over this newest development, and "whether it proved to be of any value or not," to try to find out what Uncle Lee had really WANTED for them all, and then agree to do that in a friendly manner, out of court. Alix turned from the wheel, to face Cherry in the back seat, and Anne leaned on the door of the tonneau.

"My first feeling, when Frenny told me," said Anne, chatting pleasantly in the shade, "was one of such RELIEF! For I hadn't wanted all that money one bit," she confessed, gaily. "I only wanted to do what was FAIR. Only two or three nights ago I said to Frenny that it really belonged to us all, and last night we talked and talked about it, and the result was that I said that I must see the girls—we three are the only ones concerned, after all, and"—Anne's old half-merry and half-pouting manner was unchanged- -"what we decide is what really matters!" she finished.

"Why, there is no question that it's Daddy's handwriting," Cherry said, with what, for her, was sharpness, "and it seems to me—it seems to me Anne—" she added, hesitatingly.

"That you have a nerve!" Alix finished, not with any particular venom. "That document throws the case out of court," she said, flatly. "Peter is confident of that!"

Anne's pale face flushed a trifle, and her eyes narrowed.

"Yes, but it doesn't throw the WILL out of court," she said quickly.

"You proposed to break the Will!" Alix reminded her, getting angry.

"I know I did, but it might be valid, after all, and under that Will I inherit only a fifth less than you and Cherry!" Anne answered, also with feeling. "That's just what I came over to talk about," she added, still smiling. "Isn't it better," and all friendliness and appeal were in her voice, "isn't it better to do it all in a kindly manner, than to fight about it? Why, we can easily settle it among ourselves," she assured them, sensibly.

Alix shrugged, and looked down at the wheel of her car with a doubtful shake of her head. Cherry, now standing beside it on the platform, was flushed and uncomfortable. There was an awkward pause.

"Board?" shouted a trainman, with a rising inflection. The sisters looked at each other in a panic of haste.

"I can't leave this car here." Alix exclaimed. "I've got to park her and lock her and everything! Run get on board, Cherry, I don't have to go in anyway—you've got a date!"

Cherry's heart leaped, sank coldly, and leaped again, as with a swift nod of parting she hurried for her train. The other two women watched her with forced interest as she climbed on board, and as the train slipped noiselessly out of sight. It curved among the redwoods, and was gone before either spoke again. Then, as her eyes met Anne's friendly, questioning smile, Alix said awkwardly:

"I think the only thing to do is for you and Justin to take this up with Peter, Anne. I mean—I mean that you were the ones who proposed to bring it into court in the first place, and—and I don't understand much about it!"

"Alix, don't let's talk in a cold, hard, legal way," Anne pleaded. She had gotten into the back seat, and was leaning on the front seat in an informal sort of way. "Let's just try to get each other's point of view!" she suggested. "The idea is that Uncle Lee wanted all his girls to inherit alike—"

"That idea didn't seem to impress you much a week ago!" Alix said, glad to feel herself getting angry.

"My dear, I was going to divide it to the last PENNY!" Anne assured her, widening her eyes.

Alix was silent, but the silence shouted her unbelief.

"Truly, I was," Anne went on. "This—this discovery only complicates matters. Why, the last thing in the world that dear Uncle Lee would wish would be to have us drag the family name into a law-suit—"

"You and Justin began it!" Alix reminded her, goaded into reluctant speech.

"I beg your pardon!" It was a favourite phrase of Anne's. "But it was Peter who said he would fight!"

"Well, because you made the claim!" Alix, hating herself for being betrayed into argument, said hotly. "But I won't talk about it, Anne," she added, firmly, "and as far as coming to any agreement with me is concerned, you might just as well have gone back on the train with Cherry. I hate to talk this way—but we all think you acted very—well, very meanly!" Alix finished rather flatly.

"Perhaps it's just as well to understand each other!" Anne said, with hot cheeks. They exchanged a few more sentences, wasted words and angry ones, and then Anne walked over to a seat in the shade, to wait for another train, and Alix, with her heart beating hard and her colour high, drove at mad speed back to the mountain cabin.

"I didn't ask her to lunch—I don't care!" Alix said to herself, in agitation. "She and Justin know they're beaten—they're just trying to patch it up before it's too late—I don't care—I won't have her think she can get away with any such scheme—!"

And so muttering and scolding, Alix got back to her dog and her barnyard, and soothed herself with great hosing and cleaning of the duck-pond, and much skimming and tasting of Kow's preserves. After all, she had grudged this perfect summer day to the city, and she was always happiest here, in the solitude of the high mountain.

CHAPTER XV

Meanwhile, Cherry, in the sick flutter of spirits that had become familiar to her of late, kept her dentist appointment, and at noon looked at a flushed and lovely vision of herself in the dentist's mirror.

"Doctor has given me red lips!" said Cherry, trembling, and trying to smile to the nurse in attendance.

"I guess the good Lord gave you your looks," Miss Maloney said generously. "You're the youngest-looking—to be married!" she added. "I said to my sister last week, 'That lady has been married nearly six years!' 'What!' she said, 'That little girl of eighteen—!'"

"Why—why don't you come and have lunch with me, at the 'Pheasant'?" Cherry said, suddenly, pushing up the golden hair under her hat.

"I'd love it," Miss Maloney said, appreciatively, "but Doctor has a one o'clock appointment after this one, and I shan't get a bite until nearly three. I've got crackers here—"

Cherry went out into the blazing street; it was one of the hot noontides of the year. At two o'clock a wild wind would spring up, and send papers and dust flying, but just now the heat was dry and clear and still.

She was carrying a parasol, and she opened it now and walked slowly toward Geary Street. She could go and have a cup of tea and a salad at the Pheasant—she could go to the Pheasant—

But she made not the slightest effort to go there. Beyond saying the words, she had no intention of doing so. She could not even frame in her thoughts the utter blankness of the feeling that swept over her at missing an opportunity to see Peter. She turned and went slowly up past the big shop windows that reflected the burning Plaza, and so came to the cool, great doorway of the St. Francis. Inside was tempered light and much noiseless coming and going, meeting and parting. Chinese boys in plum colour and pale blue went about with dustpans gathering fallen cigar and cigarette ashes; a pleasant traffic in magazines and cigarettes and candy and flowers was incessant, back in the dim wide passageways.

Cherry drifted into the big, deep-carpeted waiting-room; there were other women there, sunk into the big leather chairs, watching the doors, and glancing at the clock. The high windows gave directly upon Powell Street, where cable-cars were grating to and fro, and where motor-horns honked, but all noises were filtered here to a sort of monotone, and the effect of the room was of silence. When a man came hastily in the door one woman rose, there was a significant smile, a murmured greeting, before the two vanished.

In a luxurious chair Cherry waited. Peter certainly would not come in until half-past twelve, perhaps not then. Long before that time she might decide to go away; meanwhile, this was a pleasant and restful place to be. It was cool in here, and the murmuring and waiting women left in the air the delicate scents of perfumes and of the flowers they wore.

Suddenly, with a spring of her heart against her ribs, she saw Peter's dark head with its touches of iron gray. Groomed and brushed scrupulously as always, with the little limp, yet as always dignified and erect, he came to stand before her, and she stood up, and their hands met. Flushed and a little confused, she followed him to an inconspicuous table in a corner of the dining room. Then the dreamlike unreality and beauty of their hours together began again. Cherry felt adjusted, untrammelled, at ease; she felt that all the uncomfortable sensations of the past two hours were absurd, forgotten.

"Did you expect me to meet you?" she smiled. For answer he looked at her thoughtfully a minute before his own face lighted with a bright smile.

"I don't think I thought of your not being there," he confessed. "I was simply moving all morning toward the instant of meeting. I had a mental picture of you, always before my eyes, and when you stood up there, it was just my picture come real!"

"If THIS is real!" she said, musingly. "Sometimes my thoughts get so—so mixed," she added, "that I feel as if Alix and the valley— and Martin especially—were all a dream, and this the true thing."

"I know how you feel!" Peter answered. He watched her, almost with anxiety, for a moment, then turned his attention to the bill of fare. But Cherry was not hungry, and she paid small attention to the order, or to the food when it came.

Presently they were talking again, in that hunger for self- analysis that is a part of new love. They thrilled at every word, Cherry raising her eyes, shining with eagerness, to his, or Peter watching the little down-dropped face in an agony of adoration. An hour passed, two hours, after awhile they were walking, still with that strange sense of oneness and of solitude, and still as easily as if they had been floating, to the ferry.

Alix met them in Mill Valley with vivid accounts of the day; she had been pondering the brief talk with Anne, and was anxious to have Peter's view of it. Peter was of the opinion that Anne's conduct indicated very clearly that she and Justin realized that their case was lost.

"Then you're fixed for life, Cherry," was Alix's first remark. "Oh, say!" she added, in a burst. "Let's go down to the old house to-morrow, will you? Let's see what it needs, and how much would have to be done to make it fit to live in!"

Cherry flushed, staring steadily at her sister, and Peter, too, was confused, but Alix saw nothing. The next day she carried her point, and took them with her down to the old house. It had stood empty since her marriage, for winter storms had gone hard with it, and the small rent it would have brought them through the summer months was not enough to warrant the expense of putting it in order. It looked neglected and shabby; it was almost buried in the dry over-growth of the untended garden. There was a drift of colourless leaves on the porch, the steps were deep in the dropped needles of the redwoods, the paths were quite lost to sight under a fine wash of winter mud, and the roses and lilacs were grown woody and wild.

Alix was suddenly silent, and Cherry was pale and fighting tears, as they crossed the porch, and fitted the key in the door. Inside the house the air was close and stale, odorous of dry pine walls and of unaired rooms. Peter flung up a window, the girls walked aimlessly about, through the familiar yet shockingly strange chairs and table that were all coated thickly with dust. Somehow this dust gave Cherry a desolate sensation, it covered everything alike: the spectacle case and the newspaper that still lay on her father's desk; the cups and glasses that remained, face downward at the sink, from some last meal. Her hands and Alix's were speedily coated with it, too; they felt sad and unnatural here, in the house where they had spent so many years.

"It needs everything!" Alix said, after a first quick tour of inspection, eyeing a great weather streak on the raw plaster of the dining-room wall. "It needs air, cleaning, straightening, flowers—-Gosh, how it does need people!"

"I—I can't bear it!" Cherry said softly, in a sick undertone.

Alix, who was rapidly recovering her equilibrium, sprang upstairs without hearing her, but Cherry did not follow. She went to the open front doorway and stood there, leaning against the sill, and gazing sadly out at the shabby, tangled garden that had sheltered all the safety and joy and innocence of her little girl days.

"Peter," she said, as he came to stand beside her, "I'm so unhappy!"

"I'm sorry!" he said, simply.

"I can't—I can't ever be here!" Cherry half-whispered. "At least I can't until some day—years from now—years from now!—when you and I have forgotten—-"

"I never shall forget," he said. And after awhile he added, "Shall you?"

"No," she whispered, her eyes brimming until the dry and dusty green of the garden swam before her.

"Cherry, will you end it?" he asked her, huskily.

She gave him a startled look.

"End it?" she faltered.

"Will you—do you think you are brave enough to give everything else up for me?" he asked.

"Peter!" said Cherry, hardly above a breath.

"Will you go away with me?" Peter went on, feverishly. "That's the only way, now. That's the only way—now. Will you go away?"

"Go away!" Cherry's face was ashen as she moved her tragic and beautiful eyes to his. "Go away where?"

"Anywhere!" Peter answered, confusedly. "Anywhere!" He did not meet her look, his own went furtively about the garden. Immediately he seemed to regain self-control. "I'm talking like a fool!" he said, quickly. "I don't know what I'm saying half the time! I'm sorry—I'm sorry, Cherry. Don't mind me. Say that you'll forgive me for what I said!"

He had taken her hands, and they were looking distressedly and soberly at each other when an unexpected noise made them step quickly apart. Cherry's heart beat madly with terror, and Peter flushed deeply.

It was Martin Lloyd's aunt, Mrs. North, their old neighbour, who came about the corner of the house, and approached them smilingly. How much had she seen? Cherry asked herself, in a panic. What were they doing?—what were they saying as she appeared?—how much had their attitude betrayed them?

Mrs. North was the same loud-laughing, cheerful woman as of old. She had moved to Portland to be near Martin's mother, some years before, and was delighted with the chance that had brought her back to the valley on the very day that brought the Strickland girls back to the old house.

She kissed Cherry, and was full of queries for Martin.

"Durango? Belle told me something about his going there," she said. "Isn't he the wandering Ayrab? And ain't you the good- natured little wife to follow him about everywhere? How long you been here, Cherry?"

"I've been with Alix and Peter for—for several weeks," Cherry said, uneasily. Her eyes met Peter's, and he conveyed reassurance to her with a look.

"When you going back, dear?" Mrs. North asked, with so shrewd a glance from Cherry's exquisite rosy face to Peter's that he felt a fresh pang of suspicion. She HAD seen something—-

"Why, I've been rather—rather kept here by the—the law-suit, haven't I, Peter?" Cherry explained. "But I expect to go as soon as it's all settled! Here's Alix," she said, gladly, as Alix came downstairs with an old kodak album in her hands.

"Look, Cherry—I'd forgotten this!" Alix said, in deep amusement, holding out the book. But she immediately put it aside to greet the old friend.

"I'll bet you three are having real good times!" Mrs. North said, with a curious look from one to the other.

"You know what I hope," Alix told her, "is that Cherry and Martin will always keep the old place open now. They could get a Chinese boy for very little to keep it in order, and then, you see, with all Martin's moving about, she'd always have headquarters here. And I don't believe Cherry'll ever love another place as she does the valley—will you, Sis?" Alix ended, eagerly. Cherry met the arm her sister linked around her, half-way, and gave her a troubled smile.

And yet a few moments later, when some quest took Peter suddenly from the group, she watched the shabby corduroy suit, the laced high boots, and the black head touched with gray, disappear in the direction of the kitchen with a tearing pain at her heart, and the words the other women were saying hummed without meaning in her ears.

"When you three girls got started, you all went off together!" Mrs.

North commented. "I used to say I thought you girls never would marry—you never seemed to take much interest in the men!"

"I never thought we'd marry!" Alix agreed, pleasantly. "Did you, Kirschwasser?"

"I don't think I ever thought about it—much," Cherry said, rousing herself from a musing mood.

"According to age," Alix pursued, in one of her absurdly argumentative moments, "Anne should have married Peter, Cherry, Justin, and I, Martin. But the truth is, we didn't seem to give the matter sufficient thought!"

"Girls never do; it isn't expected!" Mrs. North said, with her indulgent laugh, as they followed Peter into the empty kitchen which smelled of dry woods and drains. Dust was thick on Hong's range, and one of his old white aprons was flung limply across a chair. Cherry's eyes were thoughtful, filled with a look of pain. It was true; girls didn't think anything about it, it wasn't expected of them. And yet, in these very rooms, her father had urged her to consider; consideration simply wasn't in that feather-brained little head of hers in those days. Words seemed to have no meaning, or were transmuted into different meanings by Martin Lloyd's voice. Her father had asked her to wait, wait until she was nineteen! Nineteen had seemed old then. She had felt that at nineteen she would have merely delayed the great joy of life for nothing; at nineteen she would be only so much older, so much more desperately bent upon this marriage.

And Peter was there then, was coming and going, advising and teasing her—so near, so accessible, loving her even then, had she but known it! That engagement might as easily—and how much more wisely!—have been with Peter; the presents, the gowns, the wedding would have been the same, to her childish egotism; the rest how different! The rest would have been light instead of darkness, joy instead of pain, dignity and development and increasing content instead of all the months of restless criticism and doubt and disillusionment. The very scene here, with Mrs. North and Alix, might easily have been, with Cherry as the wife of Peter, Cherry as her sister's hostess, in the mountain cabin—

At the thought her heart suffocated her. She stood dazedly looking out of the old kitchen window, and her senses swam in a sudden spasm of pain.

And Alix? Well, Alix might have been Mrs. Lloyd. Martin had told her more than once that he had "a crush on Alix, right off the bat!" And Alix had liked him, too—any girl would like any man under the same circumstances of age and environment. Alix would have made Martin a better wife; she would have loved the mining towns, the muddy railroad stations, and the odd women. She would have had her dogs, perhaps a child or two now. Anyway, ran Cherry's thoughts, she would have had the old home now, and that, to Alix, would have meant a very triumph of joy. She would have come to stay with Peter and Cherry while it was put in order; she would have revelled in cows and ducks and dogs here.

"Cherry, child, come and lend us a hand!" Peter said. They were trying to push aside the ice-box that blocked the unlocked kitchen door. Cherry went to them at once; the little word "child" danced in her heart all day, and warmed it when she was lying wakeful and restless deep into the summer night.

CHAPTER XVI

"You and I must go away!" said Peter. "I can't stand it. I love you. I love you so dearly, Cherry. I can't think of anything else any more. It's like a fever—it's like a sickness. I'm never happy, any more, unless my arms are about you. Will you let me take you somewhere, where we can be happy together?"

Cherry turned her confident, childish face toward him; her lashes glittered, but she smiled.

"I love you, Peter!" she said. And the words, sounding softly through the silence of the garden, died away on the warm night air like music.

It was night, the third night of the harvest moon. Through the branches of the oak tree under which they were sitting blots of silver were falling; between them the shadows were inky black. The grass was a sheen of pearly light, the little cabin was like an enchanted dwelling, wreathed with flowers, and steeped in moonshine. Toward the ocean, over the moon-flooded ridge, a great fold of creamy fog was silently pushing, and Cherry had a scarf of creamy lace caught about her shoulders. Her coil of corn-coloured hair was loosened; she and Peter had been moving geranium slips all afternoon, and at supper-time, when a telephone message from Alix had advised them that she was obliged to stay in town to dine with an exacting old family friend, they had parted only to bathe and change, before sitting down for dinner in the sunset beauty of the porch.

It had been a memorable meal, an hour always to have its place in their hearts. In the two weeks since the day at the old house they had not chanced to be often alone, and to-night, for the first time, Cherry admitted that she could fight no longer. A few days before she had again gone to the dentist, and again had waited for Peter at the great hotel. But on this occasion he had not known of her engagement in town, and had lunched elsewhere, so that Cherry had waited, growing weary, headachy, and heartsick as the slow moments went their way. Peter, happening to telephone to Alix, at about two o'clock, had learned that Cherry was in the city, and hanging up the receiver, had sat wrapped in agitated thought for a few minutes before rushing to the hotel on the desperate hazard of finding her there.

The sight of the little patient figure, the irradiation of her face, as they met, the ecstasy of delight with which their hands were joined, and the flood of joy in their hearts, as he took her to tea, was illuminating to them both. Cherry had spent two long hours waiting only for the sight of that eager, limping, straight- shouldered form, and Peter had experienced enough anguish as he sped to find her to tear the last deception away.

To-night they talked as lovers, his arm about the soft little clinging figure, her small, firm fingers tight in his own. He had squared about on the great log that was their seat so that his ardent eyes were closer to her; the world held nothing but themselves. It was eight o'clock.

"So this is the thing that was waiting for us all these years, Cherry, ever since the time you and Alix used to dam my brook and climb my oak trees!"

"I never dreamed of it!" Cherry said, with wonder in her tone.

"If we had dreamed of it—" Peter began, and stopped.

"Ah, if we had, it would all be different," Cherry said, with a look of pain. "That's the one thing I can't bear to think of!"

"What is?" he asked, watching the lovely face that was only dimly visible in the moonlight.

"Oh, that it all might have been so simple—so easy and right!" the girl answered. "That we might have been so happy instead of so sad—"

"It makes you sad, dear?"

"Peter, how could it make me anything else? Why, what can come of it?" Cherry asked, sorrowfully. "I cannot stay on here, now. I cannot—" She freed herself from his arms, and walked away from him restlessly through the moonshine, twisting her arms above her head. "I cannot go back to Martin!" he heard her whisper, in an agony. "I can't leave you—I can't leave you!"

"Shall we go away?" Peter asked, simply, when she stopped at the great stone that Alix, for the view it commanded, had christened Sunrise Rock. Cherry dropped down upon it, facing away from him across the soft green luminous light of the valley.

"Go where?" she asked.

"Go anywhere!" he answered. "We have money enough; we can leave Alix rich—she will still have her cabin and her dogs and the life she loves. But there are other tiny places, Cherry; there are little cabins in Hawaii, there are Canadian villages—Cherry, there are thousands of places in the south of France where we might live for years and never be questioned, and never be annoyed."

"France!" she whispered, and the downcast face he was watching so eagerly was thoughtful. "How could we go," she breathed. "You first, and then I? To meet somewhere?"

"We would have to go together," he decided, swiftly. "Everyone must know, dear; you realize that?"

Wide-eyed, she was staring at him as if spellbound by some new hope; now she shrugged her shoulders in careless disdain.

"That isn't of any consequence!"

"You don't feel it so!" He sat down beside her, and again they locked hands.

"Not that part," she answered, simply. "I mind—Alix," she added, thoughtfully.

"Yes, I mind Alix!" he admitted.

"But the injury is done to Alix now," Cherry said, slowly. "Now it is too late to go back! You and I couldn't—we couldn't deceive Alix here, Peter," Cherry added, and as she turned to him he saw her thin white blouse move suddenly with the quick rising of her heart. "That—that would be too horrible! But I could take this love of ours away, leave everything else behind, simply—simply recognize," stammered Cherry, her lips beginning to tremble, "that it is bigger than ourselves, that we can't help it, Peter. I'd fight it if I could," she added, piteously, "I'd go away if I didn't know that no power on earth could keep me from coming back!"

She buried her head on his shoulder, and he put his arm about her, and there was utter silence over the great brooding mountain, and in the valley brimming with soft moonshine, and in the garden.

"I believe that even Alix will understand," Peter said after awhile. "She loves you and me better than any one else in the world; she is not only everything that is generous, but she isn't selfish, she is the busiest and the most sensible person I ever knew. I know—of course I know it's rotten," he broke off in sudden despair, "but what I'm trying to say is that Alix, of all people I know, is the one that will make the least fuss about it— "

Cherry was staring raptly before her; now she grasped his hand and said breathlessly:

"Oh, Peter, are we talking about it? Are we talking about our going away, and belonging to each other?"

"What else?" he said, quick tears in his eyes.

"Oh, but I've been so unhappy, I've been so starved!" she whispered. "I thought I wanted people—cities—I thought I wanted to go on the stage. But it was only you that I wanted. Oh, Peter, what a life it will be! The littlest cottage, the simplest life, and perhaps a beach or woods to walk in— and always talking, reading, always together. I never want to come back; I never want to see any one; I never want anything but that."

"France it must be, I think," he said, "for then we can go about— no one will know us—-"

"But we will meet people we know in the trains, going," Cherry said, suddenly. "I know what I am doing," she added, "but that would be so hard, to have them identify us, perhaps come up to us, whisper and point!"

"But why not go by sea?" he mused, "why not to Japan and through India, and so on to France?"

"No!" she said quickly. "On a long sea-trip someone would surely know us—isn't there some way we can get away, disappear as if we had never been?"

"Cherry!" he said, kneeling before her in the wet grass. "You know what it means!"

"It means you!" she answered, after a silence. She had laid her hands softly about his neck, and her shining eyes were close to his.

"And you trust me?" he whispered. "You know that when I am free and you are free—"

She put her fingers over his mouth.

"Peter! Haven't I known you ever since I was little enough to sit in your lap and have you read 'Lady Jane' to me? It's so beautiful—it's so wonderful—to love this way," she said, in her innocent, little-girl voice, "that it seems to me the only thing in the world! I'd come to you, Peter, if it meant shame and death and horror. It doesn't mean that, it only means a man and a woman settling down somewhere in the south of France, a big quiet man who limps a little, and a little yellow-headed woman in blue smocks and silly-looking hats—"

"It means life, of course!" he interrupted her. "The hour that makes you mine, Cherry, will be the exquisite hour of my whole life!"

They were silent for a while, and below them the white moonlight deepened and brightened and swam like an enchantment.

"If you will face it," Peter said, presently, "I will give every instant of my life to you!"

"I know you will," she said, dreamily.

"There will be no coming back, Cherry."

"Oh, I know that!"

"There can't ever be—there mustn't be—you've thought of that?" he said, uncertainly. In the curious, unreal light that flooded the world, he saw her turn, and caught the gleam of her surprised eyes.

"You mean children—a child?" she said, surprisedly. "Why not, Peter?" she added, tightening her fingers, "what could be more wonderful than that we should have a child? Can you imagine a happier environment for a child than that little sunshiny, woodsy beach cottage; can't you see the little figure—the two or three little figures!—scampering ahead of us through the country roads, or around the fire? Oh, I can," said Cherry, her extraordinary voice rich and sweet with longing, "I can! That would be motherhood, Peter, that wouldn't be like having a baby whose father one didn't—one COULDN'T love, marriage or no marriage!"

And as he watched, amazed at the change that love had brought to quiet, little inarticulate Cherry, she added, earnestly:

"I've been thinking how BITTER it was, Peter, to have the greatest thing in life come to us this way, but just lately—just this last hour it's come to me that it is right—it's best!—to have it so. We give all the world up, and we get only each other, and yet how little it seems to give, and how much to get! Why, every hour of it, every minute will hold more joy than we've ever known! I couldn't," she said, suddenly grave, "I couldn't take you from any one who loved you as I do; I couldn't hurt any one, to be happy. But Alix will forgive us; you'll see she will!"

"Alix—I know her!—will only be sorry for me," Cherry mused. "She'll only think me mad to disgrace the good name of Strickland; she'll think we're both crazy. Perhaps she'll plunge into the orphanage work, or perhaps she'll go on here, gardening, playing with Buck, raising ducks—she says herself that she has never known what love means—says it really meaning it, yet as if the whole subject was a joke—a weakness!"

"I believe she will forgive us, for she is the most generous woman in the world," Peter said, slowly. "Anyway—we can't stop now! We can't stop now! It will take me only a few days now to close everything up, to arrange matters so that she shall have plenty of money, and so that I can carry on the affairs of my mother's estate at long range. Spencer will attend to the rents, mail me quarterly checks; the whole thing is simple. And I will let you know—"

"It all seems so unreal!" Cherry said, with her heart beginning to hammer with excitement. "It doesn't seem as if it was you and me, Peter. I shall not need a trunk; I shall buy new things—it will be a new life—-"

"There is the steamer line that goes to Los Angeles," Peter mused. "Yes—I believe that is the solution," he added, with a brightening face. "Nobody you know goes there on it; it leaves daily at eleven, and gets into Los Angeles the following morning. From there—-"

"I don't know ANYBODY there!" Cherry said, eagerly.

"You wouldn't see anybody anyway. From there we can get a drawing- room to New Orleans; that's only a day and a half more; and we can keep to ourselves if by any unlucky chance there should be any one we know on the train—"

"Which isn't likely!"

"Which isn't likely! Then at New Orleans we go either to the Zone, or to South America, or to any one of the thousand places—New York, if we like, by water. By that time we will be lost as completely as if we had dropped into the sea. I'll see about reservations—the thing is, you're too pretty to go quite unnoticed!" he added, ruefully.

He saw a smile flicker on her face in the moonlight, but when she spoke, it was with almost tearful gravity:

"You arrange it, Peter, and somehow I'll go. I'll write Alix—I'll tell her that where she's sane, I'm mad, and where she's strong, I'm weak! And we'll weather it, dear, and we'll find ourselves somewhere, alone, with all the golden, beautiful future before us. But, Peter, until this part of it's over we mustn't be alone again—you mustn't kiss me again! Will you promise me?"

As stirred as she was, he gathered her little fingers together, and kissed them.

"I'll promise anything!"

"I'll make it up to you," Cherry said, with a sort of feverish weariness. "I'm all confused and frightened now; I only want it somehow—somehow, to be over! I want you to take me away somewhere," she whispered, with the hands he was clasping resting on his breast, and her flowerlike face raised to his, "take me somewhere, and take care of me! I only want you!"

"Cherry, my darling—my dearest!" Peter said. "I will take care of you. Only trust me for a few days more, and we will be away from it all. And now you put it all out of your mind, and run in and go to bed. You're exhausted, and if Alix gets the eight o'clock train she will be here in a few minutes. I'll wander down the road a little way, and meet the car if she drives it up."

"Good-night!" she breathed, and he saw the white gown flicker against the soft light on the lawn, and saw the black shadow creeping by it, before she mounted the porch steps, and was gone.

CHAPTER XVII

Swept along by a passionate excitement that seemed actually to consume her, Cherry lived through the next three days. Alix noticed her mood, and asked her more than once what caused it. Cherry would press a hot cheek to hers, smile with eyes full of pain, and flutter away. She was well, she was quite all right, only she—she was afraid Martin would summon her soon—and she didn't want to go to him—!

Alix was puzzled, watching her sister with anxious eyes. The cleaning and refurnishing of the old home was proceeding rapidly, and Alix feared that the constant memory of the old times would be too much for Cherry. She tried to induce her to rest, to spend this morning or that afternoon in the hammock, but Cherry gently but irresistibly refused. Her one hope was to be busy, to tire her brain and body before night.

Suspecting something gravely amiss, Alix tried to win her confidence regarding Martin. But briefly, quickly, and with a sort of affectionate and apologetic impatience, Cherry refused to discuss him.

"I shall not go back to him!" she said, breathing hard, and with the air of being more absorbed in what she was doing than what she was saying. She and Alix were dusting the books in their father's old library, and arranging them on the shelves, on a quiet September morning.

"But, Cherry, dear, you were saying yesterday that you dreaded his sending for you!" Alix said, in a troubled surprise.

"Yes, I know I was!" Cherry admitted, quickly.

"But did you mean that you are really going to leave him?" the older sister questioned. And as Cherry was silent she repeated: "Are you going to leave him, dear?"

"I don't know what I'm going to do!" Cherry half sobbed.

"But, dearest—dearest, you're only twenty-four; don't you think you might feel better about it as time goes on?" Alix urged. "Now that the money is all yours, Cherry, and you can have this nice home to come to now and then, isn't it different?"

Cherry, an old volume in her hand, was looking at her steadily.

"You don't understand, Sis!" she said.

"I understand that you don't love Martin," Alix said, perplexed. "But can't people who don't love each other live together in peace?" she added, with a half smile.

"N-n-not as man and wife!" Cherry stammered.

Alix sat back on her heels, in the ungraceful fashion of her girlhood, and shrugged her shoulders.

"Think of the people who are worrying themselves sick over bills, or sick wives, or children to bring up!" she suggested, hopefully. "My Lord, if you have enough money, and food, and are young, and well—!"

"Yes, but, Alix," Cherry argued, eagerly, "I'm NOT well when I'm unhappy. My heart is like lead all the time; I can't seem to breathe! People—isn't it possible that people are different about that?" she asked, timidly.

"I suppose they are!" Alix conceded, thoughtfully. "Anyway, look at all the fusses in history," she added, carelessly, "of GRANDE PASSIONS, and murders, and elopements, and the fate of nations— resting on just the fact that a man and woman hated each other too much, or loved each other too much! There must be something in it that I don't understand. But what I DO understand," she added, after a moment, when Cherry, choked with emotion, was silent, "is that Dad would die of grief if he knew you were unhappy, that your life was all broken up in disappointment and bitterness!"

"But is that my fault!" Cherry exclaimed, with sudden tears.

Alix, after watching her for a troubled minute, went to her, and put her arm about her. "Don't cry, Cherry!" she pleaded, sorrowfully.

Cherry, regaining self-control, resumed her work silently, with an occasional, sudden sigh. Alix, clapping the heavy covers of a leatherbound volume in Buck's inquisitive nose, presently laughed gaily as he sneezed and pawed.

She had opened the subject with reluctance; now she realized that they had again reached a blank wall.

Three days after their talk in the moonlit garden Peter found chance to speak alone to Cherry.

"Are you ready?" he asked.

"Quite!" she said, raising blue eyes to his.

"What about your suitcase?"

"I took it into San Francisco yesterday; Alix went in early, and I followed at noon. It's checked in the ferry building, waiting."

"It's to-morrow then, Cherry!" he said.

"To-morrow!" He saw the colour ebb from her face as she echoed him. This was already late afternoon; perhaps her thoughts raced ahead to to-morrow afternoon at this time when they two would be leaning on the rail of the little steamer, gazing out over the smooth, boundless blue of the Pacific, and alone in the world.

"To-morrow you will be mine!" he said.

"That's all I think of," she answered. And now the colour came up in a splendid wave of flame, and the face that she turned toward his was radiant with proud surrender.

He told her the number of the dock; they discussed trains.

"We sail at eleven," said Peter, "but I shall be there shortly after ten. I'll have the baggage on board, everything ready; you only have to cross the gangplank. You have your baggage check; give it to me."

They were waiting in the car while Alix marketed; Cherry opened her purse and gave him the punched cardboard.

"I'll tell Alix that I have a last dentist appointment at half- past ten," she said. "If she goes in with me, we'll go to the very door. But she says she can't come in to-morrow, anyway. I'll write her to-night, and drop the letter on the way to the boat."

"Better wait until we are in Los Angeles," he said, pondering. "I'm writing, too, of course. I'm simply saying that it is one of the big things that come into people's lives and that one can't combat. Perhaps some day—but I can't look forward; I can't tell what the future holds. I only know that we belong to each other, and that life might as well be ended as love!"

"To-morrow, then!" was Cherry's only answer. "I'm glad it's so soon."

"Good-bye!" said Cherry, leaning over the side of the car to kiss her sister. Alix received the kiss, smiled, and stretched in the sun.

"Heavenly day to waste in the city!" said Alix.

"I know!" Cherry said, nervously. She had been so strangely nervous and distracted in manner all morning that Alix had more than once asked her if there was anything wrong. Now she questioned her again.

"You mustn't mind me!" Cherry said, with a laugh. "I'm desperately unhappy," she said, her eyes watering. "And sometimes I think of desperate remedies, that's all."

"I'd do anything in the world to help you, Cerise!" Alix said, sympathetically.

"I know you would, Sis! I believe," Cherry said, trembling, "that there's nothing you wouldn't give me!"

"That's easily said," Alix answered, carelessly, "for I don't get fond of things, as you do! My dear, I'd go off with Martin to Mexico in a minute. I mean it! I don't care a whoop where I live, if only people are happy. I'd work my hands to the bone for you— as a matter of fact, I do work 'em to the bone," she added, laughing, as she looked at the hands that were stained and rough from gardening.

"How about Buck?" Cherry said, as the dog leaped to his place on the front seat, and licked his mistress's ear.

Alix embraced him lovingly.

"Well—if he wanted to go with you!" she conceded, unwillingly. "But he wouldn't!" she added, quickly. Cherry, going to the train, gave her an April smile, and as she took her seat and the train drew on its way, it seemed to her suddenly that she might indeed meet Peter, but it would only be to tell him that what they had planned was impossible.

But on the deck of the Sausalito steamer, dreaming in the sunshine of the soft, lazy autumn day, her heart turned sick with longing once more. Alix was forgotten, everything was forgotten except Peter. His voice, his tall figure, erect, yet moving with the little limp she knew so well, came to her thoughts. She thought of herself on the other steamer, only an hour from now, safe in his care, Martin forgotten, and all the perplexities and disappointments of the old life forgotten, in the flood of new security and joy. Los Angeles—New Orleans—France—it mattered not where they wandered, they might well lose the world, and the world them, from to-day on.

"So that is to be my life—one of the blamed and ignored women?"

Cherry mused, leaning on the rail, and watching the plunge of the receding water. "Like the heroines of half the books—only it always seemed so bold and so frightful in books! But to me it just seems the most natural thing in all the world. I love Peter, and he loves me, and the earth is big enough to hide us, and that's all there is to it. Anyway, right or wrong, I can't help it," she finished, rejoicing to find herself suddenly serene and confident, as the boat made the slip, and the passengers streamed downstairs and so across the ferry place and into the city.

It was twenty minutes past ten, a warm, sweet morning, with great hurrying back and forth at the ferry, women climbing to the open seats of the cable-cars, pinning on their violets or roses as they climbed. In the air was the pleasant mingling of the scents of roasting coffee, salt bay-water, and softening tar in the paving, that is native only to San Francisco. Cars clanged about the circle, hummed their way up into the long vista of Market Street, disturbing great flights of gulls that were picking dropped oats from the very feet of feeding horses.

Cherry sped through it all, beside herself now with excitement and strain, only anxious to have the great hands of the clock drop more speedily from minute to minute, and so round out the terrible hour that joined the old life to the new. She was hurrying blindly toward the docks of the Los Angeles Line, absorbed in her one whirling thought, when somebody touched her arm, and a voice, terrifyingly unexpected and yet familiar, addressed her, and a hand was laid on her arm.

In utter confusion she looked up. It was Martin who had stopped her.

CHAPTER XVIII

For a few dreadful seconds a sort of vertigo seized Cherry and she was unable to collect her thoughts or to speak even the most casual words of greeting. She had been so full of her extraordinary errand that she was bewildered and sick at its interruption, her heart thundered, her throat was choked, and her knees shook beneath her. Where was she—what was known—how much had she betrayed—Her thoughts jumbled together in a tangle of horrified questioning.

Gasping, trying to smile, she looked up at him, while the ferry place whirled about her, and pulses drummed in her ears. She had automatically given him her hand; now he kissed her.

"Hello, Cherry, where you going?" for the third time.

"I came into town to shop," she faltered.

"You what?" She had not really been intelligible, and she felt it, with a pang of fright. He must not suspect—the steamer was there, only a short block away; Peter might pass them; a chance word might be fatal—he must not suspect—

"I'm shopping!" she said distinctly, with dry lips. And she managed to smile.

"Well," Martin said, smiling in turn, "surprised to see me?"

"Oh, Martin—" said her fluttered voice. Even in the utter panic of heart and soul she knew that for safety's sake she must find his vanity.

"I'm going to tell you something that will surprise you," he said. "I'm through with the Red Creek people!"

"Martin!" Cherry enunciated, almost voicelessly.

"You remember I wrote you that they fired Mason, and that I was doing his work and mine, too?"

"I—I remember!" Cherry, seized by deadly nausea and chill, looked from a flower vendor to a newsboy, looked at the cars, the people- -she must not faint. She must not faint.

"Well—but where are you going? Home?"

"I was going to the dentist a minute, but it's not important." They had turned and were walking across to the ferry. She knew that there was no way in which she might escape him. "What did you say?" she said.

"I asked you when the next boat left for Mill Valley?"

"We can—go—find out." Cherry's thoughts were spinning. She must warn Peter somehow. It was twenty minutes of eleven by the ferry clock. Twenty minutes of eleven. In twenty minutes the boat would sail. She thought desperately of the women's waiting-room upstairs; she might plead the necessity of telephoning from it. But it had but one door, and Martin would wait at that door. The glow of meeting had already faded from his face, but he was loitering by her side, quite as a matter of course.

Suddenly she realized that her only hope of warning Peter was to send a messenger. But if Martin should chance to connect her neighbourhood with the boat, when he met her, and her sending of a message to Peter here—

"I think there's a boat at eleven something," she said, collectedly. "Suppose you go and find out?"

She glanced toward the entrance of the Sausalito waiting-room, a hundred yards away, and a mad hope leaped in her heart. If he turned his back on her—

"What are you going to do?" he asked, somewhat surprised.

"I ought to telephone Alix!" Her despair lent her wit. If he went to the ticket office, and she into a telephone booth, she might escape him yet! While he dawdled here, minutes were flying, and Peter was watching every car and every passer-by, torn with the same agony that was tearing her. "If you'll go find out the exact time and get tickets," she said, "I'll telephone Alix."

"Tickets?" he echoed, with all Martin's old, maddening slowness. "Haven't you got a return ticket?"

"I have mileage!" she blundered.

"Oh, then I'll use your mileage!" Martin said. "Telephone," he added, nodding toward a row of booths, "no hurry; we've got piles of time!"

She remembered that he liked a masculine assumption of easiness where all trains, tickets, railroad connections, and transit business of any sort were concerned. He liked to loiter elaborately while other people were running, liked to pull out his big watch and assure her that they had all the time in the world. She tried to call a number, left the booth, paid a staring girl, and rejoined him.

"Busy!" she reported.

"I was just thinking," Martin said, "that we might stay in town and go to the Orpheum; how about it? Do we have to have Peter and Alix?"

Cherry flushed, angered again, in the well-remembered way, under all her fright and stir. Her voice had its old bored note.

"Well, Martin, I've been their guest for two months!"

"I'd just as soon have them!" Martin conceded, indifferently.

But the diverted thought had helped Cherry, irritation had nerved her, and the reminder of Martin's old, trying stupidities had lessened her fear of him.

"I've got to send a telegram-for Alix," she said.

"What about?" he asked, less curious than ill-bred.

"Good-bye to some people who are sailing!" Cherry answered, calmly. "Only don't mention it to Alix, because I promised it would go earlier!" she added.

"I saw the office back here," he told her. They went to it together, and he was within five feet of her while she scribbled her note.

"Martin met me. Nothing wrong. We are returning to Mill Valley. C. L." She glanced at her husband; he was standing in the doorway of the little office, smoking. Quickly she addressed the envelope. "DON'T READ THAT NAME OUT LOUD," she said, softly but very slowly and distinctly, to the girl at the desk. She put a gold piece down on the note. "Keep the change, and for God's sake get that to the Harvard, sailing from Dock 67, before eleven!" she said.

The girl, who had been pencilling a large "10:46" on the envelope, looked up in surprise; but rose immediately to the occasion. Cherry's beauty, her agonized eyes and voice, were enough to awaken her sense of the dramatic. A sharp rap of the clerk's pencil summoned a boy.

"George, there's a dollar in that for you if you deliver it before eleven to the Harvard!" said she. The boy seized it, stuck it in his hat, and fled.

"And now for the boat!" Cherry said, rejoining Martin, and speaking in almost her natural voice. They went back to the Sausalito ferry entrance again, and this time telephoned Alix in real earnest, and presently found themselves on the upper deck of the boat, bound for the valley.

Until now, and in occasional rushes of terror still, she had been absorbed in the hideous necessity of deceiving, of covering her own traces, of anticipating and closing possible avenues of betrayal. But now Cherry began to breathe more easily, and to feel rising about her, like a tide, the half-forgotten consciousness of her relationship with this man in the boldly-checked suit who was sitting beside her. She had thought to escape the necessity of telling him that she was not willing to return to him; she had been wrapped in dreams so great and so wonderful that the thought of his anger and resentment had been as nothing to her. But she had all that to face now.

She had it to face immediately, too. She knew that every hour of postponement would cost her fresh humiliations and difficulties. He did not love her, but he was quietly taking her for granted again, and until she could summon courage to speak to him with utter frankness and finality, he would of course claim his position as her husband.

The thought threw her into a nervous agitation almost as frightful as that of meeting him had been, and again she felt the dizzy faintness and sickness of that moment.

The trip from San Francisco to Sausalito occupies exactly half an hour; after that there was a train trip of twenty minutes. Cherry knew that what was done must be done in that time. In Mill Valley Alix would meet them, perhaps willing to take any cue that Cherry gave her, as to their relationship, but of course anxious to have that relationship as pleasant and normal and friendly as possible.

Her head was still rocking from the shock of the experiences of the last hour and the last fortnight. Even had she met Peter it might have been to yield with a sort of collapse to mental and physical exhaustion. But to be forced to make a fresh effort now, one of the crucial and fearful struggles of a lifetime, to present her case to Martin now, and force him to her viewpoint, was almost impossible.

Yet Cherry knew that it must be done, and as the boat slipped smoothly past the island that roughly marked the halfway point, she gathered all her forces for the trial.

Martin was meanwhile energetically presenting to her the arguments that had convinced him that he must give up the Mexico position. She vaguely appreciated that someone named Murry was a traitor, and that the "whole bunch" were "rubes," but her mind was busy with its own problem all the while, and the one distinct impression she had from Martin was the appalling one that he did not dream that she had decided to sever their union completely and finally.

"Well, how's the valley? Bore you to death?" he interrupted the flow of his own topic to ask carelessly.

"Oh, no, Martin!" she quivered. "I—I love it there! I always loved it!"

"Alix is a fine girl—she's a nice girl," Martin conceded. "But I can't go Peter! He may be all right, all that lah-di-dah and Omar Khayyam and Browning stuff may be all right, but I don't get it!" And he yawned contentedly in the sunshine.

After a few seconds he gave Cherry an oblique glance, expecting her resentment. But she was thinking too deeply even to have heard him. Her mind was working as desperately as a caged animal, her thoughts circling frantically, trying windows, walls, and doors in the prison in which she found herself, mad for escape.

She blamed herself bitterly now for allowing him, in the surprise and fear she felt, in the shock of their unexpected meeting, to arrange this domestic and apparently reconciled return to the valley house. Had she known beforehand that they were to meet she would have steeled herself to suggest to him coldly that they lunch somewhere, and talk. She could imagine now the quiet significance with which she would have stressed the phrase, "Martin, I want to talk to you."

Better still, she would have anticipated that meeting with a letter that would have warned him that his position as a husband was changed. But it was too late now! Too late for anything but a bald and brave and cruel half-hour that should, at any cost, sunder them.

Quick upon the thought came another: what should she and Peter plan now? For to suppose that their lives were to be guided back into the old hateful channel by this mere mischance was preposterous. Within a few days their interrupted trip must be resumed, perhaps to-morrow— perhaps this very night they would manage it successfully. Alix was unsuspicious, Martin utterly unconcerned, and perhaps it would be even easier to do now, than when Alix must at once communicate with Martin, and perhaps bring him away from his work, to adjust life to the new conditions.

But meanwhile, until she could see Peter alone, there was Martin to deal with, Martin who was leaning forward, vaingloriously reciting to her long speeches he had made to this superior or that.

"Martin," she said, impetuously interrupting him, "I've got to talk to you! I've meant to write it—so many times, I've had it in my mind ever since I left Red Creek!"

"Shoot!" Martin said, with his favourite look of indulgent amusement.

But she knew the little twitch to his lips that was neither indulgent nor amused.

"There are marriages that without any fault on either side are a mistake," Cherry began, "any contributory fault, I mean—"

"Talk United States!" Martin growled, smiling, but on guard.

"Well, I think our marriage was one of those!" Cherry said.

"What have you got to kick about?" Martin asked, after a pause.

"I'm not kicking!" Cherry answered, with quick resentment. "But I wish I had words to make you realize how I feel about it!"

Martin looked gloomily up at her, and shrugged.

"This is a sweet welcome from your wife!" he observed. But as she regarded him with troubled and earnest eyes, perhaps her half- forgotten beauty made an unexpected appeal to him, for he turned toward her and eyed her with a large tolerance. "What's the matter, Cherry?" he asked. "It doesn't seem to me that you've got much to kick about. Haven't I always taken pretty good care of you? Didn't I take the house and move the things in; didn't I leave you a whole month, while I ate at that rotten boarding-house, when your father died; haven't I let you have—how long is it?— seven weeks, by George, with your sister?"

It poured out too readily to be unpremeditated; Cherry recognized the tones of his old arraigning voice. He had brooded over his grievances. He felt himself ill-treated.

"Now you come in for this money," he began. But she interrupted him hotly:

"Martin, you know that is not true!"

"Isn't it true that the instant you can take care of yourself you begin to talk about not being happy, and so on!" he asked, without any particular feeling. "You bet you do! Why, I never cared anything about that money, you never heard me speak of it. I always felt that by the time the lawyers and the heirs and the witnesses got through, there wouldn't be much left of it, anyway!"

Too rich in her new position of the woman beloved by Peter to quarrel with Martin in the old unhappy fashion, Cherry laid an appealing hand on his arm.

"I'm sorry to meet you with this sort of thing," she said, simply, "I blame myself now for not writing you just how I've come to feel about it! But I just want it SAID before we meet Alix—"

"Have what said?" he asked, surlily.

"Have it understood," she pursued, patiently, "that we must make some arrangement for the future—things can't be as they were!"

"You've had it all your way ever since we were married," he began. "Now you blame me—"

"I DON'T blame you, Martin!"

"Well, what do you want a divorce for, then?"

"I don't even say anything about a divorce," Cherry said, fighting for time only. "But I can't go back!" she added, with a sudden force and conviction that reached him at last.

"Why can't you?"

"Because you don't love me, Martin, and—you know it!—I don't love you!"

"Well, but you can't expect the way we felt when we got married to last forever," he said, clumsily. "Do you suppose other men and women talk this way when the—the novelty has worn off?"

"I don't know how they talk. I only know how I feel!" Cherry said, chilled by the old generalization.

Martin, who had stretched his legs to their length, crossed them at the ankles, and shoved his hands deep into his pockets, staring at the racing blue water with sombre eyes.

"What do you want?" he asked, heavily. "I want to live my own life!" Cherry answered, after a silence during which her tortured spirit seemed to coin the hackneyed phrase.

"That stuff!" Martin sneered, under his breath. "Well, all right, I don't care, get your divorce!" he agreed, carelessly. "But I'll have something to say about that, too," he warned her. "You can drag the whole thing up before the courts if you want to—only remember, if you don't like it much, YOU DID IT. It never occurred to me even to think of such a thing! I've done my share in this business; you never asked me for anything I could give you that you didn't get; you've never been tied down to housework like other women; you're not raising a family of kids—go ahead, tell every shop-girl in San Francisco all about it, in the papers, and see how much sympathy you get!"

"Oh, you BEAST!" Cherry said, between her teeth, furious tears in her eyes. The water swam in a blur of blue before her as they rose to go downstairs at Sausalito. The boat had made the slip, and the few passengers, at this quiet noontime, were drifting off.

Martin glanced at her with impatience. Her tears never failed to anger him.

"Don't cry, for God's sake!" he said, nervously glancing about for possible onlookers. "What do you want me to do? For the Lord's sake don't make a scene until you and I have a chance to talk this over quietly—"

Cherry's thoughts were with Peter. In her soul she felt as if his arm was about her, as if she were pouring out to him the whole troubled story, sure that he would rescue and console her. She had wiped her eyes, and somewhat recovered calm, but she trusted herself only to shrug her shoulder as she preceded Mart to the train.

There was time for not another word, for Alix suddenly took possession of them. She had had time to bring the car all the six miles to Sausalito, and meant to drive them direct to the valley from there.

She greeted Martin affectionately, although even while she did so her eyes went with a quick, worried look to Cherry. They had been quarrelling, of course—it was too bad, Alix thought, but her own course was clear. Until she could take her cue from them, she must treat them both with cheerful unconsciousness of the storm. She invited Martin to share the driver's seat with her, pushing the resentful Buck into the tonneau with Cherry.

Alix, in the months that she had not seen him, had had time to develop a certain generous sympathy for Martin, but as she took the car swiftly through the warm, sweet summer day, she began to realize afresh just how serious Cherry's problem was. It was not merely that Martin chewed a toothpick as he talked to her, and took out a pen-knife to trim a finger-nail; it was not that he was somewhat vain, stupid, and opinionated, for the minor social deficiencies might have been remedied in a larger nature by an affectionate word, and there were times, Alix felt, when the best of men are insistent upon perverse and perverted views, and unashamed or unconscious of their limitations. Martin had coarsened in the six years since they had first known him. There had been something unspoiled, vigorous, and fresh about him then that was gone now. Alix sensed that his associates in the mining towns in which he had lived had been men and women of a low type. The defiling influence had left its mark. Missing entertainment in his home, he had sought it elsewhere.

But besides these things Martin had a certain complacency, an assurance that would have been inexcusable even in great genius, a mental arrogance that nothing in his life in the least degree warranted. He made no slight effort to adapt himself to the atmosphere in which he found his wife and her sister, interested himself for not one moment in their concerns, put out no feelers toward the mood that might have made him an agreeable addition to their group. He conceded nothing; he was Martin Lloyd, mining engineer, philosopher, man of the world, and it was for them to listen to him, admire him, and praise and tease and flatter him in all he did. Humility and shyness were never a part of Martin's nature, but to-day he was galled by his talk with Cherry, and less inclined even than usual to abase himself.

"Does Peter let you drive the car on these mountain roads?" he demanded of Alix.

"Oh, yes, indeed. I love to run the car!" she said, with a swift, smiling glance.

"Well, you want to keep your eyes on the road," he warned her. "There's nothing worries me like having a lady at the wheel," he went on, good-naturedly, "that's the time I say my prayers!"

"Plenty of women running cars now, Martin!" Alix said, cheerfully, wishing that Martin didn't always and infallibly nettle her.

"But it's no business for a woman," he assured her, in a suddenly serious and confidential undertone. "No business for them! They haven't the strength, in the first place, and they haven't—well, they're too nervous, in the second. Mouse cross the road," said Martin, sucking in deep breaths as he lighted a cigar, "and—whee! Over she goes into a ditch. No," he said, kindly, "I'm a great friend of all the ladies, but I think they make a mistake when they think they're men."

"Only one accident in ten is with a woman driver," Alix argued.

"That may be true, too," Martin conceded, largely. She knew that he was drawing his words merely to cover any impression of being caught unprepared. "That may be true, too. But don't you believe that half the cases of women's accidents get into the courts," he added, knowingly. "You bet your life they don't! You bet your sweet life they don't. Oh, no—pretty girl smiles at the policeman—" He smoked a few seconds in triumphant silence. "Why, you knew that, didn't you?" he asked, in kindly patronage.

"I suppose so!" Alix said, briefly, after swallowing a more spirited answer with a gulp.

"Oh, sure!" Martin agreed, in great content.

They reached the valley, and Martin was magnanimous about the delayed lunch. Anything would do for him, he said, he was taking a couple of days' holiday, and everything went. Kow was chopping wood after lunch, and he sauntered out to the block with suggestions; Alix, laying a fire for the evening, simply because she liked to do that sort of work, was favoured with directions. Finally Martin pushed her aside.

"Here, let me do that," he said. "You'd have a fine fire here, at that rate!"

Later he went down to the old house with them, to spend there an hour that was trying to both women. It was almost in order now; Cherry had pleased her simple fancy in the matter of hangings and papering, and the effect was fresh and good. The kitchen smelled cleanly of white paint, and the other rooms wore almost their old, hospitable aspect.

"Girls going to rent this?" Martin asked.

"Unless you and Cherry come live here," Alix said, boldly. He smiled tolerantly.

"Why should we?"

"Well, why shouldn't you?"

"Loafing, eh?"

"No, not loafing. But you could transfer your work to San Francisco, couldn't you?" Martin smiled a deep, wise, long- enduring smile.

"Oh, you'd get me a job, I suppose?" he asked. "I love the way you women try to run things," he added, "but I guess I'll paddle my own canoe for awhile longer!"

"There is no earthly reason why you shouldn't live here," Alix said, pleasantly.

"There is no earthly reason why we should!" Martin returned. He was annoyed by a suspicion that Alix and Cherry had arranged between them to make this plan the alternative to a divorce. "To tell you the honest truth, I don't like Mill Valley!"

Alix tasted despair. Small hope of preserving this particular relationship. He was, as Cherry had said, "impossible."

"Well, we must try to make you like Mill Valley better!" she said, with resolute good-nature. "Of course, it means a lot to Cherry and to me to be near each other!"

"That may be true, too," Martin agreed, taking the front seat again for the drive home. He told Cherry later that he liked Alix, and Alix was interested enough in keeping him happy to deliberately play upon his easily touched self-confidence. She humoured him, laughed at his jokes, asked him the questions that he was able to answer, and loved to answer.

She was surprised at Cherry's passivity and silence, but Cherry was wrapped in a sick and nervous dream, unable either to interpret the present or face the future with any courage. Before luncheon he had followed her into her room, and had put his arm about her. But she had quietly shaken him off, with the nervous murmur: "Please—no, don't kiss me, Martin!"

Stung, Martin had immediately dropped his arm, had shrugged his shoulders indifferently, and laughed scornfully. Now he remarked to Alix, with some bravado:

"You girls still sleeping out?"

"Oh, always—we all do!" Alix had answered, readily. "Peter has an extra bunk on his porch, Cherry and I have my porch. But you can be out or in, as you choose!"

Martin ventured an answer that made Cherry's eyes glint angrily, and brought a quick, embarrassed flush to Alix's face. Alix did not enjoy a certain type of joking, and she did not concede Martin even the ghost of a smile. He immediately sobered, and remarked that he himself liked to be indoors at night. His suitcase was accordingly taken into the pleasant little wood-smelling room next to Peter's, where the autumn sunlight, scented with the dry sweetness of mountain shrubs, was streaming.

He began to play solitaire, on the porch table, at five, and Kow had to disturb him to set it for dinner at seven. Alix was watering the garden, Cherry was dressing. It was an exquisite hour of long shadows and brilliant lights; bees from Alix's hives went to and fro, and the air was full and fragrant, as if a golden powder had been scattered through it.

Kow had put a tureen of soup on the table, and Alix had returned with damp, clean hands and trimly brushed hair, for supper, when Peter came up through the garden. Cherry had rambled off in the direction of the barn a few moments before, but Martin had followed her and brought her back, remarking that she had had no idea of the time, and was idly watching Antone milking. She slipped into her place after they were all eating, and hardly raised her eyes throughout the meal. If Alix addressed her she fluttered the white lids as if it were an absolute agony to look up; to Peter she did not speak at all. But to Martin she sent an occasional answer, and when the conversation lagged, as it was apt to do in this company, she nervously filled it with random remarks infinitely less reassuring than silence.

"How long do we stay here?" Martin cautiously asked his wife, when after dinner, Peter could be heard in the kitchen, interrogating Kow, and when the drip and splash of Alix's hose was sounding steadily from the other end of the garden.

"Stay here?" she echoed, at a loss.

"Yes," he answered, decidedly. "I can stand a little of it, but I don't think much of this sort of life! I thought maybe we could all go into town for dinner and the theatre to-morrow or Saturday. But on Monday we'll have to beat it."

"Monday!" Cherry's heart bounded.

"My idea was, you to come up with me," Martin continued, "we'll see the folks in Portland—"

"Martin, isn't it a mistake to go on pretending—" she began bitterly. But Peter's voice, in the drawing room, interrupted her. "I'll let you know—we'll talk about it!" she had time to say, hurriedly, before he came out to them. He flung himself into a chair. Martin at once opened a general conversation, in which Alix, still diligently watering, was presently near enough to take part.

CHAPTER XIX

The evening dragged. Alix had suggested bridge, but Martin did not play bridge. So she presently scattered anagrams over the table, reminding Peter of some of their battles with word-making in the long winter nights, and they had a half-hearted game, in which Martin showed no interest at all, and Peter deliberately missed chances to score.

Alix glanced furtively at her wrist-watch; it was twenty minutes of ten. As Martin flung himself into a chair beside the fire, and lighted one of his strong cigars, she went to the piano, and began to ramble through various songs, hoping that somebody would start to sing, or suggest a favourite, or in some way help to lighten the dreadful heaviness of the atmosphere.

Cherry and Peter, left at the table, did not speak to each other; Peter leaned back in his chair, with a cigarette; Cherry dreamily pushed to and fro the little wooden block letters.

But presently her heart gave a great plunge, and although she did not alter her different attitude, or raise her eyes, her white hand moved with directed impulse, and Peter's casual glance fell upon the word "Alone."

When he laid his finished cigarette in the tray, it was to finger the letters himself, in turn, and Cherry realized with a great thrill of relief that he was answering her. Carelessly, and obliterating one word before he began another, he formed the question: "My office to-morrow?"

"Martin always with me," Cherry spelled back. She did not glance at Peter, but at Martin, who was watching the fire, and at Alix, whose back was toward the room.

"Come on, have another game!" Peter asked, generally, while he spelled quickly: "Will arrange sailing first possible day."

Alix, humming along with her song, said: "Wait a few minutes!" and Martin glanced up to say, "No, I'm no good at that thing!"

Then Cherry and Peter were unobserved again, and she spelled "Mart goes Monday. Plans to take me."

Peter had reached for a magazine; he whirled through the pages, and yawned. Then he began to play with the anagrams again.

"Can you get away without him?" he spelled.

"How?" Cherry instantly asked. And as Peter's hands went on building a little bridge of wooden letters, she went on: "Alix to train, Martin with me to city, impossible."

"Give him the slip," Peter spelled. And after a pause he added, "Life or death."

"Difficult to evade," Cherry spelled, wiping the words away one by one.

"Must wait—" Peter began. Alix, ending her song on a crash of chords, came to the table, interrupting him. Cherry was now lazily reading a magazine; Peter had built a little pen of tiny blocks.

"I'll go you!" Alix said, with spirit. But the game was rather a languid one, nevertheless, and when it was over they gathered yawning about the mantel, ready to disperse for the night.

"And to-morrow night we dine in town and go to the Orpheum?" Alix asked, for the plan had been suggested at dinner-time.

"I'll blow you girls to any show you like," Martin offered. He took out his big watch—Cherry remembered just how smoothly this watch always seemed to slip in and out of his pocket—and smiled at them. "Ten o'clock," he grinned. "I'll set up awhile longer, and have a look at the evening papers."

"Well—" Peter conceded. Cherry was shocked by the sudden chill and sternness of his face. Immediately, remarking that he was tired, he went to his room. Cherry, with only a general good- night, also disappeared, to find Alix arranging beds and pillows on their sleeping porch.

"Oh, Alix—I'm so worried—I'm so sick with worry!" Cherry whispered. Alix, sitting still in the circle of light thrown from the reading lamp light, over her bed, nodded, with a stricken face. "He won't listen to me," said Cherry. "He won't hear of a divorce!"

"I know!" Alix said, distressedly.

"But what shall I do—I can't go with him!" Cherry protested.

Alix was silent.

"What shall I do?" Cherry pleaded again.

"Why, I don't see what else you CAN do, but go with him!" Alix said, in a troubled voice. "I should think that no man would want his wife, knowing that she didn't want to be with him! And I should think that to leave you here, with enough money to live on, and your own old home, would suit him better than to drag you—" She sighed. "But if it doesn't," she finished, "of course it doesn't alter your obligation, in a way. You ARE his wife. 'For better or worse, for richer or poorer, till death—-'"

It was said so kindly, with Alix's simple and embarrassed fashion of giving advice, that poor Cherry could not resent it. She could only bow her head desolately upon her knees, as she sat, child- fashion, in her bed, and cry.

"A nice mess I've made of my life!" she sobbed. "I've made a nice mess of it! I wish—oh, my God, how I wish I was dead!"

"My own life has been so darned easy," Alix mused, in a cautious undertone, sitting, fully dressed, on the side of her own bed, and studying her sister with pitying eyes. "I've often wondered if I could buck up and get through with it if some of that sort of thing had come to me! I don't know, of course, but it seems to me that I'd say: 'Who loses his life shall gain it!' and I'd stand anything—people and places I hated, loneliness and poverty—the whole bag of tricks! I think I would. I mean I'd read the Bible and Shakespere, and enjoy my meals, and have a garden—" Her voice sank. "I know it's terribly hard for you, Cherry!" she ended, suddenly pitiful.

Cherry had stopped crying, dried her eyes, and had reached resolutely for the book that was waiting on the little shelf above the porch bed.

"You're bigger than I am," she said, quietly. "Or else I'm so made that I suffer more! I wish I could face the music. But I can't do anything. Of course, just—just loathing some things about a man isn't valid cause for divorce, I know that. But I'd rather live with a man that drank, and stole, and beat me—I'd rather he should disgrace me before the whole world, and drag me to prison with him, than to feel as I feel! I would, Alix. I tell you—" Her voice was rising, but suddenly she interrupted herself, and spoke in a lifeless and apologetic tone: "I'm sorry," she said. "One knows of unhappy marriages, everywhere, without quite fancying just what a horrible tragedy an unhappy marriage is! Don't mind me, Alix. The Mill Valley Zeus will have an item in it this week that Mr. and Mrs. Martin Lloyd have gone to visit relatives in Portland, Oregon, and nobody'll know but what we're the happiest couple in the world—and perhaps we are!"

Alix laughed uncomfortably. She was conscious, as she went out to speak to Kow about breakfast, and to give a final glance at fires and lights, that this was one of the times when girls needed a wise mother, or a father, who could decide, blame, and advise.

Coming back from the kitchen, with a pitcher of hot water, she saw Martin, in a welter of evening papers, staring at the last pink ashes of the wood fire. Upon seeing her he got up, and with a cautious glance toward the bedroom doors he said:

"Look here a minute! Can they hear us?" Alix set down her pitcher of water, and came to stand beside him.

"Hear us—Peter and Cherry? No, Cherry's out on our porch, and Peter's porch is even farther away. Why?"

"Take a look, will you?" he said. "I want to speak to you!"

Alix, mystified, duly went to glance at Cherry, reading now in a little funnel of yellow light, and then crossed to enter Peter's room. His porch was dark, but she could see the outline of the tall figure lying across the bed.

"Asleep?" she asked.

"Nope!" he answered.

"Well, don't go to sleep without pulling a rug over you!" she commanded. "Good-night, Pete!"

"Good-night, old girl!" Something in the tone touched her, with a vague hint of unhappiness, but she did not stop to analyze it. She went back through his room, and through the little passage, and rejoined Martin. The freedom of Peter's apartment Alix had always taken as naturally as she did the freedom of her father's.

"Can't hear us, eh?" Martin asked, when again she stood beside him.

"Positively not!" she answered.

"Look here," he said, abruptly. "What brought me up here is this. Who's making love to Cherry?"

Indignant, and with rising colour, she stared at him.

"Who—WHAT!"

"She's having a nice little quiet flirtation with somebody," Martin said, with a significant and warning smile. "Who is it?"

"I don't know who's been talking to you about Cherry, Martin," Alix said, sharply, "but you know you can't repeat that sort of rotten scandal to me!"

"I don't mean any harm—I don't mean any harm!" he assured her, with a quick attempt to quiet the storm he had raised. "Don't get mad— don't get mad! But I happen to know that there's some attraction that's keeping Cherry here, and I came up to look over the ground for myself, do you see?"

His look, which was almost a leer, seemed to imply that Alix was in the secret, a party to Cherry's foolishness, and did imply very distinctly that Martin felt himself to be more than a match for all their cunning. The woman was silent, looking straight into his eyes.

"Come on, now, put me on!" he said.

Alix made an effort at self-control.

"Martin, you're mistaken!" she said, quietly. "You have no right to listen to any one who tells you such things, and if it wasn't that you're Cherry's husband, I wouldn't listen to you! But you'll have to take my word for it that it's a lie. We three have lived up here without seeing any one- ANY ONE! Cherry has hardly spoken to a man, except Peter and Antone and Kow, since she came!"

"Who's this George Sewall?" he asked, shrewdly. "The lawyer! Oh, heavens, Martin! Why, George was a beau of mine; he's a widower of fifty, and has just announced his engagement to the trained nurse that took care of his boy!"

"H'm!" Martin commented.

"If any one mentioned Cherry's name in connection with George," Alix said, firmly, "that was a perfectly malicious slander—"

"Sewall's wasn't mentioned!" Martin said, hastily.

"Whose name WAS mentioned, then?" Alix pursued, hotly.

"Well, nobody's name was mentioned." Martin took a great many creased and rubbed papers from his vest pockets, and shifted them over. Finally, with a fat, deliberate hand he selected one, and put the others away.

"This is from my mother," he said. "My aunt, Mrs. North—"

"We saw her here, a week or two ago!" Alix said as he paused.

"Well, she was in Portland, and saw the folks," said Martin. "And my mother writes me this—" And after a few seconds of searching, he read from the letter: "Bessie North saw Cherry and Mrs. Joyce in Mill Valley, and if I was you I would not let Cherry stay away too long. A wife's place is with her husband, especially when she is as pretty as Cherry, and if Bessie is right, somebody else thinks she is pretty, too, and you know it doesn't take much to start people talking. It isn't like she had a couple of children to keep her busy. Why don't you bring her up here and leave her with Papa and me while you look over the Mexican proposition?"

"That's all of that," said Martin, folding the letter. He eyed Alix keenly. "Well, what do you think?" he asked, triumphantly.

"I think that's a mean, wicked thing to say!" she said, indignantly. "No, Martin," she said, silencing him, as he would have interrupted her, "I know she is beautiful and young, and I know—because she's told me—that you and she feel that your marriage is a mistake, but if you think—"

"Oh, she said that, did she?"

"Don't use that tone!" Alix commanded him quickly. "She didn't blame you or herself, except in that she didn't listen to my father, who thought she was too young to marry any one! But if you want to lose her, Martin," Alix said, with heat, "just let her suspect all this petty suspicion and scandal! Cherry's proud—"

"Now, look here," he said, with his air of assurance, "I'm proud, too. And if I don't choose to stand before the world as a divorced man—"

"Nobody's talking of divorce!" Alix hushed him. "But no woman would stand having other women spy and suspect—"

"How about this Sewall!" he muttered. "By George, she had SOMETHING on her mind when she met me to-day. She was fussed, all right, and it wasn't all the surprise of seeing me, either. First she wanted to telephone you—then she fussed over your message—"

"Cherry gets fluttered very easily!" Alix reminded him.

"Well, she was fussed all right this morning. She said not to mention it to Alix, because she had promised that it should go on time. I thought maybe she meant that you wanted her to go herself; no, she said, a note would do—"

"I don't know what you're talking about!" Alix said, puzzled.

"Your note!" Martin explained.

"What note! I didn't write any note. Cherry telephoned—"

"No," he said, patiently and perfunctorily, "you wanted—Cherry—to-say—good-bye—to—those—people—who—were—sailing! That was all. She wrote it; it got there in time, I guess. Anyway, I heard the girl say to rush it to the boat!"

"Oh!" Alix said. "Oh—" she added. Her tone betrayed nothing, but she was thoroughly at sea. "Did I ask Cherry to say good-bye to any one?" she asked herself, going back to the beginning of the long day. Instinct warned her that nothing would be gained by sharing her perplexity with Martin. "I give you my word that she hasn't been five minutes alone with any one but Peter and me!" she said, frankly, looking into Martin's eyes. "Now, are you satisfied?"

"Sure, I'm satisfied!" he answered. "She didn't go into town to lunch with any one?" he asked.

"No!" Alix said, scornfully. "She always lunches with us! You don't deserve her, to talk so about her, Martin!" she said.

"Well, I'm not anybody's fool, you know!" he assured her. "All right, I'll take your say-so for it. He yawned, "Trouble with Cherry is, she hasn't enough to do!" he finished, sapiently.

"I'm a poor person with whom to discuss Cherry!" Alix hinted, with an unsmiling nod for good-night.

And she looked at Cherry's corn-coloured head, ten minutes later, with a thrill of maternal protectiveness. Cherry was evidently asleep, buried deep under the blue army blankets. But Alix did not get to sleep that night.

She did not even undress. For it was while sitting on the side of her bed, ready to begin the process, that through her excited and indignant and whirling thoughts the first suspicion shot like a touch of flame.

"How dares Martin—how dares he!" her thoughts had run. And then suddenly she had said: "Why, she has seen no one but Peter—she has seen no one but Peter!

"I'll tell Peter all this when Martin has gone," Alix decided. "He'll be furious—he adores Cherry—he'll be furious—he thinks that there is no one like Cherry—"

The words she had said came back to her, and she said them again, half-aloud, with a look of pain and almost of fear suddenly coming into her eyes.

"Peter adores Cherry—"

And then she knew. Even while the sick suspicion formed itself, vague and menacing and horrible, in her heart, she knew the truth of it. And though for hours she was to weigh it and measure it, to remember and question and compare all the days and hours that she and Peter and Cherry had been together; from the moment the thought was born she knew that it was to be with her as an accepted fact for all time to come.

CHAPTER XX

For a few seconds Alix felt ill, dazed, and shocked almost beyond enduring. She sat immovable, her eyes fixed, her body held rigid, as a body might be in the second before it fell after a bullet had cleanly pierced the heart.

Then she put her hand to her throat, and looked with a sort of terror at the silent figure of Cherry. Nobody must know—that was Alix's first clear thought. She was breathing hard, her breast rising and falling painfully, and the blood in her temples began to pound; her mouth was dry.

With a blind instinct for solitude she went quickly and silently from the sleeping porch, and into the warm sitting room. The lamps were all extinguished, but the fire was still burning, low and pink, where the hearts of the logs had fallen apart to show the flame.

For a few minutes Alix stood, with one foot on the chain that linked the old brass fire dogs, her elbow on the mantel, and her cheek resting against her arm.

"No," she whispered, almost audibly, "no—it can't be that! It can't be Cherry and Peter—Oh, my God! Oh, my God, it has been that, all the time, THAT, all the time—and I never knew it—I never dreamed it!"

The end of a log blazed up with a sudden bright flame, and in the light it cast about the quiet room Alix glanced nervously behind her. Silence and shadow held the place; the bedroom doors were shut. The fugitive red warmth picked out the backs of books—Alix knew them all, had browsed over those shabby rows during a hundred winter nights— touched the green shaded lamps, and the roses that were dropping their petals from the crystal bowl, and the polished legs of the old mahogany table.

Nothing moved, nothing stirred. Everything in the little mountain cabin was at rest except the woman who stood, with aching heart and feverish mind, resting her arm on the level of the low mantel, and staring with desolate eyes into the fading heart of the fire.

"It's Peter and Cherry! They have come to care for each other— they have come to care for each other," she said to herself, her thoughts rushing and tumbling in mad confusion as she tested and tried the new fear. "It must be so. But it CAN'T be so!" Alix interrupted herself in terror, "for what shall we do—what shall we do! Cherry in love with Peter. But Peter is my husband—he is MY husband—" And in a spasm of pain she shut her eyes, and flung her head as if suffocating. The beating of her heart frightened her. "I shall be sick if I go on this way!" she reminded herself. "And then they will know. They mustn't know. But Peter—" she whispered suddenly. "Peter, who has always been so good to me—so generous to me— and it was Cherry all the time! While we were up here, reading and talking, and—" her lips trembled, "—and cooking," she told herself, "he was thinking of Cherry—he was always thinking of Cherry! Even those years ago, when we used to tease him about the lady with the crinolines and ringlets, it was she. But why didn't he ask her instead of me?" wondered Alix, and with an aching head, and a frowning brow, she began to piece it all together.

The terrible truth rose triumphant from all her memories. Sometimes for a second hope would flood her with almost painful joy, but inevitably the truth shut down upon her again, and hope died, and she realized afresh that sorrow, stronger than before, was waiting to seize upon her again.

Sorrow and fear and pain, these wrestled with her spirit, that spirit that had never known them before. She had grieved for her father a few years ago; she would always miss him and need him— perhaps never more than to-night. But that was natural loss, softened by everything that love and loyalty and faith could give her, and this was a living anguish, which wrung and twisted her heart more terribly with every instant of its realization.

"Well—I can't stand it in here!" Alix said, suddenly. The walls, the peaceful room, seemed to smother and stifle her. She crossed to the door, and opened it, and slipped noiselessly out into the night, catching a coat from the rack as she passed.

The night was wrapped in an ocean fog, there was no moon and no stars, but the air was soft and warm. The garden was so black that Alix, familiar with every inch of it as she was, groped her way confusedly between the wet bushes and shrubs. Roses drenched her with fog and dew, a wall-flower springing erect as she passed by sent a wave of velvety perfume into her face.

When she gained the woods she made better progress, for under the great shafts of the redwoods there was little growth, and the ground was unencumbered and almost as smooth as a floor. With no goal in view, Alix climbed upward, walking rapidly, breathing hard, and frequently speaking aloud, as some poignant thought smote her, or standing still, too sick with pain, under an unexpected rush of emotion, to move.

Sometimes some small woodland animal scrambled noisily through the dry brush, in escape, and now and then an owl, perhaps a mile away, broke the silence with a mournful and muffled cry. Tiny squeaks and sleepy chirps from birds and chipmunks recognized the disturbance of a stranger's passage through the wood, and once the ugly snarling of wild-cats, always alert in the night, sounded suddenly near, and then died as suddenly away.

Of these things Alix heard nothing. In a trance of feverish dread she went on and on, trying to escape from the conviction that grew momentarily more and more clear.

"He would have told me about it—why didn't I let him!" ran Alix's thoughts. "I thought of some older woman, I don't know why— anyway, I didn't care so much then. But I care now! Peter, I care now! I can't give you up, even to Cherry. It is nonsense to talk of giving him up," Alix told herself, sitting down in the inky dark, on a log against which her wild walk had suddenly brought her, "for we are all married people, and we all love each other. But oh, I am so sorry! I am so sorry, Peter," she whispered, as if she were speaking to him. "You couldn't help it, I know that. She is so pretty and so sweet, Cherry—and she turns to you as if you were her big brother!"

She sat motionless, her hands clasped, and raised so that her cheek was pressed against them. For awhile she seemed to have no thoughts; she was merely vaguely aware that the hands she had plunged into the pockets of one of Peter's old coats were scented with tobacco now, and so reminded her of him. She pressed them hard against her face, as if to ease the pain of her forehead.

But the thoughts, exactly like a pain, began to creep back. With choking bitterness it was upon her again, and she got to her feet and went on.

"What am I thinking about—it's absurd! Can't people like each other, in this world, just because they happen to be married! Peter would be the first to laugh at me. And is it fair to Cherry even to think that she would—

"Oh, but it's true!" the honester impulse interrupted, mercilessly. "It is true. Whether it's right or wrong, or sensible or absurd, they DO love each other; that's what has changed them both."

And she began to remember a hundred—a thousand—trifles, that made it all hideously clear. Words, glances, moods subtler than either, came back to her. Cherry's confusion of late, when the question of her return to Martin was raised, her indifference to her inheritance, her restless talk during one hour of immediate departure, and during the next of an apparently termless visit; all these were significant now.

"I am desperately unhappy!" Cherry had said. And immediately after that, Alix recalled wretchedly, had come a brief and apparently aimless talk about Alix's rights, and her eagerness to share them with her sister.

Cherry had been in misery, of course. Alix knew her too well not to know with what suffering she would admit that the one desire of her heart was for something to which Alix had the higher, if not the stronger, claim.

"Poor Cherry!" the older sister said aloud, standing still for a moment, and pressing both hands over her hot eyes. "Poor little old Cherry—life hasn't been very kind to her! She and Peter must be so sorry and ashamed about this! And Dad would be so sorry; of all things he wanted most that Cherry should be happy! Perhaps," thought Alix, "he realized that she was that sort of a nature, she must love and be loved, or she cannot live! But why did he let her marry Martin, and why wasn't he here to keep me from marrying Peter? What a mess—mess—mess we've made of it all!"

As she used the term, she realized that Cherry had used it, too, this same evening, and fresh conviction was added to the great weight of conviction in her heart.

"She was thinking of that," Alix told herself, "and it has been in

Peter's mind all these weeks. Oh, Peter—Peter—Peter!" she moaned, writhing as the cry escaped her. "Why couldn't it have been me, why couldn't it have been me! Why couldn't you have loved me that way? I know I am not so pretty as Cherry," Alix went on, resuming her restless walk, "and I know that those things don't seem to mean as much to me as to most women! But, Peter," she said softly, aloud, "no wife ever loved a man more than I love you, my dear!" She remembered some of his half-laughing, half-fretful reproaches, when he had told her that she loved him much as she loved Buck, and that, in these respects, she was no more than a healthy child. "I may be a child," said Alix, feeling that a dry flame was consuming her heart, "but a child can love! My dear—my dear—

"I wish I could cry," she said suddenly, finding herself sitting on a log where low oaks met the forest and the open meadows, and where they had often paused in mountain climbs to look far across the panorama of hills and valley below. "But now we must face this thing sensibly. What is to be done? They must not know that I know, and in some way we must get out of this tangle. Even if Peter were free, Cherry would not be free," she decided, "and so the only thing to do is to help them, until it dies away."

No suspicion of the truth stabbed her, although she remembered Martin and his strange tale of a message and wondered about it a little in her thoughts. To whom had Cherry been sending that telegram if not to Peter? And if to Peter, why had she not simply telephoned? Because she had known that Peter was not in his office, because she had been going to meet him somewhere. But where? Well, at the boat. Martin had heard her tell the boy that he must catch that boat.

Alix did not guess the truth. But she guessed enough to make her feel frightened and sick. She could not suppose that Cherry and Peter had planned to go away on that boat together, because at most her thoughts would have grasped the idea of one or two days' absence only, and they had given her no warning of that. But until this instant the thought of the passionate desire that enveloped them had not reached her; she had imagined Cherry's feeling for Peter to be something only a little stronger than her own.

Now she thought of Cherry's beauty, her fragrance and softness, the shine in her blue eyes and the light on her corn-coloured hair, and knew that life for them all, of late, had been mined with frightful danger.

"Cherry would be disgraced, and Martin—Martin would kill her, if he found her out! ... Oh, my little sister! She would be town talk; she is so reckless, she would do anything—she would be a public scandal, and the papers would have her pictures—Dad's little yellow-headed Charity! Oh, Dad," she said, looking up into the dark, "tell me what to do! I need you so! Won't you somehow tell me what to do!"

Silence and darkness. But even in the gloom Alix could tell that fog was lifting, and a sudden sweep of breeze, like a tired breath, went over the tops of the redwoods.

Steadily came the change. The darkness, by imperceptible degrees, lifted. The world grew gray as if with moonshine, trees and bushes began to stand out dimly from the mass of shadows. On the road below her Alix heard a wagon rattle, the mud-spattered wagon from the Portuguese dairy upon the ridge; and past her, leaving a dark wake of brushed dewdrops on the pearled grass, a cottontail fled silently.

She noted with surprise that she could see the grass now, although it had been invisible a few moments ago. She could see it, and presently its brownness showed, and the rich, solid green of the oaks lifted from the dull twilight that had enveloped the world.

"Light!" Alix whispered, awestruck And a few moments later she added, "Dawn!"

It was dawn indeed that was creeping into the valley, and as it brightened and deepened and warmed momentarily, Alix felt some of the peace and glory of it swelling in her tired heart. The sky grew pale, grew white, gradually turned to blue, and the little clouds drifting across it vanished, lost in a swimming vapour of pink and pearl.

Suddenly a first shaft of sunlight struck across the mountain ridge, and lay bright on the hilltop opposite, the fog that still clung to the peak of the mountain was steadily ascending into the brilliant air, dew sparkled, and the hoary, lichened limbs of the sprawling oaks glistened in the light. The sun came up, and Alix felt the blessed warmth against her chilled and cramped shoulders, and stretched her arms out to welcome the flood of brightness and new courage after the darkness and doubts of the night.

She was still sitting on the log, dreamily watching the expanding beauty of the new day, when there was a crashing in the underbrush behind her, and wild with joy, and with twigs and dried brown grasses on his wet coat, Buck came bounding out of the forest, and leaped upon her.

"Bucky!" she faltered, as he stood beside her, his quick tongue flashing ecstatically, close to her face, every splendid muscle of his body wriggling with eager affection. "Did you miss me, old fellow? Did you come to find me?"

She had not cried during the long vigil of the night, when a storm had raged in her heart, and had left her weak and sick with dread. But there was peace now, and Alix locked her arms about the dog's shoulders, and laid her face against his satiny head, and cried.

CHAPTER XXI

When Cherry came out to breakfast, a few hours later, she found Alix already at the porch table. Alix looked pale, but fresh and trim; she had evidently just tubbed, and she wore one of the plain, wide-striped ginghams that were extremely becoming to her rather boyish type.

She looked up, and nodded at Cherry composedly. Cherry always kissed her sister in the morning, but she did not to-day. She felt troubled and ashamed, and instinctively avoided the little caress.

"No men?" she asked, sharing her grapefruit with her mail.

"Peter had to go to San Rafael with Mr. Thomas in his car, to do something about the case," Alix explained. "I drove them down, and at the last minute Martin decided to go. So I marketed, and got the mail, and came back, and the understanding is that we are to meet them at the St. Francis for dinner, at six, and go to the Orpheum."

"Is it almost ten?" Cherry said sleepily, gazing in surprise at the clock that was visible through the open door. "I'm terribly ashamed! And when did you get up, and silently make your bed, and hang up your things?"

"Oh, early!" Alix answered, noncommittally. "I had a bath, and this is my second breakfast!"

Cherry, who was reading a letter, did not hear her. Now she made some inarticulate sound that made Alix look at her in quick concern.

"Cherry, what is it?" she exclaimed.

For answer Cherry tossed her the letter, written on a thick sheet of lavender paper, which diffused a strong odour of scent.

"Read that!" she said, briefly. And with a desperate air she dropped her head on the table, and knotted her hands high above it.

Fearfully, Alix picked up the perfumed sheet, and read, in a coarse and sprawling, yet unmistakably feminine handwriting, the following words:

DEAR MRS. LLOYD: Perhaps you would not feel so pleased with yourself if you knew the real reason why your husband left Red Creek? It was because of a quarrel he had with Hatty Woods.

If you don't believe it you had better ask him about some of the parties he had with Joe King's crowd, and where they were on the night of August 28th, and if he knows anybody named Hatty Woods, and see what he says. Ask him if he ever heard of Bopps' Hotel and when he was in Sacramento last. If he denies it, you can show him this letter.

There was no signature.

Alix, who had read it first with a bewildered and suspicious look, read it again, and flushed deeply at the sordid shame of it. She laid it down, and looked in stunned conviction at her sister.

Cherry, who was breathing hard, raised her head, rested her chin on her hands, elbows on the table, and stared at Alix defiantly.

"There!" she said, almost with triumph. "There! Now, is that so easy? Now, am I to just smile and agree and say 'Certainly, Martin,' 'Of course, Martin dear!' Now you see—now you see! Now, am I to bear THAT," she rushed on, her words suddenly violent. "And go on with him—as his wife—when a common woman like that—"

"Cherry, dear!" Alix said, distressedly.

"Ah, well, you can't realize it; nobody but the woman to whom it happens can!" Cherry interrupted her, covering her face with her hands. "But let him say what he pleases now," she added, passionately, "let him do what he pleases—I'll follow my own course from to-day on!"

Alix, watching her fearfully, was amazed at the change in her. Cherry's eyes were blazing, her cheeks pale. Her voice was dry and feverish, and there was a sort of frenzy in her manner that Alix had never seen before. To bring sunny little Cherry to this—to change the radiant, innocent child that had been Cherry into this bitter and disillusioned woman—Alix felt as if the whole world were going mad, and as if life would never be sane and serene again for any one of them.

"Cherry, do you believe it?" she asked.

Cherry, roused from a moment of brooding silence, shrugged her shoulders impatiently.

"Oh, of course I believe it!" she answered.

"But, darling, we don't even know who wrote it. We have only this woman's word for it—"

"Oh, LOOK at it—LOOK at it, Alix!" Cherry burst forth. "Do DECENT men have letters like that sent to their wives? Is it probable that a good man would do anything to rouse some busybody woman to write such a letter about him?"

"Well, but who is she, and what do you suppose she wrote it for?" Alix wondered.

"Oh, I don't know. She got mad at him, perhaps. Or perhaps she is a champion of this Woods woman. They had some quarrel—how do I know? But you can see that she is mad, and this is the way she gets even!"

"Cherry, at least do Martin the justice to ask him about it!" Alix pleaded, really frightened now.

Her sister seemed not to hear her. She stopped her angry pacing, and sat down at the table, and the misery in her beautiful eyes made Alix's heart sink.

"And that," Cherry said in a whisper, "is my husband!"

She paused, staring down at the table, one hand supporting her forehead, the other wandering idly among the breakfast things. Her look was sombre and far away. Alix, standing, watched her distressedly, through a long minute of silence.

"Well!" Cherry said lifelessly, looking up at her sister with dulled eyes. "What now? It's still 'for better or worse,' I suppose?"

Alix sat down, and for a moment covered her face with a tight-pressed hand. When she took it away, there was new serenity and resolution in her tired face.

"No," she said, with a great sigh, "I think perhaps you're right! He hasn't—he should have no claim on you now!"

"Alix," Cherry demanded, "would you forgive him?"

"Perhaps I wouldn't," Alix said, after thought.

"PERHAPS you wouldn't!" Cherry echoed, incredulously.

"Well, I'm not very good," Alix said, hesitatingly. "But a vow is a vow, you know. If it was limited, then my—my fulfillment of it would be limited, I suppose. Of course," she added, honestly, "I'm talking for myself only!"

"And you would quietly forgive and forget!" demanded the little sister, in bitter scorn.

"I say I HOPE I would!" Alix corrected her. "Even if this IS true"— she added, with a glance at the lavender letter—"still, I suppose the rule of forgiving seventy times seven times—"

Cherry interrupted her with a burst of bitter and rebellious weeping.

"Oh, my God, what shall I do!" she sobbed, with her bright head dropped on her arm. Alix saw Kow come to the door, look at them speculatively, and disappear, and thought in her shaken soul that things in a household were demoralized indeed when pretense before the servants was no longer maintained.

"Don't cry, Cherry, Cherry!" she said, her own tears brimming over. She came to kneel beside her sister, and they locked their arms about each other, and their wet cheeks touched. "Don't cry, dear!" she said, tenderly. "It'll all come straight, somehow, and we'll wonder why we took it so hard!"

"The thing that breaks—my—heart!" sobbed Cherry, clinging tight, "is that it is all my fault!"

"Oh, no; it's not, Cherry. You were too young. And it's only one of so many thousands of unhappy marriages!" Alix argued, soothingly. "Now listen to me, Sis," she began briskly, as soon as Cherry had somewhat regained her composure. "We'll ascertain about this letter; that's only fair. If Martin denies it—"

"Of course he'll deny it!" Cherry interrupted, from the bitter knowledge she had of him.

Alix again felt daunted for a second by the sheer ugliness and sordidness of the matter, but she returned to the charge bravely.

"Suppose we get Peter to ask him," she suggested suddenly. "Peter has a wonderful way of getting the truth out of people! Poor Cherry, the very mention of his name makes her wince," Alix thought, watching her sister sorrowfully. "If Martin can convince Peter that it is not true, then that makes all the difference in the world," she added, aloud. "Then you tell Martin frankly that you have the old house ready to live in, and you want to live there. He—"

"He'll never agree to that!" Cherry said, shaking her head. "But if this is true?" she asked, again indicating the letter.

"Then tell him that unless he agrees absolutely to a separation," Alix said, "that you will get a divorce!"

"And live here, alone, under that sort of a cloud?" Cherry said, with watering eyes. "Oh, well!" she said, rising, and going toward the door. "It's horrible—horrible—horrible—whatever I do! What is your idea—that we should dine, and go to the Orpheum tonight as if nothing had happened, and let all this wait until you can ask Peter to cross-examine Martin?"

"I wonder if Martin would tell ME?" Alix mused.

"He'd tell you sooner than Peter!" Cherry prophesied.

"Why couldn't I pretend that I opened that letter by mistake," Alix said, thoughtfully, "and frighten him into admitting it, if it's true!"

"You could," Cherry admitted, lifelessly. "But you may be sure it is true enough!" she added.

"Then leave it to me!" Alix said. "And don't feel too sad, Cherry. You're young, and life may take a turn that changes everything for you. You always have Peter—Peter and me, back of you!"

"Alix, you're the best sister a girl ever had!" Cherry said, passionately, putting her hand on Alix's shoulder. "I wish I were as big as you are! And he's made me so wretched," whispered Cherry, with trembling lips, "that sometimes I've been sick of life! But I will investigate this letter, and if it's not true, I'll try again, Alix! I'll go away with him, if he wants me to, or I'll live here—and study French—and go to lectures with you—"

"You darling!" Alix said, with an aching heart. And they smiled through tears as they kissed each other.

That night it was simply managed that Martin should be next to Alix, in the loge at the theatre, and she began to question him seriously at once. All through the strange, unnatural day that followed her night of vigil she had been planning what she should say to him, but she and Cherry had not spoken of the subject again. Cherry had dressed herself with her usual dainty care, and now, with the violets Alix had given her spraying in a great purple bunch at her breast, and her blue eyes ringed and thoughtful under her soft little feathered hat, she was so arrestingly lovely that Alix was well aware of the admiring glances from all sides to which she was so superbly indifferent.

"Martin," Alix began, "I read a letter intended for Cherry this morning. I—I open all the mail!"

She had to repeat it twice before he realized that there was something behind her earnest and significant tone. Then she saw him stop twisting his program, and veer about toward her. She murmured a question.

"Do I what?" he asked, in an undertone instantly lowered.

"Do you know a girl named Hatty Woods?" Alix repeated, cautiously.

All hope died when she saw his face. He shot her a quick, suspicious look, and his big mouth trembled with a scornful and contemptuous smile and he looked away indifferently. Then he faced her, on guard.

"What about her?" he asked, almost inaudibly.

"Somebody wrote this letter about her," Alix stated, quietly.

"Who wrote you about her? What'd she say?" he demanded quickly.

"Just—I'll let you see it," she said. "I don't know who wrote it- -it wasn't signed. Do you—do you know her? Do you know Hatty Woods?"

Martin smiled again, a superior yet ugly smile. It was the look of a man approached in his own realm, threatened in his infallible fastness.

"The less you have to do with girls like Hatty, the better!" he told her. "You've got plenty to do without mixing up with her!"

"She said—" Alix began. "The letter said—"

"Oh, sure, I know what she'd say!" Martin conceded, furious at Alix's interference, trembling with anger and resentment, and only anxious to close the conversation. "I know all about her and her kind. I think I know who wrote that letter, too. I guess Joe King's wife knows something about it. They're all alike! You give it to me to-morrow and I'll manage it. There won't be any more!"

"Martin," Alix whispered, gravely, "if you have given Cherry any cause—" Her voice fell, and there was a silence.

"There are a great many things in life that you don't understand, my dear sister-in-law," Martin said reluctantly, nettled, but still maintaining his air of lofty superiority, "a man's life is not a woman's—isn't intended to be! If this woman says she has anything on me—"

"She said that you went to a place called Bopps' Hotel in Sacramento—" Alix began, but he interrupted her.

"Oh, she did, did she?" he said, furiously, yet always in a cautious undertone. "Well, now, I'll tell you something! She's going to have a nice time proving that, and you can tell your sister—if this is a frame-up, that I'll fight Hatty Woods and fifty Hatty Woods! I—"

"Martin—for Heaven's sake!" Alix warned him, as she pressed her violets against her face.

"Well," he said, surlily, "now you know how I feel about it!"

"Martin," Alix pleaded, feeling that her last hope was sinking away from her, "can you deny her story?"

He was silent, while a beaming young Jewess in an outrageous gown took an encore for her song and dance. Then he turned again toward Alix with the smile she had learned to hate.

"You get Cherry to deny that she's never lost a chance to beat it away from home ever since she was married," he said. "You get her to deny that she has said over and over again that she never wanted children, that her marriage was a mistake! You ask her to show you the letters I've written her, asking her to come back, and then I'll show you the answers I got!"

"Mart," Alix said, sharply, "there's no use in your taking that tone with me! I'm simply sick over the whole affair. I would do anything in the world—I would put my hand in the fire to straighten it out!"

She paused, arrested by some sudden thought.

"I tell you I would put my hand in the fire to help," she said again, in quieter tones. "But taking that attitude will do no good! If this poor girl, this Hatty—"

"I tell you to leave Hatty OUT of it!" Martin said. "The best thing you can do is to let the whole thing alone!"

But she saw that he was both nervous and apprehensive, and she knew that the inference she and Cherry had drawn from the letter was a true one.

"Does Cherry know anything of this?" Martin presently muttered.

"Do you want her to?" Alix asked, pointedly.

He shrugged his shoulders with a great assumption of indifference.

"If she wants to have it all dragged to light, why, she can go ahead!" he remarked, carelessly. "I've left Red Creek, and—as I tell you!—that woman will never write another letter, for I know the way to shut her up, and I intend to do it. But if you and Cherry want the whole thing aired in public, why, go ahead! I'm not stopping you!"

"At least I think you ought to let Cherry lead her own life after this!" Alix countered with spirit.

"Live in your old house, eh?" he asked, resentfully, as he flipped the pages of his program with a big thumb and stared at it with unseeing eyes. "What does she want to live there for?"

"The fact remains that she DOES," Alix persisted.

"Yes, and have just as good a time as if she never had been married at all!" he said.

"You KNOW—"

Alix was beginning the denial that she had given him so confidently last night, but she interrupted herself, and stopped short. The conviction rushed upon her in an overwhelming wave that she had no right to repeat that denial now that the last dreadful twenty-four hours had changed the whole situation, and that she herself had better reason to suspect Cherry than either Martin or his gossiping aunt. She sat sick and silent, unable to speak again, thinking only that it was Peter that Mrs. Lloyd had seen with Cherry that day, and that there must have been something in their attitude that revealed their secret even to her first casual look.

The vaudeville show whirled and crashed and rattled on its way. Martin applauded heartily but involuntarily; Alix applauded mechanically. Their conversation was closed.

Meanwhile, Cherry and Peter had their first opportunity to speak to each other alone. It occurred to neither of them that it was strange to find this chance in the rustling darkness of the big vaudeville house, with several thousand of persons pressing all about them. To both the thirst for speech was a burning necessity, and it was with an almost dizzy sense of relief that Cherry turned to him with her first words.

"Peter, I don't dare say much! Can you hear me?"

"Perfectly!" he answered, looking at his folded program.

"Peter, I've been thinking—about our plan, I mean! Martin plans to go on Monday. But something has happened since I saw you this morning, something that makes a difference! I had a letter, a letter from some woman connecting his name with another woman, a Hatty Woods—she's notorious in Red Creek—and this Joe King crowd that he went with—I don't know who wrote the letter, or why she wrote," she said, hastily, as Peter interpolated a question. "And I don't care! I haven't spoken to Martin about it. But I've been thinking about it all day. And of course it makes a difference to us—to you and me. As far as Martin goes, I am free now; what is justice to Martin, and kindness to Martin, will never count with me any more!"

Peter wasted no words. His face was thoughtful.

"He goes Monday," he said. "We can go Sunday."

"Does the boat sail Sunday?"

"I am sure of it. This is Thursday night. Your suitcase I checked again yesterday. Was it only yesterday?"

"That's all!"

"We would have been on the train to-night, Cherry, flying toward New Orleans!"

Her small hand gripped his in the darkness.

"If we only were!" he heard her breathe.

He turned to her, so exquisite in her distress. Her breast was rising and falling quickly.

"Patience, sweetheart!" he said. "Patience for only a few days more! To-morrow I'll make the arrangements. Sunday is only two days off."

"Sunday will be day after day after to-morrow," she said whimsically.

"Is Sunday the best day?" he questioned, thoughtfully.

"Oh, much the best!" Cherry said, her whole face glowing suddenly. "You see, it's already arranged that I come in to the Olivers' Saturday night, and help them get ready for their tea on Sunday. Alix is to stay in the valley, and play the organ Sunday morning, and come in with Martin at ten."

"I suppose I'll have to come when they do!" he mused.

"But isn't there that breakfast at the club on Sunday?" Cherry asked.

"Porter's breakfast—yes. But I'm not going to that," Peter said, stupidly.

"Couldn't you say that you were?" she supplied, simply.

"Yes, by George!" he agreed, brightening. "That fixes me! But now how about you?"

"Why, I am at the Olivers'!" she reminded him. "All I have to do is walk out of the house at ten!"

Their eyes met in a wild rush of triumph and hope.

"This time we shall do it!" Peter said. "Your suitcase I'll have. You have money?"

"Oh, plenty!"

"Martin thinks you go with him Monday, eh?"

"I hardly know what he thinks!" she answered, with a fluttered air. "I've hardly known what I was doing or saying! He was to go to-morrow, you know. But I told him that I wanted to get the whole house in perfect order, in case Alix should ever find a tenant. We've worked like beavers there!"

"I know you have!" He smiled down at her, Peter's kind and radiant smile. "After day after day after to-morrow," he said, "I shall see to it that you never work too hard again!"

"Oh, Peter—you'll never be sorry?" she whispered.

"Sorry! My dearest child, when you give your beauty and your youth to a man almost twice your age, who has loved you all your life— do you think there is much chance of it?"

"Why SHOULDN'T it be one of the happy—marriages?" said Cherry after a silence.

"It will," he answered, confidently. "My dearest girl, I know something of life and its disappointments and disillusionments! And I tell you that I know that every hour you and I have together is going to be more wonderful than the hour before! I tell you that as the weeks become months, and the months become years, and the beauty and miracle of it go on and on, we will think that what we feel for each other now is only the shadow—the dream!"

"But the beginning will be wonderful enough!" Cherry mused. "You and I, breakfasting together, walking together, talking together, always just we two! But, Peter," she said, suddenly, "one of us might die!"

"Ah, THAT," he conceded, soberly, "that! It's all I'm afraid of, now!"

"I am terribly afraid of it!" said Cherry, beginning to tremble. "If you should die now, before Sunday! I never thought of it before—"

"You mustn't think of it now, and I won't!" he said, quickly. "Why, we have only two days to wait—!"

"Only two!" she echoed, nervously. "I promised him to-night that I would write to his mother about our coming—"

"You talk as if you meant to go with Martin!" he said, smiling.

"I know I do, sometimes, and that's one of the things that worries me!" she answered, quickly. "So many things have happened, and I get so confused, thinking," she went on, "that I am all mixed most of the time! I arrange one thing as if I were going to do what Martin thinks I am—go with him to Portland, I mean—at another time I'll get into long talks with Alix of what divorces would mean, and all the time I am straining toward you— and escape from it all! It worries and frightens and puzzles me so," she confided, raising her lovely eyes to him, "that I am almost afraid to speak at all for fear of betraying myself!"

"Don't speak at all then!" he answered, smiling whimsically.

"Shall I just let him think I am quietly going away with him on Monday?" she asked, after a silence in which she was deeply thinking.

"Does he know you had that letter?" Peter said.

"No; Alix is going to speak to him about it." Cherry outlined the talk that she and her sister had had at breakfast.

"Then I shouldn't bring up the question at all," Peter decided, quickly. "It would only mean an ugly and unnecessary scene. If you were going to be here, it would be very different. Even then you might have to face a terrible publicity and unpleasantness. But as it is, it's much wiser to let him continue to think that you don't know anything about it, and to let Alix think that you are ignoring the whole thing!"

"Until Sunday!" she whispered.

"Until Sunday." Peter glanced at Martin and Alix, who were talking together absorbedly, in low tones. "My little sweetheart, I'll make all this misery up to you!" he whispered. Her little hand was locked in his for the rest of the evening.

The vaudeville performance ended, and they went out into the cool night, decided against a supper, found the car where Alix had parked it in a quiet side street, and made their way to the ferry, and so home under the dark low arch of a starless and moonless sky. Cherry shared the driver's seat with her sister to-night; they spoke occasionally on the long drive; everybody was weary and silent. Alix, racing between Sausalito's low hills and the dark, odorous marshes, wondered if in the packed theatre any other four hearts had borne the burden that these four were bearing.

The car flew on its way; the men, in the back seat, occasionally exchanged brief, indifferent remarks. Cherry, staring straight ahead of her, neither moved nor spoke, and Alix, at the wheel, watching the road and the lights keenly, and listening to the complicated breathing of the machinery, resumed again the endless chain of thought. Peter—Cherry—Martin—Dad—the few people with whom her life concerned wheeled in unceasing confusion through her brain, and always it was herself, Alix, who would have died for them, who must somehow find the solution.

Morning came, a crystal autumn morning, and life went on. Peter and Martin went away before Cherry came out to the porch, to find her breakfast waiting, and Alix, in striped blue linen, cutting food for the ducks. The peaceful day went by, and if there was any change at the cabin it was a change for the better. Alix, who had been silent and troubled for a little while, was more serene now, as usual concerned for the comfort of her household, and as usual busy all day long with her poultry and pigeons, her bee-keeping, stable, and dogs. Peter was his courteous, gentle, interested self, more like the old Peter, who had always been occupied with his music and his books, than like the passionately metamorphosed Peter who had been so changed by love for Cherry. Martin, satisfied with the general respects and consideration with which he found himself surrounded, accepted life placidly enough; perhaps he had been disturbed by the advent of the letter, perhaps he was willing to let the question of an adjustment between Cherry and himself rest. If she had been innocently indiscreet, he had also yielded to temptation, not so innocently, and although Martin was not a man to consider the question of morals between the sexes as evenly balanced, still he had winced very uncomfortably under Alix's cross-examination, and was not anxious to reopen the subject. "Let by-gones be by-gones!" Martin said to himself, contentedly, as he ate, slept, and smoked his endless cigars, chatted with Peter, followed Alix about the farmyard, and expressed an occasional opinion that was considerately received by the others. It amused him to help get the house ready for a tenant, and from the fact that Cherry talked no more of living there, and made no comment upon his frequent reference to their departure on Monday, he deduced that she had come to her senses.

Cherry, too, was less unhappy than she had been. By avoiding Peter, by refraining even in words and looks from the companionship for which she so hungered by devoting herself to Alix, she managed to hold her feelings tightly in leash. It cost her dear, for sometimes the thought of what she was about to do swept her with a feeling of agony and faintness hard to conceal, and the need for perpetual watchfulness was exhausting to body and spirit. But even though Alix found that the knowledge of the secret they shared without ever mentioning stood between them like a screen, the sisters, busy about the house, had wonderful hours together.

Saturday came, a perfect day that filled the little valley to the brim with golden sunshine. The mountain swam in a pale haze of gray-blue, the sky was soft, unclouded, faintly azure. In the forest about the old Strickland house not a breath of air stirred. Alix, driving alone to the mountain cabin, stared in the morning freshness at the blue overhead and said aloud, "Oh, what a day of gold!"

The dog, sitting beside her on the front seat, flapped his tail in answer to her voice, and she laughed at him. But the laugh was quickly followed by a sharp sigh.

"Saturday," she mused, "and Martin expects Cherry to go with him on Monday! Expects her to go back with him to a life of misery for her, existence with a man she hates! Oh, Cherry—my little sister!—there can be no happiness for you there! And Peter! Peter is left behind to me, who cannot comfort him, or still the ache that is tearing his heart! My two loved ones, and what can I do to help them!"

Driving slowly, on the noiseless pine-needles, she looked up at the great, brown shafts of the trees through which the roadway wound like a shelf. Streaks of sunlight filtered through them; the September air was soft and sweet. The forest was like an old friend to Alix, and the time she spent in it was always her quietest time. The tempered light, the air scented with piney sweetness, the delicate summer humming of tiny forest voices, the brief snap of twigs, and the rustling of tiny bodies in the underbrush, these made the world in which she was most at home.

"Oh, why can't we always be like children, just happy to be free!" she mused, as she left the forest and came in sight of the cabin. "How happy we used to be, playing in these woods and going home tired and hungry to Dad and supper! Buck," she said aloud, "a dog is happier than a man, and perhaps"—and Alix smiled her whimsical smile, as the car moved under the last oaks and was brought to a standstill close to the house—"perhaps a tree is the happiest of all!"

She had come up to the cabin to do the usual last little daily fussing among the ducks and chickens and to bring Peter, if Peter had not gone into town, back with her to Cherry's house. They had all dined in the old Strickland house the night before, and because of a sudden rainfall had decided to spend the night there, too. The Chinese boy who had been helping the sisters with their housecleaning had been persuaded to cook the dinner and get breakfast, and the evening about the old fireplace had been almost too poignantly sweet. Martin, who had been mixing cocktails, liked the role of host, and to the other three every inch of the house was full of happy memories, softened and saddened by all that had happened since the old days, by all that they knew and felt now, and accompanied by the softly dripping rain on the roof and eaves as by a plaintive obbligato.

But suddenly, at about ten o'clock, Peter had surprised them all by getting to his feet. He was going up to the cabin, he said— must go, in fact.

"In all the rain!" they had protested.

"In all the rain," he answered, shaking himself into his coat; he liked rain. He would rather walk, please, he told Alix, when she offered to drive him up in the car. Bewildered and a little apprehensive, she let him go. To Cherry, who seemed to feel suddenly sad and uneasy, Alix laughed about it, but she was secretly worried herself, and immediately after breakfast the next morning decided to run up to the cabin in the car and assure herself that everything was right there.

Cherry, who had not slept and who was pale, had come out to the car, her distracted manner increasing Alix's sense that something was gravely amiss. The sisters had loitered at the car a moment in the exquisite morning freshness.

"Remember the day the rose vine came down and you crawled through it?" Alix had asked, looking back at the house.

"Oh, don't!" Cherry had protested faintly.

"Why not?" her sister had asked, tenderly reproachful.

"Oh, because it makes me so sad to think how happy we were!" Cherry had answered, making an effort to speak lightly. "It's such a glorious morning," she had added, "I wish I were going to drive up with you."

"Why don't you?" Alix had said, eagerly.

"Oh—too much to do here!" Cherry had answered, vaguely. She had looked at her sister as if she would like to speak, smiled uncertainly, and had gone back to the house. Alix had started on her trip with a heavy heart, but the half-hour's run soothed her in spite of herself, and now she reached the cabin in a much more cheerful mood.

Peter was nowhere about, and as she plunged into the work of house and farmyard she supposed, without giving the matter a conscious thought, that he had gone to the city.

"Mis' Peter not go train," Kow announced, presently.

All Alix's vague suspicions awakened.

"Not go train?" she asked, with a premonitory pang.

Kow made a large gesture, as indicating affairs disorganized.

"Him no go to bed," he further stated.

Alix stopped the busy chopping that she was carrying on at the end of the kitchen table, and looked at the Chinese boy fearfully.

"Mr. Peter not go to bed?" she echoed with a sick heart.

"No sleep!" Kow announced, positively. And pleased with her tense interest, he added, "Boss come late. He walkin' on porch."

"He came in late and walked on the porch!" Alix echoed in a low tone, as if to herself. "And you say he didn't sleep, Kow?"

"Bed all same daytime," the boy said. And with the artless laugh of his race he added, "*I* go sleep."

"You slept, of course," Alix answered, absently. "Where Mr. Peter go now?" she asked. "He have some coffee?"

"No eat," the boy answered. He indicated the direction of the creek, and after a while Alix, with an icy heart, went to the bridge and the pool where Peter had first found Cherry only a few weeks ago.

He was standing, staring vaguely at the low and lisping stream, and Alix felt a great pang of pity when she saw him. He came to her smiling, but as Cherry had smiled, with a wan and ghastly face.

"Peter, you're not well?" Alix said. "I think—I am a little upset," he answered. They walked back to the house together. Alix ordered him to take a hot bath, and made him drink some coffee, when, refreshed and grateful, he came out to the porch half an hour later. They shared the little meal that was her luncheon and his breakfast.

"And now we've got to go down and get the others, for they're coming up here for dinner," Alix said. "Do you—do you feel up to tennis?" she asked, anxiously.

"Sure I do!" Peter answered with an effort.

"Don't have to, you know," she assured him, feeling a great desolation sweep her.

"Oh, I'd like it. It's a wonderful day," he answered, politely.

He followed her to the car and got in the front seat beside her.

"You're awfully good to me," he said, briefly, when they were going down the long grade.

Alix did not answer immediately, and he thought that she had not heard. She ran the big machine through the valley, where the dry, glaring heat of the day burned mercilessly, stopped at the post- office, and still in silence began the climb toward the old house. The roads were all narrow here, but she could have followed them in the dark, he knew, and he understood that it was not her driving that made her face so thoughtful and kept her eyes from meeting his.

On one side of the shelf-like mountain road rose the sharp hillside, clothed in close-packed, straight-rising redwoods; on the other the ground fell away so precipitously to the tiny thread of creek below that they looked down upon the water through the top branches of the trees. Years ago, when he had first entrusted her with the car, Peter had been somewhat concerned for Alix's safely, but now he was secretly proud of her sureness of touch and of the generosity and self-confidence that prompted her to give the inner right of way to every lumbering express van or surrey that she met, and risk the more dangerous passing herself.

"You say I'm good to you, Pete," she surprised him by saying suddenly. "I hope I am. For you've been very good to me, my dear.

There's only one thing in life now that I haven't got, and want. And that, you can't, unfortunately, get for me."

He had flushed darkly, and he spoke with a little effort.

"I'd like to try!"

She ignored the invitation for a few minutes, and for an instant of panic he thought he saw her lip tremble. But when she turned to him, it was with her usual smile.

"It's only that I would like to have you—and—and Martin—and Cherry, as happy as I am!" she said, quickly. And a second later the mood was gone as she turned the car in at the home gate and exclaimed, "There's Cherry now!"

There was Cherry; Peter's heart gave a leap at the sight of her. Just a woman's slender figure, half obscured by blowing lines of fresh, dry linen, just white arms, where the snowy frill of her gown fell back, and blue eyes under bright, loose, corn-coloured hair, but Peter could see nothing else in all the world.

"Martin's somewhere about," Cherry said, as Peter joined her, and Alix stopped the car within conversational range. "I was passing these, and I thought I'd help the boy get his clothes in."

"Here, let me do that," Peter exclaimed. Alix remarking that she would turn the car so that she might later start on the grade, disappeared, and the two were alone with their arms full of the stiff and fragrant cleanness of the linen in the sweetness of the afternoon.

"Just—just fold them roughly," stammered Cherry, hardly conscious of what she was saying, "and put them in the basket—"

Peter did not hear the words. But he heard the wonderful voice; he saw the red sweetness of the mouth, saw the quick glances of the averted eyes, the white neck with its film of gold hair blowing across it.

He murmured something inarticulate in reply, trying to control the great wave of happiness and emotion that rose over him. They were together again, after what a night—and what a day!—and that was all that mattered. They spoke confusedly, in brief monosyllables, and were silent, their hands touching on the line, their eyes meeting only furtively and briefly.

"Can you walk up to the cabin with me?" Peter asked. "I want so much to speak to you. Everything's all arranged for tomorrow. I've got tickets and reservations. Your suitcase is checked in the Oakland ferry waiting-room. All you have to think of is yourself. Now, in case of missing the boat again—which isn't conceivable, but we must be ready for anything!—I shall go straight to the club. You must telephone me there. Just go off to-night quietly, get as much sleep as you can, and keep your wits about you."

"Tell me our plans again," Cherry faltered.

"It's perfectly simple," he said, giving her anxious face a concerned glance. "You are going to the Olivers'. I go in, in the morning, presumably for the Porter breakfast, but really to get your suitcase and my own and get to the boat. I shall be there at half-past ten. You get there well before eleven—you won't see me. But go straight on board, and ask for Mrs. Joyce's cabin. Wait for me there!"

"But—but suppose you don't come!"

"I'll be there before you. It is better for us not to meet upstairs. But to be sure, I'll telephone you at Minna Oliver's at about nine o'clock tomorrow morning. I'll just tell you that I'm on my way and that everything is all right! Have you your heavy coat?"

"I will have," she answered. "I've not got much in the suitcase," she added with an enchanting flush.

"You shall buy more in New Orleans on Tuesday," he promised her. "I've made no plans beyond that."

"A hat?" Cherry asked, with uplifted, silky lashes giving a childish look to her blue eyes.

Peter, tightening his fingers on hers, gave a great, joyous laugh of utter surprise and adoration, as, leaning toward her, he caught her bashful murmur.

"You need that?" he whispered.

"Well—MOST" she answered, seriously.

"Do you realize," he asked, "that you are the most delicious child that ever lived?"

"No, I don't know that," she said, drooping her head, suddenly self-conscious.

"Do you realize that by this time tomorrow we shall be out at sea," he added, "leaning on the rail—watching the Pacific race by—and belonging to each other forever and ever?"

The picture flooded her face with happy colour. "It's tomorrow at last!" she said, wonderingly, as they walked slowly toward the house. "I thought it would never be. It's only a few hours more now."

"How will you feel when it's TO-DAY?" he asked.

"Oh, Peter, I shall be so glad when it's all over, and when the letters are written, and when we've been together for a year," she answered, fervently. "I know it will be all as we have planned, but—but if it were over!"

They had reached the side door now, and were mounting the three steps together.

"Be patient until tomorrow," he whispered.

"Oh," she said softly, "I shan't breathe until tomorrow."

Leaning across her to push back the light screen door, he found himself face to face with Alix. In the dark entryway Peter and Cherry had not seen her, had not heard her move. Peter cursed his carelessness; he could not remember, in the utter confusion of the moment, just what he and Cherry had said, but if it was of a betraying nature, they had betrayed themselves. One chance in a hundred that she had not heard!

Yet, if she was acting, she was acting superbly. Cherry had turned scarlet and had given him an open glance of consternation, but Alix did not seem to see it. She addressed Peter, but when he found himself physically unable to answer, she continued the conversation with no apparent consciousness of his stumbling effort to appear natural.

"There you are! Are we going to have any tennis? It's after two o'clock now."

"Two seventeen," Martin said, following her out of the house and slipping his big watch back into his pocket. They all gathered in one of the reclaimed garden paths, assuming a deep interest in the time.

"I had no idea it was so late," Peter said.

"I knew it was getting on," Cherry added, utterly at random.

"Go in and tell the boy we won't be back until tomorrow," Martin suggested to his wife. "Unless you told him, Alix?" he added, turning toward her.

"I beg your pardon?" Her face was very pale, and she started as if from deep thought as she spoke.

"You could all come down here to sleep," Cherry said, "and have breakfast here!"

"I have to go into town rather early tomorrow," Peter remarked. "Porter's giving a breakfast at the Bohemian Club."

"Why not walk up to the cabin?" Cherry suggested in a shaking voice.

"I have to take the car up. You three walk! Come on, anybody who wants to ride!" Alix said.

"They can walk," Martin said, getting into the front seat. "Me for the little old bus!"

Cherry came out of the house with her hat on, and Buck leaped before her into the back seat. Alix watched her as she stepped up on the running board, and saw the colour flicker in her beautiful face.

"I thought you were going to walk?" Peter said, nervously. He had sauntered up to them with an air of indifference.

"Shall I?" faltered Cherry. She looked at Alix, who had not yet climbed into the car and was pulling on her driving gloves. Alix, toward whose face the dog was making eager springs, did not appear interested, so Cherry turned to Martin. "Walk with us, Mart?" she said.

"Nix," Martin said, comfortably, not stirring.

"I'll be home before you, Pete, and wait for you," Alix said. She looked at him irresolutely, as if she would have added more, but evidently decided against it and spoke again only in reference to the dog. "Keep Buck with you, will you, Pete?" she said. "He's getting too lazy. No, sir!" she reproached the animal affectionately. "You shall not ride! Well, the dear old Bucky-boy, does he want to come along?"

And she knelt down and put her arms about the animal, and laid her brown cheek against his head.

"You old fool!" she said, shaking him gently to and fro. "You've got to stay with Peter. Old Buck—!" Suddenly she was on her feet and had sprung into her place.

"Hold him, Pete!" she said. "Goodbye, Sis dear! All right, Martin?"

The engine raced; the car slipped smoothly into gear and vanished. Peter and Cherry stood looking at each other.

"Give them a good start, or Buck will catch them," Peter said, his body swaying with the frantic jumping of the straining dog. But to himself he said, with a sense of shock: "Alix knows!"

Buck was off like a rocket when he finally set him free; his feathery tail disappeared between the columns of the redwoods. Without speaking, Cherry and Peter started after him.

"And now that we are alone together," Cherry said, after a few minutes, "there seems to be nothing to say! We've said it all."

"Nothing to say!" Peter echoed. "Alix knows," he said in his heart.

"Whatever we do, it all seems so—wrong!" Cherry said with watering eyes.

"Whatever we do is wrong," he agreed, soberly.

"But we go?" she said on a fluttering breath.

"We MUST go!" Peter answered. And again, like the ominous fall of a heavy bell-tongue, the words formed in his heart: "Alix knows. Alix knows."

He thought of the afternoon, only a few weeks ago, when Cherry's beauty had made so sudden and so irresistible an appeal to him, and of the innocent delight of their luncheons together, when she had first confided in him, and of the days of secret and intense joy that her mere nearness and the knowledge that he would see her had afforded him. It had all seemed so fresh, so natural, so entirely their own affair, until the tragic day of Martin's reappearance and the hour of agonized waiting at the boat for the Cherry who did not come. There had been no joyous self-confidence in that hour, none in the distressed hour at the Orpheum, and the hour just past, when Cherry's rarely displayed passion had wrenched from him his last vestige of doubt.

But this was the culminating unhappiness, that he should know, from Alix's brave and gentle and generous look as they parted, that Alix knew. He had, in the wild rush and hurry of his thoughts, no time now to analyze what their love must mean to her, but it hurt him to see on her happy face those lines of sternness and gravity, to see her bright and honest eyes shadowed with that new look of pain.

It was too late now to undo it; he and Cherry must carry their desperate plan to a conclusion now, must disappear—and forget. They had tried, all this last dreadful week, they had both tried, to extinguish the flames, and they had failed. But to Peter there was no comforting thought anywhere. Wrong would be done to Martin, to Alix, to Cherry—and more than even these, wrong to himself, to the ideal of himself that had been his for so many years, to the real Peter Joyce.

"If I had it all to do over again, I should not come here," Cherry began, breathlessly.

"Ah, if we had it all to do over again!" Looking back half a dozen years, how simple it all seemed! How uncomplicated life was, in those old days when the doctor and his girls had teased him, and consulted him, and made him one of themselves. "What a web, Cherry!" he said, sadly. "If Anne hadn't made her claim, you would not have been kept here all these weeks; if the financial question hadn't been raised, you must have stayed in Red Creek, simply because you couldn't well have done anything else."

"And if I had been with Martin, this horrible business of that girl's letter wouldn't have happened," she added, bravely. "Oh, yes—that's quite true!" she interrupted him, as he interpolated a bitter protest. "Mart has no particular principle about it, but he never would have got in with that crowd if I had been there. So that once more," she ended, sadly, "I can say that I have made a mess of things. Listen, that's Buck!" she interrupted herself, as the dog's loud and violent barking reached them from beyond a turn in the twisting road. "He didn't catch them, then."

The next instant a woman came up the road, running, and making a queer, whimpering noise that Cherry never forgot. She was a stranger to them, but she ran toward them, making the odd, gasping noise with much dry mouthing, and with wild eyes.

Horror was in her aspect, and horror was the emotion that the first glimpse of her awakened vaguely in their hearts, but as she saw them she suddenly found voice for so hideous a scream that Cherry's knees failed her, and Peter sprang forward with a shout.

He gripped the woman's arm, and her frantic eyes were turned to him.

"Oh, my God!" she cried in a hoarse, cawing voice. "My God! They're over the bank—they're over the bank!"

"Who?" Peter shouted, his heart turning to ashes.

"Oh, the car—the automobile!" the woman mouthed. "Oh, my God— I saw it go! I saw it fall! Oh, God, save them-oh, God, take them, don't let them suffer that way!"

They were all running now, running with desperate speed down the long road, about the curves, on and on toward the frantic noise of the dog's barking, and toward another noise, the sound of a human voice twisted and wild with agony.

The strange woman was crying out wildly; Cherry was sobbing a prayer. Peter, without knowing that he spoke at all, was repeating over and over again the words: "Not Alix-my God!—it cannot be— she has never had an accident before-not Alix!"

A last curve, and they knew. Over one of the sharpest and ugliest of the descending precipices, crashing down through the saplings and underbrush and striking the trunks of a score of trees on its way, the heavy car had fallen like a boulder. And Peter saw that it was Alix's car, and with a great cry he sprang over the bank and, slipping and stumbling, followed its mad course down almost to the dry creek-bed in the canyon, and fell on his knees beside the huddled figure that, erect and strong, in its striped blue gingham, had been Alix only a few short minutes ago.

She had been flung clear of the car, and although almost every bone in her body was broken, by some miracle the face, except for a deep cut where the brown hair met the tanned forehead, was untouched. And as he caught her in his arms and bent over her with the bitterness of death stopping his own heart, a soft, thick braid loosened and fell like the touch of her hand upon his own, and it seemed to him that in the tranquil face and in the very look of the closed and fast-shadowing eyelids he caught a glimpse of Alix's old smile.

Peter forgot everything else in the world. He held her close to him and put his face against her face, and perhaps she had never so truly been his own as in this moment of their parting, when the quiet autumn woodland, shot with long shafts from the sinking sun, rang with his bitter cry:

"No, Alix—not dead! My wife—my wife!"

There were other men and women gathering fast now, and the whole little valley was beginning to ring with the tragedy. After a while some sympathetic man touched Peter on the arm to say that Mrs. Lloyd had fainted, and that if he would please tell them what to do about the other man—he was not yet dead—

Peter roused himself, and with help from half a dozen hands on all sides he carried Alix up to the road and laid her upon a motor robe that some kindly spectator had spread in the deep dust. AH about he heard the quick, horrified breathing and muttering of the shocked and sympathetic neighbours who had gathered, but to him there was a brassy light in the world and a hideous taste of inky bitterness in the very air he breathed, and he recognized nobody.

Presently he was conscious that a small, slight woman with disorderly fair hair and with her face streaked with dust and tears was standing beside him, and looking down at her, he saw that it was Cherry.

"Yes, Cherry?" he said, moistening his dry lips.

"Peter," she said, "they say Martin's living—he was screaming—" She grew deathly pale, and faintness swept over her, but she mastered it. "He was caught by that tree," she said. "And he is living. Will you tell them—tell one of these men—that if he will help me, we can drive him home. If you'll tell him that, then I'll get a doctor—"

"Yes, I will," Peter said, not stirring. His eyes had the look of a sleep-walker; he nodded slowly and gravely at her, like a very old man. "You—" he said to a man who had stopped his car near by and who was pressing sympathetically close. "Will you—?"

"If you'll sit in the back seat, dear, and just rest his poor head," a woman said to Cherry. Peter saw that they were lifting Martin's big, senseless form in tender hands and carrying it through the little group. There was a shudder as Martin moaned deeply. Peter went and sat on the low bank by Alix again, and lifted one of her limp hands, and held it. Ah, if in God's mercy and goodness she might moan, he thought, that one slight ray of hope would flood all the world with light for him again! But she did not stir.

"Gone?" said Cherry's heartrending voice, a mere whisper, beside him.

He turned upon her lifeless eyes.

"Gone," he echoed.

"Oh, Alix—my darling! My own big sister!"

Cherry sobbed, falling to her knees and passionately kissing the peaceful face. "Oh, Alix, dearest!"

The women about broke into tears. Peter pressed his hand close against his aching eyeballs, wishing that he might cry.

"She drove here," he heard a man's voice saying in the silence, "and she must have lost control of her car for a minute. Then—do you see?—the wheel slipped on the bank. Once it got this far, no power in God's earth—"

"No power in God's earth!" another man's voice said in solemn confirmation.

"Peter," Cherry said, "will you come to me as soon as you can? I shall need you."

"As soon as I can," he answered, absently.

The car drove away, and he heard Martin moan again as it moved.

"Joyce," said a man's kind voice close beside him. He recognized the voice rather than the distressed face of an old friend and neighbour. "Joyce, my dear fellow," he urged, affectionately, "tell us what we may do, and we'll see to it. Pull yourself together, my dear old chap. Now, shall I telephone for an—an ambulance? You must help us just a little here, and then we'll spare you everything else."

"Thank you, Fred," Peter answered after a moment, during which he looked seriously and studiously at his friend, as if ascertaining through unseen mists and barriers the identity of the speaker. "Thank you," he said. "Will you help me take—my wife—home?"

"You wish it that way?" the other man said, anxiously.

"Please," Peter answered, simply. And instantly there was moving and clearing in the crowd, a murmuring of whispered directions.

After a while they were at the mountain cabin, and Kow, with tears running down his yellow face, was helping them. Then Peter and his friend were walking up over the familiar trails, he hardly knew where, in the late twilight, and then they went into the old living room, and Alix was lying there, splendid, sweet, untouched, with her brave, brown forehead shadowed softly by her brown hair, and her lashes resting upon her cheeks, and her fingers clasped about the stems of three great, creamy roses.

There were other flowers all about, and there were women in the room. White draperies fell with sweeping lines from the merciful veiling of the crushed figure, and Alix might have been only asleep, and dreaming some heroic dream that lent that secret pride and joy to her mouth and filled those closed eyes with a triumph they had never known in life.

Peter stood and looked down at her, and the men and women drew back. But although the muscles of his mouth twitched, he did not weep. He looked long at her, while an utter silence filled the room, and while twilight deepened into dark over the cabin and over the mountain above it.

Something cold touched his hand, and he heard the dog whimper. Without turning his head or moving his eyes from Alix's face, he pressed his fingers on the silky head; his breast rose on one agonized breath, but he controlled it. Buck was as still as his master, sensing, in unfailing dog-fashion, that something was wrong.

"So that was your way out, Alix?" Peter said in the depth of his soul. "That was your solution for us all? You would go out of life, away from the sunshine and the trees and the hills that you loved, so that Cherry and I should be saved? I was blind not to see it. I have been blind from the very beginning."

Silence. The room was filling with shadows. On the mantel was a deep bowl of roses that he remembered watching her cut—was it yesterday or centuries ago?

"I was wrong," he said. "But I think you would be sorry to have me face—what I am facing now. You were always so forgiving, Alix; you would be the first to be sorry."

He put his hand over the tigerish pain that was beginning to reach his heart. His throat felt thick and choked, and still he did not cry.

"An hour ago," he said, "if it had been that the least thought of what this meant to you might have reached me an hour ago, it would not have been too late. Alix, one look into your eyes an hour ago might have saved us all! Fred," Peter said aloud, with a bitter groan, clinching tight the hands of the old friend who had crept in to stand beside him "Fred, she was here, in all her health and joy and strength only today. And now—"

"I know—old man—" the other man muttered. He looked anxiously at Peter's terrible face. In the silence the dog whimpered faintly. But when Peter, after an endless five minutes, turned away, it was to speak to his friend in an almost normal voice.

"I must go down and see Cherry, Fred. She took her husband to the old house; they were living there."

"Helen will stay here," the man assured him, quickly. "I'll drive you down and come back here. We thought perhaps a few of us could come here to-morrow afternoon, Peter," he added timidly, with his reddened eyes filling again, "and talk of her a little, and pray for her a little, and then take her to—to rest beside the old doctor—"

"I hadn't thought about that," Peter answered, still with the air of finding it hard to link words to thought. "But that is the way she would like it. Thank you—and thank Helen for me—"

"Oh, Peter, to do anything—" the woman faltered. "She came to us, you know, when the baby was so ill—day after day—my own sister couldn't have been more to us!"

"Did she?" Peter asked, staring at the speaker steadily. "That was like her."

He went out of the house and got into a waiting car, and they drove down the mountain. Alix had driven him over this road day before yesterday—yesterday—no, it was today, he remembered.

"Thank God I don't feel it yet as I shall feel it, Thompson!" he said, quietly. The man who was driving gave him an anxious glance.

"You must take each day as it comes," he answered, simply.

Peter nodded, folded his arms across his chest, and stared into the early dark. There was no other way to go than past the very spot where the horror had occurred, but Thompson told his wife later that poor Joyce had not seemed to know it when they passed it. Nor did he give any evidence of emotion when they reached the old Strickland house and entered the old hallway where Cherry had come flying in, a few short years ago, with Martin's first kiss upon her lips.

Two doctors, summoned from San Francisco, were here, and two nurses. Martin had been laid upon a hastily moved bed in the old study, to be spared the narrow stairs. The room was metamorphosed, the whole house moved about it as about a pivot, and there was no thought but for the man who lay, sometimes moaning and sometimes ominously still, waiting for death.

"He cannot live!" whispered Cherry, ghastly of face, and with the utter chaos of her soul and brain expressed by her tumbled frock and the carelessly pushed back and knotted masses of her hair. "His arm is broken, Peter, and his leg crushed—they don't dare touch him! And the surgeon says the spine, too—and you see his head! Oh, God! it is so terrible," she said in agony, through shut teeth, knotting her hands together, "it is too terrible that he is breathing NOW, that life is there NOW, and that they cannot hold it!"

She led Peter into the sitting room, where the doctors were waiting. The nurses came and went; the lamps had been lighted. Both the physicians rose as Peter came in, and he knew that they had been told that this was the man whose wife had been killed that day. Their manner expressed the sympathy they did not voice. Peter sat down with them.

"Is there any hope?" he asked, when Cherry had gone away on one of the restless, unnecessary journeys with which she was filling the endless hours. One man shook his head, and in the silence they heard Martin groan.

"It is possible he may weather it, of course," the older man said, doubtfully. "He is coming out of that first stupor, and we may be able to tell better in a short time. The fact that he is living at all indicates a tremendous vitality."

Thoughtfully and gravely they exchanged technical phrases. Cherry's Chinese boy brought in a tray, and both the other men ate and drank. Peter nodded a negative without a change of expression, but presently he roused himself to replenish the fire. The clock ticked and ticked in the stillness.

Cherry came to the door to say "Doctor!" on a burst of tears. The physicians departed at once to the study, and Peter was immediately summoned to assist them in handling the big frame of the patient. Martin was thoroughly conscious now; his face chalk white. Cherry, agonized, knelt beside the bed, her frightened eyes moving from face to face.

There was a brief consultation, then Cherry and Peter were banished.

"Don't worry, dear," said one of the nurses, coming out of the sick-room. "It's just that Doctor Henry thinks he would be more comfortable if we could get the arm and leg set! You see, now that he's conscious and is running just a little temperature—"

"Much fever?" Cherry asked, sharply.

"Oh, nothing at all, dear!" the nurse hastened to say. "The only thing is, that setting the arm and leg will ease the pain and save his strength." She bustled off for basins, bandages, and hot water. In the silence Martin's groans occasionally broke.

Cherry, her eyes on the study door, stood biting her fingers in frenzy. When from the sound of Martin's voice she realized that he was being hurt, she looked at Peter in agony.

"Oh, why do they do that—why do they do that? Torturing him for nothing!" he heard her whisper. "Go in and—go in and do something!" she urged, incoherently.

But the sounds had stopped, and there was a blessed interval of silence. The clock on the mantel sounded eight in swift, silvery strokes, and presently a sympathetic nurse came silently in with a tray holding two cups of hot soup. Cherry shut her eyes and shook her head.

"Please, Cherry—you need it!" Peter pleaded, carrying her a smoking cup. She protested again with a gesture, looked wearily into his eyes, and drank the soup docilely, like a child.

"You, too, Peter!" she said, suddenly rousing herself. Peter gulped down his own cupful, waved away the sandwiches that were on the tray, and took the chair opposite the one in which Cherry was sitting.

The clock presently struck the half-hour, but neither spoke. Cherry's pallor, her air of fatigue and bewilderment, and the familiar setting of the old environment made her seem a child again. Peter watched her with a confused sense that the whole frightful day had been a dream. Once she looked up and met his eyes.

"He can't live," she said in a whisper.

"Perhaps not," Peter answered very low. Cherry returned to her sombre musing.

"We didn't see this end to it, did we?" she said with a pitiful smile after a long while.

"Oh, no—NO!" Peter said, shutting his eyes, and with a faint, negative movement of his head.

"We wouldn't have had this happen—" Cherry began. Her lips trembled, her whole face wrinkled, and she put her hand across her eyes and pressed it there with a gesture of forlornness and sorrow that wrenched Peter's heart. Her tears began to fall fast.

"Poor Cherry—if I could spare you all this!" he said, knotting his fingers and feeling for the first time the prick of bitter tears against his eyelids.

"Oh, there is nothing you can do," she said faintly and wearily after a while. And she whispered, as if to herself, "Nothing— nothing—nothing!"

Then there was silence again. The lamps burned softly; the fire sucked and flickered; a chilling air, full of autumn sadness, began to creep from the corners of the room. Peter's eyes moved over the backs of the old books, Dickens and Thackeray and the "Household Book of Verse," moved to the faded photograph of Cherry's mother on the mantel, a beautiful woman in the big sleeves of the late nineties.

The doctors came back; there was a little stir and rearrangement as they seated themselves.

"Any change?" Cherry asked, cautiously.

"No change." Both men shook their heads.

"Any—any hope?" she faltered.

The physicians exchanged glances. No word was spoken, but the look in their faces, the faint narrowing of eyes and compressing of lips, gave her her answer.

CHAPTER XXII

It was all strange and bewildering, thought Peter. It was not like anything he had ever connected in his thoughts with Alix, yet it was all for her.

The day was warm and still, and the little church was packed with flowers, and packed with people. Women were crying, and men were crying, too, rather to his dazed surprise. The organ was straining through the warm, fragrant air, and the old clergyman, whose venerable, leonine head, in its crown of snowy hair, Peter could see clearly, spoke in a voice that was thickened with tears. Strangers, or almost strangers, had been touching Peter's hand respectfully, timidly, had been praising Alix. She had been "good" to this one, "good" to that one, they told him; she had always been so "interested," and so "happy."

Her coffin was buried in flowers, many of them the plain flowers she loved, the gillies and stock and verbena, and even the sweet, sober wallflowers that were somehow like herself. But it was the roses that scented the whole world for Alix to-day, and fresh creamy buds had been placed between the waxen fingers. And still that radiant look of triumphant love lingered on her quiet face, and still the faint ghost of a smile touched the once kindly and merry mouth.

They said good-bye to her at the church, the villagers and old friends who had loved her, and Peter and two or three men alone followed her down along the winding road that led to the old cemetery. Cherry was hanging over the bedside of her husband, who still miraculously lingered through hours of pain, but as Peter, responsive to a touch on his arm, crossed the church porch to blindly enter the waiting motor-car, he saw, erect and grave, on the front seat, in his decent holiday black, and with his felt hat held in his hands, Kow, claiming his right to stand beside the grave of the mistress he had loved and served so faithfully. The sight of him, in his clumsy black, instead of the usual crisp white, and with a sad and tear-stained face shook Peter strangely, but he did not show a sign of pain.

The twisted low branches of oak trees threw shadows on the grave when they finally reached it, and sheep were cropping the watered grass of the graveyard. It was silent and peaceful here, on the very top of the world, not a sound intruded, and nothing stirred but the shadow of a flying bird, and the slowly moving, rounded woolly backs of the sheep.

The soft autumn sky, the drift of snowy clouds across the blue, the clear shadows on brown grass under the oaks, all these were familiar. But Peter still looked dazedly at his black cuff and at the turned earth next to the doctor's headstone, telling himself again that this was for Alix. How often he had seen her sitting there, with her bright face sobered and sweet, as she talked lovingly, eagerly, of her father! They had often come here, Peter the more willingly because she was so sensible and happy about it;

she would pack lunch, button herself into one of the crisp blue ginghams, chatter on the road in her usual fashion. And if, for a few moments, the train of memory fired by the sight of the old doctor's grave became too poignant, and tears came, she always scolded herself with that mixture of childish and maternal impatience that was so characteristic of her, and that Peter had seen her use to this very father years ago!

He remembered her, a tall, awkward girl, with a volume of Dickens slipping from her lap as she sat on a hassock by the fire, teasing her father, scolding and reproaching him. Blazing red on high cheek-bones, untidy black hair, quick tongue and ready laugh; that was the Alix of the old days, when he had criticized and patronized her, and told her that she should be more like Anne and little Cherry!

He remembered being delegated, one day, to take her into town to the dentist, and that upon discovering that the dentist was not in his office, he had taken her to the circus instead. She had been about thirteen, and had eaten too many peanuts, he thought, and had lost a petticoat in full sight of the grand-stand. But how grateful and happy she had been!

"Dear little old blue petticoat!" he said. "Dear little old madcap Alix—!"

There was silence, the silence of inanition, about him. He came to himself with a start. He was up on the hills, in the cemetery— this was Alix's grave, newly covered with wilting masses of flowers, and he was keeping everybody waiting. He murmured an apology; the waiting men were all kindness and sympathy.

He got back into the motor-car; Kow got in; the man who drove them quickly toward the valley talked easily and steadily to Peter, attempting to interest him in the affairs of some water company in San Francisco. When they got to the valley a city train was arriving, and Peter saw people looking at him furtively and sorrowfully. He remembered the many, many times Alix had waited for him at the trains; he glanced toward the big madrone under which she always parked her car. She was usually deep in a book as he crossed from the train, but she would fling it into the back seat, and make room for him beside her. The dog would bound into the tonneau, Alix would hand her husband his mail, the car would start with a great plunge toward the mountain—toward the cool garden high up on the ridge—

"She never had an accident, Fred," he said, simply.

"Alix?" The other man nodded gravely, but there was a worried look in his eyes. He did not like Peter's quiet tone. "It may be that her steering-gear broke," he said. "I don't believe it was her fault. Never will! No, it was just one of those things—" He emptied his lungs with a great breath of nervousness and sympathy. "Now, we want you to-night—" he began, pleadingly.

"No—no—no!" Peter said, quickly. "I had better go to her sister. Poor Lloyd is dying, and she is on the verge of a collapse. The nurse said this morning that they could not get her to undress or to leave the room. Poor girl—poor Cherry! I had better go there, Fred. She will need me!"

"No chance for him?" the driving man asked, turning his car.

"No—it's only a matter of time!"

"She came in for the old doctor's money, didn't she?"

"Yes—all of it, now. And my wife had some property—some I had given her; that will go to the sister now. She will be well fixed," Peter said, in a dull tone. "That would have pleased Alix."

"She's a beautiful woman, and young still," said the other man, after awhile. Peter did not hear him.

Cherry looked small and pathetic in her fresh black, and her face was marked by secret incessant weeping. But the nurses and doctors could not say enough for her self-control; she was always composed, always quietly helpful and calm when they saw her, and she was always busy. From early morning, when she slipped into the sick-room, to stand looking at the unconscious Martin with a troubled, intent expression that the nurses came to know well, until night, she moved untiringly about the quiet, shaded house. She supervised the Chinese boy, saw that the nurses had their hours for rest and exercise, telephoned, dusted, and arranged the rooms, saw callers sweetly and patiently, filled vases with flowers.

Every day she had several vigils in the sick-room, and every day at least one long talk with the doctors. Peter would find her deep in letters and documents, or find her—who had loved to be idle, a few weeks ago— busily sewing. Sometimes she gave him a long list of things to do for her in the village and the city, and every day she wrote notes—Cherry, who had always hated to write notes!—to thank the friends who had sent in flowers, soups, and jellies, and custards for the patient. Every afternoon and evening had its callers; she and Peter were rarely alone.

Martin was utterly unconscious of the life that flowed on about him; sometimes he seemed to recognize Cherry, and would stare with painful intentness into her face, but after a few seconds his gaze would wander to the strange nurses, and the room that he had never known, and with a puzzled sigh he would close his eyes again, and drift back into his own strange world of pain, fever, and unconsciousness.

Almost every day there was the sudden summons and panic in the old house, Peter going toward the sick-room with a thick beating at his heart, Cherry entering, white-faced and with terrified eyes, doctors and nurses gathering noiselessly near for the last scene in the drama of Martin's suffering. But the release did not come.

There would be murmuring among the doctors and nurses; the pulse was gaining, not losing; the apparently fatal, final symptoms were proving neither fatal nor final. The tension would relax; a doctor would go, a nurse slip from the room; Cherry, looking anxiously from one face to another, would breathe more easily. It was inevitable, she knew that now— but it was not to be this minute, it was not to be this hour!

"My dear—my dear!" Peter said to her, one day, when spent and shaken she came stumbling from Martin's bedside, and stood dazedly looking from the window into the soaking October forest, like a person stunned from a blow. "My poor little Cherry! If I could spare you this!"

"Nobody can spare me now!" she whispered. And very simply and quietly she added, "If I have been a fool—if I have been a selfish, wicked girl, all my life, I am punished!" She was clinging to the unpainted wood that framed the window, her hand above her head, and her face resting against her arm. "I am punished!" she added.

"Cherry!" he protested, heartsick to see her so.

"Was it wrong for us to love each other, Peter?" she asked, in a low tone. "I suppose it was! I suppose it was! But it never seemed as if—" she shut her eyes and shivered—"as if—THIS—would come of it!" she whispered.

"This!" he echoed, aghast.

"Oh, I think this is punishment," Cherry continued, in the same lifeless, weary tone.

There was a silence. The rain dripped and dripped from the redwoods, the room in which they stood was in twilight, even at noon. Peter could think of nothing to say.

About two weeks after the accident there was a change in the tone of the physicians who had been giving almost all their time to Martin's case. There was no visible change in Martin, but that fact in itself was so surprising that it was construed into a definite hope that he would live.

Not as he had lived, they warned his wife. It would be but a restricted life; tied to his couch, or permitted, at best, to move about within a small boundary on crutches.

"Martin!" his wife exclaimed piteously, when this was first discussed. "He has always been so strong—so independent! He would rather—he would infinitely rather be dead!" But her mind was busy grasping the possibilities, too. "He won't suffer too much?" she asked, fearfully.

They hastened to assure her that the chance of his even partial recovery was still slight, but that in case of his convalescence Martin need not necessarily suffer.

Another day or two went by, in the silent, rainwrapped house under the trees; days of quiet footsteps, and whispering, and the lisping of wood fires. Then Martin suddenly was conscious, knew his wife, languidly smiled at her, thanked the doctors for occasional ease from pain.

"Peter—I'm sorry. It's terrible for you—terrible!" he said, in his new, hoarse, gentle voice, when he first saw Peter. They marvelled among themselves that he knew that Alix was gone. But to Cherry, in one of the long hours that she spent, sitting beside him, and holding his big, weak, strangely white hand, he explained, one day. "I knew she was killed," he said, out of a silence. "I thought we both were!"

"How did she ever happen to do it?" Cherry said. "She was always so sure of herself—even when she drove fast!"

"I don't know," he answered. "It was all like a flash, of course! I never watched her drive—I had such confidence in her!"

His interest dropped; she saw that the tide of pain was slowly rising again, glanced at the clock. It was two; he might not have relief until four. In his own eyes she saw reflected the apprehension of her own.

"You might ask Peter to play some of that—that rambly stuff he was playing yesterday?" he suggested. Cherry, only too happy to have him want anything, to have him helped by anything, flew to find Peter. Busy with one of the trays that were really beginning to interest and please the invalid now, she told herself that the house was a different place, now that one nurse was gone, the doctors coming only for brief calls, and the dear, familiar sound of the old piano echoing throughout the rooms.

Martin came from the fiery furnace changed in soul and body. It was a thin, gentle, strangely patient man who was propped in bed for his Thanksgiving dinner, and whose pain-worn face turned with an appreciative smile to the decorations and the gifts that made his room cheerful. His thick beard had grown; for weeks they had not dared disturb him to cut it, and as he recovered, Cherry found it so becoming that she had persuaded him to let it remain. He wore a blue-and-gray wrapper that was his wife's gift; the sling was gone, but his hands were oddly thin and white.

The big room, once the study, and still shaded by the old banksia rose, had been turned into as luxurious a bedroom as Cherry could make it. The signs of extreme illness gradually were banished, and all sorts of invalid comforts took their place; daylight and lamplight were alike tempered for Martin; there were pillows, screens; there was a noiseless deep chair always waiting for Cherry at his side. As his unconscious and feverish times lessened, and he was able feebly to request this small delicacy or that, Cherry rejoiced to gratify him; her voice had something of its old content as she would say: "He loved the oysters, Peter!" or "Doctor said he might have wine jelly!"

The heavy cloud lightened slowly but steadily; Martin had a long talk, dreaded by Cherry from the first hours of the accident, with his physicians. He bore the ultimatum with unexpected fortitude.

"Let me get this straight," he said, slowly. "The arm is O. K. and the leg, but the back—"

Cherry, kneeling beside him, her hands on his, drew a wincing breath. Martin reassured her with an indulgent nod.

"I've known it right along!" he told her. He looked at the doctors. "It's no go?"

"I don't see why I should deceive you, my dear boy," said the younger doctor, who had grown very fond of him. "You can still beat me at bridge, you know, you can read and write, and come to the table, after awhile; you have your devoted wife to keep finding new things for you to do! Next summer now—a chair out in the garden—"

Cherry was fearfully watching her husband's face.

"We'll all do what we can to make it easy, Mart!" she whispered, in tears.

He looked at her with a whimsical smile.

"Mind very much taking care of a helpless man all your life?" he asked, with a hint of his old confident manner.

"Oh, Mart, I mind only for you!" she said. Peter, standing behind the doctors, slipped from the room unnoticed.

Late that evening, when Martin was asleep, Cherry came noiselessly from the sick-room, to find Peter alone in the dimly lighted sitting room. The fire had burned low, and he was sitting before it, sunk into his chair, and leaning forward, fingers loosely locked, and sombre eyes fixed on the dull pink glow of the logs. He looked tired, Cherry thought, and was so buried in thought that she at first attempted to go quietly through the room without rousing him. But he glanced at her, feeling rather than hearing her presence, and called her.

"Come over here, will you, Cherry? I want to speak to you."

Something in his voice fluttered her for a second; she had not heard the echo of the old mood for a long time. She came, with an inquiring and yet not wholly unconscious look, to the fireside, and he stood up to greet her.

"Tired?" he asked, in an unnatural voice.

"I—I was just going to bed," she answered, hesitatingly. But she sat down, nevertheless; sank comfortably into the chair opposite his own, and stretched her little feet, crossed at the ankle, before her, as if she were indeed tired. "I don't know what should make me—always—so weary!" she said, smiling. "I don't do a thing, really, all day!"

Utterly relaxed, her small figure in its plain black gown, with the childish white she always wore at collar and wrist, looked like the figure of a child. Her golden hair shone with a dull gleam in the dim light; there was a glint of firelight in her dropped lashes.

"Perhaps it's the nervous strain," Peter suggested. "Of course, you would feel that." There was a silence in which neither moved. Cherry did not even raise her eyelids, and Peter, standing with one arm on the mantel, looked down at her steadily. "Cherry," he said, suddenly, "are you and I going to talk to each other like that?"

A flood of colour rose in Cherry's pale face, and she gave him one appealing glance.

"I don't—I don't think I know what you mean, Peter!"

"Oh, yes; you do!" he said. He knelt down beside her chair, and gathered her cold hands into one of his own. "What are you and I going to do?" he asked.

She looked at him in terror.

"But all that is changed!" she said, quickly, fearfully.

"Why is it changed?" he countered. "I love you—I have always loved you, since the days long ago, in this very house! I can't stop it now. And you love me, Cherry!"

"Yes, I shall always love you," she answered, agitatedly, after a pause in which she looked at him with troubled eyes. "I shall always love you, and always dream of the time when we—we thought we might belong to each other, Peter. But—but—you must see that we cannot—cannot think of all that now," she added with difficulty. "I couldn't fail Martin now, when he needs me so!"

"He needs you now," Peter conceded, "and I don't ask you to do anything that must distress him now. But in a few months, when his mother comes down for a visit, what then?"

Cherry's exquisite eyes were fixed on his.

"Well, what then?" she whispered.

"Then you must tell them honestly that you care for me," he said.

Cherry was trembling violently.

"But how could I!" she protested. "Tell him that I am going away, deserting him when he most needs me!"

Peter had grown very pale.

"But—" he stammered, his face close to hers—"but you cannot mean that this is the end?"

She moved her lips as if she was about to speak; looked at him blankly. Then suddenly tears came, and she wrenched her hands free from his, and laid her arms about his neck. Her wet cheek was pressed to his own, and he put his arms tightly about the little shaken figure.

"Peter!" she whispered, desolately. And after a time, when the violence of her sobs was lessened, and she was breathing more quietly, she said again: "Peter!"

He took out his handkerchief, and dried her eyes, and she remained, resting against him like a spent bird, her blue eyes fixed mournfully on the fire, her hands, which had slipped to his breast, gathered in his own, and her bright head on his shoulder.

"We can never dream that dream again," she said.

"We shall dream it again," he corrected her.

Cherry did not answer for a long while. Then she gently disengaged herself from his arms, and sat erect. Her tears were ended now, and her voice firmer and surer.

"No; never again!" she told him. "I've been thinking about it, all these days, and I've come to see what is right, as I never did before. Alix never knew about us, Peter—and that's been the one thing for which I could be thankful in all this time! But Alix had only one hope for me, and that was that somehow Martin and I would come to be—well, to be nearer to each other, and that somehow he and I would make a success of our marriage, would spare—well, let's say the family name, from all the disgrace and publicity of a divorce—"

"And you feel that this has drawn you and Martin nearer together?" Peter asked, in a simple, expressionless voice, as she paused.

"Well—he needs me now."

"But, Cherry, my child—" Peter expostulated. "You cannot sacrifice all your life to the fancy that no one else can take your place with him—"

"That," she said, steadily, "is just what I must do!"

Peter looked at her for a few seconds without speaking. "You don't love him," he said.

"No," she admitted, gravely. "I don't love him—not in the way you mean."

"He is nothing to you," Peter argued. "As a matter of fact, it never was what a marriage should be. It was always—always—a mistake."

"Yes," she conceded, sadly, "it was always a mistake!"

"Then there is nothing to bind you to him!" Peter added.

"No—and there isn't Alix to distress now!" she agreed, thoughtfully. "And yet," she went on, suddenly, "I do this more for Alix than for any one!"

Peter looked at her in silence, looked back at the last flicker of the fire.

"You will change your mind after awhile!" he said.

Cherry rose from the chair, and stood with dropped head and troubled eyes, looking down at the flame.

"No, I shall never change my mind!" she said, in a low tone that was still strangely firm and final for her. "I have thought about it, about the sacrifices I shall have to make, and about what my life will be as the years go on! And I know that I never will change. This is as much my life as it would be my life if you and I were alone in that little French village somewhere. There would be no going back then, no thinking of what might have been; there is no going back now. This is my life, that's all! For five or ten or twenty or thirty years I shall always be where Martin is, caring for him, amusing him, making a life for him." And Cherry raised her glorious blue eyes in which there was a pure and an uplifted look that Peter had never seen there before. "It is what Dad and Alix would have wished," she finished, solemnly, "and I do it for them!"

Peter did not answer; and after a moment she went quietly and quickly from the room, with the new air of quiet responsibility that she had worn ever since the accident.

CHAPTER XXIII

Peter saw, with a sort of stupefaction, that life was satisfying her now as life had never satisfied restless, exacting little Cherry before. Not that she knew it; she was absolutely unconscious of the truth, and he realized that she would have been genuinely shocked by it. But there was a busy energy about her now, an absorbed and contented concentration upon the duties of the day, a cheerfulness, a philosophy, that were new.

There had been touched by all this terrible time unexpected deeps of maternal tenderness in childish little Cherry; there had been unsuspected qualities of domesticity and sacrifice. A new Cherry had been born, a Cherry always beautiful, always resourceful, always admired. Busy with Martin's trays, out in the garden searching for shy violets, conferring with the Chinese boy, pouring tea for afternoon callers, Cherry was newly adequate and newly happy.

She spent much of her free time by her husband's side, amusing him as skillfully as a mother. What was she doing? Why, she was simply basting fresh cuffs into her afternoon gown. He was getting so popular that she had to be ready for callers every day. Would he like her to keep George Sewall for dinner, then they could play dominoes again? Would he like the table with the picture puzzle? He would like just to talk? Very well; they would talk.

Martin's day was so filled and divided with small pleasures that it was apt to amaze him by passing too quickly. He had special breakfasts, he had his paper, his hair was brushed and his bed remade a dozen times a day. Cherry shared her mail, which was always heavy now, with him; she flitted into the sick-room every few minutes with small messages or gifts. With her bare, bright head, her busy white hands, her voice all motherly amusement and sympathy and sweetness, she had never seemed so much a wife. She had the pleasantest laugh in the world, and she often laughed. The sick-room was kept with exquisite simplicity, with such freshness, bareness, and order as made it a place of delight. One day Cherry brought home a great Vikory bowl of silvery glass, and a dozen drifting goldfish, and Martin never tired of watching them idly while he listened to her reading.

"Cherry," Peter said, on a wet January day, when he came upon her in the dining room, contentedly arranging a fragrant mass of wet violets, "I think Martin's out of the woods now. I believe I'll be moving along!"

"Oh, but we want you always, Peter!" she said, innocently regretful.

The ghost of a pained smile flitted across his face.

"Thank you," he said, gently. "But I think I will go," he added, mildly. She made no further protest.

"But where?" she asked, sympathetically.

"I don't know. I shall take Buck—start off" toward the big mountains. I'll write you now and then, of course! I'm going home, first!"

"Of course!" she answered. "But you won't stay in that lonely cabin all alone," she added, almost timidly.

"No, I shan't be there long!" he assured her, briefly. "Everything's finished up now. I'm leaving Kow in charge, of course. I'll be back one of these days!"

"Just now," Cherry mused, sadly, "perhaps it is best—for you—to get away! Now that Martin is so much better," she added, in a little burst. "I do feel so sorry for you, Peter! I know how you feel. I shall miss her always, of course," said Cherry, "but I have him."

"I try not to think of her," Peter said, flinging up his head.

"When you do," Cherry said, earnestly, giving him more of her attention than had been usual, of late, "Here is something to think, Peter. It's this: we have so much to be thankful for, because she never—knew! It was madness," Cherry went on, eagerly, "sheer madness—that is clear now. I don't try to explain it, because it's all been washed away by the frightful thing that happened. I'm different now; you're different—I don't know how we ever thought we could—

"But I forget all that," she went on, after a moment of shamed thought. "I don't let myself think of it any more! I was unhappy, I was overwrought; there's no explanation for what I felt and said but that! And, Peter, you know that if I was false in thought to Martin, he had been unkind to me, and he had—" she paused, interrupted herself. "But men are different, I suppose," she mused. There was a silence during which she looked at him anxiously, but the expression on his face did not alter, and he did not speak.

"And what I think we ought to be thankful for," she resumed, "is that Alix would rather—she would rather have it this way. She told me that she would be heartbroken if there had been any actual separation between me and Martin, and how much worse that would have been—what we planned, I mean. She was spared that, and we were spared—I see it now—what would have ruined both our lives. We were brought to our senses, and the awakening only came a little sooner than it would have come anyway!"

Peter had walked to the window, and was looking out at the shabby winter trees that were dripping rain, and at the beaten garden, where the drenched chrysanthemums had been bowed to the soaked earth. A wet wind swished through the low, fanlike branches of the redwoods; the creek was rushing high and noisily.

"Here, in Dad's home," Cherry said, coming to stand beside him, "I see how wicked and how mad I was. In another twenty-four hours it would have been too late—you don't know how often I wake up in the night and shiver, thinking that! And as it is, I am here in the dear old house; and Martin—well, you can see that even Martin's life is going to be far happier than it ever was! Yesterday Mrs. Porter spoke to me about getting him a player-piano when he is stronger, you know. Doctor Young comes in to play cribbage with him—it's amazing how the day fills itself! It's such a joy to me," she added, with the radiant look she often wore when her husband's comfort was under consideration, "to feel that we need never worry about the money end of things—there's enough for what we need forever!"

"You must never worry about money," he told her. "And if ever you need it—if it is a question of a long trip, or of more operations—if there is any chance—"

"I shall remember that I have a big brother!" she said.

The room was scented by the sweet, damp flowers, and by the good odour of lazily burning logs; yet to Peter there was chill and desolateness in the air. Cherry took up the glass bowl in both careful hands, and went away in the direction of the study, but he stood at the window for a long time staring dully out at the battered chrysanthemums and the swishing branches, and the steadily falling rain.

CHAPTER XXIV

A few days later, on a day of uncertain sunshine and showers, Peter left them. Martin was the sorrier of the two to see him go, for it seemed to Martin that the tragedy had united Cherry and himself in a peculiar manner, had rounded and secured their relationship, and had made for them a new life that had no place for Peter. With a sort of affectionate pity for the older man he would have been glad to have him stay longer, to play the old piano, work in the old garden, and share their talks of Alix and of all the old days. But to Cherry Peter's going was a relief; it burned one more bridge behind her. It confirmed her in the path she had chosen; it was to her spirit like the cap that marks the accepted student nurse, or like the black coif that replaces the postulant's white veil of probation.

He had been in the downstairs bedroom, talking with Martin, for perhaps an hour; he had drawn them a rough sketch of the little addition to the house that Cherry meant some day to build next to the study, and he and Martin had been discussing the details. Cherry had left them there, and was sweeping the wet, dun-coloured leaves from the old porch, in a pale shaft of sunshine, and thinking that there must be a wide railing here next summer for Martin's books, and a gay awning to be drawn or furled as Martin fancied, when a sudden step in the doorway behind her made her look up.

Peter had come out of the house, with Buck curving beside him. He wore his old corduroy clothes and his shabby cap, but there was something in his aspect that made her ask:

"Not going?"

"Yes, I'm going now!" he said.

She rested her broom against the thick trunk of the old banksia, and rubbed her two hands together, and came to the top of the steps to say good-bye. And standing there, under the rose tree, she linked her arm about it, looking up through the branches, where the shabby foliage of last year lingered.

"How fast it's grown since that terrific pruning we gave it all that long time ago!" she said.

"Little more than six years ago, Cherry!" he reminded her.

"Only six years—" She was obviously amazed.

"It doesn't seem possible that all this has happened in six years!" she exclaimed. "Those were wonderful old days, with Anne and Alix scolding you, and Dad here, looking out for us all," she mused, tenderly. "We'll never be so happy again."

He did not answer. He had her hand now for farewells, and perhaps, with the thought of those short six years had come also the thought that this slender figure in the housewifely blue linen, this exquisite little head, so trim and demure despite all its rebel tendrils of gold, this lovely face, still the face of a child, with a child's trusting, uplifted eyes, might have been his. The old home might have been their home, and perhaps—who knows, there might have been a new Cherry and a new Peter beginning to look eagerly out at life through the screen of the old rose vine.

Too late now. A single instant of those lost years might have bought him all this, but there was no going back. He put his arm about her, and kissed her forehead, and said: "God bless you, Cherry!"

"God bless you, dear!" she answered, gravely. She watched the tall figure, with its little limp, and with the dog leaping and circling about it in ecstasy, until the redwoods closed around, him. Then she took up the broom again, and slowly and thoughtfully crossed the old porch, and shut the door.

Peter, walking with long strides, and with a furrowed brow and absent eyes, crossed the village, and climbed once more the old trail that led up to the cabin. His great boots made simple work of the muddy roads, his hands were thrust deep into the pockets of his shabby old coat, and his cap pulled low. The rain had stopped, but every branch that hung down over his path, or stretched an arm to stop him, was charged with water; the creeks were swollen and yellow, and raced along between crumbling banks with a fresh rushing sound that mingled with the creaking of wet boughs and the wild spring chant of the wind high up in the tops of the redwoods.

Coming out of the forest, on the ridge, where the dim road ran under the scattered oaks, he saw the last of the battle of the dying storm raging over the valley below. Great masses of cloud were in travail; when the sun was hidden, the world was wrapped in shade and chill; when it burst forth, every wet tree and spear glistened and twinkled in the flood of warmth and light, the dried brown grass sparkled with jewels, and the great roadside rain pools flashed back the azure of the sky. The mountain was partly obscured by rapidly shifting masses of mist; the air was pungent and seemed to hum with a thousand tiny, electric voices.

Already there was new grass showing a timid film of emerald under the brown growth of last year. While Peter climbed, the good earth giving soddenly under his feet, and grasses tangling in the clasps of his walking shoes, the sunlight conquered, the sky cleared, and the last of the storm drifted and spread and vanished in a bath of dazzling blue. Birds began to circle in brief flights; cloud shadows fell clear-cut on the west, dark flank of the mountain; and in the saturated marshy spots, where a scummy green growth already was spread over the crystal pools of the little hillside springs, frogs were exultant.

The roof of the little cabin and the outbuildings smoked up into the pure warm air; the Jersey, placidly awaiting her hour, looked at him with soft, great eyes; and Alix's chickens picked and squawked on the steaming mound near the stable. Kow was hanging out the blue glass-towels, everything—everything was as he had found it a hundred, a thousand, happy times!

Peter spoke to the Chinese and went into the cabin. It was dusted, orderly, complete; he and Alix might have left it yesterday. Kow had seen him coming, he thought, and had had time to light the fire, which was blazing freshly up to the chimney's great throat. He sat down, staring at the flames.

Buck pushed open the swinging door between the pantry and the sitting room, and came in, a question in his bright eyes, his great plumy tail beating the floor as he lay down at Peter's side. Presently the dog laid his nose on Peter's knee and poured forth a faint sound that was not quite a whine, not quite a sigh, and rose restlessly, and went to the closed door of Alix's room, and pawed it, his eager nose to the threshold.

"Not here, old fellow!" Peter said, stroking the silky head under his hand.

He had not been in this room since the day of her death. It struck him as strangely changed, strangely and heartrendingly familiar. The windows were closed, as Alix had never had them closed, winter or summer, rain or sunshine. Her books stood in their old order, her student's Shakespere, and some of her girlhood's books, "Little Women," and "Uncle Max." In the closet, which exhaled a damp and woody smell, were one or two of the boyish-looking hats he had so often seen her crush carelessly over her dark hair, and the big belted coat that was as plain as his own, and the big boots she wore when she tramped about the poultry yard, still spattered with pale, dry mud. Her father's worn little Bible lay on the table, and beside it another book "Duck Raising for the Market," with the marks of muddy and mealy hands still lingering on its cover.

Suddenly, evoked by these silent witnesses to her busy and happy life, the whole woman seemed to stand beside Peter, the tall, eager, vital woman who had been at home here, who had ruled the cabin with a splendid and vital personality. He seemed to feel her near him again, to see the interested eyes, the high cheek-bones touched with scarlet, the wisp of hair that would fall across her face sometimes when she was deep in baking, or preserving, or poultry-farming, and that she would brush away with the back of an impatient hand, only to have it slip loose again.

One of her kitchen aprons, caught in the current of air from the opened door, blew about on its hook. He remembered her, on many a wintry day, buttoned into just such a crisp apron, radiantly busy and brisk in her kitchen, stirring and chopping, moving constantly between stove and table. With strong hands still showing traces of flour she would come to sit beside him at the piano, to play a duet with her characteristic dash and finish, only to jump up in sudden compunction, with an exclamation: "Oh, my ducks—I'd forgotten them! Oh, the poor little wretches!"

And she would be gone, leaving a streak of wet, fresh air through the warm house from the open door, and he would perhaps glance from a window to see her, roughly coated and booted, ploughing about her duck yard, delving into barrels of grain, turning on faucets, wielding a stubby old broom.

She loved her life, he mused, with a bitter heartache, as he stood here in her empty room. Sometimes he had marvelled at the complete and unquestioning joy she had brought to it. Books, puzzles, music, and fires sufficed her in the few hours that she ever spent in her own drawing room. For the rest she had the kitchen and the farmyard, and the world out of doors, the oaks and the grass, the great stretches of dim forest, the muddy trails, the blowing airs on the crest of the ridge that made her shout and stagger in their wild onslaught. Peter reminded himself that never in their years together had he heard her complain about anything, or seem to feel bored or at a loss.

"We've always thought of Cherry as the child!" he thought. "But it was she, Alix, who was the real child. She never grew up. She never entered into the time of moods and self-analysis and jealousies and desires! She would have played and picnicked all her life——"

His heart pressed like a dull pain in his chest. Dully, quietly, he went out to the fire again, and dully and quietly moved through the day. Her books and music might stand as they were, her potted ferns and her scattered small possessions—the sewing-basket that she always handled with a boy's awkwardness, and the camera she used so well—should keep their places. But he went to her desk, thinking in this long, solitary evening, to destroy various papers that she might wish destroyed before the cabin was deserted. And here he found her letter.

He found it only after he had somewhat explored the different small drawers and pigeonholes of the desk, drawers and pigeonholes which were, to his surprise, all in astonishing order for Alix. Everything was marked, tied, pocketed; her accounts were balanced, and if she had anywhere left private papers, they were at least nowhere to be found.

Seeing in all this a dread confirmation of his first suspicion of her death, Peter nevertheless experienced a shock when he found her letter. It had been placed in an empty drawer, face up, and was sealed, and addressed simply with his name.

He sat holding it in his hand, and moments passed before he could open it.

So it had been true, then, the fear that he had tried all these weeks to crush? He had been weighing, measuring, remembering, until his very soul was sick with the uncertainty. His mind had been a confused web of memories, of this casual word and that look, of what she had possibly heard, had probably seen, had suspected—known—

Now he would know. He tore open the envelope, and the dozen written lines were before his eyes. The letter was dated, a most unusual thing for Alix to do, and "Saturday, one o'clock" was written under the date. It was the day of her death.

He read:

PETER DEAR, Don't feel too badly if I find a stupid way out. I've been thinking for several days about it. You've done so much for me, and after you, of course there's no one but Cherry. She could be free now, he couldn't prevent it. When I saw your face a few minutes ago I knew we couldn't fight it. Remember, this is our secret. And always remember that I want you to be happy because I love you so!

It was unsigned.

Peter sat staring at it for awhile without moving, without the stir of a changing expression on his face. Then he folded it up, and put it in the pocket of his coat, and went out to the backyard, where Kow was feeding the chickens. The wet, dark day was ending brilliantly in a wash of red sunset light that sent long shadows from the young fruit trees, and touched every twig with a dull glow.

"Kow," Peter said, after an effort to speak that was unsuccessful. The Chinese boy looked at him solicitously; for Peter's face was ashen, and about his mouth were drawn lines. "Kow," he said, "I go now!"

"Go now other house?" Kow nodded, glancing down toward the valley.

But Peter jerked his head instead toward the bare ridge.

"No, I go now—not come back!" he said, briefly. "To-night—maybe Bolinas—to-morrow, Inverness. I don't know. By and by the big mountains, Kow—by and by I forget!"

Tears glittered in the Chinese boy's eyes, but he smiled with a great air of cheer.

"I keep house!" he promised.

The dog came fawning and springing from the stables, and Peter whistled to him.

"Come on, Buck! We're going now!"

He opened the farmyard gate where her hand had so often rested, crossed the muddy corral, opened another gate, and struck off across the darkening world toward the ridge. The last sunlight lingered on crest and treetop, tangled itself redly in the uppermost branches of a few tall redwoods, and was gone. Twilight- -a long twilight that had in it some hint of spring—lay softly over the valley; the mountain loomed high in the clear shadow.

Gaining the top of the first ridge, he paused and looked back. Lights were beginning to prick forth in the brown houses of the valley, buried in their trees. The busy little mountain train, descending, puffed forth smoke and steam. Far away, the silver ribbons of the canals wound through the marsh, and beyond the bay, the Oakland shore lay like a chain of gems in the pale twilight.

Peter looked at the cabin, the little brown house that he had built almost fifteen years ago. He remembered that it was in the beginning a sort of experiment; his mother and he were too much alone in their big city house, and she had suggested, with rare wisdom, that as he did not care for society, and as his travels always meant great loneliness For her, he should have a little eyrie of his own, to which he might retreat whenever the fancy touched him.

She liked Del Monte and Tahoe, herself, but she had come to Mill Valley now and then in the days of his first wild delight in its freedom and beauty, silk-gowned and white-gloved and very much disliking dust. She had sent him plants, roses, and fruit trees, and she had told him one day that he had a neighbour in the valley who was an old friend of hers, a Doctor Strickland, a widower, with children.

He remembered sauntering up the opposite canyon to duly call upon this inventor-physician one day, and his delight upon finding a well-read, music-loving, philosophic, erratic man, who had at once recognized a kindred spirit, and who had made the younger man warmly welcome.

Presently, on the first call, an enchanting little girl In a shabby smock had come in, a little girl all dimples, demureness, and untouched babyish beauty. She had said that "Anne wath mad wiv her, and that Alix—" she managed to lisp the name, "wath up in the madrone!"

A somewhat older child, named Alix, a freckled, leggy little person with enormous front teeth, had proved the claim by falling out of the madrone, and had received no sympathy for a bump, but a—to him—rather surprising censure. He had yet to realize that nothing ever hurt Alix, but that she always ruined her clothes, and frequently hurt other persons and other things. He found her a spirited, enthusiastic little person, extremely articulate, and quite unselfconscious, and she had entertained him with an excited account of a sex feud that was being pushed with some violence at her school, and had used expressions that rather shocked Peter. A quiet third girl—a niece, he gathered—had joined the group, a girl with braids and clean hands, who elucidated:

"Alix and I don't like our teacher!"

"She's a sneak and a skunk," Alix had frankly contributed. Cherry, now quietly established in her father's lap, had smiled with mischievous enjoyment; nobody else, to Peter's surprise, had paid this extraordinary remark the slightest attention. He remembered that he had fancied only the smallest of these children, and had been glad when they all went out of the room.

But after that Alix used often to amuse him, and he always felt more at home with her than with the other two. She had only been a gawky and thin fifteen or sixteen when she began to assert herself in his kitchen, dictate to Kow, and waste good butter and eggs on experiments. He had secretly rather admired her quick tongue and her daring, he liked her to ride his horses, and was amazed at the speed with which she grasped the controlling principles of the motor-car. He had seen her move plants, treat sick chickens, sew up the gashed head of a horse with her own fingers, while Cherry, lovely, round-eyed, immaculate in white ruffles, watched her with fear and admiration.

Looking down at the cabin, the years slipped past him like a flying film, and it was the present again, and Alix—Alix was gone.

He roused himself, spoke to the dog, and they went on their way again. Mud squelched beneath Peter's boots in the roadway; the dog sprang lightly from clump to clump of dried grass. But when they left the road, and cut straight across the rise of the hillside, the ground was firmer, and the two figures moved swiftly through the dark night. The early stars came out, and showed them, silhouetted against the sky above Alix's beloved Tamalpais, the man's erect form with its slight limp, the dog following faithfully, his plumy tail and feathered ruff showing a dull lustre in the starlight.

Cherry, with her violet eyes and corn-coloured hair, Cherry, with her little hands gathered in his, and her heart beating against his heart, and Alix, his chum, his companion, his comrade on so many night walks under the stars—he had lost them both. But it was Alix who was closest to his thoughts to-night, Alix, the thought of whom was gradually gripping his heart and soul with a new pain.

Alix was his own; Cherry had never been his own. It was for him to comfort Cherry, it had always been his mission to comfort Cherry, since the days of her broken dolls and cut fingers. But Alix was his own comforter, and Alix might have been laughing and stumbling and chattering beside him here, in the dark, wet woods, full of a child's happy satisfaction in the moment and confidence in the morrow.

"Alix, my wife!" he said softly, aloud. "I loved Cherry—always. But you were mine—you were mine. We belonged to each other—for better and for worse—and I have let you go!"

He went on and on and on. They were plunging down hill now, under the trees. He would see a light after awhile, and sleep for a few hours, and have a hunter's breakfast, and be gone again. And he knew that for weeks—for months—perhaps for years, he would wander so, through the great mountains, with their snow and their forests, over the seas, in strange cities and stranger solitudes. Always alone, always moving, always remembering. That would be his life. And some day—some day perhaps he would come back to the valley she had loved—

But even now he recoiled in distaste from that hour. To see the familiar faces, to come up to the cabin again, to touch the music and the books—

Worse, to find Cherry a little older, happy and busy in her life of sacrifice, not needing him, not very much wanting the reminder of the old tragic times—

An owl cried in the woods; the mournful sound floated and drifted away into utter silence. Some small animal, meeting the death its brief life had evaded a hundred times, screamed shrilly, and was silent. Great branches, stirred by the night wind, moved high above his head, and when there was utter silence, Peter could hear the steady, soft rush of the ocean, dulled here to the sound of gigantic, quiet breathing.

Suddenly she seemed again to be beside him. He seemed to see the dark, animated face, the slender, tall girl wrapped in her big, rough coat. He seemed to hear her vibrating voice, with that new, tender note in it that he had noticed when she last spoke to him.

"I'll go home ahead of you, Peter, and wait for you there!"

Tears suddenly flooded his eyes, and he put his hand over them, and pressed it there, standing still, while the wave of tender and poignant and exquisite memories broke over him.

"We'll go on, Buck," he whispered, looking up through the trees at a strip of dark sky spangled with cold stars. "We'll go on. She's— she's waiting for us somewhere, old fellow!"

www.ingramcontent.com/pod-product-compliance
Lightning Source LLC
Chambersburg PA
CBHW050938120626
46552CB00001B/273